THE EVENTS IN THIS BOOK ARE REAL.

NAMES AND PLACES HAVE BEEN CHANGED
TO PROTECT THE LORIEN SIX,
WHO REMAIN IN HIDING.

OTHER CIVILIZATIONS DO EXIST.

SOME OF THEM SEEK TO DESTROY YOU.

ALSO BY PITTACUS LORE

I AM NUMBER FOUR

I AM NUMBER FOUR: THE LOST FILES: SIX'S LEGACY

THE POWER OF SIX

BOOK TWO OF THE LORIEN LEGACIES

PITTACUS LORE

HARPER

An Imprint of HarperCollinsPublishers

Library of Congress Cataloging-in-Publication Data is available.

ISBN 978-0-06-197455-7 (trade bdg.)

ISBN 978-0-06-207062-3 (intl. ed.)

ISBN 978-0-06-211163-0 (special edition)

Typography by Ray Shappell

11 12 13 14 15   CG/BV   10 9 8 7 6 5 4 3 2 1

❖

First Edition

CHAPTER ONE

MY NAME IS MARINA, AS OF THE SEA, BUT I WASN'T called that until much later. In the beginning I was known merely as Seven, one of the nine surviving Garde from the planet Lorien, the fate of which was, and still is, left in our hands. Those of us who aren't lost. Those of us still alive.

I was six when we landed. When the ship jolted to a halt on Earth, even at my young age I sensed how much was at stake for us—nine Cêpan, nine Garde—and that our only chance waited for us here. We had entered the planet's atmosphere in the midst of a storm of our own creation, and as our feet found Earth for the very first time, I remember the wisps of steam that rolled off the ship and the goose bumps that covered my arms. I hadn't felt the wind in a year, and it was freezing outside. Somebody was there waiting for us. I don't know who he was, only that he handed each Cêpan two sets of clothes and a large envelope. I still don't know what was in it.

As a group we huddled together, knowing we might never see one another again. Words were spoken, hugs were given, and then we split up, as we knew we must, walking in pairs in nine different directions. I kept peering over my shoulder as the others receded in the distance until, very slowly, one by one, they all disappeared. And then it was just Adelina and me, alone. I realize now just how scared Adelina must have been.

I remember boarding a ship headed to some unknown destination. I remember two or three different trains after that. Adelina and I kept to ourselves, huddled against each other in obscure corners, away from whoever might be around. We hiked from town to town, over mountains and across fields, knocking on doors that were quickly slammed in our faces. We were hungry, tired, and scared. I remember sitting on a sidewalk begging for change. I remember crying instead of sleeping. I'm certain that Adelina gave away some of our precious gems from Lorien for nothing more than warm meals, so great was our need. Perhaps she gave them all away. And then we found this place in Spain.

A stern-looking woman I would come to know as Sister Lucia answered the heavy oak door. She squinted at Adelina, taking in her desperation, the way her shoulders drooped.

"Do you believe in the word of God?" the woman asked

in Spanish, pursing her lips and narrowing her eyes in scrutiny.

"The word of God is my vow," Adelina replied with a solemn nod. I don't know how she knew this response—perhaps she learned it when we stayed in a church basement weeks before—but it was the right one. Sister Lucia opened the door.

We've been here ever since, eleven years in this stone convent with its musty rooms, drafty hallways, and hard floors like slabs of ice. Aside from the few visitors, the internet is my only source to the world outside our small town; and I search it constantly, looking for some indication that the others are out there, that they're searching, maybe fighting. Some sign that I'm not alone, because at this point I can't say that Adelina still believes, that she's still with me. Her attitude changed somewhere over the mountains. Maybe it was with the slam of one of the doors that shut a starving woman and her child out in the cold for another night. Whatever it was, Adelina seems to have lost the urgency of staying on the move, and her faith in the resurgence of Lorien seems to have been replaced by the faith shared by the convent's Sisters. I remember a distinct shift in Adelina's eyes, her sudden speeches on the need for guidance and structure if we were to survive.

My faith in Lorien remains intact. In India, a year and a half ago, four different people witnessed a boy move objects with his mind. While the significance behind the

event was small at first, the boy's abrupt disappearance
shortly thereafter created much buzz in the region, and
a hunt for him began. As far as I know, he hasn't been
found.

A few months ago there was news of a girl in Argentina
who, in the wake of an earthquake, lifted a five-ton slab of
concrete to save a man trapped beneath it; and when news
of this heroic act spread, she disappeared. Like the boy in
India, she's still missing.

And then there's the father-son duo making all the
news now in America, in Ohio, who the police are hunting after the two allegedly demolished an entire school by
themselves, killing five people in the process. They left no
trace behind other than mysterious heaps of ash.

"It looks like a battle took place here. I don't know how
else to explain it," the head investigator was quoted as
saying. "But make no mistake, we will get to the bottom
of this, and we will find Henri Smith and his son, John."

Perhaps John Smith, if that's his real name, is merely
a boy with a grudge who was pushed too far. But I don't
think that's the case. My heart races whenever his picture appears on my screen. I'm gripped with a profound
desperation that I can't quite explain. I can feel it in my
bones that he's one of us. And I know, somehow, that I
must find him.

CHAPTER TWO

I PERCH MY ARMS ON THE COLD WINDOWSILL AND watch the snowflakes fall from the dark sky and settle on the side of the mountain, which is dotted with pine, cork oak, and beech trees, with patches of craggy rock mixed throughout. The snow hasn't let up all day, and they say it will continue through the night. I can barely see beyond the edge of town to the north—the world lost in a white haze. During the day, when the sky is clear, it's possible to see the watery blue smudge of the Bay of Biscay. But not in this weather, and I can't help but wonder what might lurk in all that white beyond my line of sight.

I look behind me. In the high-ceilinged, drafty room, there are two computers. To use one we must add our name to a list and wait our turn. At night there's a ten-minute time limit if somebody is waiting, twenty minutes if there isn't. The two girls using them now have been on for a half hour each, and my patience is thin. I haven't checked the news since this morning when I snuck in before breakfast. At that time nothing new about John Smith had been reported, but I'm almost shaking in anticipation over what might have sprung up since then. Some new discovery has been uncovered each day since the story first broke.

Santa Teresa is a convent that doubles as an orphanage for girls. I'm now the oldest out of thirty-seven, a distinction I've held for six months, after the last girl who turned eighteen left. At eighteen we must all make the choice to strike out on our own or to forge a life within the Church. The birthday Adelina and I created for me when we arrived is less than five months away, and that's when I'll turn eighteen, too. Of all who've reached eighteen, not a single girl has stayed. I can't blame them. Like the others, I have every intention of leaving this prison behind, whether or not Adelina comes with me. And it's hard to imagine she will.

The convent itself was built entirely of stone in 1510 and is much too large for the small number of us who live here. Most of the rooms stand empty; and those that aren't are imbued with a damp, earthy feel, and our voices echo to the ceiling and back. The convent rests atop the highest hill overlooking the village that shares the same name, nestled deep within the Picos de Europa Mountains of northern Spain. The village, like the convent, is made of rock, with many structures built straight into the mountainside. Walking down the town's main road, Calle Principal, it's impossible not to be inundated by the disrepair. It's as though this place was forgotten by time, and the passing centuries have turned most everything to shades of mossy green and brown, while the pervasive smell of mildew hangs in the air.

It's been five years since I started begging Adelina to leave, to keep moving like we were instructed to. "I'm going to be getting my Legacies soon, and I don't want to discover them here, with all of these girls and nuns around," I'd said. She had refused, quoting La Biblia Reina Valera that we must stand still for salvation. I've begged every year since, and every year she looks at me with blank eyes and talks me down with a different religious quote. But I know my salvation does not lie here.

Past the church gates and down the gently sloping hill, I can see the faint dimness of the town lights. In the midst of this blizzard, they look like floating halos. Though I can't hear the music from either of the two cantinas, I'm sure both of them are packed. Aside from those, there is a restaurant, a café, a market, a bodega, and various vendors that line Calle Principal most mornings and afternoons. Towards the bottom of the hill, on the southern edge of town, is the brick school we all attend.

My head snaps around when the bell dings: prayers are five minutes away, followed directly by bed. Panic sweeps through me. I have to know if anything new has been reported. Perhaps John's been caught. Perhaps the police have found something else at the demolished school, something originally overlooked. Even if there's nothing new at all, I have to know. I'll never get to sleep otherwise.

I fix a hard stare on Gabriela García—Gabby for short—who sits at one of the computers. Gabby's sixteen and very pretty, with long dark hair and brown eyes; and she always dresses slutty when she's outside the convent, wearing tight shirts that show off her pierced navel. Every morning she dresses in loose, baggy clothes, but the second we're out of sight of the Sisters she removes them, revealing a tight, skimpy outfit underneath. Then she spends the rest of the walk to school applying makeup and redoing her hair. It's the same with her four friends, three of whom also live here. And when the day ends, they wipe their faces clean during the walk back and re-dress in their original clothes.

"What?" Gabby asks in a snotty voice, glaring at me. "I'm writing an email."

"I've been waiting longer than ten minutes," I say. "And you're not writing an email. You're looking at guys with their shirts off."

"So what? Are you gonna tell on me, tattletale?" she asks mockingly.

The girl beside her, whose name is Hilda but who most kids in school call La Gorda—"the fat one"—(behind her back, never to her face) laughs.

They're an inseparable pair, Gabby and La Gorda. I bite my tongue and turn back to the window, folding my arms across my chest. I'm seething inside, partly because I need to get on the computer and partly because I never know how to respond when Gabby mocks me. There are four minutes left. My impatience segues to full-on desperation. There could be news right now—breaking news!—but I have no way of knowing because these self-ish jerks won't give up one of the computers.

Three minutes left. I'm nearly shaking with anger. And then an idea pops into my head, and a grin plays across my lips. It's risky, but worth it if it works.

I pivot just enough to see Gabby's chair in my peripheral vision. I take a deep breath and, focusing all my energy on her chair, use my telekinesis to jerk it to the left. Then I quickly thrust it right so hard it nearly topples over. Gabby jumps up and yelps. I look at her in mock surprise.

"What?" La Gorda asks.

"I don't know; it felt like somebody just kicked my chair or something. Did you feel anything?"

"No," La Gorda says; and as soon as the word is uttered, I move her chair a few centimeters backwards, then jerk it to the right, all the while remaining at my spot by the window. Both of the girls scream this time. I thrust Gabby's chair, then La Gorda's again; and without giving their computer screens a second glance, they flee the room, screaming as they go.

"Yes!" I say, rushing to the computer Gabby was using and quickly typing the web address of the news site I've deemed most reliable. Then I wait impatiently for the page to load. The old computers, combined with the slow internet here, are the bane of my existence.

The browser goes white and, line by line, the page forms. When a quarter of it has loaded, the final bell rings. One minute until prayers. I'm inclined to ignore the bell, even at the risk of being punished. At this point I don't really care. "Five more months," I whisper to myself.

Half of the page is now up, revealing the top of John Smith's face, his upturned eyes, which are dark and confident, though within them there's a sense of discomfort that seems almost out of place. I lean on the edge of my seat, waiting, the excitement bubbling up inside me, causing my hands to tremble.

"Come on," I say to the screen, trying in vain to hurry it. "Come on come on come on."

"Marina!" a voice barks from the open doorway. I jerk around and see Sister Dora, a portly woman who's the head cook in the kitchen, staring daggers at me. This is nothing new. She stares daggers at everyone who walks through the lunch line holding a tray, as though our needing sustenance is a personal affront. She presses her lips together in a perfect straight line, then narrows her eyes. "Come! Now! And I mean *right* now!"

I sigh, knowing I have no choice but to go. I clear the

browser's history and close it, then follow Sister Dora down the dark hallway. There was something new on that screen; I just know it. Why else would John's face have taken up the entire page? A week and a half is long enough for any news to turn stale, so for him to command so much of the screen means there's some significant new piece of information.

We walk to Santa Teresa's nave, which is huge. Towering pillars lead to a high, vaulted ceiling and stained glass windows line the walls. Wooden pews run the length of the open room and can seat nearly three hundred people. Sister Dora and I are the last to enter. I sit alone in one of the center pews. Sister Lucia, who opened the door to Adelina and me when we first arrived and who still runs the convent, stands at the pulpit, closes her eyes, lowers her head and presses her hands together in front of her. Everyone else does the same.

"*Padre divino*," the prayer begins in somber unison. "*Que nos bendiga y nos proteja en su amor . . .*"

I tune it out and look at the back of the heads before me, all of which are bowed in concentration. Or just bowed. My eyes find Adelina, sitting in the very first row six pews in front of me and slightly to the right. She is on her knees, deeply meditative, her brown hair pulled into a tight braid that falls to the middle of her back. She doesn't look up once, doesn't try to find me at the back of the room like she used to during our first few years here, a covert smile on each of our faces as our eyes met, acknowledging our shared secret. We still share that secret, but somewhere along the way Adelina has stopped acknowledging it. Somewhere along the way the plan to bide our time until we felt strong enough and safe enough to leave has been replaced with Adelina's desire to simply stay—or her fear to leave.

Before the news of John Smith, which I'd told Adelina about when it broke, it had been months since we last talked about our mission. In September I had shown her my third scar, the third warning that said another Garde has died and that she and I are one step closer to being hunted and killed by the Mogadorians, and she had acted like it didn't exist. Like it didn't mean what we both know it means. Upon hearing the news about John, she merely rolled her eyes and told me to stop believing in fairy tales.

"*En el nombre del Padre, y del Hijo, y del Espíritu Santo. Amén,*" they say, and everyone in the room makes the sign of the cross in unison with this last sentence, myself included to keep up appearances: forehead, chest, left shoulder, right shoulder.

I had been asleep, dreaming of running down a mountain with my arms out at my sides as if I was about to take flight, when I had been awoken by the pain and glow of the third scar wrapping itself around my lower leg. The light had woken several girls in the room, but thankfully not the attending Sister. The girls thought I had

a flashlight and a magazine under the covers and that
I was breaking the rules of curfew. On the bed next to
mine, Elena, a quiet sixteen-year-old with jet-black hair
she often sticks in her mouth when speaking, had thrown
a pillow at me. My flesh had begun to bubble, and the
pain had been so intense I had to bite on the edge of my
blanket to remain quiet. I couldn't help but cry, because
somewhere Number Three had lost his or her life. There
were six of us left now.

Tonight I file out of the nave with the rest of the girls
and head to our sleeping quarters filled with creaky twin
beds evenly spaced apart, but in my mind I'm hatching a
plan. To compensate for the hard beds and the concrete
chill of every room, the linens are soft and the blankets
heavy, the only real luxury we're afforded. My bed is in
the back corner, farthest from the door, which is the most
sought after spot; it's the quietest, and it took me a long
time to get it, moving one bed closer as each girl left.

The lights are shut off once everyone is settled in. I
lie on my back and stare at the faint, jagged outline of
the high ceiling. An occasional whisper breaks the silence,
followed immediately by the attending Sister shushing
whoever it came from. I keep my eyes open, waiting impatiently for everyone to fall asleep. After a half hour the
whispers fade, replaced by the soft sounds of sleep, but I
don't dare risk it yet. Too soon. Another fifteen minutes
and still no sounds. Then I can't stand it any longer.

I hold my breath and inch my legs over the edge of the bed, listening to the rhythm of Elena's breathing beside me. My feet find the icy floor, and turn cold instantly. I stand slowly to keep the bed from creaking and then tiptoe across the room and towards the door, taking my time, being careful not to bump any beds. I reach the open doorway and rush out into the hall and down to the computer room. I pull out the chair and push the computer's power button.

I fidget waiting for the computer to boot up and keep peering towards the hallway to see if anyone has followed. I'm finally able to type in the web address and the screen goes white, then two pictures take shape in the center of the page, surrounded by text with a top headline in bold black letters too blurry to read. Two images now—I wonder what changed since I tried to check earlier. And then, at last, they come into focus:

INTERNATIONAL TERRORISTS?

John Smith, with his square jaw, shaggy dark blond hair, and blue eyes, fills the left side of the screen, while his father—or more likely Cêpan—Henri takes up the right. What's there isn't a photo but a black-and-white artist's sketch done in pencil. I skim the details I already know—demolished school, five deaths, abrupt disappearance—and then come to the breaking news only now being reported:

> In a bizarre twist, FBI investigators today un-
> covered what is believed to be the tools of
> a professional counterfeiter. Several machines
> typically used for the creation of documents were
> found in the Paradise, Ohio, home rented by Henri
> and John Smith in a hatch beneath the floorboards
> of the master bedroom, leading investigators to
> consider possible links to terrorism. Creating
> local uproar within the Paradise community, Henri
> and John Smith are now considered a threat to
> national security, fugitives; and investigators are
> asking for any and all information that might lead
> to their whereabouts.

I scroll back to John's image, and when my gaze meets his, my hands begin to shake. His eyes—even in this sketch there's something familiar about them. How could I know them if not from the yearlong journey that brought us here? Nobody can convince me now that he isn't one of the six remaining Garde, still alive in this foreign world.

I lean back and blow my bangs out of my eyes, wishing I could go in search of John myself. Of course Henri and John Smith are able to elude police; they've kept hidden for eleven years now, just as Adelina and I have. But how can I possibly hope to be the one to find him when the whole world is looking? How can any of us hope to come together?

The eyes of the Mogadorians are everywhere. I have no idea how One or Three were found, but I believe they located Two because of a blog post he or she had written. I had found it, and then I'd sat there for fifteen minutes thinking how best to respond without giving myself away. Though the message itself had been obscure, it was very obvious to those of us looking: **Nine, now eight. Are the rest of you out there?** It had been posted by an account called Two. My fingers found the keyboard and I'd typed a quick response, and just before I hit the Post button, the page refreshed—somebody else had responded first.

We are here, it read.

My mouth had dropped open, and I'd stared in utter shock. Hope flooded through me from those two brief messages, but just as my fingers had typed a different reply, a bright glow appeared at my feet and the sizzling sound of burning flesh reached my ears, followed closely by a searing pain so great that I'd dropped to the floor and writhed in agony, screaming at the top of my lungs for Adelina, holding my hands over my ankle so no one else would see. When Adelina arrived and realized what was happening, I'd pointed at the screen, but it was blank; both posts had been deleted.

I look away from John Smith's familiar eyes on the screen. Beside the computer sits a small flower that's been forgotten. It's wilted and tired, shrunken down to half its normal height, a brown, crispy tinge at the edge of its leaves. Several petals have dropped, now dry and crinkled on the desk around the pot. The flower isn't dead yet, but it's not far off. I lean forward and cup my hands around it, move my face near enough so that my lips brush against the edge of its leaves, and then I blow hot air over it. An icy feeling shoots down my spine and, in response, life bursts through the small flower. It springs upward and a verdant green floods the leaves and stalk and new petals bloom, colorless at first, then turning a brilliant purple. A mischievous grin sprouts on my face, and I can't help but think of how the Sisters would react if they were to see such a thing. But I'll never let them. It would be misinterpreted, and I don't want to be cast out into the cold. I'm not ready for that. Soon, but not just yet.

I turn off the computer and hurry back to bed while thoughts of John Smith, somewhere out there, swim in my head.

Be safe and stay hidden, I think. *We'll find each other yet.*

CHAPTER THREE

A LOW WHISPER FINDS ME. THE VOICE IS COLD. I can't seem to move but I listen intently.

I'm not asleep anymore, but I'm not awake either. I'm paralyzed, and as the whispers increase, my eyes are whisked away through the impenetrable darkness of my motel room. The electricity I feel as the vision breaks above my bed reminds me of when my first Legacy, Lumen, lit up my palms in Paradise, Ohio. Back when Henri was still here, still alive. But Henri's gone now. He's not coming back. Even in this state I can't escape that reality.

I completely enter the vision above me, blazing through its darkness with my hands turned on, but the glow is swallowed by the shadows. And then I snap to a halt. Everything falls silent. I lift my hands in front of me but touch nothing, my feet off the ground, floating in a great void.

More whispering in a language I don't recognize, but somehow still understand. The words burst forth anxiously. The darkness fades, and the world I'm in turns a shade of gray on its way to a white so bright I have to squint to see. A mist drifts in front of me and filters away, revealing a large open room with candles lining the walls.

"I—I don't know what went wrong," a voice says, clearly shaken.

The room is long and wide, the size of a football field. The acrid smell of sulfur burns my nostrils, makes my eyes water. The air is hot and stuffy. And then I see them at the far end of the room: two figures shrouded in shadows, one much bigger than the other, and menacing even from a distance.

"They got away. Somehow they got away. I don't know how. . . ."

I move forward. I feel the sort of calm that sometimes comes in dreams when you're aware you're asleep and that nothing can really hurt you. Step by step, nearing the growing shadows.

"All of them, all of them killed. Along with three piken and two krauls," the smaller of the two says, standing with fidgeting hands beside the larger man.

"We had them. We were about to—," comes the voice, but the other cuts him off. He scans the air to see what he's already sensed. I stop, stand motionless, and hold my breath. And then he finds me. A shudder runs up my spine.

"John," somebody says, the voice a distant echo.

The larger figure comes towards me. He towers over me, twenty feet tall, muscular, a chiseled jaw. His hair isn't long like the others', but cut short instead. His skin is tan. Our eyes stay locked as he slowly approaches. Thirty feet away, then twenty. He stops ten feet short. My pendant grows heavy and the chain cuts into my neck. Around his throat, like a collar, I notice a grotesque, purplish scar.

"I've been expecting you," he says, his voice level and calm. He lifts his right arm and pulls a sword from the sheath on his back. It comes alive at once, keeping its shape while the metal turns nearly liquid. The wound in my shoulder, from the soldier's dagger during the battle in Ohio, screams with pain as though I'm being stabbed all over again. I fall to my knees.

"It's been a very long time," he says.

"I don't know what you're talking about," I say in a language I've never spoken before.

I want to leave immediately, wherever this place is. I try to rise, but it's as if I'm suddenly stuck to the ground.

"Don't you?" he asks.

"John," I hear again from somewhere on the periphery. The Mogadorian doesn't seem to notice, and there's something about his gaze that holds my own. I can't look away.

"I'm not supposed to be here," I say. My voice sounds watery. Everything dims until it's just the two of us and nothing else.

"I can make you disappear if that's what you want," he says, slashing a figure eight with the sword, leaving a stark white streak hanging in the air where the blade passes through. And then he charges, his sword held high and cracking with power. He swings, and it comes down like a bullet, aimed for my throat, and I know that there's nothing I can do to stop the blow from decapitating me.

"John!" the voice screams again.

My eyes whip open. Two hands grip me hard by the shoulders. I'm covered in sweat and out of breath. I focus first on Sam standing over me, then on Six, with her stark hazel eyes that sometimes look blue and sometimes green, kneeling beside me, appearing tired and worn as though I just woke her, which I probably did.

"What was that all about?" Sam asks.

I shake my head, letting the vision dissipate, and I take in my surroundings. The room is dark with the curtains drawn, and I'm lying in the same bed I've spent the last week and a half in, healing from the battle wounds. Six has been recovering beside me, and neither she nor I have left this place since we arrived, relying on Sam to head out for food and supplies. A shabby motel room with two full beds off the main street in Trucksville, North Carolina. To rent the room, Sam had used one of the seventeen driver's licenses Henri created for me before he was killed, and luckily the old man at the front desk was too busy watching TV to study the photograph. Situated on the northwestern edge of the state, the motel is a fifteen-minute drive from both Virginia and Tennessee, a location chosen mainly because we had traveled as far as we could go given the extent of our injuries. But our wounds have slowly healed, and our strength is finally returning.

"You were talking in a foreign language I've never heard before," Sam says. "I think you made it up, dude."

"No, he was talking in Mogadorian," Six corrects him. "And even a little Loric."

"Really?" I ask. "That's totally weird."

Six walks to the window and pulls back the right side of the curtains. "What were you dreaming about?"

I shake my head. "I'm not really sure. I was dreaming, but I wasn't dreaming, you know. Having visions, I guess, and they were about them. We were about to have a battle; but I was, I don't know, too weak or confused or something." I look up at Sam, who is frowning and looking at the TV. "What?"

"Bad news." He sighs, shaking his head.

"What?" I sit up, wipe the sleep from my eyes.

Sam nods to the front of the room, and I turn to the glow of the television. My face takes up the entire left half of the screen, while an artist's rendering of Henri's is on the right. The drawing looks nothing like him: his face seems sharp and haggard to the point of emaciation, giving him the appearance of being twenty years older than he really is. Or *was*.

"As if being called a threat to national security or a terrorist wasn't bad enough," Sam says. "They're now offering a reward."

"For me?" I ask.

"For you and Henri. A hundred thousand dollars for any information leading to your and Henri's capture, and two hundred and fifty thousand if somebody brings either of you in on their own," Sam says.

"I've been on the run all of my life," I say, rubbing my eyes. "What difference does it make?"

"Yeah, well, I haven't and they're offering a reward for me, too," Sam says. "A measly twenty-five grand, if you can believe that. And I don't know how good of a fugitive I am. I've never done this before."

I gingerly scoot up the bed, still a little stiff. Sam sits on the other bed and places his head in his palms.

"You're with us, though, Sam. We have your back," I say.

"I'm not worried," he says into his chest.

I chew on the insides of my cheeks, thinking about how I'm going to keep him safe, and me and Six alive, without Henri. I turn to face Sam, who is stressed enough to be picking a hole in his black NASA T-shirt. "Listen, Sam. I wish Henri was here. I can't even tell you how much I wish he was here, for so many reasons. Not only did he keep me safe when we were running from one state to the next, but he also had all this knowledge about Lorien and my family, and he had this amazing calming way about him that's kept us out of trouble for so long. I don't know if I'm ever going to be able to do what he did to keep us safe. I bet if he were alive today, he wouldn't have let you come with us. There's just no way he would have put you in this kind of danger. But, listen, you're here and that's that, and I promise that I won't let anything happen to you."

"I want to be here," Sam says. "This is the coolest thing that's ever happened to me." There is a pause, and then he looks me in the eyes. "Plus you're my best friend, and I've never had a best friend."

"Neither have I," I say.

"Just hug already," Six says. Sam and I laugh.

My face is still on the screen. The photo on the TV is the one Sarah took on my very first day of school, the day I'd met her; and I have an awkward, uncomfortable look on my face. The right side of the screen is now filled with smaller photos of the five people we're being accused of killing: three teachers, the men's basketball coach, the school janitor. And then the screen changes yet again to images of the wrecked school—and it really is wrecked; the entire right side of the building is nothing more than a heap of rubble. Next come various interviews with Paradise residents, the last being Sam's mom. When she comes on screen she's crying, and looking straight into the camera she desperately pleads with the "kidnappers" to "please please please return my baby safely to me." When Sam sees this interview, I can tell something inside of him shifts.

Scenes from the past week's funerals and candle-light vigils come next. Sarah's face flashes on the screen, and she's holding a candle as tears stream down her cheeks. A lump forms in my throat. I'd give anything to hear her voice. It kills me to imagine what she must be dealing with. The video of us escaping Mark's burning house—which is what started all of this—has blown up on the internet, and while I was blamed for starting *that* blaze as well, Mark stepped in and swore up and down that I had no part in it, even though using me as a scapegoat would have let him off the hook completely.

When we had left Ohio, the damage to the school had first been attributed to an out-of-season tornado; but then rescue crews filtered through the rubble, and in no time all five bodies had been found lying equal distances from each other—without a single mark on them—in a room untouched by the battle. Autopsies reported that they had died of natural causes, with no trace of drugs or trauma. Who knows how it really happened. When one of the reporters had heard the story of me jumping through the principal's window and running away from the school, and then when Henri and I couldn't be found, he'd run a story blaming us for everything; and the rest had been quick to follow. With the recent discovery of Henri's forgery tools, along with a few of the fake documents he had left at the house, the public outrage has grown.

"We're going to have to be very careful now," Six says, sitting against the wall.

"More careful than staying inside a crummy motel room with the curtains drawn?" I ask.

Six goes back to the window and pulls aside one of the curtains to peer out. A sliver of sunlight cuts across the floor. "The sun will set in three hours. Let's leave as soon as it's dark."

"Thank God," Sam says. "There's a meteor shower tonight we can see if we drive south. Plus if I have to spend one more minute inside this crappy room, I'm going to go nuts."

"Sam, you've been nuts since the first time I met you," I kid. He throws a pillow at me, which I deflect without lifting a hand. I twist the pillow over and over in the air with my telekenisis and then send it like a rocket at the television, shutting it off.

I know Six is right that we should keep moving, but I'm frustrated. It seems like there's no end in sight, no place where we'll be safe. At the foot of the bed, keeping my feet warm, is Bernie Kosar, who's hardly left my side since Ohio. He opens his eyes and yawns and stretches. He peers up at me, and through my telepathy communicates that he's also feeling better. Most of the small scabs that covered his body are gone, and the larger ones are healing nicely. He's still wearing the makeshift splint on his broken front leg, and he'll limp for a few more weeks; but he almost looks like his old self. He offers a subtle wag and paws at my leg. I reach down and pull him up to my lap and scratch his tummy.

"How about you, buddy? You ready to get out of this dump?"

Bernie Kosar thumps his tail against the bed.

"So where to, guys?" I ask.

"I don't know," Six says. "Preferably somewhere warm to ride out the winter. I'm pretty sick of this snow. Though I'm even more sick of not knowing where the others are."

"For now it's just us three. Four plus Six plus Sam."

"I love algebra," Sam says. "Sam equals x. Variable x."

"Such a nerd, dude," I say.

Six enters the bathroom and then exits a second later with a handful of toiletries. "If there's any consolation in what happened, at least the other Garde know John not only survived his first battle, but that he won it. Maybe they'll find a bit of hope in it. Our biggest priority now is finding the others. And training together in the meantime."

"We will," I say, then look at Sam. "It's not too late to go back and put things straight, Sam. You can make up any story about us you want. Tell them we kidnapped you and held you against your will, and that you escaped the first chance you got. You'll be considered a hero. Girls will be all over you."

Sam bites his lower lip and shakes his head. "I don't want to be a hero. And girls are already all over me."

Six and I roll our eyes, but I also see Six blush. Or maybe I imagine it.

"I mean it," he says. "I'm not leaving."

I shrug. "I guess that's settled. Sam equals x in this equation."

Sam watches Six walk to her small duffel bag beside the TV, and his attraction to her is painted all over his face. She's wearing black cotton shorts and a white tank top with her hair pulled back. A few strands fall loose around her face. A purple scar is prominent on the front of her left thigh, and the stitch marks around it are a tender pink, still scabbed over. Stitches she not only sewed herself, but also removed. When Six looks up, Sam shyly diverts his gaze. Clearly there's another reason Sam wants to stick around.

Six bends down and reaches into her bag, removing a folded map. She opens it on the foot of the bed.

"Right here," she says, pointing to Trucksville, "is where we are. And here," she continues, moving her finger from North Carolina to a tiny red star made in ink close to the center of West Virginia, "is where the Mogadorians' cave is, the one I know of, anyhow."

I look where she's pointing. Even on the map it's obvious the location is very isolated; there doesn't appear to be any sort of main road within five miles, nor any town within ten.

"How do you even know where the cave is?"

"That's a long story," she says. "Probably one better left for the road."

Her finger takes up a new route on the map, heading southwest from West Virginia, traversing Tennessee, and coming to rest on a point in Arkansas near the Mississippi River.

"What's there?" I ask.

She puffs her cheeks and releases a deep breath, undoubtedly remembering something that happened. Her face takes on a special look when deep in concentration.

"This is where my Chest was," she says. "And some of the stuff Katarina brought from Lorien. This is where we hid it."

"What do you mean, where it *was*?"

She shakes her head.

"It's not there anymore?"

"No. They were tracking us, and we couldn't risk them getting it. It was no longer safe with us, so we stowed it and Katarina's artifacts in Arkansas and fled as fast as we could, thinking we could stay ahead of them . . ." She trails off.

"They caught up to you, didn't they?" I ask, knowing her Cêpan Katarina died three years ago.

She sighs. "That's another story better left for the road."

It takes minutes to throw my clothes into my duffel bag, and as I'm doing it I realize the last time this bag was packed, Sarah had done it. Only a week and a half has passed, but it feels like a year and a half. I wonder if she's been interrogated by police, or singled out at school. Where is she even going to school since the high school was destroyed? I'm certain she can hold her own, but still, it can't be easy on her, especially since she has no idea where I am, or even if I'm okay. I wish I could contact her without putting us both in danger.

Sam turns the TV back on the old-fashioned way—
with the remote—and he watches the news while Six
goes invisible to check on the truck. We assume Sam's
mom noticed it missing, which surely means the police
are keeping an eye out for it. Earlier in the week Sam
stole the front license plate off another truck. It might
help us until we get to where we're going.

I finish packing and set my bag beside the door.
Sam smiles when his picture pops up on the television
screen, again on the same news cycle, and I know he's
enjoying his small bit of celebrity even at the risk of
being considered a fugitive. Then they show my picture
again, which means they also show Henri's. It rips me
apart to see him, even though the sketch looks nothing
like him. Now isn't the time for guilt or misery, but I
miss him so much. It's my fault he's dead.

Fifteen minutes later Six walks in carrying a white
plastic bag.

She holds up the bag and shakes it at us. "I bought
you guys something."

"Yeah, what is it?" I ask.

She reaches in and pulls out a pair of hair clippers.
"I think it's time for a haircut for you and Sam."

"Oh come on, my head's too small. It's going to make
me look like a turtle," Sam objects. I laugh and try to
picture him without his shaggy hair. He has a long,
skinny neck, and I think he might be right.

"You'll be incognito," Six replies.

"Well, I don't want to be incognito. I'm Variable *x*."

"Stop being a wuss," Six says.

He scowls. I try to be upbeat. "Yeah, Sam," I say, peeling off my shirt. Six follows me into the bathroom, ripping the packaging away from the clippers as I bend over the tub. Her fingers are a little cold, and goose bumps sprinkle down my spine. I wish it was Sarah who was holding my shoulder steady and giving me a makeover. Sam watches from the doorway, sighing loudly, making his displeasure known.

Six finishes, and I wipe away the loose hair with a towel, then stand and look in the mirror. My head is whiter than the rest of my face, but only because it's never seen the sun. I think that a few days in the Florida Keys, where Henri and I lived before coming to Ohio, would fix the problem in no time.

"See, John looks tough and rugged like that. I'm going to look like a turd," Sam groans.

"I *am* tough and rugged, Sam," I reply.

He rolls his eyes while Six cleans the clippers. "Down," she says.

Sam obeys, dropping to his knees and bending over the tub. When she's done, Sam stands and flashes me a pleading look.

"How bad is it?"

"You look good, buddy," I say. "You look like a fugitive."

Sam rubs his head a few times and finally looks in the mirror. He cringes. "I look like an alien!" he exclaims in mock disgust, then glances at me over his shoulder. "No offense," he adds lamely.

Six collects all the hair from the tub and drops it in the toilet, careful to flush every strand. She coils the cord of the clippers into a neat, tight loop, then slips it back into its bag.

"No time like the present," she says.

We strap our bags across her shoulders and she grabs them both with her hands, then makes herself invisible, causing the bags to disappear as well. She rushes out the door to take them to the truck without being seen. While she's gone I reach up into the far right corner of the closet, toss aside a few towels, and grab the Loric Chest.

"You ever going to open that thing or what?" Sam asks. He's been excited to see what's inside ever since I told him about it.

"Yeah, I will," I say. "As soon as I feel safe."

The motel door opens, then closes. Six reappears and glances at the Chest.

"I won't be able to make you and Sam disappear *and* that. Only what I hold in my hands. I'll run it back to the truck first."

"No, that's okay. Take Sam with you, and I'll follow behind."

"That's stupid, John. How are you going to follow behind?"

I pull on my hat and jacket, then zip it and pull the hood over my head so that only my face shows.

"I'll be fine. I have advanced hearing, like you," I say.

She eyes me skeptically and shakes her head. I grab Bernie Kosar's leash and clip it to his collar.

"Only until we get to the truck," I tell him, since he hates walking on a leash. On second thought, I lean down to carry him since his leg is still healing, but he tells me he'd rather walk himself.

"Ready when you are," I say.

"All right, let's do this," Six says.

Sam offers his hand to her a little too enthusiastically. I stifle a laugh.

"What?" he asks.

I shake my head. "Nothing. I'll follow you as best I can, but don't get too far ahead."

"Just cough if you can't follow and we'll stop. The truck is only a few minutes' walk from here, behind the abandoned barn," Six says. "Can't miss it."

As the door flings open, Sam and Six disappear.

"That's our cue, BK. Just the two of us now."

He follows me out, trotting happily with his tongue

dangling. Aside from quick bathroom trips to the small plot of grass beside the motel, Bernie Kosar's been cooped up like the rest of us.

The night air is cool and fresh, carrying a scent of pine, and the wind on my face brings me instantly back to life. As I walk I close my eyes and try to sense Six by combing the air with my mind, reaching out and feeling the landscape with telekinesis, the same way I was able to stop the speeding bullet in Athens by grabbing everything in the air. I feel them, a few feet ahead of me and slightly to the right. I give Six a nudge and she startles, her breath catching in her throat. Three seconds later she shoulders into me, nearly causing me to fall. I laugh. And so does she.

"What are you guys doing?" Sam asks. He's annoyed with our little game. "We're supposed to be quiet, remember?"

We make it to the truck, which is parked behind a dilapidated old barn that looks as though it's ready to collapse. Six releases Sam's hand and he climbs into the middle of the cab. Six jumps behind the wheel, and I slide in next to Sam with BK at my feet.

"Holy crap, dude, what happened to your hair?" I goad Sam.

"Shut up."

Six starts the truck and I smile as she steers us onto the road, flicking on the headlights when the wheels touch the asphalt.

"What?" Sam asks.

"I was just thinking that, out of the four of us, three are aliens, two are fugitives with terrorist ties, and not a single one of us has a valid driver's license. Something tells me things might get interesting."

Even Six can't help but smile at this.

CHAPTER
FOUR

"I WAS THIRTEEN WHEN THEY CAUGHT UP TO us," Six says when we cross into Tennessee, fifteen minutes after leaving the Trucksville Motel behind. I'd asked her to tell us about how she and Katarina were captured. "We were in West Texas after fleeing Mexico because of a stupid mistake. We had both been completely entranced by some stupid internet post that Two had written, though we didn't know it was by Two at the time, and we responded. We were lonely in Mexico, living in some dusty town in the middle of nowhere, and we just had to know if it really was a member of the Garde."

I nod, knowing what she's talking about. Henri had also seen the blog post while we were in Colorado. I had been in a school spelling bee, and the scar had come while I was onstage. I'd been rushed to the hospital and the doctor saw the first scar, and the fresh burn all the way to the bone of the second. When Henri arrived, they'd accused him of child abuse, which was the catalyst behind our fleeing the state and assuming new identities, another new start.

"'Nine, now eight. Are the rest of you out there?'" I ask.

"That's the one."

"So you guys are the ones who responded," I say. Henri had taken screen shots of the post so I could see it. He had tried furiously to hack the computer to delete it before the damage could be done, but he hadn't been quick enough. Two was killed. Somebody else deleted the post right after. We'd assumed it was the Mogadorians.

"We did, simply writing 'We are here'; and not a minute later the scar appeared," Six says, shaking her head. "It was so stupid of Two to post that, knowing she was next. I still can't understand why she'd risk it."

"Do you guys know where she was?" Sam asks.

I look at Six. "Do you? Henri thought it was England, but he couldn't say for sure."

"No idea. All we knew was that if they'd gotten to her that quickly, it wouldn't take long for them to get to us."

"But, how do you even know she posted it?" Sam asks.

Six glances at him.

"What do you mean?"

"I don't know; you guys can't even say for sure where she was, so how do you know it *was* her?"

"Who else would it be?"

"Well, I mean, I watch the way you and John are so cautious. I can't imagine either of you doing something so stupid like that if you knew you were next. Especially with everything you know about the Mogadorians. I don't think you would have posted something to begin with."

"True, Sam."

"So maybe they had already captured Two and were trying to draw some of you guys out before they killed her, which could explain why she was killed seconds after you responded. It could have been a bluff. Or maybe she knew what they were doing, and she killed herself to warn you guys away or something. Who knows. Those are just some guesses, right?"

"Right," I say. But they are good guesses. Ones I hadn't thought about. Ones I wonder if Henri had.

We ride in silence thinking about it. Six drives the speed limit and a few cars cruise past us. The highway itself is lined with overhead lights that make the rolling hills beyond look spooky.

"She could have been scared and desperate," I say. "That could have led her to do something stupid, like write a careless post on the internet."

Sam shrugs. "Just seems kind of unlikely to me."

"But they could have already killed her Cêpan, and she could have become frantic. She must have been twelve, maybe thirteen. Imagine being thirteen and on your own," I say before I realize I'm describing Six's exact scenario. She glances at me, then turns back to the road.

"We never once thought it was a trick," she says. "Though it kind of makes sense. Back then we were just scared. And my ankle was on fire. Kind of hard to think straight when it feels as though your foot is being sawed off."

I nod my head gravely.

"But even after the initial fear, we still didn't consider that angle. We replied, which is what put them on our tail. It was ridiculous for us to do. Maybe you're right, Sam. I can only hope we've grown a little wiser, those of us still left."

Her last sentence hangs in the air. There are only six of us left. Six of us against any number of them. And no way of knowing how we might possibly find one another. We're the only hope. Strength in numbers. The power of six. The thought makes my heart pump at twice its normal speed.

"What?" Six asks.

"There're six of us left."

"I know there are. So what?"

"Six of us, and maybe some of the others still have their Cêpans; maybe they don't. But six to fight who knows how many Mogadorians? A thousand? A hundred thousand? A *million*?"

"Hey, don't forget about me," Sam says. "And Bernie Kosar."

I nod. "Sorry, Sam; you're right. Eight of us." And then all of a sudden I remember something else. "Six, do you know about the second ship that left Lorien?"

"A ship aside from ours?"

"Yeah, it left after ours. Or, at least, I think it did. Loaded with Chimæra. Fifteen or so, and three Cêpan, and maybe a baby. I had visions of it when Henri and I were training, though he was skeptical. But so far all my visions have proven true."

"I had no idea."

"It took off in an old rocket that kind of looked like a NASA shuttle. You know, powered by fuel that left a trail of smoke behind it."

"Then it wouldn't have made it here," Six says.

"Yeah, that's what Henri said."

"Chimæra?" Sam asks. "The same kind of animal as Bernie Kosar?" I nod. He perks up. "Maybe that's how Bernie made it here? Could you imagine if they *all* made it? After seeing what Bernie did during the fight?"

"It'd be amazing," I agree. "But I'm pretty sure old

Bernie here was on our ship."

I run my hand down the length of Bernie Kosar's back and can feel matted scabs still covering most of his body. Sam sighs, leans back in his seat with a look of relief on his face, probably imagining an army of Chimæra coming to our aid at the last minute to defeat the Mogadorians. Six looks into the rearview mirror, and the headlights from the car behind us illuminate a band of light across her face. She looks back to the road wearing the same introspective gaze that Henri always did when driving.

"The Mogadorians," she begins softly, swallowing as Sam and I turn our attention to her. "They caught up to us the day after we responded to Two's post, in a desolate town in West Texas. Katarina had driven fifteen straight hours from Mexico, and it was getting late and we were both exhausted because neither of us had slept. We stopped at a motel off the highway, not all that different from the one we just left. It was in a tiny town that looked like something out of an old Western movie, full of cowboys and ranchers. There were even hitching posts outside some of the buildings so that the people could tie up their horses. It was very weird, but we had just come from a dusty town in Mexico, so we didn't think twice about stopping."

She pauses as a car cruises past us. She follows it with her eyes and checks the speedometer before turning back to the road.

"We went to get something to eat at a diner. About halfway through our meal, a man entered and took a seat. He was wearing a white shirt and tie, but it was a Western tie and his clothes looked outdated. We ignored him, even though I noticed the others in the diner staring at him, the same way they were staring at us. At one point he turned and gazed our way, but since everyone else had done the same, I didn't piece it together. I was only thirteen then, and it was hard to think of anything at that point other than sleep and food. So we finished eating and went back to our room. Katarina jumped into the shower; and when she stepped out, wrapped in a robe, there was a knock at the door. We looked at each other. She asked who it was, and the man answered that he was the motel manager and had brought fresh towels and ice; and without thinking twice, I walked to the door and opened it."

"Oh no," Sam says.

Six nods. "It was the man from the diner with the Western tie. He walked straight into the room and shut the door. I was wearing my pendant in plain view. He knew immediately who I was, and Katarina and I knew immediately who he was. In one fluid motion he pulled a knife from the waistband of his trousers and swung for my head. He was fast, and I had no time to react. I had no Legacies yet, no defenses. I was dead. But then the weirdest thing happened. As the knife dug into my skull, it was *his* skull that split open. I didn't feel a thing. I learned later they had no idea how the charm worked, that he couldn't kill me until numbers one through five were dead. He dropped to the ground and burst into ash."

"Wicked," Sam says.

"Wait," I interrupt. "From what I've seen, Mogadorians are pretty recognizable. Their skin is so white it looks bleached. And their teeth and eyes . . ." I trail off. "How could you not have known it in the diner? Why'd you let him into the room?"

"I'm pretty sure only the scouts and soldiers look like that. They're the Mogadorians' version of the military. That's what Katarina said, anyway. The rest of them look as much like normal humans as we do. The one who came into the diner looked like an accountant, wearing wire-rimmed glasses, black slacks, and a white short-sleeved dress shirt and that tie. He even had a really dorky mustache. I remember him being tan. We had no idea they had followed us."

"That's reassuring," I say sarcastically. I replay the image of the knife plunging into Six's skull and killing the Mogadorian instead. If one of them tried the same thing with a knife on me, right now, I would be killed. I push the thought away and ask, "Do you think they're still in Paradise?"

She says nothing for a minute, and when she finally speaks, I wish she had stayed silent instead. "I think they might be."

"So Sarah's in danger?"

"Everyone's in danger, John. Every person we know in Paradise, every person we don't know in Paradise."

All of Paradise is probably under surveillance, and I know it's not safe to go within fifty miles of it. Or to call. Or even to send a letter, or they'd learn the pull Sarah has on me, the connection we have.

"Anyway," Sam says, wanting to get back to the story. "The Mogadorian accountant falls to the floor and dies. Then what?"

"Katarina threw the Chest to me and grabbed our suitcase, and we sprinted out of the motel room, Katarina still in her robe. The truck was unlocked, and we jumped inside. Another Mog came charging out from behind the motel. Kat was so flustered that she couldn't find the keys. She locked the doors, though, and the windows were rolled up. But the guy wasted no time at all and punched straight through the passenger-side glass and grabbed me by the shirt. Katarina screamed, and some men nearby jumped into action.

"Others poured out of the diner to see what was happening. The Mogadorian had no choice but to let go of me to face the men.

"'The keys are in the motel room!' Katarina yelled.

She looked at me with these big, huge, desperate eyes. She was panicking. We both were. I jumped out of the truck and sprinted back to our room for the keys. Those men in Texas, they were the only reason we got away then; they saved our lives. When I came out of the motel room with the keys, one of the Texans was aiming a gun at the Mogadorian.

"We have no idea what happened after that because Katarina sped away and we didn't look back. We hid the Chest a few weeks later, right before they caught up to us for good."

"Don't they already have the Chests from the first three?" Sam asks.

"I'm sure they do, but what use are they? The second we die the Chest unlocks itself, and everything inside becomes useless," she says, and I nod, knowing that much from past conversations with Henri.

"Not only are the objects worthless," I say, "but they completely disintegrate the same way the Mogadorians do when they're killed."

"Wicked," Sam says.

And then I remember the sticky note I found when saving Henri in Athens, Ohio.

"Those guys Henri visited who ran the *They Walk Among Us* magazine?"

"Yeah?"

"They had this source who apparently caught a

Mogadorian and tortured it for information, and he supposedly knew that Number Seven was being trailed in Spain and that Number Nine was somewhere in South America."

Six thinks about it a moment. She bites her lip and glances in the rearview mirror. "I know for a fact that Number Seven is a girl; I remember that much from the ride in the ship." The second this leaves her mouth, a siren blares behind us.

CHAPTER
FIVE

THE SNOW STOPS ON SATURDAY NIGHT. THE SCRAP-
ing sound of shovels against asphalt fills the night air.
From the window I can see the faint silhouettes of residents throwing snow to less cumbersome places, readying
themselves for the morning walk for Sunday obligations.
There's a certain tranquillity to the town at work on a
quiet night, everyone bound by the same cause, and I wish
I was out there among them. And then the bedtime bell
tolls. In the room fourteen girls find their beds within
the minute, and the lights are shut off.

The second I close my eyes the dream begins. I stand
in a field of flowers on a warm summer day. To my right,
in the distance, the outline of a jagged mountain range
stands against the backdrop of the setting sun; to my left
lies the sea. A girl dressed in black, with raven hair and
striking gray eyes, appears out of nowhere. She wears a
smile, both fierce and confident. It's just the two of us.

Then a great disturbance kicks up behind me, as though an isolated earthquake has just begun, and the ground is split open and torn apart. I don't turn to see what's actually happening. The girl lifts her hand, beckoning me to take it, her eyes locked on mine. I reach for it. My eyes open.

Light streams in through the windows. While it feels as though minutes have passed, in reality the whole night has gone by. I shake my head free of the dream. Sunday is the day of rest, though ironically for us it's the busiest day of the week, starting with a long Mass.

Ostensibly the large Sunday crowd is because of religious devotion within the community, but really it's because of El Festín, the grand dinner that follows Mass. All of us who live here must work it. My place is in the cafeteria line. It's only after dinner that we're finally free. If I'm lucky we'll finish by four, then we're not due back until the sun sets. This time of year it comes a little after six.

We rush to the showers, quickly bathe, brush our teeth and our hair, then dress in our Sunday best, identical black-and-white outfits that leave only our hands and heads showing. When most of the other girls have fled the room, Adelina walks in. She stands in front of me and fixes the neck of my tunic. It makes me feel much younger than I really am. I can hear the throng of people filing into the nave. Adelina remains silent. So do I. I look at the gray streaks in her auburn hair, which I hadn't noticed before. There are wrinkles at her eyes and mouth. She's forty-two but looks ten years older.

"I had a dream about a girl with raven hair and gray eyes who reached her hand out to me," I say, breaking the silence. "She wanted me to take it."

"Okay," she says, unsure of why I'm telling her about a dream.

"Do you think she could be one of us?"

She gives the collar a final tug. "I think you shouldn't read into your dreams so much."

I want to argue with her, but I'm not sure what to say. So instead I utter, "It felt real."

"Some dreams do."

"But you said a long time ago that on Lorien we could sometimes communicate with each other over long distances."

"Yes, and right after that I would read you stories about a wolf who could blow down houses and a goose who laid golden eggs."

"Those were fairy tales."

"It's all one big fairy tale, Marina."

I grit my teeth. "How can you say that? We both know it's not a fairy tale. We both know where we came from and why we're here. I don't know why you act as if you didn't come from Lorien and you don't have a duty to teach me."

She puts her hands behind her back and looks at the ceiling. "Marina, since I've been here, since we've been here, we've been fortunate to learn the truth about creation and where we came from and what our real mission is on Earth. And that's all found in the Bible."

"And the Bible isn't a fairy tale?"

Her shoulders stiffen. She furrows her brows and flexes her jaw.

"Lorien isn't a fairy tale," I say before she can respond, and, using telekinesis, I lift a pillow from a nearby bed and spin it in the air. Adelina does something she's never done before: she slaps me. Hard. I drop the pillow and press my hand to my stinging cheek with my mouth wide-open.

"Don't you dare let them see you do that!" she says furiously.

"What I did right there, that's not a fairy tale. I am not part of a fairy tale. You are my Cêpan, and *you* are not part of a fairy tale."

"Call it what you will," she says.

"But haven't you read the news? You know the boy in Ohio is one of us; you have to! He could be our only chance!"

"Our only chance at what?" she asks.

"A life."

"And what do you call this?"

"Spending our days living the lies of an alien race is no life," I say.

She shakes her head. "Give it up, Marina," she says, and walks away. I have no choice but to follow.

Marina. The name sounds so normal now, so *me.* I don't think twice when Adelina hisses the name at me or when one of the other girls in the orphanage yells it on the way out the school doors, waving my forgotten math book. But it hasn't always been my name. Back when we were aimlessly looking for a warm meal or a bed, back before Spain and Santa Teresa, before Adelina was Adelina, I had been Geneviève. Adelina was Odette. Those were our French names.

"We should change our names with every new country," Adelina had whispered when she was Signy and we were in Norway, where our ship landed after months at sea. She'd chosen Signy because it had been written on the woman's shirt behind the counter.

"What should my name be?" I'd asked.

"Whatever you want it to be," she'd said. We'd been at a café in the middle of a bleak village, enjoying the heat from the mug of hot chocolate we'd shared. Signy had stood and retrieved the weekend's newspaper from a nearby table. On the front page was the most beautiful woman I had ever seen. Blond hair, high cheekbones, deep blue eyes. Her name was Birgitta. My name had become Birgitta.

Even when we were on a train and the countries zipped past the window like trees, we'd always change our names, if just for a few hours. Yes, it was to stay hidden from the Mogadorians or anyone else who might be following us, but it was also the one thing that raised our spirits among so much disappointment. I'd thought it was so much fun, I wish we'd traveled over Europe several times. In Poland I was Minka and she chose Zali. She was Fatima in Denmark; I was Yasmin. I had two names in Austria: Sophie and Astrid. She fell in love with Emmalina.

"Why Emmalina?" I'd asked.

She laughed. "I don't know exactly. I guess I love that it's almost two names in one. Either one is beautiful, but you smash them together and you get something extraordinary."

In fact, I wonder now if that was the last time I heard her laugh. Or the last time we hugged or made proclamations about our destinies. I believe it was the last time I sensed she cared about being my Cêpan or what happened to Lorien—what happened to me.

We arrive at Mass just before it begins. The only available seats are in the very last row, which is where I prefer to sit anyhow. Adelina shuffles to the front where the Sisters sit. Father Marco, the priest, begins with an opening prayer in his always-somber voice, and most of his words are muffled beyond recognition by the time they reach me. I like it this way, sitting through Mass with detached apathy. I try not to think about Adelina smacking me, filling my mind instead with what I will do when

El Festín finally ends. None of the snow has melted, but I'm determined to make it to the cave anyway. I have something new to paint, and I want to finish the picture of John Smith that I started last week.

Mass drags on forever, or at least it feels that way, with rites, liturgies, communion, readings, prayers, rituals. When we reach the final prayer I'm exhausted and don't even bother pretending to pray like I normally do, and instead sit there with my head lifted and eyes open, scanning the backs of the heads of those in attendance. Almost all of them are familiar. One man sleeps upright in his pew, arms crossed and chin touching his chest. I watch him until something in his dream startles him awake with a grunt. Several heads turn his way as he gathers his bearings. I can't help but smile; and as I look away, my eyes find Sister Dora scowling at me. I drop my head, close my eyes, and feign prayer, mouthing the words that Father Marco recites up front, but I know I've been caught. It's what Sister Dora thrives on. She goes out of her way to catch us in the act of doing something we shouldn't.

Prayer concludes with the sign of the cross, finally bringing an end to Mass. I'm up out of my seat before anyone else, and I hurry from the nave to the kitchen. Sister Dora may be the largest among all the Sisters, but she shows surprising agility when it's needed, and I don't want to give her the chance to catch me. If she doesn't, I might escape punishment. And I do, because when she enters the cafeteria five minutes later as I'm peeling potatoes beside a gangly fourteen-year-old named Paola and her twelve-year-old sister, Lucia, she only glares at me.

"What's up with her?" Paola asks.

"She caught me smiling during Mass."

"Good thing you weren't paddled," Lucia says out of the corner of her mouth.

I nod and go back to what I'm doing. As fleeting as they are, it's these small moments that bring us girls together, the fact that we share a common enemy. When I was younger, I thought commonalities like this, and of being orphaned and living under this same tyrannical roof, would unite us all as immediate and lifelong friends. But really it only worked to further divide us, creating small factions within our already small group—the pretty girls huddling together (La Gorda excepted, but still a part of their crowd), the smart girls, the athletic ones, the young ones—until I was left all alone.

A half hour later when everything's ready, we carry the food from the kitchen to the serving line. The crowd of waiting people clap. At the back of the line I see my favorite person in all of Santa Teresa: Héctor Ricardo. His clothes are dirty and wrinkled, and his hair is tousled. He has bloodshot eyes, an almost scarlet complexion to his face and cheeks. Even from as far away as I am I notice he has a slight shake in each hand, as he always does on Sundays—the only day in the week he swears off drinking.

He looks especially rough today, though when he finally approaches, he holds his tray out and fixes on his face the most optimistic smile he can muster.

"And how are you, my dear Queen of the sea?" he asks.

I curtsy in return. "I'm doing well, Héctor. And you?"

He shrugs, then says, "Life is but a fine wine, to be sipped and savored."

I laugh. Héctor always has some old adage to share.

I first met Héctor when I was thirteen. He had been sitting outside the lone café on Calle Principal drinking a bottle of wine by himself. It was midafternoon, and I had been on my way home from school. Our eyes met as I passed.

"Marina, as of the sea," he had said, and I'd found it odd that he knew my name, though I shouldn't have since I'd seen him every week at the church pretty much since the day I'd arrived. "Come keep a drunk man company a few minutes."

I did. I'm not sure why. Maybe because there's something entirely agreeable about Héctor. He makes me feel relaxed, and doesn't pretend to be somebody he isn't like so many other people do. He exudes the attitude of "This is who I am; take it or leave it."

That first day we had sat and talked long enough for him to finish one bottle of wine and order a second.

"You stick with Héctor Ricardo," he'd said when I had to get back to the convent. "I'll take care of you; it's in my name. The Latin root of Hector means 'to defend and hold fast.' And Ricardo means 'power and bravery,'" he'd said, thumping his chest twice with his right fist. "Héctor Ricardo will take care of you!"

I could tell he meant it.

He'd gone on. "Marina. 'Of the sea.' That's what your name means; did you know that?"

I'd told him I did not. I'd wondered what Birgitta meant. And Yasmin. What Emmalina was rooted in.

"That means you are Santa Teresa's own Sea Queen," he'd said with a sideways grin.

I'd laughed at him. "I think you've been drinking too much, Héctor Ricardo."

"Yes," he'd replied. "I am the town drunk, dear Marina. But don't let that fool you. Héctor Ricardo is a defender all the same. And besides, show me a man without vice and I'll show you one without virtue!"

Years later, he's one of the few people I can call a friend.

It takes twenty-five minutes for the few hundred people to receive their due today; and after the last person leaves the line, it's our turn to eat, sitting away from the others. As a group we eat as fast as we can, knowing that the quicker we clean up and get everything put away, the sooner we'll be on our own.

Fifteen minutes later the five of us who work the line are scraping pots and pans and wiping counters. At its best, cleanup takes an hour, and that's only if everyone leaves the cafeteria after they're done eating, which rarely happens. As we're cleaning, when I know the others aren't looking, I throw into a bag the nonperishable items I plan to take to the cave today: dried fruits and berries, nuts, a can of tuna fish, a can of beans. This has become another weekly tradition of mine. For a long time I convinced myself I was doing it so I could snack when painting the cave's walls. But the truth is I'm creating a stockpile of food in case the worst arrives and I have to hide. And by the worst, I mean *them*.

CHAPTER
SIX

WHEN I FINALLY WALK OUTSIDE AFTER CHANGING into warmer clothes and rolling my bed blanket under my arm, the sun is shifted to the west and there's not a cloud in the sky. It's half past four, which gives me an hour and a half at best. I hate the rushed quality of Sundays, the way the day creeps by until the very moment we're free, at which point time flies. I look to the east, and the light reflected off the snow causes me to squint. The cave is over two rocky hills. With as much snow as there is on the ground now, I'm not even sure I'll see the opening today. But I pull on my hat, zip up my jacket, tie the blanket around my neck like a cape, and head east.

Two tall birch trees mark the trail's start, and my feet turn cold the second I enter the deep drifts. The blanket-cape sweeps the snow behind me, erasing my footprints. I pass a few recognizable fixtures that show the way—a rock jutting out past the others, a tree that leans at a slightly different angle. After about twenty minutes I pass the rock formation identical to a camel's back, which tells me I'm almost there.

I have the faint sensation of being watched, possibly followed. I turn and scan the mountainside. Silence. Snow, nothing else. The blanket around my neck has done a great job of hiding my tracks. A slow, prickly feeling crawls up the back of my neck. I've seen the way rabbits blend into the landscape, going unnoticed until you're almost on top of them, and I know that just because I can't see somebody doesn't mean they can't see me.

Five minutes later I finally spot the rounded shrub that blocks the entrance. The cave's mouth looks like an oversized groundhog hole cutting into the mountain, and that's exactly what I had mistaken it for years ago. But when I'd looked more closely I knew I was wrong. The cave was deep and dark, and back then I could see next to nothing in the little light that entered. There was an implicit desire to discover the cave's secrets, and I wonder if this is what caused the Legacy to develop: my ability to see in the dark. I can't see in the dark as easily as I can in the day, but even the deepest recesses of black glow as though lit by candlelight.

On my knees, I knock away just enough snow to be able to slip down and in. I drop the bag ahead of me, untie the blanket from my neck and sweep it across the snow to hide my footprints, then hang it on the other side of the opening to keep out the wind. The entrance is narrow for the first three meters, followed by a slightly wider passageway that winds down a steep decline large enough to navigate while standing; and after that the cave opens, revealing itself.

The ceiling is high and echoing, and its five walls smoothly transition into one another, creating an almost perfect polygon. A stream cuts through the back right corner. I have no idea where the water comes from or where it goes—springing up through one of the walls only to disappear into the earth's deeper depths—but the level never changes, offering a reservoir of icy cold water regardless of the time of day or season. With the constant fresh source of water, this is the perfect place to hide. From the Mogadorians, the Sisters, and the girls—even Adelina. It's also the perfect place to use and hone my Legacies.

I drop the bag beside the stream, remove the nonperishables, and place them on the rock ledge, which already holds several chocolate bars, small bags of granola, oatmeal, cereal, powdered milk, a jar of peanut butter, and various cans of fruits, vegetables, and soup. Enough for weeks. Only when everything is put away do I stand and allow myself to be greeted by the landscapes and faces I've painted on the walls.

From the very first time a brush was put into my hand

at school, I fell in love with painting. Painting allows me to see things as I want to and not necessarily as they are; it's an escape, a way to preserve thoughts and memories, a way to create hopes and dreams.

I rinse the brushes, rubbing the stiffness from the bristles, and then mix the paint with water and sediment from the creek bed, creating earthy tones that match the gray of the cave's walls. Then I walk to where John Smith's partially completed face greets me with his uncertain grin.

I spend a lot of time on his dark blue eyes, trying to get them just right. There's a certain glint that's hard to replicate; and when I tire of trying, I start on a new painting, that of the girl with the raven hair I had dreamed about. Unlike John's eyes, I have no trouble at all with hers, letting the gray wall do its magic; and I think that if I were to wave a lighted candle in front of it, the color would slightly change, as I'm sure her eyes do depending on her mood and the light around her. It's just a feeling I get. The other faces I've painted are Hector's, Adelina's, a few of the town's vendors I see every weekday. Because this cave is so deep and dark, I believe my paintings are safe from anyone's eyes but mine. It's still a risk, I know, but I just can't help myself.

After a while I go up and push aside my blanket, poking my head out of the cave. I see nothing but drifts of white and the bottom of the sun kissing the horizon line—which tells me it's time to go. I haven't painted nearly as much or as long as I would have liked. Before cleaning the brushes I walk to the wall opposite John and look at the big red square I've painted there. Before it was a red square I'd done something foolish, something I know would have exposed me as a Garde, and painted a list.

I touch the square and think of the first three numbers that are underneath, running my fingertips over the dried, cracked paint, deeply saddened by what those lines meant. If there is any consolation in their deaths, it's that they can now rest easy and no longer have to live in fear.

I turn from the square, from the hidden and destroyed list, clean the brushes, and put everything away.

"I'll see you guys next week," I say to the faces.

Before leaving the cave I take in the landscape painted on the wall beside the passageway leading in and out. It's the first painting I'd ever attempted here, sometime around the age of twelve; and while I have touched it up a bit over the years, mostly it has remained the same. It's the view of Lorien from my own bedroom window and I still remember it perfectly. Rolling hills and grassy plains accentuated with tall trees. A thick slice of blue river that cuts across the terrain. Small bits of paint here and there that represent the Chimæra drinking from its cool waters. And then, off in the far distance at the very top, standing tall over the nine archways representing the planet's nine Elders, is the statue of Pittacus Lore, so small it's almost indistinct; but there's no mistaking it for what it really is, standing out among the others: a beacon of hope.

I hurry from the cave and back to the convent, keeping an eye open for anything out of place. The sun is just below the horizon when I leave the path, which means I'm running late. I push through the heavy oak doors to find the welcome bells ringing; somebody new has arrived.

I join the others on their way to our sleeping quarters. We have a welcoming tradition here, standing next to our beds with our hands behind our backs, facing the new girl and introducing ourselves one by one. I'd hated it when I had first arrived; hated feeling on display when all I wanted to do was hide.

In the doorway, standing beside Sister Lucia, is a small girl with auburn hair, curious brown eyes, and petite features not unlike a mouse. She stares at the stone floor, shifting her weight uncomfortably from one leg to the other. Her fingers fiddle with the waist of her gray wool dress, which is patterned with pink flowers. There's a small pink clip in her hair, and she wears black shoes with silver buckles. I feel sorry for her. Sister Lucia waits for us all to smile, all thirty-seven of us, and then she speaks.

"This is Ella. She's seven years old and will be staying

with us from here on out. I trust that you will all make her feel welcome."

A rumor is later whispered that her parents had been killed in an automobile accident and she's here because she has no other relatives.

Ella flutters her eyes up as each person says their name, but mostly she keeps her gaze on the floor. It's obvious she's scared and sad, but I can tell she's the kind of girl people will fall for. She won't be here for very long.

We all walk to the nave together so Sister Lucia can explain to Ella its importance to the orphanage. Gabby García stands yawning in the back of the group, and I turn to look at her. Just beyond Gabby, framed in one of the clear panes of the stained glass window at the far wall, a dark figure stands outside looking in. I can just make him out in the oncoming nightfall, his black hair, heavy brows, and thick mustache. His eyes are trained on me; there's no doubt about it. My heart skips a beat. I gasp and take a step backwards. Everyone's head snaps around.

"Marina, are you okay?" Sister Lucia asks.

"Nothing," I say, then shake my head. "I mean, yes, I'm fine. Sorry."

My heart pounds and my hands shake. I clasp them together so it's not noticeable. Sister Lucia says something else about welcoming Ella, but I'm too distracted to hear it. I turn back to the window. The figure is gone. The group's dismissed.

I rush across the nave and look outside. I don't see anyone, but I do see a single set of boot prints in the snow. I step away from the window. Perhaps it's a potential foster parent assessing the girls from afar, or perhaps it's one of the girl's real parents sneaking a glance at the daughter he can't provide for. But for some reason I don't feel safe. I don't like the way his eyes settled on me.

"Are you okay?" I hear behind me. I jump, then turn around. It's Adelina, standing with her hands clasped in front of her waist. A rosary dangles from her fingers.

"Yes, I'm fine," I say.

"You look like you've seen a ghost."

Worse than a ghost, I think, but I don't say that. I'm scared after this morning's slap, and I pocket my hands.

"There was somebody at the window watching me," I whisper. "Just now."

Her eyes squint.

"Look. Look at the prints," I say, turning back and motioning to the ground.

Adelina's back is straight and rigid, and for a moment I think she's actually concerned; but then she softens and steps forward. She takes in the prints.

"I'm sure it's nothing," she says.

"What do you mean it's nothing? How can you say that?"

"I wouldn't worry. It could have been anyone."

"He was looking right at me."

"Marina, wake up. With today's new arrival there are thirty-eight girls here. We do the best we can keeping you girls safe, but that doesn't mean the occasional boy from town doesn't wander up here to sneak a peek. We've even caught some of them. And don't think for a minute we don't know the way that some of the others dress, changing clothes on the walk to school to look provocative. There are six of you turning eighteen soon, and everyone in town knows it. So, I wouldn't worry about the man you saw. He was probably nothing more than a boy from school."

I'm sure this was no boy from school, but I don't say so.

"Anyway, I wanted to apologize for this morning. It was wrong of me to strike you."

"It's okay," I say, and for a minute I think of bringing John Smith up again, but I decide against it. It would create more friction, which I want to avoid. I miss the way we used to be. And it's hard enough living here without having Adelina angry at me.

Before she says anything further, Sister Dora hurries over and whispers something into Adelina's ear. Adelina looks at me and nods and smiles.

"We'll talk later," she says.

They walk away, leaving me to myself. I look back down at the boot prints, and a shiver runs up my back.

For the next hour I pace from room to room looking

down the hill at the dark town cast in shadow, but I don't see the looming figure again. Perhaps Adelina is right.

But no matter how hard I try convincing myself, I don't think she is.

CHAPTER
SEVEN

SILENCE FALLS IN THE TRUCK. SIX GLANCES IN the rearview mirror. Flashing red and blue plays along her face.

"Not good," Sam says.

"Shit," Six says.

The bright lights and screaming siren rouse even Bernie Kosar, who peers out the back window.

"What do we do?" Sam asks, his voice frightened and desperate.

Six takes her foot off the accelerator and steers the truck to the right side of the highway.

"It might mean nothing," she says.

I shake my head. "Doubtful."

"Wait. Why are we stopping?" Sam asks. "Don't stop. Step on it!"

"Let's see what happens first. We'll never make it if we lead this cop on a high-speed chase. He'll call for backup and they'll get a helicopter. Then we'll never get away."

Bernie Kosar begins growling. I tell him to chill out and he stops, but he keeps vigil out the window. Gravel pings against the truck as we slow along the shoulder. Cars speed past in the left lanes. The cop car pulls to within ten feet of our rear bumper, and its headlights fill the truck's interior. The cop flips them off, then aims a spotlight straight through the rear window. The siren stops wailing but the lights still flash.

"What do you think?" I ask, watching from the side mirror. The spotlight is blinding; but when a car passes, I can see that the officer is holding the radio up in his right hand, probably running our license plate, or calling for backup.

"Our best bet is to flee on foot," Six says. "If that's what it comes to."

"Turn off your vehicle and remove the key from the ignition," the cop barks through a speaker.

Six turns off the truck. She looks at me and removes the key.

"If he radios us in, you have to assume that *they'll* hear it," I say.

She nods, says nothing. From behind us the officer's car door creaks. His approaching boots click bleakly on the asphalt.

"Do you think he'll recognize us?" Sam asks.

"Shhh," Six says.

When I look in the side mirror again, I realize the officer isn't walking towards the driver's side, and has instead veered right and is coming towards me. He taps my window with his chrome flashlight. I hesitate for a moment, then roll it down. He shines the light in my face, causing me to squint. Then he moves the beam to Sam, then Six. He forces his brows together, studying each of us closely while he tries to determine why we look so familiar.

"Is there a problem, officer?" I ask.

"You kids from around here?"

"No, sir."

"Ya care tellin' me why y'alls drivin' through Tennessee in a Chevy S-10 with North Carolina plates belonging to a Ford Ranger?"

He glares at me, waiting for an answer. My face feels warm as I struggle to find one. I have nothing. The officer bends down and again flashes the light on Six. Then at Sam.

"Anyone wanna try me?" he asks.

He's met with silence, which causes him to chuckle.

"Of course not," he says. "Three kids from North Carolina driving through Tennessee in a stolen truck on a Saturday night. Ya kids are on a dope run, aren't ya?"

I turn and stare into his face, which is ruddy and clean shaven.

"What do you want to do?" I ask.

"What do *I* wanna do? Ha! Ya kids are going to jail!"

I shake my head at him. "I wasn't talking to you."

He leans forward with his elbows on the door.

"So where's the dope?" he says, and then sweeps the flashlight across the interior of the truck. He stops when the light hits the Chest at my feet, then a smug smile spreads along his lips. "Well, never mind, looks like I found it myself."

He reaches to open the door. In one lightning-quick motion I shoulder-open the door and knock the officer backwards. He grunts and moves for his gun before he even hits the ground. Using telekinesis, I rip it away, bringing it to me as I step out. I open the chamber and empty the bullets into my hand and snap the gun shut.

"What the . . ." The officer is dumbfounded.

"We're not dealing dope," I say.

Sam and Six are out of the truck now and standing beside me.

"Put these in your pocket," I say to Sam, handing him the bullets. Then I hand him the gun.

"What do you want me to do with this?" Sam asks.

"I don't know; put it in your bag with your dad's gun."

Off in the distance, two miles away, the whine of a

second siren reaches me. The officer stares intently at me, his eyes wide in recognition.

"Aw hell, you the boys from the news, aren't ya? Y'all are those terrorists!" he says, and spits on the ground.

"Shut up," Sam says. "We're not terrorists."

I turn around and grab Bernie Kosar, who's still in the cab because of his broken leg. As I'm lowering him to the ground, an agonizing scream rips through the night. I jerk around and see Sam convulsing, and it takes a second to realize what's happened. The officer has Tasered him. I tear the Taser from him while I'm ten feet away. Sam falls to the ground and shakes as though he's having a seizure.

"What the hell is the matter with you!" I yell at the officer. "We're trying to save you; don't you see that!"

Confusion crosses his face. I press the button of the Taser as it hovers in the air. Blue currents snap across the top of it. The cop scrambles away. I use telekinesis to drag him through the pebbles and trash on the side of the road. He kicks and tries in vain to get away.

"Please," he begs. "I'm sorry, I'm sorry."

"Don't, John," Six says.

I refuse to listen to her. I'm blind to anything other than retribution, and I don't feel a shred of remorse as I slam the Taser into the officer's gut and hold it there for a full two seconds.

"How do you like it, huh? Big, tough guy with a

Taser? Why can't anyone see we're not the bad guys!"

He shakes his head, his face locked in a horrified grimace, sweat beads glistening on his forehead.

"We have to get out of here fast," Six says as the red and blue lights of the second police car appear on the horizon.

I lift Sam and pull him over my shoulder. Bernie Kosar is able to run on his own on only three legs. I carry the Chest under my left arm while Six carries everything else.

"This way," she says, jumping over the guardrail and entering a barren field leading to the dark hills a mile away.

I sprint as fast as I can with Sam and the Chest. Bernie Kosar tires of hobbling and morphs into a bird and speeds ahead of us. Not a minute later the second car arrives on the scene, followed by a third. I can't tell if the officers are pursuing us on foot; but if they are, Six and I can easily outrun them even as weighed down as we are.

"Put me down," Sam finally says.

"Are you okay?" I put him down.

"Yeah, I'm fine." Sam is a little unsteady. Sweat beads his forehead, and he wipes it away with the sleeve of his jacket and takes a deep breath.

"Come on," Six says. "They aren't going to let us go that easily. We have ten minutes, fifteen at the most, until we're hiding from a helicopter."

We make for the hills, Six in the lead, then me, then Sam struggling to keep up. He moves much faster than when we ran the mile in gym class a few months ago. It feels like years ago. None of us looks back; but as soon as we reach the first incline, the howl of a bloodhound fills the air. One of the officers has brought a police dog.

"Any ideas?" I ask Six.

"I was hoping we could hide our stuff and go invisible. That would elude a copter, but the dog will still pick up our scent."

"Shit," I say. I look around. There's a hill to our right.

"Let's get to the top and see what's on the other side," I say.

Bernie Kosar zips ahead and disappears into the night sky. Six leads, stumbling wildly up. I follow behind her; and Sam, who is breathing heavily yet still moving swiftly, brings up the rear.

We stop at the top. Faint outlines of more hills as far as I can see, nothing more. Very softly I hear the trickle of running water. I spin around. Eight sets of flashing lights line the highway, sandwiching Sam's father's truck. In the distance, coming from both directions, two more cop cars are speeding towards the scene. Bernie Kosar lands beside me and turns back into a beagle, tongue dangling. The police bloodhound barks, closer than before. There's no doubt that it's following our scent, which means that officers on foot can't be far behind.

"We have to get the dog off our trail," Six says.

"Can you hear that?" I ask her.

"Hear what?"

"The sound of water. I think there's some kind of stream at the bottom of this. Maybe a river."

"I hear it," Sam chimes in.

An idea pops into my head. I unzip my jacket and remove my shirt. I wipe it across my face, my chest, soaking up every bit of sweat and scent I might have. I throw it at Sam.

"Do what I just did," I say.

"No way, that's disgusting."

"Sam, the entire state of Tennessee is hot on our trail. We don't have much time."

He sighs but obeys me. Six does too, unsure of what I have planned but willing to go along with it. I put on a new shirt and slip on my jacket. Six tosses me the soiled shirt and I rub it over Bernie Kosar's face and body.

"We're going to need your help, buddy. You up for it?"

I can hardly see him in the dark, but the sound of his tail thumping excitedly on the ground is unmistakable. Always eager to assist, happy to be alive. I can sense within him the odd thrill of being chased, and I can't help but feel it myself.

"What's your plan?" Six asks.

"We have to hurry," I say, taking the first steps downhill towards the running water. Bernie Kosar again turns himself into a bird and we race down, occasionally hearing the bloodhound bark and howl. It's closing the gap. If my idea fails, I wonder if I might communicate with it and tell it to stop following us.

Bernie Kosar waits for us at the bank of the wide river, which has a still quality to its surface that tells me it's much deeper than it sounded from the top of the hill.

"We have to swim across," I say. There's no other choice.

"What? John, do you understand what happens to the human body when it's in freezing water? Cardiac arrest from shock, for one. And if that doesn't kill you, then the loss of feeling in your arms and legs will make it impossible to swim. We'll freeze and drown," Sam objects.

"It's the only way to get the dog from following our scent. At least we'll have a chance this way."

"This is suicide. Remember for a second that I'm not an alien."

I drop to a knee in front of Bernie Kosar. "You have to

take this shirt," I say to him. "Drag it across the ground as fast as you can, for two or three miles. We'll cross the river so the bloodhound loses our scent and follows this one instead. Then we'll run some more. You should have no trouble catching up to us if you fly."

Bernie Kosar transforms into a large bald eagle, takes the shirt into his talons, and speeds off.

"No time to waste," I say, gripping the Chest in my left arm so I can swim with my right. Just as I'm about to jump into the water Six grabs my bicep.

"Sam's right; we'll *freeze*, John," she urges. She looks afraid.

"They're too close. We have no other choice," I say. She bites her lip, her eyes sweeping the river, and turns back to me, giving my arm another squeeze.

"Yes we do," she says. She lets go of my arm, and the whites of her eyes glisten in the dark. She pushes me behind her and takes a step towards the water, then tilts her head in a gesture of concentration. The bloodhound barks, closer than before.

She exhales slowly. At the same time she lifts her hands out in front of her, and as they come up, the waters of the river begin to part right there before us. With a loud rushing sound, the water foams and churns as it recedes upward to reveal a muddy path five feet wide that cuts across to the other bank. The water hovers, looking like a wave ready to crash. But instead it hangs suspended while icy mist coats our faces.

"Go!" she orders, her face strained in concentration, her eyes on the water.

Sam and I jump down from the bank. My feet sink and the mud comes nearly to my knees, but it still beats swimming in forty-degree temperatures in the dead of night. We tramp through it, taking big steps and struggling to lift our feet from the heavy mud. Once we're across Six follows, rotating her hands as she passes through the massive waves ready to crash into each other, waves of her own creation. She climbs up the bank and then lets it go. The waves smash down with a deep hollow thud as though someone has just done a cannonball into it. The water rises and falls, and then looks no different than it did before.

"Amazing," Sam says. "Just like Moses."

"Come on, we have to get into the trees so the dog can't see us," she says.

The plan works. After just a few minutes, the dog pauses at the riverbank and sniffs wildly. He circles several times and then rushes after Bernie Kosar. Sam, Six, and I take off in the opposite direction, just inside the tree line but near enough to still see the river, going as fast as Sam's legs will permit.

The sound of men's voices yelling to one another reaches us for the first few minutes until we outrun them. Ten minutes after that we hear the first whir of

a helicopter. We stop and wait for it to appear. A minute later, a spotlight shines high in the sky a few miles
away in the direction Bernie Kosar has flown. The light
sweeps the hills, shining one way, rushing the other.

"He should have been back already," I say.

"He's fine, John," Sam says. "He's BK, the most resil-
ient beast I know."

"He has a broken leg."

"But two healthy wings," Six counters. "He's fine.
We have to keep going. They'll figure it out soon, if they
haven't already. We have to stay ahead. The longer we
wait, the closer they'll get."

I nod. She's right. We have to keep going.

After a half mile the river takes a sharp turn to the
right, back towards the highway, away from the hills.
We stop and huddle beneath the low branches of a tall
tree.

"Now what?" Sam asks.

"No idea," I say. We turn in the direction in which
we had just fled. The helicopter is closer now, its spotlight still sweeping back and forth across the hills.

"We have to leave the river," I say.

"Yes, we do," Six says. "He'll find us, John. I promise."

We hear an eagle's scream high in the treetops not far
off. It's too dark to see where he is, and perhaps too dark
for him to see us. I don't think twice about it, even if it

will give away our position—I aim my palms towards the sky and turn my lights on, letting them shine as brightly as I can for a full half second. We wait, listening with our breaths held and heads craned. And then I hear a dog's pant, and Bernie Kosar, changed back into a beagle, comes charging up from the riverbank. He's out of breath but excited, his tongue falling from his mouth and his tail whipping in the air a thousand miles an hour. I bend down and pet him.

"Good job, buddy!" I say, planting a kiss on the top of his head.

And then it happens, a quick end to a celebration that was only just beginning.

While I'm on bended knee, a second copter shoots up over the hill behind us, instantly hitting us with its bright spotlight.

I bolt to my feet, blinded at once by the glaring beam.

"Run!" Six says.

We do, sprinting up the nearest hill. The helicopter drops down and hovers so the wind off its rotors beats against our backs and causes the trees to bow. The forest floor is a haze of debris, and I drape my arm across my mouth to breathe, keeping my eyes squinted to alleviate the stinging dirt. How long until the FBI is called?

"Stay where you are!" a male voice blares from the copter. "You're all under arrest."

We hear shouts. The officers on foot can't be more than five hundred feet away.

Six stops running, which causes Sam and me to do the same.

"We're toast!" Sam yells.

"Okay, you bastards. We'll do this the hard way," Six says under her breath. She drops the bags, and for a second I think she plans to make Sam and me invisible. While I have no problem with leaving the bags behind, what does she expect me to do with the Chest? She can't make all of us invisible and that, too.

A brilliant stroke of lightning splits the night sky in two, followed by the deep groan of rolling thunder.

"John!" she yells without looking away.

"Right here."

"Take care of the cops. Keep them away from me."

Now I understand. I shove the Chest into Sam's arms, who stands beside me, unsure of what to do. "Guard this with your life," I tell him. "And stay down!" I turn to Bernie Kosar and communicate that he needs to stay with Sam in case our plan falls apart.

I sprint down the hill as another bolt of lightning, chased by a clap of thunder dark and menacing in tone, flashes across the sky. *Good luck, fellas,* I think, knowing full well the power of Six's abilities. *You're going to need it.*

I reach the bottom and hide behind an oak. The

voices draw near, moving swiftly towards both pillars of light. Rain begins to fall, cold and heavy. I glance up through the thick drops and see both helicopters struggling against the gale-force winds, but somehow still keeping their beams steady. That won't last for long.

The first two officers blow past me, followed closely behind by a third. I reach out with my mind when they're fifteen feet away, grab all three in midstride, and yank them towards the thick oak. They surge backwards so fast I have to leap out of the way to keep from being hit. Two of them fall lifelessly to the ground, knocked unconscious by the tree. The third lifts his head, confused, then reaches for his gun. I tear it from its holster before his hand even touches it. The metal feels cold against my palm, and I turn to the two copters and hurl it like a bullet at the nearest. That's when I see the eyes, doleful and black in the middle of the storm. Soon the old, withered face takes shape. The same face I saw in Ohio when Six killed the beast that wrecked the school.

"Don't move a muscle!" I hear behind me. "Hands in the air!"

I turn to the officer. Without his gun, he aims his Taser straight at my chest.

"Which is it, hands in the air or don't move a muscle? I can't do both."

He cocks the Taser. "Don't be a smartass, kid," he says.

Lightning cracks, followed by a roar of thunder that makes the officer jump in surprise. The officer looks towards the sound, and his eyes open wide in alarm. The face in the clouds, it's awoken.

I rip the Taser from his hand, then punch him hard in the chest. He sails thirty feet backwards and crashes into the side of a tree. While my back is still turned, the crack of a nightstick slams against my skull. I fall face-first in the mud and sparkling fuzz fills my vision. I turn as quickly as I can, lift my hand towards the cop who hit me, and get a firm grip around him before he's able to hit me again. He grunts, and with all of my might I throw him as hard as I can straight up in the air. He screams until he's up so high I can no longer hear him over the copter blades and rumbling thunder. I feel the back of my head and look at my hand. It's covered with blood. I catch the officer when he's within five feet of dying. I let him hover a few seconds before tossing him against a tree, knocking him unconscious.

A loud explosion tears through the night, and the whir of the copters cuts off. The wind stops. The rain stops, too.

"John!" Six screams from the top of the hill; and somehow in the pleading, desperate tone of her voice, I know what she needs me to do.

The lights in my hands snap on, two glowing spot-lights every bit as bright as those just extinguished. Both helicopters are wrecked and twisted, and smoke pours from them as they free fall. I don't know what the face has done to them, but Six and I must save the people aboard.

As they torpedo down, the helicopter farthest from me jerks upwards. Six is trying to stop it. I don't think she'll be able to, and I know that I can't. It's too heavy. I close my eyes. *Remember the basement in Athens, the way you captured everything inside the room to stop the speeding bullet.* And that's what I do, feeling every-thing inside the cockpit's interior. The controls. The weapons. The chairs. The three men sitting in them. I grab hold of the men, and as the trees begin to snap under the weight of the falling copter, I yank all three out. The copter crashes to the ground.

Six's copter hits the ground at the same time as mine. The explosions reach out over the treetops, two red balls of fire floating up from the twisted steel. I hold the three men in the air a safe distance from the damage, and bring them carefully to the ground. Then I race back up the hill to Six and Sam.

"Holy crap!" Sam says, his eyes wide-open.

"Did you pull them free?" I ask Six.

She nods. "Just in time."

"Me too," I say.

I grab the Chest from Sam and thrust it into Six's arms. Sam picks up our bags.

"Why are you giving me this?" Six asks.

"Because we have to get the hell out of here!" I say. I grab Sam and drape him across my shoulders. "Hold on!" I yell.

We sprint away, deeper into the hills away from the river, Bernie Kosar in the lead as a hawk. *Let the cops try to keep up now,* I think.

It's hard running with Sam on my shoulders, but I still keep a pace three times faster than what he could run on his own. And a far faster pace than any of the officers. Their yelling voices fade away, and after both helicopters just crashed in a heaping mess, who's to say they're even following?

After twenty minutes of a full-on sprint, we stop in a small valley. Sweat runs down my face. I shrug Sam off and he drops the bags. Bernie Kosar lands.

"Well, I imagine we're going to be all over the news again after that," Sam says.

I nod. "Staying hidden is going to be a lot harder than I thought." I bend over at the waist, catching my breath with my hands on my knees. I smile, which quickly changes to a kind of incredulous half laugh over what just happened.

Six grins crookedly, adjusts the Chest in her arms, and begins climbing the next hill.

"Come on, guys," she says. "We're far from out of the woods just yet."

CHAPTER EIGHT

WE HOP A FREIGHT TRAIN IN TENNESSEE, AND once we are settled Six tells us about her and Katarina being captured while they were in upstate New York, just a month after narrowly escaping the Mogadorians in West Texas. This second time around, after botching the first attempt, the Mogadorians had planned well; and when they stormed the room, they totaled more than thirty in number. Six and Katarina had been able to take a few down, but they were quickly bound, gagged, and drugged. When Six woke up—having no idea how much time had passed—she was alone in a cell in a hollowed-out mountain. She didn't discover she was in West Virginia until some time later. Six learned the Mogadorians had been trailing them the entire time, observing, hoping the two might lead them to the others, because, in Six's words, "Why kill one when the others might be near?" I shift uneasily when she says this. Maybe she is still being followed and they are waiting for the perfect time to kill us.

"They had bugged our car when we were eating in the diner in Texas, and it never once occurred to either of us to check," she says, and then gives herself over to a long silence.

Aside from an iron door containing a sliding hatch in its center for food to be delivered through, her tiny cell was made entirely of rock, measuring eight feet on each side. She had no bed or toilet, and the cell was pitch-black. The first two days passed in total darkness and silence, without food or water (though she never felt hungry or thirsty, which, she said she later learned, was due to the charm's effect), and she had started to believe she'd been forgotten. But her luck hadn't been that good, and on the third day they came for her.

"When they opened the door I was huddled in the far corner. They threw a bucket of cold water on me, picked me up, blindfolded me, and pulled me away."

After being dragged down a tunnel, they'd let her walk on her own while surrounded by ten or so Mogs. She could see nothing, but heard plenty—screams and cries from other prisoners there for who knows what reasons (when he heard this, Sam perked up and seemed about to interrupt and ask questions, but said nothing), the roars of beasts locked away in their own cells, and metallic clanking. And then she had been thrust in a room, had her wrists chained to a wall, and been gagged. They'd ripped off her blindfold, and when her eyes finally adjusted, she saw Katarina on the opposite wall, also chained and gagged and looking far worse than Six felt.

"And then he finally entered, a Mogadorian who looked no different from someone you're likely to pass on the street. He was small, had hairy arms and a thick mustache. Almost all of them had mustaches, as though they had learned to blend in by watching movies from the early eighties. He wore a white shirt, and the top button was undone; and for some reason my eyes focused on the thick tuft of black hair poking out. I looked into his dark eyes, and he smiled at me in a way that told me he was looking forward to doing what he was about to do, and I started to cry. I slid down the wall until I dangled from the shackles around my wrists, watching through my tears as he pulled razor blades, knives, pliers, and a drill from the desk they had in the center of the room."

When the Mogadorian had finished removing over twenty instruments, he'd gone to Six and stood inches from her face so that she could smell his sour breath.

"Do you see all of these?" he'd asked. She didn't respond. "I intend to use each and every one of them on you and your Cêpan, unless you truthfully answer every question I ask. If you don't, I assure you that both of you will wish you were dead."

He picked one up—a thin razor blade with a rubber-coated handle—and caressed the side of Six's face with it.

"I've been hunting you kids for a very long time," he'd said. "We've killed two of you, and now we have one right here, whatever number you are. As you might imagine, I hope you are Number Three."

Six had made no response, pushing herself against the wall as though she might disappear into it. The Mogadorian grinned, the flat end of the razor still touching her face. Then he twisted it so the blade pressed against her cheek, and while looking deep into her eyes, he jerked the razor down and made a long, thin gash along her face. Or rather he tried too, but it had been his own face that was slit open. Blood instantly poured down his cheek and he screamed in pain and anger, kicking the desk over, sending all of his tools flying, and he stormed from the room. Six and Katarina had been dragged back to their cells, kept in darkness another two days before finding themselves again gagged and chained to the walls of the room. Sitting on the desk with his cheek bandaged sat the same Mog, looking far less certain of himself than he had before.

He'd jumped from the desk and removed Six's gag, grabbed the same razor he had tried cutting her with, and held it up in front of her face, twisting it so that the light glimmered along the blade. "I don't know what number you are. . . ." For a second she'd thought he would try to cut her again, but he turned and crossed the room to Katarina instead. He stood at her side while looking at Six, and then he touched the blade to Katarina's arm. "But you're going to tell me right now."

"No!" Six had screamed. And then very slowly the Mogadorian made an incision down Katarina's arm just to be certain he could. His grin widened, and beside the original cut he made another, this one deeper than the first. Katarina groaned in pain while the blood ran down her arm.

"I can do this all day. Do you understand me? You're going to tell me everything I want to know, starting with what number are you."

Six had closed her eyes. When she reopened them he was at the desk, turning over a dagger that changed colors with movement. He'd held it up, wanting Six to see the blade twist and glow as it came to life. Six could feel its hunger, its desperation for blood.

"Now . . . your number. Four? Seven? Are you lucky enough to be Number Nine?"

Katarina had shaken her head in an attempt to keep Six quiet, and Six knew that no amount of torture would ever cause her Cêpan to talk. But she also knew she preferred death to seeing Katarina maimed and mutilated.

The Mogadorian had gone to Katarina, lifted the dagger so the tip was just over her heart. It jerked in his hand, as though the heart was a magnet pulling it forward. He looked into Six's eyes.

"I have all the time in the galaxies for this," he'd said without emotion. "While you are in here with me, we are out there with the rest of you. Don't think anything has stopped us from moving forward because we have you. We know more than you think. But we want to know *everything*. If you don't want to see her sliced into little pieces, then you better start talking, and fast. And every single word that comes out better be true. I *will* know if you're lying."

Six had told him everything she remembered about leaving Lorien and the trip here, the Chests, where they'd been hiding. She talked so fast that most of it came out jumbled. Six told him she was Number Eight—not wanting to tell him the whole truth—and there was something about the desperation in her voice that caused him to believe it.

"You really are weak, aren't you? Your relatives on Lorien, as easy as they fell, at least they were fighters. At least they had some bravery and dignity. But you," he'd said, and shook his head as if disappointed. "You have nothing, Number Eight."

And then he'd jammed the knife forward, through Katarina's heart. All Six could do was scream. Their eyes had met for a single second before Katarina drifted away, her mouth still gagged, slowly sliding down the wall until the chain had run out of slack and she hung limply by her wrists as the light drained from her eyes.

"They were going to kill her anyway," Six says softly. "Telling them what I did, at least I spared her from horrible torture, as if there's any comfort in that."

Six wraps her arms around her knees and stares at some abstract point out the window of the train.

"Of course there's comfort in that," I offer, wishing I were brave enough to stand and wrap my arms around her.

To my surprise, Sam is that brave. He stands, and makes his way over to her. He doesn't say a word when he sits down next to her, instead opening his arms. Six buries her face in Sam's shoulder and cries.

She eventually pulls back and wipes her cheeks. "When Katarina was dead, they tried everything, and I mean everything, they could to kill me—electrocution, drowning, explosives. They injected me with cyanide, which did nothing—I didn't even feel the needle going into my arm. They threw me in a chamber filled with poisonous gas, and it was like the air inside was the freshest I'd ever breathed. The Mogadorian who pushed the button on the other side of the door, though, he was dead within seconds." Six takes another swipe at her cheek with the back of her hand. "It's funny, you know,

that I think I killed more Mogadorians when I was captured than I did at the school in Ohio. They finally
threw me in another cell, and I think they'd planned
on keeping me there until they killed Three through
Seven."

"I love that you told them you were Number Eight,"
Sam says.

"I feel bad that I did it now. It's like I tarnished Katarina's legacy, or the real Number Eight's."

Sam places his hands on both her shoulders. "No
way, Six."

"How long were you in there?" I ask.

"One hundred and eighty-five days. I think."

My mouth drops open. Over half a year locked away,
completely and utterly alone, waiting to be killed. "I'm
so sorry, Six."

"I was just waiting and praying for my Legacies
to finally develop so I could get the hell out of there.
And then one day, the first one finally did. It was after
breakfast. I looked down and my left hand just wasn't
there. Of course, I freaked out, but then I realized I
could still feel my hand. I tried to pick up my spoon,
and sure enough, I could. And that's when I understood
what was happening—and invisibility was the thing I
needed in order to escape."

How it started for Six wasn't all that different from
how it had started for me, when my hand began to glow

in the middle of my first class at Paradise High.

Two days later Six had been able to make herself completely invisible, and when dinner rolled around that day, and the slot on the door was slid open and her meal pushed through, the Mogadorian guard saw an empty cell. He'd looked wildly around and then hit an alarm that sent a piercing wail through the cave. The iron door had been flung open and four Mogs charged in. While they stood there, dumbfounded as to how she'd escaped, she slid by and rushed out the door and down the tunnel, seeing the cave for the very first time.

It had been a massive labyrinthine network of long, interconnected tunnels that were dark and drafty. There were cameras everywhere. She'd passed thick glass windows revealing chambers that looked like scientific labs, clean and brightly lit. The Mogadorians inside had worn white plastic suits and goggles, but she'd raced by so swiftly she couldn't tell what they were doing. A sprawling room housed a thousand or so computer screens with a Mogadorian sitting in front of each, and Six assumed they were looking for signs of us. *Just like Henri,* I thought. One tunnel was lined with heavy steel doors she had been sure held other prisoners. But she sped on, knowing her Legacy was far from developed and terrified she wouldn't stay invisible for very long. The siren had continued to wail. And then she reached the heart of the mountain, a great, cavernous hall a half mile wide and so dark and murky she could hardly see to its other side.

The air had been stifling and Six was already sweating. The walls and ceiling were lined with huge wooden trellises to keep the cave from collapsing, and narrow ledges chiseled into the rock face connected the tunnels dotting the dark walls. Above her, several long arches had been carved from the mountain itself to bridge the great divide from one side to the other.

She had pressed herself against a rocky crag, her eyes darting back and forth for a way out. The number of passageways had been endless. She'd stood there overwhelmed, her eyes sweeping across the hollow darkness, seeing nothing at all that looked promising. But then she did—far across the ravine, a pale pinprick of natural light at the end of a wider tunnel. Just before she climbed the wooden trellis to reach the stone bridge that led to it, something else caught her eye: the Mogadorian who had killed Katarina. She couldn't let him get away. She followed him.

He entered the room where he had killed Katarina.

"I went straight to his desk and took the sharpest razor I saw, then grabbed him from behind and slit his throat. And as I watched the blood gush and spread across the floor, followed by him bursting into ash, I found myself wishing that it would have been possible to kill him a little more slowly. Or to kill him again."

"What did you do when you finally got out?" I ask.

"I hiked up the opposite mountain, and when I got up there I stared down at the cave for an hour, trying to remember every little detail I could. Once I was sat-isfied with that, I took note of everything I passed on the five-mile run to the nearest road, and from there I jumped on the back of a slow pickup truck. When it stopped a few miles down the road to get gas, I stole his map, a notepad, and a couple of pens from the cab. Oh, and a bag of potato chips."

"Niiiiice. What kind of chips?" Sam asks.

"Dude," I say.

"What?"

"They were barbecue, Sam. I marked the cave's loca-tion on the map I showed you guys back at the motel, and in the notepad I drew a diagram of everything I remembered, like a chart that would lead whoever read it straight to its entrance. I kind of panicked and hid the diagram not far from the town but kept the map, then I stole a car and drove straight to Arkansas; but of course by then my Chest had long since been taken."

"I'm so sorry, Six."

"Me, too," she says. "But they can't open it without me anyway. Maybe I'll get it back someday."

"At least we still have mine," I reply.

"You should open it soon," she says, and I know she's right. I should have opened it already. Whatever's in that Chest, whatever secrets it holds, Henri had wanted me to know them. *The secrets. The Chest.* He had said as much in his final breaths. I feel stupid for having put it off this long; but whatever's in the Chest, I have a feeling it's going to set the four of us on a long, uphill journey.

"I will," I say. "Let's just get off this train and find a safe place first."

CHAPTER NINE

I'M THE FIRST ONE OUT OF BED WHEN THE MORN-
ing bell rings. I always am. It's not necessarily because I'm
a morning person but because I prefer being in and out of
the bathroom before anyone else.

I rush through making my bed, which I've gotten very
good at over time. The key is getting the sheet, blanket, and
comforter tucked deeply in at the foot. From there it's just
a matter of pulling the rest to the head, tucking the sides,
and adding pillows to give it that clean, a-quarter-could-
be-bounced-off-it finish.

By the time I'm done, across the room in the bed nearest to the door, Ella, the girl who arrived on Sunday, is
the only other one up. Like the previous two mornings,
she's trying to emulate the way I make my bed, though
she's struggling with it. Her problem is that she's trying to work from the top down instead of the bottom
up. While Sister Katherine has been lenient with Ella,

her rotation ends today and Sister Dora's weeklong shift begins tonight. I know she won't allow Ella to skimp on perfection, regardless of how new she is or what she's going through.

"Would you like help?" I ask, crossing the room.

She looks at me with sad eyes. I can see she doesn't care about the bed. I imagine she doesn't care about much of anything right now, and I can't blame her, given the death of her parents. I'd like to tell her not to worry, that unlike those of us who are "lifers," she'll be out of this place within the month, two at the most. But what consolation can that be to her now?

I bend down at the foot of the bed and pull the sheet and blanket until there's enough to tuck them both beneath the mattress, then I stretch her comforter over them both.

"Want to grab that side?" I ask, nodding to the left of the bed while I go to the right. Together we give the whole bed the same tight, clean look as my own.

"Perfect," I say.

"Thank you," she replies in her soft, timid voice. I look down into her big brown eyes and can't help but like her and feel some need to look after her.

"I'm sorry to hear about your parents," I say.

Ella looks away. I think I've overstepped my boundaries, but then she offers me a slight smile. "Thank you. I miss them a lot."

"I'm sure they miss you, too."

We leave the room together, and I notice she walks on the balls of her feet so as not to make a sound.

At the bathroom sink, Ella grips her toothbrush near the top, almost touching the bristles with her small fingers, making the toothbrush appear larger than it really is. When I catch her staring at me in the mirror, I grin. She grins back, showing two rows of tiny teeth. Toothpaste pours from her mouth and runs down her arm, dripping from her elbow. I watch it, thinking the *S* pattern it creates is familiar, and I let my mind wander.

A hot summer day in June. Clouds drift in the blue sky. Cool waters ripple in the sun. The fresh air carries hints of pine. I breathe it in and let the stress of Santa Teresa melt away into nothingness.

Though I believe my second Legacy developed shortly after the first, I didn't discover it until almost a full year later. It was an accident I discovered it at all, which makes me wonder if I have other Legacies waiting to be uncovered.

Every year when school lets out for summer, to reward those of us who have been what the Sisters deem "good," a four-day trip to a nearby mountain camp is organized. I've always loved the trip for the same reason I love the cave that sits hidden in the opposite direction. It's an escape— a rare opportunity to spend four days swimming in the huge lake nestled in the mountains, or a chance to hike, to sleep beneath the stars, to smell the fresh air away from the musty corridors of Santa Teresa. It is, in essence, a chance to act our age. I've even caught some of the Sisters laughing and smiling when they think nobody's looking.

In the lake, there's a floating dock. I'm a horrible swimmer, and for many summers I just sat and watched from shore while the others laughed and played and did flips off the dock into the water. It took a couple summers of practicing alone in the shallow water, but the summer of my thirteenth year, I finally learned an imperfect and slow doggy paddle that kept my head above water. It got me to the dock, and that was enough for me.

At the dock, the game is to try to push each other off it. Groups team up until they're the only ones left, and then it's every girl for herself. As the biggest and strongest at Santa Teresa, I used to think it'd be an effortless victory for La Gorda, but it rarely is; she's often outsmarted by the smaller, more wily girls, and I don't think anyone has won as many times as a girl named Bonita.

I didn't want to play *La Reina del Muelle*, Queen of the Dock. I was content to sit on the side and let my feet dangle in the water, but Bonita shoves me hard from behind anyway, sending me headlong into the lake.

"Play the game or go back to shore," Bonita says, flicking her hair over her shoulder.

I climb back up and rush straight towards her. I shove her as hard as I can, and she falls backwards and crashes into the lake.

I don't hear La Gorda behind me, and suddenly two strong hands shove me hard from behind. My feet slip on the wet wood, and the side of my head and shoulder smack against the edge of the dock, clouding my vision with stars. I'm knocked unconscious for a second, and when my eyes open I'm underwater. I see nothing but darkness and instinctively kick upward, flailing my arms to reach the surface. But my head smacks against the bottom of the dock, and I realize there are only a few inches of space between the water and the wooden boards of the dock. I try to tilt my head backwards to put my nose and mouth above the surface, but water instantly laps into my nostrils. I panic, my lungs already burning. I scramble to the left but there's nowhere to go; I'm trapped by the dock's plastic barrels. Water fills my lungs while the absurdity of death by drowning pops into my head. I think of the others, how their ankles are about to be seared. Will they believe that Number Three has been killed, or will they somehow know it's me? Will it burn differently than if I'd died at the hands of the Mogadorians instead of my own stupidity? My eyes slowly close and I begin to sink. Just as I feel the last stream of bubbles escape my lips, my eyes snap open, and an odd sort of calm sweeps in. My lungs are no longer burning.

I'm breathing.

The water tickles my lungs, but at the same time satisfies every desperate need I have to breathe, and that's when I know I've discovered my second Legacy: the ability to breathe underwater. I've found it only because I was pushed to the brink of death.

I don't want to be found just yet by the girls diving into the water looking for me, so I let myself drift down to the deep bottom, the world slowly fading to black until my feet finally sink into the cold mud. I can see through the brown, murky water once my eyes adjust. Ten minutes pass. Then twenty. Finally the girls swim away from the dock. I assume the lunch bell's been rung. I wait until I'm absolutely sure they've all left, then I walk slowly along on the lake's bottom towards shore, my feet sinking into the mud as I inch forward. After a while the icy water begins to warm and brighten and the mud segues to rocks and then to sand, and finally my head emerges. I listen to the girls, La Gorda and Bonita included, scream and splash towards me in relief. I take inventory of myself on shore, noticing a gash on my shoulder is bleeding, leaving a trail of blood down my arm in the shape of a subtle *S*.

The Sisters make me sit the rest of the afternoon at a picnic table under a tree, but I didn't mind. I had another Legacy.

In the bathroom, Ella catches me watching the toothpaste run down her arm in the mirror. She looks embarrassed, and as she tries to replicate the way I brush my teeth, even more frothy toothpaste pours from her mouth.

"You're like a bubble factory," I say with a smile, grabbing a towel to clean her up.

We leave the bathroom as the others are arriving, dress quickly in the room and walk out of it as the others are coming in, keeping just ahead of the group, as I prefer to do. We grab our lunches from the cafeteria and head out into the cold morning. I eat my apple on the walk to school. Ella does the same. I'm about ten minutes early today, which will give me a little time to get on the internet to see if there's anything new about John Smith. The thought of him makes me smile.

"Why are you smiling? Do you like school?" Ella asks. I look over at her. The half-eaten apple looks big in her small hand.

"It's a nice morning, I guess," I say. "And I have good company today."

We walk through town as street vendors set up shop. The snow hasn't melted and is piled along both sides of Calle Principal, but the road itself is clear. Up ahead on the right Héctor Ricardo's front door opens, and out comes his mother in a wheelchair, being pushed by Héctor. She's had Parkinson's disease for a very long time. She's been in a wheelchair for the last five years, and she's been unable to speak for the last three. He positions her in a sliver of sunlight and applies her wheel brakes. While the sun seems to bring her some comfort, Héctor slinks away and sits in the shade, dropping his head.

"Good morning, Héctor," I call out. He lifts his head and squints one eye open. He waves with a shaky hand.

"Marina, as of the sea," he croaks. "The only limits of tomorrow are the doubts we have today."

I stop and smile. Ella stops, too.

"That's one of your better ones."

"Don't doubt Héctor; he has a few nuggets left," he says.

"Are you doing okay?"

"Strength, confidence, humility, love. Héctor Ricardo's four tenets of a happy life," he says, which makes no sense whatsoever considering the question I asked, but it makes me feel good anyway. He turns his gaze on Ella. "And who's this little angel?"

Ella grabs my hand and hides behind me.

"Her name is Ella," I say, looking down at her. "This is Héctor. He's my friend."

"Héctor is one of the good guys," he says, though Ella remains behind me.

He waves at us as we walk the rest of the way to school.

"Do you know where you're going?" I ask her.

"I have Señora Lopez's class," she says, smiling.

"Ahh, you're a lucky girl. I had her, too. She's one of the good ones in this town, like Héctor," I say.

I'm devastated; all three of the school computers are occupied, a trio of younger girls from town are desperately trying to finish a science assignment, their fingers flying across the keyboards. I coast through the day, keeping to myself as one thing runs through my mind. John Smith, on the run in America, somehow staying ahead of the law, and I'm stuck here, in Santa Teresa, an old, moldy town where nothing happens. I'd always thought I'd leave when I turned eighteen. But now that John Smith is out there, being hunted, I know I have to leave as soon as I can, to join him. The only question now is how to find him.

My last class is Spanish history. The teacher drones on about General Francisco Franco and the Spanish Civil War of the 1930s. I tune her out and instead write in my notebook about John, what I know based on the most recent article I read.

John Smith

Lived 4 months in Paradise, OH

Pulled over by an officer in Tennessee, driving west in a pickup truck. Middle of the night, with 2 other people around the same age.

Where were they driving?

One of the two people he was with is believed to be Sam Goode, also from Paradise, originally thought to be a hostage, now considered an accomplice.

Who is the third person? A girl with black hair. Girl in my dream had black hair.

Where is Henri?

How did they get away from 2 helicopters and 35 police officers? How did the 2 copters crash?

How can I contact him OR the others?
Post something on internet?
Too dangerous. Is there a way to do so that eludes the Mogs?
If so, will any of the others even see it?
John is on the run. Ever checking internet?
Does Adelina know something that I don't?
Can I bring it up to her without being obvious?

The pen hovers over the page. The internet and Adelina, my only two ideas, neither of which seems promising. What more can I do, though? Everything else seems as futile as walking up the mountain and sending smoke signals into the air. But I can't help but feel like I'm missing something—some crucial element that's so obvious it's staring me right in the face.

The teacher drones on. I close my eyes and think it all through. Nine Garde. Nine Cêpan. An airship that brought us to Earth, the same airship to take us back eventually, hidden somewhere on Earth. All I remember about it is that we landed in a remote place in the midst of a thunderstorm. A charm was cast to protect us from the Mogadorians, which went into effect only when we scattered, and that only works if we stay away from each other. But why? A charm that keeps us apart seems pretty

counterintuitive in helping us fight and defeat the Mogadorians. What's the point in it? While asking myself this
question my mind stumbles on something else. I close my
eyes and let the logic carry me.

We were meant to hide, but for how long? Until our
Legacies developed and we had the tools to fight, to win.
What's the one thing we're able to do when that first Leg-
acy finally arrives?

The answer seems too obvious to be correct. With the
pen still in my hand, I write the only answer I can come
up with:

The Chest

CHAPTER
TEN

I NO LONGER SLEEP WITHOUT NIGHTMARES. Every night I'm stricken by Sarah's face, there for only a second before it's swallowed by darkness, followed by her calling out for help. No matter how furiously I search, she's nowhere to be found. She keeps calling, a scared voice, bleak and alone, but I can never find her.

And then there's Henri, his body twisted and smoking as he looks at me, knowing our end together has finally come. It's never fear I see in his eyes, or regret, or sadness, but rather pride, relief, and love. He seems to tell me to go on, to fight, to win. Then, right at the end, his eyes widen in a plea for more time. "Coming here, to Paradise, it wasn't by chance," he says again, and I still have no idea what he means. Then, "I wouldn't have missed a second of it, kiddo. Not for all of Lorien. Not for the whole damn world." This is my curse, that every time I dream of Henri I'm forced to watch him die. Over and over again.

I see Lorien, the days before the war, the jungles and oceans I've dreamed of a hundred times. Myself as a kid, running wild through the tall grass while those around me smile and laugh, unaware of the horrors to come. Then I see the war, the destruction, the killing, and the blood. Sometimes, on nights like tonight, I have distinct visions of what I believe is the future.

My eyes aren't closed for long before I'm whisked away. And even as it begins, I feel myself entering a landscape I know I've never seen before, but still find familiar.

I run down a pathway lined with litter and debris. Broken glass. Burned plastic. Twisted, rusted steel. Acrid mist fills my nose and causes my eyes to water. Decaying buildings stand tall against the gray sky. A dark, stagnant river lurks to my right. There's commotion up ahead. The sounds of yelling and metallic clattering swell in the thick air. I come to an angry mob surrounding a tarmac where a large airship prepares for takeoff. I go through a barbed-wire gate and enter the airstrip fenced off from the crowd.

The tarmac is marked with small rivulets the color of magma. Mogadorian soldiers keep the crowd at bay while swarms of scouts ready the ship, an onyx orb hovering in midair.

The crowd roars against the fence as soldiers knock them back. They're smaller than the soldiers, but have the same ashy skin tone. A low rumble grows from somewhere beyond the ship. The crowd hushes, taking panicked steps backwards, while those on the tarmac file into orderly lines.

Then something drops from the hazy sky. A dark vortex absorbs the surrounding clouds, leaving a thick, black discharge in its wake. I cover my ears before the object crashes to the ground, shooting vibrations through the soil that nearly knock me off my feet. Everything falls silent as the dust clears, revealing a perfectly spherical ship, milky white like a pearl. A round door slides open, and a monstrous creature steps out. The same creature that tried to behead me in the rock castle.

A brawl breaks out along the fence, with everyone scrambling to get away from this monster. He's even more enormous than I remember, with muscular, chiseled features and short, cropped hair. Tattoos crawl up his arms, scars are branded into his ankles, the largest of which stands out on his neck, grotesque and purple. A soldier retrieves a golden cane from the ship, its head curved like a hammer, a black eye painted on its side. When the creature holds it in his hand, the eye comes alive, rolling left and then right, taking in its surroundings, until it finds me.

The Mogadorian scans the crowd, sensing me nearby. His eyes narrow. He takes a giant step towards me, lifting the golden cane. Its eye pulses.

Just then an onlooker shouts at the Mogadorian, furiously rattling the fence. The Mogadorian turns towards the protester, thrusting the rod in his direction. The rod's eye glows red and the man is instantly ripped to shreds, torn through the barbed-wired fence. Pandemonium erupts as everyone fights to get away.

The Mogadorian returns his attention to me, pointing the rod at my head. I'm hit with the sensation of falling. Weightlessness rises in my gut until I'm on the brink of vomiting. What I see around his neck is so disturbing, so haunting, that I'm jolted awake as though struck by a bolt of blue lightning.

Early dawn breaks through the windows, bathing the small room in the hard morning light. The shapes of things return. I'm sweat covered and out of breath. And yet I'm here, the ache and confusion in my heart telling me I'm still alive, no longer in a dreadful place where a man can be ripped through the small holes of a barbed-wired fence.

We found an abandoned house bordering a conservation area a few miles from Lake George. The kind of house Henri would have loved: isolated, small and quiet, offering security without any personality. It's one story, the exterior painted lime green while the interior is various shades of beige, with brown carpeting. We couldn't be luckier that the water hasn't been turned off. By the heavy dust in the air, I can only assume it's been a while since anyone lived here.

I roll to my side and glance at the phone beside my head. Having seen what I just did, the only thing that could take it all away is Sarah. I remember the time in my room when she'd just returned from Colorado— the way we'd held one another. If I'm allowed to save a single moment with her then I choose that one. I close my eyes and imagine what she's doing at this very moment, what she's wearing, who she's talking to. The news reported that each of the six school districts surrounding Paradise absorbed a portion of the displaced students until a new building is built. I wonder which of them Sarah's attending, if she's still taking photographs.

I reach for my cell phone, the one prepaid and registered under the name Julius Seazar. Henri's sense of humor. I turn it on for the first time in days. All I have to do is dial her number to hear her voice. It's that simple. I press the familiar numbers one by one until reaching the last. I close my eyes, take a deep breath, then turn the phone off and flip it shut. I know I can't punch the tenth number. Fear for Sarah's safety, for her life—and all of ours, too—stops me.

Out in the living room, Sam streams CNN with one of Henri's laptops on his thighs. Luckily Henri's wireless internet card, under whatever pseudonym he chose at the time, still works. Sam furiously scribbles notes on a legal pad. It's been three days since the mess in Tennessee, and we only arrived in Florida last night, having hopped aboard three different semis—one of which carried us two hundred miles in the wrong direction—before jumping a train that brought us here. Without the use of our Legacies—our speed, Six's invisibility—we would have never made it. It's our intent to lie low for a bit and let the news dissipate. We'll regroup, start training, and avoid any further mishaps like the one involving the helicopters at all costs. First order of business, find a new car. Second order of business, figure out what to do next. None of us really knows for sure. Again, I feel the enormity of Henri's absence.

"Where's Six?" I ask, stumbling into the living room.

"Out back swimming laps or something," Sam replies. The one cool thing about the house is the pool in the backyard, which Six immediately filled by directing a heavy rainstorm overhead.

"I'd think you'd want to catch a glimpse of Six in her bathing suit." I nudge Sam.

His face reddens. "Shut up, dude. I wanted to check the news. You know, be productive."

"Anything?"

"Aside from now being considered an accomplice and having the reward for me increased to a half million dollars?" Sam asks.

"Oh come on, you know you love it."

"Yeah, it's pretty cool," he says, grinning. "Anyway, no, nothing new. I don't see how Henri kept up with all this. There're literally thousands of stories every day."

"Henri never slept."

"Don't *you* want to go check out Six in her bathing suit?" Sam asks, turning back to the screen. I'm surprised by the lack of sarcasm in his voice. He knows how I feel about Sarah. And I know how he feels about Six.

"What's that supposed to mean?"

"I see the way you look at her," Sam says. He clicks on a link about a plane crash in Kenya. One survivor.

"And how do I look at her, Sam?"

"Never mind." The survivor is an old woman. Definitely not one of us.

"The Loric fall in love for life, man. And I love Sarah. You know that."

Sam looks over the screen of the laptop. "I know you do. It's just that, I don't know. You're the kind of guy she'd go for, not some math nerd obsessed with aliens and outer space. I just don't see how Six could fall for someone like me."

"You kick ass, Sam. And don't forget it."

I walk out the rear sliding glass door leading to the pool. Beyond the pool lies an overgrown yard enclosed by a brick wall offering privacy from anyone who might wander by. The nearest neighbor is a quarter mile away. The nearest town is a ten-minute drive.

Six zips across the water, skimming the top like some water-borne insect, and beside her, going twice as fast, is a platypus-shaped mammal with long white hair and a beard—I have no idea what animal Bernie Kosar's copying. Six senses me and stops at the edge, pulling herself halfway out of the water and resting her arms on the deck. Bernie Kosar jumps out and returns to his beagle form, shaking himself dry and covering me with water. It's refreshing, and I can't help but think how nice it is to be down South again.

"You better not be killing my dog out here," I say. I catch myself staring at her perfect shoulders, her slender neck. Maybe Sam is right. Maybe I am looking at Six the same way he does. I want more than ever to run back inside, turn on my phone, and hear Sarah's voice.

"More like he's killing me. The little guy swims like he's totally healed. Speaking of which, how's your head?"

"Still hurts," I say, running a hand over it. "But nothing I can't handle. I'm ready to start training today, if that's why you're asking."

"Good," she says. "I'm getting antsy. It's been a long time since I've trained with somebody."

"You're sure you want to train with me? You know you'll probably end up hurt, right?"

She laughs, and then spits a mouthful of water at me. "Oh, it's on," I say, visualizing the surface of the pool and forcing a blast of air over it. Water rushes towards her face. She dives beneath the surface to keep from being splashed, and when she comes up she rides the crest of a huge wave that nearly empties the pool, bringing her towards me. Before I can react she moves away, but the wave keeps coming, knocking me over and sending me crashing into the back of the house. I hear her laughing. The water recedes to the pool, and I stand and try pushing her backwards into it. She deflects my telekinesis, and all at once I'm upended and sailing through the air upside down where I flail helplessly.

"What the hell are you guys doing out here?" Sam asks. He's standing at the sliding glass door.

"Um. Six was talking smack, so I decided to put her in her place. Can't you tell?"

I remain upside down, hovering four feet over the

pool's center. I can feel Six's grip around my right ankle, and the sensation is the same as if she were literally holding me up with one hand.

"Oh, totally. Got her right where you want her," Sam replies.

"I was about to make my move, you know. Biding my time."

"So what do you think, Sam?" Six asks. "Should I let him have it?"

A smile breaks across Sam's face. "Take it away."

"Hey!" I say just before she lets go and I fall head-first into the water. When I resurface, Six and Sam are laughing hysterically.

"That was only round one," I say, climbing out. I peel off my shirt and slap it to the concrete. "You caught me off guard. Just wait."

"What happened to being tough and rugged?" Sam asks. "Isn't that what you said when you buzzed your head?"

"Strategy," I say. "I'm just giving Six a false sense of security, then when she gets comfortable I'm going to pull the rug out from under her."

"Ha! Yeah, right," Sam says, then adds, "God, I wish I had Legacies."

Six stands between us in her solid black one-piece bathing suit. She's still laughing, and water runs down her arms and legs as she leans slightly forward and twists her hair to ring it out. The scar on her leg is still discolored, but it isn't nearly as purple as it was the week before. She whips her hair back over her head. Sam and I are both mesmerized.

"So, training this afternoon then?" Six asks. "Or do you still feel like I might get hurt?"

I puff my cheeks and release the air slowly. "Maybe I'll take it easy on you. I mean, that scar on your leg still looks kinda nasty. But, yeah, we're on."

"Sam, is that a yes for you, too?"

"You guys want me to train? Seriously?"

"Of course. You're one of us now," Six says.

He nods, rubbing his hands together. "I'm in," he says, grinning like a kid on Christmas morning. "But if you just want me for target practice, I'm going home."

We start at two o'clock, but by the look of the gloomy sky I don't anticipate training for very long. Sam bounces on the balls of his feet, wearing gym shorts and an oversized tee. He's all knees and elbows, but if heart and determination could be counted, I think he'd be nearly the size of the Mogadorian I'd seen aboard the ship.

To start, Six shows us what she's learned of combat techniques, which is far more than I know. Her body moves fluidly and with the precision of a machine when she throws a kick or punch, or when she does a back flip to evade an attack. She shows us how to counterassault and the merits of skill and coordination, and drills the same maneuvers until they come instinctively. Sam eats it up, even when Six pounds him backwards and he flips head over heels or has the wind knocked out of him. She does the same to me, and even though I try laughing it off like I'm playing around, I work my hardest and she still kicks the crap out of me. I can't fathom how she learned all this on her own. After my mouth is filled with grass and dirt for the second time, I realize just how much she can teach me.

The rain begins a half hour later. A light drizzle at first, but soon the skies open, sending us indoors for cover. Sam paces through the house throwing kicks and punches at phantom enemies. I sit in the chair, my fist around my blue pendant, and stare out the front window for a very long time, simply watching it all happen while remembering that the last two storms I saw both raged because Six told them to.

When I turn back I see that she's sound asleep in the corner of the living room, curled around Bernie Kosar, holding him in her arms like a pillow. It's how she always sleeps, wrapping herself into a ball on her side, her features losing their sharp edges.

The white bottoms of her feet are aimed right at me, and I use telekinesis to lightly tickle the bottom of her right foot. She twitches it as though shooing a pesky fly. I tickle her again. She twitches her foot a little harder. I wait a few seconds and then, as softly as I can, I tickle the length of her foot, from her heel up to her big toe. Six pulls her foot back and kicks her leg straight out, the telekinetic force of which sends me flying into the nearest wall, leaving a hole revealing the interior wires and studs. Sam charges into the room and jumps into the perfect fighting position.

"What happened? Who's here?" he yells.

I stand, rubbing my elbow, which took the brunt of the hit.

"Jerk," Six says, sitting up.

Sam looks from me to her.

"You guys are ridiculous," he says, retreating back to the kitchen. "Your flirting just scared the hell out of me."

"Scared the hell out of me, too," I say, ignoring the flirting comment; but he's already gone and doesn't hear it. Am I flirting? Would Sarah think that was flirting?

Six yawns, raising her arms to the ceiling. "Still raining?"

"Totally, but look on the bright side; the weather saved you from any further bruises."

She shakes her head. "The tough-guy routine is pretty tired, Johnny. And don't forget what I can do with the weather."

"Wouldn't dream of it," I say. I try to change the subject. I hate myself for flirting with another girl. "Hey, I've been meaning to ask you: who's the face in the clouds? Every time you whip up a storm I see this crazy, ominous face."

She scratches the bottom of her right foot. "I'm not sure, but ever since I've been able to mess with the weather, it's always the same face that appears. I assume it's Loric."

"Yeah, probably. And here I thought it might be a crazy ex-boyfriend you've yet to get over."

"Because obviously I have a weakness for ninety-year-old men. You know me so well, John."

I shrug. Both of us smile.

That night I cook dinner on a rusty but serviceable grill left on the back patio. Or try to cook, I guess. Since I took home economics with Sarah in Paradise, I'm the only one who knows how to make anything remotely resembling a meal. Tonight: chicken breasts, potatoes, and a frozen pepperoni pizza.

We're sitting on the living-room carpet in a triangle. Under the blanket Six has draped over her head and body, she wears a black tank top, and her pendant hangs in full view. The sight of it returns my mind to the vision I had. I long for a normal dinner around a table and a normal night's sleep where I'm not tortured by my Loric past. Was that what it was like on Lorien before we left?

"Do you think about your parents a lot?" I ask Six. "Back on Lorien, I mean?"

"Not that much anymore. I can't even tell you what they look like, really. I remember how it felt being near them, though, if that makes any sense. I think about that feeling quite a bit, I guess. What about you?"

I pick at a burned slice of pizza. I resolve never to cook frozen pizza on the grill again. "I see them a lot in my dreams. Which is really great, but at the same time it tears me up inside. Reminds me that they're dead."

The blanket slides off the top of Six's head and rests on her shoulders. "What about you, Sam? Do you miss your parents right now?"

Sam opens his mouth and closes it. I can tell he's considering telling Six that he thinks his dad was taken by aliens, abducted when he went out for milk and bread. Finally he says, "I miss them both, my mom and dad, but I know that I'm better off here with you guys. Considering what I know about everything, I don't think I could be at home."

"You know too much," I say. I feel guilty he's eating my terrible meal on the floor of an abandoned house instead of feasting on his mother's food at a dining-room table.

"Sam, I'm sorry you got caught up in this with us," Six says. "But it's nice that you're here."

He blushes. "I don't know what it is, but I feel a weird connection to the whole situation. Can I ask you something? How far away is Mogadore from Earth?"

I think back to when Henri blew on the seven glass orbs, how they came to life. Soon we were looking at a floating replica of our solar system. "It's a lot closer than Lorien is, why?"

Sam stands. "How long would it take to get there?"

"A few months maybe," Six says. "Depends on what type of ship you're flying and what type of energy it uses."

Walking in circles, Sam says, "I think the U.S. government has to have a ship built somewhere that can handle that distance. I'm sure it's a prototype and top secret and hidden under a mountain that's hidden under another mountain, but I was just thinking about what would happen if we couldn't find your ship and needed to take the fight to them—go to Mogadore. We have to have a Plan B, right?"

"Sure. What's Plan A again?" I ask, biting my tongue.

I can't fathom fighting the whole planet of Mogadore on their own turf.

"Getting my Chest," Six says. She pulls the blanket back over her head.

"And then what?"

"Training?"

"And then what?" I ask.

"We go find the others, I guess."

"It just sounds like a bunch of running and not much of anything else. I think Henri or Katarina would have us doing something more productive somehow. Like studying how to kill certain enemies. Do you know what a piken is?"

"Those are those huge beasts that destroyed the school," Six says.

"What about a kraul?"

"Those are the smaller animal things that attacked us in the gymnasium," she answers. "Why?"

"In the dream that I had in North Carolina, when you and Sam heard me speaking Mogadorian, those two names were mentioned, but I'd never heard of them before. Henri and I simply called them 'the beasts.'" I pause. "I had another dream earlier."

"Maybe you aren't having dreams," she says. "Maybe you're having visions again."

I nod. "It's hard to tell the difference at this point. I

mean, these dreams felt the same as the visions I had of Lorien, but I wasn't on Lorien during these two," I say. "Henri once said that when I have visions it's because they hold some sort of personal significance to me. And that's always been true—the past visions were always of things that had already happened. But I think what I witnessed in my dream this morning . . . I don't know. It's like I was seeing it as it was actually happening."

"Wicked," Sam says. "You're like a TV."

Six crumples her paper towel and tosses it up in the air above her head. Without thinking I set it on fire, and it wilts into nothing before landing on the carpet. Then Six says, "It's not impossible, John. Some of the Loric have been known to do it. That's what Katarina said, anyway."

"But the thing is, I think I was on Mogadore, which, by the way, is just as disgusting as I imagined it would be. The air was so thick it made my eyes water. Everything was desolate and gray. But, how did I get there? And how could this one huge dude on Mogadore seem to sense when I was there?"

"How huge?" Sam asks.

"Huge, like more than double the size of the soldiers I saw, twenty feet tall, maybe more, far more intelligent and powerful. I can tell just by looking at him. He was definitely a leader of some sort. I've seen him twice now. The first time I was overhearing information relayed to him by some little peon, and it was all about us and what had happened at the school. This second time I saw him as he was preparing to board a ship; but before he was on it, one of the others ran up and handed him something. I didn't know what it was at first, but just before the ship's door closed, he turned towards me to make sure I could see exactly what it was."

"What was it?" Sam asks.

I shake my head, ball up my paper towel, and burn it on the palm of my hand. I look out the back door at the setting sun, a blaze of orange and hot pink like the Florida sunsets Henri and I watched from our elevated porch. I wish he was still here to help make sense of all this now.

"John? What was it? What did he have?" Six asks.

I lift my hand and grab my pendant.

"This. These. He had pendants. Three of them. The Mogadorians must have taken them after each kill. And this massive leader guy, or whoever he is, he put them around his neck like Olympic medals, and then he stood there just long enough so I could see. Each one was glowing bright blue, and when I woke up, mine was too."

"So are you saying it's a premonition, like you just saw your fate? Or could you have just had a weird dream because of how stressed out you are?" Sam asks.

I shake my head. "I think Six is right and these are all visions. And I think they're all happening right now. But the thing that scares me the most is that when that guy got on that ship, there's a good chance he was headed this way. And, if Six is right about how fast a ship can travel, it won't be very long until he's here."

CHAPTER
ELEVEN

THE THINGS I REMEMBER ABOUT COMING TO SANTA Teresa are mostly just snippets of a long journey I thought would never end. I remember an empty stomach and sore feet and being impossibly tired most of the time. I remember Adelina begging for change, for food; remember the seasickness and the vomiting it caused. I remember disgusted looks from passersby. I remember every time we changed names. And I remember the Chest, as cumbersome as it was, that Adelina refused to part ways with no matter how dire our situation became. On the day we finally knocked at the door Sister Lucia answered, I remember it being on the ground tucked snug between Adelina's feet. I know she stowed it away in the shadows of some obscure corner of the orphanage. My days of searching have turned up nothing, but I still keep looking.

On Sunday, one week after Ella arrived, we sit together

in the back pew during Mass. It's her first, and it holds her attention about as well as it holds mine: not at all. Aside from class, she's pretty much been by my side since the morning I helped her make her bed. We walk to and from school together, eat breakfast and dinner together, say our nightly prayers together. I've grown very attached to her, and by the way she follows me around, I can tell she's grown attached to me as well.

Father Marco has droned on for a good forty-five minutes, and finally I close my eyes, thinking of the cave and debating whether I should bring Ella along with me today. There are several problems with it. First, there's zero light inside, and there's no way Ella will be able to see through the dark in the way that I can. Second, the snow has yet to melt, and I'm not sure she'd be able to make the trek through it. But most of all, I worry that bringing her would be putting her in harm's way. The Mogadorians could arrive at any moment, and Ella would be defenseless. But even with these obstacles and concerns, I'm eager to take her along anyway. I want to show her my paintings.

On Tuesday, minutes before we were to depart for school, I had found Ella hunched over on her bed. Still chewing on a breakfast biscuit, I looked over her shoulder to see her furiously shading a perfect drawing of our sleeping quarters. The details, the technical accuracy of each crack in the wall, her ability to capture the faintest of squares of sunrays that dropped through the windows in the morning, was astounding. It was as if I was looking at a black-and-white photograph.

"Ella!" I had blurted.

She had flipped the paper over, trapping it against her schoolbook with her tiny smudged hands. She knew it was me but didn't turn around.

"Where did you learn how to do that?" I'd whispered. "How did you learn to draw so well?"

"My father," she whispered back, keeping the drawing turned over. "He was an artist. So was my mother."

I'd sat down on her bed. "And here I thought I was a pretty good painter."

"My father was an incredible painter," she'd said plainly. Before I could ask her more questions, we had been interrupted and then ushered out of the room by Sister Carmela. That night I'd found Ella's drawing under my pillow. It's the best present I've ever received.

Sitting in Mass, I think that maybe she can help me with my cave paintings. Surely I can find a flashlight or lantern somewhere here to take with us. And then my thoughts are interrupted by a fit of giggles beside me.

I open my eyes and look over. Ella's found a red-and-black furry caterpillar that's in the process of crawling up her arm. I bring my finger to my lips in a sign of silence. It stops her for a brief moment, but then the caterpillar climbs higher and she begins giggling again. Her face turns red while trying not to laugh, but the fact that she's trying to stifle it only makes it that much harder. And then she can't help herself and a string of laughs escape. Every head snaps around to see what's happening, and Father Marco stops his sermon in midsentence. I snatch the caterpillar from Ella's arm and sit upright, staring back at those staring at us. Ella stops laughing. Slowly the heads turn back around and Father Marco, clearly flustered at having lost his spot, resumes his sermon.

I sit with my hand around the caterpillar. It tries wriggling free. After a minute I open my fist, and the sudden movement causes the furry little thing to curl into a ball. Ella raises her eyebrows and cups her hands together, and I place the caterpillar in them. She sits there smiling down at it.

I scan the front row. I'm not at all surprised to see Sister Dora glaring sternly in my direction. She shakes her head before turning back to Father Marco.

I lean over to Ella.

"When prayer ends," I whisper into her ear, "we have to get out of here as fast as we can. And keep away from Sister Dora."

Before Mass I'd fixed Ella's hair into a tight braid; and now, gazing up at me with her big, brown eyes, it looks as though the heavy braid is weighing her head back.

"Am I in trouble?"

"We should be okay," I tell her. "But just in case, we'll

rush out of here before Sister Dora can catch up to us. Got it?"

"Got it," she says.

But we don't get the chance. When there are just a few minutes left, Sister Dora stands and casually strolls to the back, and then stands waiting at the door a few steps away. When my eyes reopen as the final prayer ends with the sign of the cross, Sister Dora places a hand on my left shoulder.

"Come with me, please," she says to Ella, reaching across me to grab her by the wrist.

"What are you doing?" I say.

Sister Dora pulls Ella past me. "It's none of your business, Marina."

"Marina," Ella pleads. As she's being dragged away, Ella looks back at me with scared eyes. I panic and rush to the front of the church where Adelina is standing, talking with a lady from town.

"Sister Dora just grabbed Ella and pulled her away," I quickly say, interrupting her. "You have to make her stop, Adelina!"

She looks incredulously at me. "I will do no such thing. And it's *Sister* Adelina. If you'll excuse me, Marina, I was in the middle of a conversation," she says.

I shake my head at her. Tears form in my eyes. Adelina doesn't remember what it feels like to ask for help and not receive it.

I turn and run from the room and up the winding staircase to the church offices. To the left, at the end of the hall, the only door closed is the one leading to Sister Lucia's office. I race towards it, trying to decide what I should do. Should I knock? Should I kick straight through it? But I don't get the chance to do either. When I'm within reaching distance of the knob, I hear the crack of the paddle, followed instantly by a scream. I'm frozen in shock. Ella cries on the other side of the door and a second later the door is opened by Sister Dora.

"What are you doing here?" she snaps at me.

"I came to see Sister Lucia," I lie.

"She's not here, and you're due in the kitchen. Go on," she says, shooing me the way I came. "I'm headed there myself."

"Is she okay?"

"Marina, it's none of your concern," she says, and then grabs me by the bicep, spins me around, and gives me a shove.

"Go!" she orders.

I move away from the office, hating the fear that runs through me every time confrontation stares me in the face. It's always been that way—with the Sisters, with Gabriela García, with Bonita on the dock—I get the same feeling, the same nervousness that quickly segues to dread, that always causes me to walk away.

"Walk faster!" Sister Dora barks, following me down

the staircase and towards the kitchen where El Festín duties await.

"I have to use the restroom," I say before we reach the kitchen, which is a lie; I want to make sure Ella's okay.

"Fine. But you better make it fast. I'm timing you."

"I will."

I duck around the corner and wait thirty seconds to make sure she's gone. Then I rush back the way we came, up the staircase, down the hall. The office door is slightly ajar and I walk through it. The interior is dark, somber. A layer of dust covers the shelves that line the walls, upon which sit ancient books. The only light enters through a dirty stained glass window.

"Ella?" I say, for some reason thinking she might be hiding. No answer. I walk away and poke my head in the rooms situated off the main hallway, all of which are empty. I call her name as I go. At the hall's opposite end is the Sisters' sleeping quarters. There's no sign of her in there either. I go back down the stairs. The crowd has made its way to the cafeteria. I walk to the nave looking around for Ella. She's not in there, nor is she in either of the two sleeping rooms, nor the computer room, nor any of the storage rooms. By the time I've looked in most places I can think to check, a half hour has passed and I know I'll be in trouble if I go to the cafeteria.

Instead I hurry out of my Sunday clothes, pull my coat off its hook, swipe the blanket from my bed, and dash outside. I trudge through the snow away from town, unable to push the sound of the paddle's crack and Ella's scream from my mind. I'm also unable to forgive Adelina's scorn towards me. My whole body tense, I focus my energy on some of the large rocks I pass, using telekinesis to lift and hurl them against the mountainside. It's a great way to blow off steam. The snow's surface has hardened, creating a thin layer of ice that crunches underfoot, but it doesn't keep the rocks from skidding downhill. I'm so mad I could let them go, careening towards town. But I stop them in their tracks. My gripe isn't with the town but rather its namesake, and those who live within it.

I pass the camel's back—half a kilometer to go. The sun is warm on my face, situated high in the sky and slanted towards the east, which means I have at least five hours before I'm due back. I haven't had this much free time in a great while; and with the bright sun and crisp, fresh wind pulling me from my dismal mood, I hardly care that I'll be in trouble when I get back. I turn to see how effective my blanket cape is at hiding my prints in the hardened snow, and I'm afraid to see that it hasn't worked at all today.

Nevertheless, I push forward until I spot the rounded shrub sticking up over the snow, then I race towards it, at first not noticing the very thing my eyes should be attuned to: that the snow at the base of the cave is tossed up and pushed around. But as soon as I reach the cave's entrance, I know immediately that something is horribly off.

Approaching from the south, a single set of boot prints, double the size of my own, dot the mountainside, a perfect straight line cut into the snow leading from town to the cave. They seem to tromp around its opening, as though circling it. I'm flustered, certain there's something else here I'm missing. And then it dawns on me. The prints—they lead into the cave, but they don't lead back out.

Whoever they belong to is still inside.

CHAPTER
TWELVE

THEY'RE HERE! I THINK. AFTER ALL THESE YEARS, THE Mogadorians are finally here!

I turn so fast I slip and fall into the snow. I quickly crawl backwards away from the cave's mouth, my shoes tangled in the blanket. Tears well up in my eyes. My heart races. I manage to right myself and sprint as hard and as fast as my legs will carry me. I don't even look behind me to see if I'm being followed, sweeping across the same snowy terrain I'd just hiked through, moving so fast I hardly take note of where my feet are falling. The trees below me begin to blur, as do the clouds above. I can feel the blanket hovering behind my shoulders, flapping in the wind like a superhero's cape. I trip once and slide across the ground, but immediately scramble to my feet and sprint onward, jumping straight over the camel's back, again crashing when I land. And then I finally dash past the birch trees and make it back to the convent; the hike there took nearly twenty-five minutes; the sprint back took less than five. Like the ability to breathe underwater, the Legacy of superspeed presents itself when I need it to.

I untie the blanket from around my neck, burst through the double doors, and hear the lunchtime clatter coming from the dining room. I hurry up the winding staircase and down the narrow hall, knowing it's Adelina's turn to take Sunday off. I enter the open room where the Sisters sleep. Adelina sits regally in one of the two high-back chairs, Bible in her lap. She closes it when she sees me coming.

"Why aren't you at lunch?" she asks.

"I think they're here," I say, out of breath, my hands violently shaking. I bend over and rest them on my knees.

"Who?"

"You know who!" I yell. Then, between my closed teeth: "Mogadorians."

Her eyes narrow in disbelief. "Where?"

"I went to the cave—"

"What cave?" she interrupts.

"Who cares what cave! There was a set of boot prints outside of it, huge boot prints—"

"Slow down, Marina. Boot prints outside of a cave?"

"Yes," I say.

She smirks, and I instantly realize coming to her was a mistake. I should have known she wouldn't believe me, and I can't help feeling foolish and vulnerable standing in

front of her. I straighten. I don't know what to do with
my hands.

"I want to know where my Chest is," I say, not exactly
in a confident voice, but not in a timid one either.

"What Chest?"

"You know exactly what Chest!"

"What makes you think I held on to that old thing?"
she asks calmly.

"Because you would be turning against your own people if you didn't," I say.

She reopens her Bible and pretends to read. I think of
leaving, but then my mind returns to the boot prints in
the snow.

"Where is it?" I ask.

She continues to ignore me, so I reach out with my
mind and feel the contours of the book, its thin, dusty
pages, its rough-hewn cover. I snap the book shut. Adelina
jumps.

"Tell me where it is."

"How dare you! Who do you think you are?"

"I'm a member of the Garde, and the fate of the entire
race of Loriens depends on my survival, Adelina! How
could you turn your back on them? How could you turn
your back on the humans, too? John Smith, who I believe
is a member of the Garde, is on the run in the United
States; and when he was pulled over recently he was able
to move the officer without touching him. Just like I can

do. Like I just did with your book. Don't you see what's happening, Adelina? If we don't start helping, not only will Lorien be lost forever, but so will Earth and this stupid orphanage and stupid town!"

"How dare you call this place stupid!" Adelina steps towards me with clenched fists. "This is the only place that let us in, Marina. It's the only reason we're still alive. What did the Loric do for us? They pushed us onto a ship for a year, and then they pushed us out onto a cruel planet without any kind of plan or any instructions other than to stay hidden and train. Train for what?"

"To defeat the Mogadorians. To take back Lorien." I shake my head. "The others are probably out there right now, battling, figuring out how to come together and how to get us home, while we're stuck in this prison doing nothing."

"I'm living my life with purpose, helping the human race with my prayers and service. And you should be, too."

"Your sole purpose on Earth was to help *me*."

"You're alive, aren't you?"

"Only in the literal sense of the word, Adelina."

She sits back in her chair and opens the Bible on her lap. "Lorien is dead and buried, Marina. What does it matter?"

"Lorien isn't dead; it's hibernating. You said so yourself. And the point is, we're not dead."

She swallows hard. "A death sentence has been handed

down to us all," she says, and her voice slightly cracks. Then, in a much softer tone, she says, "Our lives were doomed from the beginning. We should do good while we're here, so we may have a good afterlife."

"How can you say that?"

"Because that's the reality. We're the last of a dying race, and soon we'll be gone, too. And may God help us when that time comes."

I shake my head at her. I have no interest in talking about God.

"Where is my Chest? In this room?" I walk around the room, casting my gaze along the ceiling's edges, and then I crouch and peer beneath a few of the beds.

"Even if you had it, you can't open it without me," she says. "You know that."

She's right. If I'm to believe what she'd told me years before, when I could still trust the things she said, then I can't open it without her. The futility of it hits me all at once. The boot prints in the snow; John Smith on the run; the sheer and utter claustrophobia of Santa Teresa; and Adelina, my Cêpan, meant to help and assist in developing my Legacies, who has given up on our mission. She doesn't even know what Legacies of mine have developed. I have the ability to see in the dark, breathe underwater, to run at superspeeds; to move things with my mind; and the means to bring plants back from the brink of death. Anxiety sweeps over me, and at the worst possible moment, Sister Dora enters the room. She props her fists on her hips.

"Why aren't you in the kitchen?"

I look at her and mirror the same scowl she's giving me.

"Oh, shut up," I say, and march out of the room before she responds. I run down the hall, down the stairs, grab my coat again and push through the double doors.

I look wildly around as I move within the shadows lining the side of the road. Though I still feel as though I'm being watched, outside nothing seems amiss. I race down the hill without letting my guard down, and when I reach the café, I enter because it's the only place open. About half of its twenty tables are occupied, which I'm thankful for; I have the urge to be surrounded by people. I'm about to sit when I notice Héctor, alone in the corner, drinking wine.

"Why aren't you at El Festín?"

He glances up. He's clean shaven, and his eyes appear clear and sharp. He seems well rested; he's even well dressed. I haven't seen him this way in quite a while. I wonder how long it will last.

"I thought you didn't drink on Sunday," I say, and immediately wish I hadn't. Héctor and Ella are my only friends at the moment, and one has already disappeared today. I don't want to upset Héctor as well.

"I thought so, too," he says, not taking offense. "If you ever know a man who tries to drown his sorrows, kindly inform him his sorrows know how to swim. Here, sit down, sit down," he says, kicking out the chair across from him. I plop down in it. "How are you?"

"I hate this place, Héctor. I hate it with everything inside of me."

"Bad day?"

"Every day is a bad day here."

"Eh, this place isn't so terrible."

"How are you always so cheerful?"

"Alcohol," he says with a sideways grin. He pours himself what looks to be his first glass from the bottle. "I wouldn't recommend it to others. But it seems to work for me."

"Oh, Héctor," I say. "I wish you wouldn't drink so much."

He chuckles. Takes a sip. "You know what I wish?"

"What?"

"That you didn't look so sad all the time, Marina of the sea."

"I didn't know that I did."

He shrugs. "It's something I've noticed, but Héctor is a very perceptive man."

I look to my left and to my right, pausing to focus on each person here. Then I take the napkin off the table and put it on my lap. I put it back on the table. Then I put it back on my lap.

"Tell me what is troubling you," Héctor says, then takes a larger sip.

"Absolutely everything."

"Everything? Even me?"

I shake my head. "Okay, not everything."

His eyebrows rise and then furrow. "Now tell me."

I have a deep urge to tell him my secret, the reason I'm here and where it is I really come from. I want to tell him about Adelina and what her role was supposed to be, and what it has instead become. I want him to know about the others, out there on the run or fighting, maybe sitting idly like me, collecting dust. If there's one person I'm certain would be my ally, who would help me in any way he could, then surely it's Héctor. He is, after all, a defender who's meant to hold fast and who was born into power and bravery by such simple means as the name he was given.

"You ever feel like you don't belong here, Héctor?"

"Sure. Some days."

"Why do you stay, then? You could go anywhere."

He shrugs. "Several reasons." He pours more wine into his glass. "For one, there's no one else to take care of my mother. Plus, this place is my home, and I'm not convinced there's much better out there. My experiences have taught me that things rarely improve with a simple change of scenery."

"Maybe so, but I still can't wait to leave. I only have a little over four months left at the orphanage, you know? And you can't tell anyone this, but I think that I'm going to leave sooner than that."

"I don't think that's a good idea, Marina. You're very young to be on your own. Where will you go?"

"America," I say without hesitation.

"America?"

"There's somebody there I need to find."

"If you're so determined, then why haven't you already left?"

"Fear," I say. "Mostly fear."

"You're not the first," he says, taking a moment to empty his entire glass. His eyes have lost their sharpness. "The key to change is letting go of fear."

"I know."

The door to the café opens, and a tall man wearing a long coat and carrying an old book enters. He moves past us and takes a table in the far corner. He has dark hair and bushy brows. A thick mustache covers his upper lip. I've never seen him before; but when he lifts his head and meets my gaze, there's something I immediately don't like about him and I quickly look away. From the corner of my eye, I can see he's still staring at me. I try ignoring it. I resume talking to Héctor, or rather I babble, hardly making sense, watching him refill his glass with red wine; and I hear next to nothing of what he says in reply.

Five minutes later the man's still staring, and I'm so bothered by it that the café seems to spin. I lean across the table and whisper to Héctor, "Do you know who the person in the far corner is?"

He shakes his head. "No, but I've noticed him watching us, too. He was in here on Friday, sitting in the same seat and reading the same book."

"There's something about him I don't like, but I don't know what it is."

"Don't worry, you have me here," he says.

"I really should leave," I say. An odd desperation to get away has come over me. I try not to look at the man, but I do anyway. He's reading the book now, the cover of which is angled toward me as though he wants me to see it. It's brittle and worn, a dusty shade of gray.

PITTACUS OF MYTILENE
AND THE
ATHENIAN WAR

Pittacus? *Pittacus?* The man is watching me again, and though I can't see the bottom half of his face, his eyes suggest a knowing grin on his lips. All at once I feel as though I've been struck by a train. Could this be my first Mogadorian?

I jump up, smacking my knee against the bottom of the table and nearly knocking over Héctor's wine bottle. My chair falls backwards, crashing to the ground. Everybody in the café turns.

"I gotta go, Héctor," I say. "I gotta go."

I stumble through the doorway and make a mad dash for home, running faster than a speeding car, not caring if anyone sees. I'm back at Santa Teresa in seconds. I crash through the double doors and quickly slam them shut. I put my back against them and close my eyes. I try to slow my breathing, the twitching in my arms and legs, my quivering bottom lip. Sweat runs down the side of my face.

I open my eyes. Adelina stands in front of me, and I fall headlong into her arms, not caring about the tension from an hour before. She tentatively hugs me back, probably confused by my sudden display of affection, which I haven't shown her in years. She pulls away and I open my mouth to tell her what I've just seen, but she brings a finger to her lips the same way I did to Ella at Mass. Then she turns and walks away.

That night, after dinner and before prayers, I stand at the bedroom window gazing out as darkness falls, scanning the landscape for anything suspicious.

"Marina? What are you doing?"

I turn around. Ella stands behind me; I hadn't heard her approach. She moves through these halls like a shadow.

"There you are," I say, relieved. "Are you okay?"

She nods, but her big brown eyes tell me otherwise. "What are you doing?" she repeats.

"Just looking outside, that's all."

"What for? You're always looking out the windows at bedtime."

She's right; every night since she arrived, since I saw the man watching me in the nave window, I've been looking outside at bedtime for any signs of him. I'm now certain he's the same man I saw in the café today.

"I'm looking for bad men, Ella. There are bad men out there sometimes."

"Really? What do they look like?"

"It's hard to say," I reply. "I think they're very tall, and they're usually very dark and mean looking. And some might even be muscular, like this," I add, doing my best bodybuilder pose.

Ella giggles, going to the window. She stands on her tippy toes and pulls herself up to see out.

It's been several hours since I was in the café, and I've managed to calm down a bit.

I place my index finger on the foggy window and trace a figure onto it with two quick squeaks.

"That's the number three," Ella says.

"That's right, kiddo. I bet you can do better than that, huh?"

She smiles, sticks her finger onto the bottom of the window, and soon there is the beginning of a beautiful farmhouse and backyard barn. I watch as my number three is absorbed by Ella's perfect silo.

Three is the only reason I was allowed to leave that café

today, it's the distance from John Smith to myself. I'm now absolutely convinced that he is Number Four by the way he is being hunted; just as I'm convinced the man at the café was a Mogadorian. This town is so small I rarely see someone I don't recognize, and his book—*Pittacus of Mytilene and the Athenian War*—plus his constant stare, are no coincidence. The name "Pittacus" is one I've heard since childhood, since long before we made it to Santa Teresa.

My number: Seven. It's my only refuge now, my greatest defense. As unfair as it might be, I'm separated from death by the three others who all must die before me. So long as the charm holds, which, I assume, is why I was left alone and not attacked right at the café table. But one thing is certain: if he is a Mogadorian, they know where I am and they could take me any time they choose and hold me until they kill Four through Six. I wish I knew what's keeping them at bay and why I'm allowed to sleep in my bed again tonight. I know the charm ensures that we can't be killed out of order, but perhaps there's more to it than that.

"You and I, we're a team now," I say. Ella puts the finishing touches on her window drawing, curling her fingernails over the heads of a few cows to give them horns.

"You want to be a team with me?" she asks in a tone of disbelief.

"You bet," I say, and hold out my pinky. "Let's pinky-swear on it."

She smiles widely and hooks her pinky around mine. I shake it once.

"There, that settles it," I say.

We turn back to the window, and Ella wipes her picture away with the heel of her palm. "I don't like it here."

"I don't like it here either, believe me. But don't worry, we'll both be out of here soon enough."

"You think so? We'll leave together?"

I turn and look at her. That wasn't what I had meant at all, but without thinking twice I nod in agreement. I hope it isn't something I'll regret promising. "If you're still here when I leave, then we'll leave together. Deal?"

"Deal! And I won't let them hurt you."

"Who?" I ask.

"The bad men."

I smile. "I would appreciate that very much."

She leaves the window and walks to another, again pulling herself up to look out. As always, she moves like a ghost, making no sound. I still have no idea where she might have hidden today, but wherever it was, it was clearly a place no one would think to look. And then an idea occurs to me.

"Hey, Ella? I need your help," I say. Ella drops from the window and looks at me expectantly. "I'm trying to find something here, but it's hidden."

"What is it?" she asks, leaning forward in excitement.

"It's a chest. It's wooden and looks very old, like you

might expect to see on a pirate ship."

"And it's here?"

I nod. "It's here somewhere, but I have no idea where. Somebody did a very good job of hiding it. You're just about the most clever girl I know. I bet you can find it in no time."

She beams, rapidly nodding her head. "I'll find it for you, Marina! We're a team!"

"That's right," I agree. "We *are* a team."

CHAPTER
THIRTEEN

SIX DRIVES OUR CHARCOAL-COLORED SUV, WHICH we saw for sale in a yard two miles down the road for fifteen hundred dollars, into town to buy groceries. While she's gone, Sam and I spar together in the backyard. The three of us have spent a week training, and I'm amazed at how good Sam's gotten in the short amount of time. Despite his small size, he's a natural; and what he lacks in strength, he makes up for in technique, which is much better than my own.

At the end of each day as Six and I retreat to the corners of the living room or to our empty rooms, Sam stays up studying fighting techniques on the internet. What Six learned from Katarina and I learned from Henri is a method of combat that loosely resembles a blend of jujitsu, Tae Kwon Do, karate and Bojuka here on Earth, a system designed to be committed to muscle memory, including grappling, blocks, fluid body movements, joint manipulation and strikes to vital points of a person's central nervous system. For Six and me, having the benefit of telekinesis, it's a matter of sensing the subtlest of motions in a radius around us and then reacting to them. Sam, however, needs to keep his enemies in front of him.

While Six ends each session without a mark, Sam and I both finish with new scrapes and bruises. But despite them, Sam never loses passion or drive. Today is no different. He comes at me, chin tucked and eyes alert. He throws a right cross that I block, then a left side kick that I counter by sweeping his right leg out from under him, sending him crashing to the ground. He stands, then charges me again. Though he connects often, with my strength, his shots aren't very effective. But sometimes I feign pain to boost his confidence.

Six gets home an hour later. She changes into shorts and a T-shirt and joins us. We drill for a while, slowly doing the same block-counterkick over and over until it becomes second nature. But while I take it somewhat easy against Sam, Six goes all out against me, thrusting me backwards with such force that the wind is knocked out of me. Sometimes I get irritated, but I can still tell I'm getting better. She's no longer able to deflect my telekinesis with a casual flick of the wrist. Now she's required to throw her whole body into it.

Sam takes a break and watches from the side with Bernie Kosar.

"You're better than that, Johnny. Show me the good stuff already," she says after she upends me when I threw a sloppy roundhouse kick.

I charge her, closing the gap between us in a tenth of a second. I throw a left hook but Six blocks it, taking hold of my bicep and using my momentum to toss me over her head. I brace myself for a painful landing, but she doesn't let go of my arm, instead twisting me back over her shoulder so my feet hit the ground.

She wraps her arms around my arms; my back is smashed against her chest. She sticks her face against mine and playfully kisses me on the cheek. Before I can react she kicks the back of my knees and my butt hits the grass. My arms are swept out from under me and I'm flat on my back. Six easily pins me, and she's so close I can count the hairs on her brow. Butterflies flood my stomach.

"Okay," Sam finally interrupts. "I think you got him pretty good. You can let him up now."

Six's smile widens, and mine does, too. We stay that way for a second longer before she leans back and hefts me up by my shoulders.

"My turn with Six," Sam says.

I take a deep breath, then shake my arms to rid them of their jitters.

"She's all yours," I say, making a beeline towards the house.

"John?" Six says just as I reach the back door.

I turn, trying to tamp down a strange fluttery sensation at the sight of her. "Yeah?"

"We've been in this house for a week now. I think it's time to lose whatever sentimentality or fear you've been holding on to."

For a second, after what just happened I think she's talking about Sarah.

"The Chest," she says.

"I know," I say, and I enter the house, sliding the door behind me.

I go to my room and pace, taking deep breaths, trying to figure out what just happened out in the yard.

I go to the bathroom and splash cold water on my face. I stare into the mirror. Sarah would kill me if she caught me looking at Six like that. I tell myself again that I have nothing to worry about because Loriens love one person for life. If Sarah is my one love, then Six is simply a crush.

Back in my room I lie on my back, fold my hands across my stomach, and close my eyes. I take deep breaths, holding each one in for a five-count before exhaling out my nose.

Thirty minutes later I open the door and creep down

the hall, hearing Sam and Six milling about in the living room. The only place I could find to hide my Chest in the house was in the utility closet, on top of the hot water heater. I struggle getting it out, making as little noise as possible. Then I tiptoe back to my room, gently closing and locking the door behind me.

Six is right. It's time. No more waiting. I grab hold of the lock. It quickly warms, then squirms against the palm of my hand, taking on an almost liquid form, and snaps open. The inside glows brightly. It's never done that before. I reach in and remove the coffee can containing Henri's ashes and his letter, still in its sealed envelope. I close the lid and relock it. I know it's stupid, but I feel like I'm somehow keeping Henri alive by not reading the letter he left behind. Once the Chest is open, and once the letter is read, he'll have nothing left to tell me, nothing left to teach—and then he'll become nothing more than a memory. I'm not ready for it yet.

I open the closet where my clothes sit in a pile, and I bury the coffee can and letter under them. Then I grab the Chest and leave the room, hovering in the hallway to listen to Sam and Six streaming a show online called *Ancient Aliens*. Sam is asking Six about all the alien theories he knows and Six quickly confirms or denies them based on the teachings of Katarina. Sam furiously scribbles answers on his legal pad, which then breeds more questions that Six patiently answers or shrugs her shoulders at. Sam eats it up, drawing parallels to what he already knows.

"The pyramids of Giza? They were built by the Loric?"

"Partly us, but mostly the Mogadorians."

"What about the Great Wall of China?"

"Humans."

"Roswell, New Mexico?"

"You know, I've asked Katarina that once and she had no idea. So I don't know either."

"Wait, how long have the Mogadorians been coming here?"

"Almost as long as we have," she says.

"So, like, this war between you two, is it new?"

"Not necessarily. What I know is that both sides have traveled to Earth for thousands of years; sometimes we were here at the same time, and from what I understand, much of it was spent on friendly terms. But then something happened that ruined the relationship, and the Mogadorians left for a very long time. Beyond that I don't know much, and I have no idea when they started coming back."

I cross the living room and plop the Chest in the middle of the dining-room floor. Sam and Six glance up. Six grins, again giving me strange flutters. I smile back, but it feels insincere.

"I figure we might as well open this thing together."

Sam begins rubbing his hands with a crazy look in his eyes.

"Jeez, Sam," I say. "You look like you're about to murder somebody."

"Oh, come on," he says. "You've been teasing me with this Chest for almost a month now and I've been patient and I've kept my mouth shut out of respect for Henri and everything, but how often do I get to see the treasures from an alien planet? I just think about how the guys at NASA would die to be sitting where I am right now. You can't blame me for being so into this."

"Would you be mad if this whole time it's been full of nothing but dirty laundry?"

"Alien dirty laundry?" Sam asks sarcastically.

I laugh, then reach down and grab hold of the lock. My hand instantly glows when touching the cold metal, and the lock again warms, shaking and twisting in my grip, protesting the ancient powers that keep it closed. When it clicks open I remove the lock, set it aside, and place my hand on the Chest's top. Six and Sam both lean forward in anticipation.

I lift the lid. The Chest is yet again ablaze with light that hurts my eyes. The first thing I do is remove the velvet bag holding the seven orbs that make up Lorien's solar system. I think of Henri and how we watched the light glow and pulsate at Lorien's core, showing that the planet is still alive, albeit hibernating. I place the bag in Sam's hand. All three of us peer down into the Chest. Something else is lit up.

"What is that glowing?" Six asks.

"No idea. It never did that before."

She reaches down and plucks a rock from the bottom of the Chest. It's a perfectly round crystal no bigger than a Ping-Pong ball, and when she touches it, the light brightens even more. And then it fades, and begins to slowly pulse. We watch the crystal, transfixed by the glow. Then, suddenly, Six lets it drop to the floor. The crystal ceases to pulse and resumes its steady glow. Sam reaches down to pick it up.

"Don't!" Six yells.

He looks up, confused.

"Something doesn't feel right about it," she says.

"What do you mean?" I ask.

"It felt like pinpricks against my palm. When I grabbed hold of it I got a really bad feeling."

"This stuff is my Inheritance," I say. "Maybe I'm the only one allowed to touch it?"

I bend down and carefully pick up the glowing crystal. Within seconds it feels as if I'm holding a radioactive cactus; my stomach compresses and acid climbs up my throat, and I instantly toss the crystal onto a blanket. I swallow. "Maybe I'm doing it wrong."

"Maybe we don't know how to use it. I mean, you said Henri kept you from seeing inside because you weren't ready. Maybe you're still not ready?"

"Well, that would be pretty lame," I say.

"This sucks," Sam says.

Six walks into the kitchen and returns with two towels and a plastic bag. She carefully grabs the glowing crystal with a towel and drops both into the bag, which she then wraps in a second towel.

"You really think that's necessary?" I ask. My stomach continues to gurgle.

She shrugs. "I don't know about you, but the feeling I got when I touched it was bad news. Better safe than sorry."

What's left in the Chest is everything comprising my Inheritance, and I'm not really sure where to start. I reach in and grab an object I've seen before, the oblong crystal Henri used to spread the Lumen from my hands to the rest of my body. It comes alive and bathes the dining room in its bright light. The crystal's center begins swirling with what looks like smoke, twisting and turning back on itself, as I have seen it do before.

"Now we're talking," Sam says.

"Here," I say, giving it to him. The crystal falls inert when it transfers hands. "I've already seen it."

Also inside the Chest are a few smaller crystals, a black diamond, a collection of brittle leaves bound with twine, and a star-shaped talisman the same pale blue as the pendant around my neck, which tells me it's Loralite, the rarest gem found only at Lorien's core. There's also a bright red oval bracelet and an amber-colored stone in the shape of a raindrop.

"What do you think that is?" Sam asks, pointing to a flat, circular stone the same milky white color as a pearl that's stuck in the corner.

"Don't know," I say.

"How about that?" he asks, this time pointing to a small dagger that looks to have a blade made of diamond.

I lift it from the Chest. The handle fits snug in my hand as though it was made for it, and I suppose it was. The blade isn't more than four inches long, and just by seeing the way the light glints along its edge, I can tell it's far sharper than any razor one might find on Earth.

"What about that thing?" Sam asks again, pointing to something else, and I have no doubt he'll ask the same question over and over until he's inquired about every object inside.

"Here," I say, setting the dagger down and removing the seven orbs in an effort to keep him occupied. "Check this out."

I blow on them, and tiny lights flicker across their surfaces. Then I toss them up in the air, and they instantly spring to life, spinning in orbit around the orange-sized sun in the center.

"It's Lorien's solar system," I say. "Six planets, one

sun. And this one here," I add, pointing to the fourth orb, which remains the same various shades of ashen gray as the last time I'd seen it, "is Lorien as it looks today, at this very moment. The glow at its center is what's left."

"Wow," Sam says. "NASA dudes would be crapping themselves right now looking at this."

"And watch this," I say, illuminating my right hand. I sweep the light over the orb, and all at once the surface changes from its depressing gray tones to vibrant blues and greens of the forests and oceans. "This is the planet as it was the day before the attack."

"Wow," Sam says again, staring in awe with his mouth hanging open; and while the rotating planets have him transfixed, I look back in the Chest.

"Do you know what any of this is? Or what it does?" I ask Six, who doesn't respond. I turn and see she's just as amazed as Sam by the solar system spinning two feet above the floor. Since Henri had told me they weren't part of my Legacy, which means they weren't locked in the Chest, I had wrongly assumed she'd seen them before. But it makes sense she hasn't; they can only be activated after the first Legacy develops.

"Six," I say again. She comes back to reality, turns to me and I find myself looking away once we make eye contact. "Do you know what any of this stuff is?"

"Not really," she murmurs, running her hands over

the stones' surfaces. "This is the healing stone Henri and I used at the school," she says, pointing out a flat, black rock I've seen before. Then she freezes, a faint gasp escaping her lips. Sam and I exchange confused expressions. She lifts a pale yellow stone, its surface waxy and smooth, from the Chest and holds it up to the light. "Oh my God," she marvels, flipping it over.

"Tell me," I prod. She looks me right in the eyes.

"Xitharis," she says. "It comes from our first moon."

She brings the small stone to her forehead, squeezing her eyes shut. The faint yellow shade of the stone darkens slightly. She opens her eyes and hands the stone to me. I frown and take it from her, my fingertips grazing the palm of her hand. Sam inhales sharply.

"What the . . ." He looks terrified, groping for me like he's blind.

"What's going on?" I ask, slapping Sam's hands away from my face.

"You're invisible," Six says quietly. I look down at my lap, and it's true: I've completely vanished. I drop the Xitharis on the floor like a hot potato, and instantly become visible.

"The Xitharis," Six explains, "allows one Garde to transfer a Legacy to another, but only for a short period of time. An hour, I think, maybe two. I can't say for sure. All you have to do is charge it by focusing your energy on the stone. Put it to your forehead, and *bam*, it's ready to go."

"Charge it, like a battery?" Sam asks.

"Exactly, and it won't start using the Legacy until it's touched again."

I look at the stone. "Sweet. Looks like somebody other than you is taking a trip into town."

"And somebody other than *you* is going to be resistant to fire," she says playfully.

"If you're nice to me, then it's definitely a possibility," I say.

Sam picks the stone up and clenches his entire body in deep concentration. Nothing happens. "Oh come on," he says to the stone. "I promise to use it for the power of good. No girls' locker rooms, I swear."

"Sorry, Sam," Six says. "I'm pretty sure this stuff only works on us."

He sets the Xitharis down and we dig through the rest of the Chest to see if anything else is activated by touch; but after an hour of studying and holding all seventeen artifacts, blowing hot air on them, squeezing them tightly, nothing else engages aside from the glowing crystal wrapped in the towel, the larger oblong crystal with the smoky center, and the solar system still rotating above us. The healing stone, however, does cure the cuts and bruises Six has been stamping my body with.

"Man, I've waited most of my life to open this

thing; and now that I have, a lot of it seems useless to me," I say.

"I'm sure their uses will reveal themselves in time," Six assures me. "Things like this need to be slept on. It's usually when they've left your mind completely that answers finally come."

I nod, looking back at everything lying around the Chest. Six is right; forcing an answer only guarantees that no answer will come.

"Yeah, maybe some of it only activates with further Legacies. Who knows," I say with a shrug. I put everything back inside, feeling compelled to keep the glowing crystal covered with the towel. I leave the solar system out, which continues its circular march. I close and lock the Chest and carry it down the hall.

"Don't be discouraged, John," Six says behind me. "As Henri said, you're probably not ready to see it all yet."

CHAPTER
FOURTEEN

I CAN'T SLEEP. PARTLY BECAUSE OF THE CHEST. For all I know, one of the gems inside could give me power to morph into different creatures like Bernie Kosar, or one could create an iron barrier around me impossible to penetrate by enemy attack. But how will I know without Henri? I feel sad. Defeated.

But mostly I can't stop thinking about Six, can't stop picturing her face hovering inches above mine, or the sugary scent of her breath, or the way the setting sun had made her eyes glow. In that moment I had an irrepressible desire to stop training and to simply wrap my arms around her and squeeze her down onto me. A pang of longing to do that even now, hours later, has anchored itself in my heart, and that's what's really keeping me up. That, and the overwhelming guilt I feel about my attraction to her. The person I'm supposed to be longing for is Sarah.

There's too much on my mind to expect sleep, too many emotions: pain, desire, confusion, guilt. I lie another twenty minutes before giving up on sleep. I whip aside my blanket and pull on a pair of pants and a gray tee. Bernie Kosar follows me from the room and down the hallway. I poke my head into the living room to see if Sam's asleep. He is, wrapped up in a blanket on the floor like a worm in a cocoon, and I turn and walk back. Six's room is directly across the hall from mine, and her door's ajar. I stand looking at it, and I hear Six rustle on the floor.

"John?" she whispers.

I cringe, and my heart immediately races.

"Yeah?" I reply, still standing outside.

"What are you doing?"

"Nothing," I whisper. "I can't sleep."

"Come in," she says. I push open the door. Her room is pitch-black, and I can't see anything. "Is everything okay?"

"Yeah, everything's fine," I say. I barely turn on my Lumen, and the faint glow is like a night-light. I keep my eyes off her and on the carpet. "Just too much on my mind, you know. I was maybe thinking of going for a walk or a run or something."

"Well, that's kind of dangerous, don't you think? Don't forget you're on the FBI's Ten Most Wanted List with a fat reward on your head," she says.

"I know, but . . . it's still dark out, and you could make us invisible, couldn't you? I mean, that's if you wanted to come along."

I increase the lights on my hands and I can see Six sitting on the floor with a couple blankets over her legs and her hair's pulled back with loose strands falling around her face. She shrugs, then tosses the blankets aside and stands. She's wearing black yoga pants and a white tank. I can't stop myself from staring at her bare shoulders. I look away when I'm hit with the absurd suspicion that she can feel my eyes on her.

"Sure," she says, pulling the band from her hair and rewrapping her ponytail. "I always have a hard time sleeping. Especially on the floor."

"I hear that," I say.

"Do you think we'll wake up Sam, though?"

I shake my head. She responds with a shoulder shrug and lifts her hand. I take it immediately. Six disappears, but my hand still glows and I can see her foot imprints in the carpet. Then I extinguish my hand and we tiptoe from the room and down the hallway. Bernie Kosar follows, and when we reach the living room, Sam lifts his head from the floor and stares right at us. Six and I stop, and I hold my breath to remain silent. I think about Sam's obvious crush on Six and how he'd be devastated if he saw us holding hands.

"Hey, Bernie," he says groggily, then drops his head

and rolls over with his back facing us. We remain silent for a few seconds, and then Six leads us across the living room and into the kitchen to leave through the back door.

The night is warm, and filled with the sounds of crickets and swaying palm fronds. I inhale deeply as Six and I walk hand in hand. I find it odd that Six's hand seems so small and delicate in mine, despite her amazing physical strength. I love the way it feels. Bernie Kosar races through the heavy brush lining the gravel drive while Six and I stroll silently down its center. It dead-ends into a narrow road and we turn left.

"I can't stop thinking about what you went through," I finally say, but what I would rather tell her is that I can't stop thinking about her. "Being held prisoner for half a year, having to witness Katarina being—well, you know what I mean."

"Sometimes I forget it happened. And other times it's all I can think about for days," she replies.

"Yeah," I say, drawing out the word. "I don't know; I guess it goes without saying that I miss Henri, and it kills me that he's gone. But after hearing your story I realize how lucky I really am. I mean, I got to say goodbye to him and everything. Plus, he was there while I went through my first Legacies. I can't imagine going through that alone like you did."

"It was really, really hard, that's for sure. I could

have used her the day I started to gain my invisibility Legacy. I could have used her even more for girl talks when I was growing up. They were pretty much our parents on Earth, right?"

"Right," I say. "What I find funny is that now that Henri's gone, the things I remember most about him are the things I usually hated. Like when we would leave some place behind and we'd drive for hours and hours and hours down the highway headed someplace I'd never even heard of when all I wanted to do was just get out of the car. Now, the conversations we had on those trips are the ones I remember most. Or when we started training in Ohio, and he made me do the same thing over and over and over again . . . I hated it so much, you know? But now I can't look back on any of it without smiling.

"Like one time after my telekinesis finally came, we were training in the snow and he was throwing all these objects so I could learn to deflect them. I had to redirect them back at the source, and he heaved a meat tenderizer really hard at me, and I used its own velocity to whip it back at him; and at the very last second he had to jump headfirst into the snow to keep from being hit," I say, smiling to myself. "The pile of snow was actually a snow-covered rosebush with all these thorns. You would not believe the noise he made. Stuff like that I won't ever forget."

A car approaches on the side of the road and we scoot off into the ditch until it passes. It whips into a stone driveway of a nearby house, and a man in a black leather jacket jumps out. He pounds on the front door, yelling for whoever is inside to open up.

"Jesus. What time is it?" I ask Six.

Six moves towards the man and the house, my hand still in hers. "Does it matter?"

As we creep within ten feet of him, the smell of alcohol hits me. He stops pounding his fist against the door to yell, "You better goddamn open this door, Charlene, or you don't wanna know what I'm gonna do!"

Six sees the revolver in his waistband the same time I do and she squeezes my hand. "Screw this guy," Six whispers.

He pounds again and again until the lights in the front window turn on. Then, through the door, a woman shouts, "Get out of here! Just get out of here, Tim!"

"Open the door right now!" he yells back. "Or else, Charlene! Or else, you hear me?"

We're within touching distance of him. I can see the faded tattoo below his left ear is a bald eagle holding a snake in its talons.

She yells back, her voice shakier than before: "Just leave me alone, Tim! Why are you here? Why won't you just leave me alone?"

He pounds and yells even harder. I'm about to put

him in a choke hold, squeeze that bald eagle and snake right off his neck, when I see the gun slowly crawl up his lower back until it floats away from him in Six's invisible hand. She puts the barrel of the gun up against the back of the man's head and buries it in his brown hair. She cocks the hammer with a loud click.

The man stops pounding on the door. He stops breathing, too. Six pushes the gun even harder into his skull and then she pushes it stiffly to the right, spinning the man around. The sight of the floating gun in front of his face makes him go white. He blinks and shakes his head violently, expecting to wake up in his bed or in the back alley of whatever bar he came from. Six moves the gun side to side and I wait for her to say something, to really spook the hell out of him, but instead she suddenly turns the gun towards his car. She shoots, and a radius of broken glass appears on the windshield. He screams, shrilly, and burst into tears.

Six aims the gun at his face again and he quiets down, letting a stream of snot hit his upper lip. "Please, please, please," he says. "I'm sorry, God. I, I, I'm gonna leave right now. I swear. I'm leaving." Six cocks the hammer again. I see the curtain of the front window move to the right, and expose the face of a large blond woman. I squeeze Six's hand and she squeezes back. "I'm leaving right now. I'm leaving, I'm leaving," the man sputters to the gun. Six aims at his car again and empties the chamber with a loud bang; the rear driver's side window explodes into a thousand pieces.

"No! Okay, okay!" the man shouts. There's suddenly a wet spot on the inner thigh of his jeans. Six motions the gun at the front window, and he makes eye contact with the blond woman inside. "And I'll never come back. I'll never, ever, ever come back." The gun bobs to the left twice, indicating he can leave. The man rips his car door open and dives in. Stones spit out from under his tires as he reverses out of the driveway and then barrels down the road. The woman in the window continues to stare at the handgun that's floating next to her front door, and that's when Six flings it over the house with such force that it's sure to land in the next county.

We run back to the road and then we continue to run until there isn't a house in sight. I wish I could see Six's face.

"I could do that kind of stuff all day," she finally says. "It's like being a superhero."

"Humans do love their superheroes," I say. "Do you think she'll call the police?"

"Nah. She's probably going to think it was all a bad dream."

"Or the best dream she's ever had," I say. Our talk turns to all the good things we could do for Earth with our Legacies if we weren't busy being hunted or hated.

"How did you train yourself, anyway?" I ask. "I can't

imagine learning the things I did if it hadn't been for Henri pushing me so much."

"What other choice did I have? Either we adapt or we perish. So I adapted. Katarina and I trained for years before we were captured, but obviously never once after my Legacies developed. When I finally got out of that cave I promised myself that her death wasn't going to be in vain, and the only way to do that was to seek revenge. So I picked up where we had left off. It was hard at first, especially on my own, but little by little I began to learn and grow stronger. Besides, I've had more time than you. My Legacies came sooner than yours, and I'm older than you."

"You know," I say, "my sixteenth birthday—or at least the day I celebrated as my birthday with Henri— was two days ago."

"John! Why didn't you tell us?" she asks, then lets go of my hand and playfully shoves me away, making me instantly visible. "We could have celebrated."

I smile and reach for her, feeling blindly in the dark. She takes my hand and interlocks her fingers in mine, allowing my thumb to rest over hers. The thought of Sarah comes into my head, and I find myself instantly pushing it out.

"So what was she like?" I ask. "Katarina?"

A moment of silence passes. "Compassionate. She was always helping others. And she was funny. We used to joke and laugh a lot, which probably seems hard to believe, seeing how serious I usually am."

I chuckle. "I didn't say it, you did."

"But hey, no changing the subject. Why didn't you say anything about your birthday?"

"I don't know. I actually forgot about it until yesterday, and then it just seemed pointless with everything else going on."

"It's your birthday, John; it's not pointless. Every birthday any of us are lucky to have is cause for celebration, considering what's hunting us. And anyway, had I known I might have even taken it easy on you in training."

"Yeah, you must feel terrible beating up a guy like that on his birthday," I say, and then nudge her. She nudges me back. Bernie Kosar leaps from the brambles and trots beside us. Several burrs are stuck to his fur like Velcro, and I let go of Six's hand to pluck them all off.

We reach the end of the road. Tall grass and a winding river lie ahead of us. We turn around and amble back towards the house.

"Does it bother you that you never got your Chest?" I ask after a few minutes of silence.

"In a way I think it fueled me that much more. It was gone; there was nothing I could do about it. So I did what I thought was smart and chose to focus on finding the rest of you. I just wish I could have found Number Three before they did."

"Well, you found me. I can't imagine I would have survived this long if you hadn't. Or Bernie Kosar, for that matter. Or even Sarah." As soon as I say Sarah's name, Six's grip loosens a little. Guilt rises in my chest as we make our way back to the house. I do love Sarah, but it's hard to imagine a life with her when I'm so far away, on the run, with no sense of where the future will take me. The only life I can imagine right now is the one I'm living. The one with Six.

We reach the house, and I find myself wishing our walk wasn't over. I try to stall, slowing my steps, hovering at the end of the driveway.

"You know, I only know you as Six," I say. "Did you have a name at one time?"

"Of course I did, but I didn't use it very often. I didn't go to school like you. Well, I did for a little while, but then we decided I was better off staying home."

"So, what was your name?"

"Maren Elizabeth."

"Whoa, really?"

"Why do you sound so surprised?"

"I don't know; Maren Elizabeth seems kind of dainty and feminine. I think I expected you to have something strong and mythic, like Athena, or maybe Xena, you know, like the warrior princess? Or even Storm. Storm would have suited you perfectly."

Six laughs, and the sound of it makes me want to pull her to me. Of course I don't, but I *want* to, and maybe that's what's most telling.

"I'll have you know, I used to be a little girl who once wore ribbons in her hair."

"Yeah, what color?"

"Pink."

"I think I'd pay money to see that."

"Forget it, you don't have enough."

"I'll have *you* know," I say, mimicking the same playful voice she just used, "I have a whole Chest of rare gems at my disposal. Just point me in the direction of a pawn shop."

She laughs, then says, "I'll keep my eyes open for one."

We continue to stand at the mouth of our driveway, and I look up at the stars and the moon, which is three-quarters full. I listen to the wind and to Six's feet on the gravel as she shifts her weight from one leg to the other. I take a deep breath.

"I'm really glad we went for that walk," I say.

"So am I."

I look where she's standing, wishing she were visible so I could read her expression. "Could you imagine if every night were like this, living your life without having to worry about what or who might be lurking out of sight, without always having to peer over your shoulder to see if you're being followed? Wouldn't it be amazing to be able to forget, just once, what's peeking over the horizon?"

"Of course it'd be nice," she says. "And it *will* be nice when we finally have that luxury."

"I hate what we have to do. I hate the situation we're in. I wish it were different." I look for Lorien in the sky and release her hand. She makes herself visible. I grab her by the shoulders and turn her towards me.

Six inhales deeply.

Just as I duck my head towards hers, an explosion rocks the back of the house. Six and I scream and tumble to the ground. A plume of fire lifts up over the roof, and flames instantly spread inside.

"Sam!" I yell. From fifty feet away I rip the front windows out. They shatter against the concrete walkway. Smoke comes billowing out.

Before I know it I've burst into a dead sprint. I take a deep breath and leap, crashing into the house and splintering the door from its hinges.

CHAPTER
FIFTEEN

EACH NIGHT LATELY I LIE AWAKE FOR HOURS, MY eyes open, ears attuned to the sounds of silence around me. Every so often I lift my head when I hear a distant noise—a drop of water hitting the floor, a person shifting in her sleep—and sometimes I crawl from bed and go to the window to be assured there's nothing out there, an obvious attempt to feel some semblance of security, however flimsy it might be.

Each night passes with less sleep than the night before. I've grown weak, exhausted to the point of delirium. I have trouble eating. I know worrying doesn't do me any good, but no amount of willing myself to rest or eat does anything to change how I feel. And when I finally do sleep, nothing keeps away the terrible dreams that wake me up again.

There's been no sign of the mustached man in the week since I saw him in the café, but I can't dismiss the notion that just because I haven't seen him doesn't mean he isn't out there. I keep returning to the same questions: who was in my cave; who *or what* was the mustached man in the café; why was he reading a book with the name *Pittacus* on the cover; and, most importantly, why did he let me go if he's Mogadorian? None of it makes sense, not even the title of his book. I've turned up nothing other than a brief summary of the plot online: a Greek general given to short, pithy statements defeats an Athenian army when they were on the verge of attacking the city of Mytilene. What does it have to do with anything?

The questions of the cave and book aside, I've come to two conclusions. The first is that nothing was done to me because of my number. For the time being, it's keeping me safe, but for how long? The second is that the crowd of people in the café kept the Mogadorian from making a move. But from what I know of them, a Mogadorian wouldn't let a few witnesses deter him. I've stopped rushing to and from school ahead of the others and have instead attached myself to their large group. To keep Ella safe, I've stopped walking with her in public. I know it hurts her feelings, but it's for the best. She doesn't deserve to be mixed up in my problems.

But there's one thing that has given me a shade of hope in all this. A noticeable change has occurred in Adelina. Worry creases her forehead. There's a nervous twitch to her eyes when she thinks nobody's watching, and they dart from one section of a room to another like a scared, threatened animal, the same way they used to years ago when she still believed. And while we haven't spoken since I fell into her arms after rushing from the café, it's these changes in her that have me thinking I might have my Cêpan back.

Darkness. Silence. Fifteen sleeping bodies. I lift my head and glance across the room. Instead of seeing a small lump in Ella's bed, the covers are thrown aside and her bed is empty. It's the third night in a row I've noticed her missing, and yet I never hear her leave. But I have bigger things to worry about than where she's gone off to.

I drop my head on the pillow and glance out the window. A full moon, bright and yellow, hangs just outside. I stare at it for a long time, entranced by the way it hovers there. I take a deep breath and close my eyes. When I reopen them, the moon has turned from bright yellow to bloodred and it seems to shimmer, but then I realize it's not the moon I'm staring at, but rather its reflection, shining brightly in the dark waters of some great pool. Steam rises off its surface, and the air reeks of pungent iron. I lift my head again, and only then do I see I'm standing amid a ravaged, bloodied battlefield.

Bodies are strewn everywhere, the dead and dying, the aftermath of some war in which there are no survivors. I instinctively bring my hands to my body, feeling for puncture wounds or cuts, but I'm unscathed. That's when

I see her, the girl with the gray eyes I've dreamed about, the one I painted on the cave's wall beside John Smith. She lies motionless at the base of the shore. I rush to her. Blood gushes from her side and soaks into the sand and is carried out to sea. Her raven hair clings to her ashen face. She's not breathing, and I'm completely and utterly anguished to know there's not a single thing I can do about it. And then behind me comes a deep, mocking laugh. My eyes close before I slowly turn around to face my enemy.

My eyes open and the battlefield disappears. The familiar bed in the darkened room has returned. The moon is normal and bright yellow. I get up and walk to the window. I scan the dark terrain, still and quiet. No sign of the mustached man, or anything else, for that matter. All the snow has melted, and the moon glistens on the wet cobblestones. Is he watching me?

I turn away and crawl back into bed. I lie on my back, taking deep breaths to calm myself. My whole body is tense and rigid. I think about the cave and how I haven't been back since the boot prints appeared. I roll to my side with my back towards the window. I don't want to see what's out there. Ella still isn't in her bed. I try to wait up for her to return, but I fall asleep. No further dreams come.

When the morning bell rings I raise my head off the pillow, my body stiff and sore. A cold rain beats against the window. I glance across the room and see Ella sitting up, lifting her arms towards the ceiling, yawning deeply.

We shuffle from the room together, saying nothing. We coast about our Sunday routines and sit through Mass with our heads hung. At one point I nudge Ella awake, and twenty minutes later she returns the favor. I survive the El Festín lunch line, doling out food while looking for anyone suspicious. When everything appears normal, I can't decide if I'm relieved or disappointed. What saddens me most is that I don't see Héctor.

Towards the end of cleanup, La Gorda and Gabby begin horsing around, spraying each other with the hose attached to the kitchen sink as I dry dishes. I ignore them, even when I get splashed in the face. Twenty minutes later when I've just finished drying the last dish, carefully placing it atop the tall stack, a girl named Delfina slips on the wet floor and bumps into me, causing me to fall into the stack and send all thirty plates back into the dirty water, where some of them break.

"Why don't you watch what you're doing," I say, and I push her with one arm.

Delfina spins around and shoves me right back.

"Hey!" Sister Dora barks from across the kitchen. "You two, knock it off! Right now!"

"You're going to pay for that," Delfina says.

I can't wait to be officially done with Santa Teresa.

"Whatever," I say, still scowling.

She nods at me, a malicious look upon her face. "Watch your back."

"If I have to come over there, Lord help me, you are going to regret it," Sister Dora says.

Instead of using telekinesis to toss Delfina through the roof—or Sister Dora or Gabby or La Gorda, for that matter—I turn back to the dishes.

When I'm finally free I walk outside. It's still raining and I stand under the eaves and look towards the cave. The mud will be thick on the mountainside, which means I'd get filthy. I use that as an excuse for why I won't go, though I know that even if it weren't raining I wouldn't have the courage, despite my curiosity of whether or not new boot prints have been made in the mud.

I walk back inside. Ella's Sunday duties require her to clean the nave after everyone leaves, wiping down pews. But when I go there, everything has already been cleaned.

"Have you seen Ella?" I ask a ten-year-old girl named Valentina. She shakes her head. I walk back to our bedroom, but there's no sign of Ella there. I sit on her bed. The bounce of the mattress causes a silver object to peek from beneath Ella's pillow. It's a tiny flashlight. I flip it on. The light shines brightly. I turn it off and put it back where I found it so that the Sisters won't see it.

I walk the halls, peeking in rooms as I go along. Because

of the rain, most of the girls have stayed in, milling about in their small groups, laughing and talking and playing games.

On the second floor, where the hallway splits and leads to the church's two separate wings, I go left, down a dark, dusty corridor. Empty rooms and ancient statues cut into the rock wall and arched ceiling, and I stick my head in the doorways, looking for Ella. No sign of her. The hallway narrows and the dusty odor segues to a damp, earthy smell. At the corridor's end stands a padlocked oak door I jimmied open a week and a half ago looking for the Chest. Beyond the door is a stone stairway that circles around the narrow tower leading up to the north belfry, which holds one of Santa Teresa's two bells. The Chest wasn't there either.

I surf the internet for a while but find nothing new about John Smith. Then I go to the sleeping quarters, lie in bed, and feign sleep. Thankfully La Gorda, Gabby, and Delfina don't come into the room, and I don't see Ella either. I crawl from bed and walk down the hall.

I enter the nave and find Ella in the back pew. I sit beside her. She smiles up at me, looking tired. This morning I had put her hair into a ponytail, but now it's come loose. I pull the band free, and Ella turns her head so I can redo it.

"Where have you been all day?" I ask. "I was looking for you."

"I was exploring," she says proudly. I instantly feel terrible all over again for ignoring her on our walks to school.

We leave and go to our room, say good night to one another. Slipping beneath the covers, waiting for the lights to be shut off, I feel hopeless and sad, wanting to simply crawl into a ball and cry. So that's what I do.

I wake in the middle of the night and I can't tell what time it is, though I assume I've slept at least a few hours. I roll over and close my eyes again, but something feels off. There's some change in the room I can't quite explain, and it amplifies the same anxiety I've felt all week.

I open my eyes again, and the second they adjust to the dark, I realize a face is staring at me. I gasp and bolt straight backwards, crashing into the wall behind me. *I'm trapped,* I think, *trapped in the far, back corner. How stupid of me to have wanted this bed.* My hands tighten, and just as I'm about to scream and kick at the face, I recognize the brown eyes.

Ella.

I instantly relax. I wonder how long she's been standing there.

Very slowly she brings her tiny index finger to her lips. Then her eyes widen and she smiles as she leans forward. She cups her hand around my ear.

"I found the Chest," she whispers.

I pull away, look earnestly into her radiant, upturned face, and know immediately she's telling the truth. My own eyes widen. I can't contain my excitement. I pull her to me and give her the tightest hug her small body can endure.

"Oh Ella, you have no idea how proud I am of you."

"I told you I'd find it. I told you, because we're a team and we help each other."

"We do," I whisper.

I let go of her. Her face brims with pride. "Come on. I'll show you where it is." She takes me by the hand, and I follow her around the bed, tiptoeing quietly.

The Chest—a bright ray of hope when I'd least expected it, when I'd needed it most.

CHAPTER
SIXTEEN

WE FLEE THE ROOM, AND I HAVE THE URGE TO
sprint to wherever Ella's leading me. She glides swiftly
and soundlessly across the cold floor. The corridor is
dark; and while I see everything clearly, every so often
Ella flicks on the flashlight to orient herself, then quickly
turns it off.

When we reach the nave I think she's going to head
towards the north tower, but she doesn't, and instead
guides me up the center aisle. We skitter past the rows
of pews. At the nave's front, stained glass saints line the
curved wall and the moonlight behind them brings a celes-
tial radiance that gives each a more biblical appearance
than they've ever had before. Water drips in a constant
patter somewhere.

Ella cuts a right turn at the front pew and sweeps
towards one of the many open recesses that run the length
of both walls. I follow. The air is cooler here than in the

nave, and a tall statue of the Virgin Mary looms over us with arms lifted from her sides. Ella goes around her, and when she reaches the back left corner, she turns to me.

"I'll have to bring it down to you," she says, putting the flashlight in her mouth. She takes hold of the stone pillar and scoots up it like a squirrel clawing up a tree. All I can do is watch in amazement, so impressed by her mobility.

When she's almost at the ceiling, she pauses and then swings around the column, disappearing into a tight little nook that's almost invisible from where I stand.

I never noticed the nook before. Lord knows how Ella did. I crane my head to listen, hearing the rough friction of her shoes scrape along the rock, which means there's just enough room for her to crawl. Some kind of tunnel. I can't help but smile. I knew the Chest was here, somewhere, but I would have never found it in a million years if it weren't for Ella. I laugh at the thought of Adelina scaling the same column with the Chest so many years ago. Ella has stopped; I hear nothing. Twenty seconds pass.

"Ella," I whisper. She sticks her head out and looks down. "Should I come up?"

She shakes her head. "It's stuck, but I almost have it. I'll bring it down to you in a minute," she whispers back, and then yanks her head back in and disappears. I can't take the suspense of not knowing what's going on up there. I look at the base of the column and take hold of it;

and just before I'm about to try climbing it, I hear a noise behind me that sounds like somebody kicking a pew. I spin around. The Virgin Mary blocks my view. I walk around her and scan the nave, but I don't see anything.

"I got it!" I hear Ella exclaim.

I rush back around the statue and look up, waiting for her to appear. I can hear her grunt and struggle to drag the Chest to the nook's opening, and I have no idea if it's because the Chest is heavy or because the tunnel is so narrow. Little by little the dragging continues. I feel nothing short of ecstasy at finally having the Chest in my possession, and I don't even consider the problem of getting it open. I'll cross that bridge when I come to it. Just as Ella is almost to the opening, I hear something else behind me.

"What are you doing up?"

I whip around. Divided equally on each side of the Virgin Mary, Gabby and Delfina stand under the statue's left arm while La Gorda and a wiry Bonita, the champion of the dock game that almost got me killed at the lake, position themselves beneath the right arm.

I glance over my shoulder and see two small eyes peering down at us from the nook's opening.

"What do you want?" I ask.

"I wanted to see what the little tattletale was up to, that's all. You know, it's funny because I saw you sneak out of the room and I thought that I would get up and *finally* see what it was you're always looking at on the computer, but you weren't there." Gabby paints a sarcastic, confused look on her face. "You were in here, which is really weird."

"Really weird. It's really weird," La Gorda says. To my relief, I don't hear Ella dragging the Chest anymore.

"Why do you even care?" I say. "Seriously. All I ever do is keep to myself and keep my mouth shut."

"I care a lot about you, Marina," Gabby says, stepping forward. She flips her long dark hair. "In fact, I care so much that I worry about you hanging out with that loser drunk, Héctor, all the time. Do you get drunk with him?" She pauses. "Do you drink from his bottle?"

I don't know if it was because she called Héctor a loser, or because she thought our friendship was anything more than just that, or because she is snooping on what I'm doing at the computer, but it just happens. I close my eyes and reach out with my mind, grabbing all four of them at once. La Gorda screams, while the other three whimper in shock. I pick them up off the ground—their bare feet kicking at the air, their shoulders smashed against each other's—and thrust them all across the smooth floor until they bounce off the steps leading to the raised dais at the back of the nave.

La Gorda slaps the floor with her open palms and gets to her feet like an angry bull ready to charge the conquistador. I run to her instead, making up the ground in a matter of seconds. La Gorda swings a wild punch and I duck, only to spring up and jam my right fist into her chin. She falls backwards with a gasp, and her head thuds against the floor. She's out cold.

Bonita jumps on my back and pulls at my hair. Someone punches me in the left cheek, and the other kicks me in the shin. Bonita slides down my back and hugs my upper arms so I can't move. Delfina swings and I duck. The punch glances off Bonita's mouth and she loosens her grip enough for me to twist away. I grab Bonita's right arm in my hands and I drive her towards Gabby.

"You're dead, Marina! You are so dead!" Bonita shrieks, and I pull her sideways and knee her in the gut, knocking the wind out of her. I shove her to the ground next to La Gorda.

Delfina's confidence is broken. She looks for the door. "You ready to leave me alone?" I ask her.

"Doesn't matter. I'm going to get you tomorrow," she says. "Right when you're not looking."

"You're going to wish you didn't say that." I fake right and lunge left, tackling her around the waist. Gabby tries to grab my hair but I whip Delfina around to block her. Then I pivot on my heels and release Delfina down the middle aisle of the nave. Her back hits the first step at the altar, and her groan echoes off the vaulted ceiling.

Gabby circles me. "I'm telling Sister Dora. You're going to be in *so* much trouble." I turn my body to keep my eyes on her. She stops right next to the column. I can tell she's about to charge and I'm ready for it.

Suddenly I see a flash of white above Gabby's head. It takes me a second to recognize that it's Ella, and she's jumped from the nook all the way down onto Gabby's shoulders. Gabby flails around until she can get her hands on Ella; and when she does, she tosses her onto the floor with a horrible cracking sound.

"No!" I yell, and then I punch Gabby in the sternum as hard as I can. Her feet leave the ground and she hits the wall, knocking dust from the stone wall's mortar.

Ella's on her back, wailing, writhing in pain, but I notice she keeps her right leg completely still. I kneel beside her and pull up the bottom of her nightgown to see a sharp white bone sticking out of her skin just below the knee. I don't know what to do. I put my hand on her shoulders to try to console her, but she's in so much pain, she doesn't feel it.

"I'm right here, Ella," I say. "I'm here right beside you, and everything is going to be okay."

Her eyes open and she gives me a pleading look. It's then that I see the damage done to her right hand. Her tiny fist is mangled, crooked; blood seeps out between her index and middle fingers. *Her talent.*

"Oh my God, Ella. I'm sorry," I cry. "I'm so, so sorry."

She just cries. I feel myself begin to sweat. Never in my life have I felt so useless.

"Try not to move," I say, knowing it's a futile plea. The nearest hospital is a half-hour drive. She'll pass out from the pain by then.

She starts to rock in a rhythm from side to side. I hover my shaking hands over the shard of bone sticking out of her leg, not knowing if I should apply pressure or try to push it back under the skin. I decide on applying pressure, and the second my fingers touch her skin, Ella stutters with a sharp intake of breath. An icy tingle inches up my spine, a feeling much like the times I've brought life back to the flower in the computer room, and the feeling spreads throughout the rest of me. Is it possible that my ability to heal plants applies to people as well? Ella stops crying and starts breathing rapidly, her tiny chest rising and falling, rising and falling. I can feel the iciness concentrate in my palms and circulate outward from my fingertips. "I think, I think I can fix you."

Her chest continues to rise and fall at an abnormal speed, but her face takes on a look of peacefulness, of detachment. I'm afraid to, but I place my hands over the piece of bone that sticks out from her leg. I feel its pebbly, broken end; and soon it begins to retreat back under the skin. The puncture wound turns from red and white back to the color of her skin; and I can see the jagged contours of her broken bone move and shift within her leg, setting itself back in place. I'm amazed at what I've just done. This could be my most important Legacy yet.

"Keep still," I say. "One more thing."

I close my eyes and wrap my hands around her thin right wrist. The iciness flows again through my fingertips. I open my eyes to watch her palm rise and her fingers spread away from each other. The cut between her index and middle fingers closes, and I see two broken knuckles straighten and mend. Ella clenches her hand and relaxes it.

I've done what Lorien has intended me to do, and that's to undo damage that's been inflicted on those who don't deserve it.

Ella turns her head to the right to look at my hands wrapped around her wrist. "You're fine," I say. "You're better than fine." She raises her head off the ground and props herself up onto her elbows. I pull her into my arms.

"We're a team," I whisper into her ear. "We take care of each other. Thanks for trying to help."

She nods her head. I squeeze her and then pull away. I look around at the girls, all of them unconscious but breathing. Sticking out of the opening of the nave, I see the edge of the Chest.

"I'm so proud of you for finding the Chest. You have no idea," I say. "Let's get it tomorrow morning after we've had some rest."

"Are you sure?" Ella asks. "I can climb back up and get it."

"No, no. You go wash up in the bathroom, and I'll be right there."

When she's finally out of my sight, I raise my eyes to the Chest. Concentrating, I float it silently down to my feet. Now I just need to get Adelina to open it with me.

CHAPTER
SEVENTEEN

AS I BURST THROUGH THE BURNING DOOR AND land on the melting brown carpet of the living room, several things race through my mind. Sam. Henri's letter. The Chest. Henri's ashes. I engulf myself purposefully in flames in order to move easily from room to room. "Sam?" I yell. "Where are you, Sam?"

Past the living room, I see that the entire back wall of the house is burning. The house could collapse in a matter of a minute. I dart into the bedrooms calling Sam's name. The bathroom door explodes with my kick. I check the kitchen, the dining room; and just when I'm about to try the living room again, I look out the window and see the Chest and a pile of our belongings, including the laptop, the coffee can of Henri's ashes, and the unopened letter, on the lip of the pool. Something small bobs in the middle of the water; it's Sam's head. He sees me and waves his arms.

I crash through the window and knock over the grill. I dive into the pool, the flames surrounding me hissing into gray and black smoke. "You okay?"

"I, I think so," he says. We pull ourselves out of the water and stand over everything Sam was able to save.

"What happened?"

"Dude, they're here. They're totally here. The Mogadorians." The moment he says these words I feel sick to my stomach. My jaw quivers. Then Sam says, "I saw them in the front window and then, *boom*, the house is on fire. I grabbed what I could. . . ."

There's movement on the roof. Between fissures of rising flames, I see a huge Mogadorian scout in a black trench coat, hat, and sunglasses marching down the decline, his feet sinking into the soft tiles with every step. He carries a long gleaming sword.

I kneel and grab ahold of the Chest's lock, and it yields under my glowing grip. Brushing aside the crystals at the bottom of the Chest, I pick up the dagger with the diamond blade. Flames dancing from the house reflect in its sharp edge. To my surprise, the handle extends and wraps itself around my entire right hand. "Get back," I say to Sam.

The scout reaches the metal eave of the collapsing roof, and he drops onto the patio below, his feet cracking the concrete when he lands. He slices the sword in the air in front of him and it leaves a glowing trail. I control my breath and go over the last week of training in my mind.

The moment my feet push me forward, the scout roars and rushes at me with his trench coat billowing behind him. I see myself in his sunglasses the second before his sword swings across my body. I lean back far enough for him to miss me; but when I right myself, I enter the glowing trail the sword left behind. Pain attaches itself to my neck and travels to my waist. I'm knocked backwards and into the pool.

When my head surfaces I see Sam squaring off with the scout. His bare hands are up and out; he bobs his shoulders left and right. The scout laughs and drops his sword to the concrete, and he then mimics Sam's fighting stance. Before I can heave myself out of the pool to help, Sam drops his weight onto his left foot and circles his right behind him. His sopping right shoe comes back around and connects with the scout's face with a force that staggers him back several feet.

The dazed scout picks up his gleaming sword. I'm up out of the pool before he can reach Sam, and I lift my dagger to block the plummeting sword. The blades meet, and there is a ball of light so bright I can't see for an instant. When the light fades, the scout's sword breaks at the exact spot my dagger collided with it. Not wasting the moment of surprise, I plunge the blade of my dagger into his chest and rip it downward. He turns to ash and it covers my feet.

The house finally collapses—beams of wood crack in different directions, windows pop and explode from the walls—the roof flattening over it all like a book with a broken spine. A storm cloud appears overhead and a lightning bolt slices through the sky, landing just on the other side of the house.

"We have to get to Six!" Sam shouts. He's right; the proximity of the lightning can only mean she's in the middle of a battle. Or finishing one. With my one free hand, I heft the Chest up and over the backyard's brick wall after making sure the coast is clear. Sam tosses the rest up to me and I then pull him to the wall's cement top. We jump and roll on the moist grass beyond the wall. Securing everything behind a thick bush, we run around to the front yard.

In the middle of the driveway, just feet from our SUV, Six has a scout in a headlock, the muscles in her arms pulsing in the squeeze. Two more scouts are approaching. One aims a long, cylindrical tube right at me and a green light blasts me backwards. I can't breathe. I can't see. I roll into the high grass and feel the heat from the house.

When I'm able to open my eyes, I see the scout with the tube standing above me. I slowly regain some feeling in my arms and legs; my breathing returns to normal. The handle of the dagger still encases my right hand. The scout adjusts a knob on the tube, perhaps going from stun to kill, and then he steps on my right wrist. I try swinging my legs up and over me, but they don't react the way I want them to, still sluggish from the paralyzing blast I just endured. The barrel of the tube is set between my eyes, and I think about the gun Six turned on the drunk man just an hour ago. *This is it,* I think. *The Mogadorians' mission is a success. Number Four, check. On to Number Five.*

I watch hundreds of lights in the tube spark to life, swirling until they become one; just as he puts his finger on the trigger, Bernie Kosar clamps down on his thigh. The scout wobbles above me for a second before his head is separated from his body by a bolt of lightning. It rolls in the grass right next to mine; our noses touch before the head crumbles into a pile of ash, and I do everything I can not to breathe it in. The body above me falls over and covers my jeans with ash.

"Get up already," Six yells, suddenly in the exact spot the scout had been.

Sam appears above me, too, his face stern and dirty. "We have to leave *right* now, John."

The sound of sirens pierces the night. A mile away, maybe less. Bernie Kosar licks my left temple and whimpers.

"What about the third one?" I whisper.

Six looks over at Sam and nods. "I got a hold of his sword and used it against him. Best moment of my life," he says.

I'm draped over Six's shoulder, and she dumps me into the backseat of the SUV. Bernie Kosar settles himself on my shins and licks my lifeless right hand. Sam takes the keys and gets behind the wheel while Six retrieves our stuff. As soon as we're on the highway and I no longer hear sirens, I'm able to relax and concentrate on my right hand. The dagger's handle transforms and retreats from my knuckles and wrist. I drop the dagger in the foot well.

Fifteen minutes later, Six tells Sam to pull over, and we screech into the lit parking lot of a closed diner. She jumps out before the car has come to a complete stop, leaving the door open.

"Help me," she orders.

"Six, I don't want to be a dick right now, but I can't really move my arms and legs."

"Dude, just really try. We have to get them off our tail," she says. "If we don't, then you're dead. Think about it."

I struggle into a seated position and feel blood circulate to my legs. I climb out of the car and waver there in my burned clothes, having no idea what she needs help with.

"Find the bug," she says. "Sam, keep the car running."

"Roger," he says.

"Find the what?" I ask.

"They use bugs to track vehicles. Trust me. They did it with me and Katarina."

"What does it look like?"

"I have no idea. But time is short, so look fast."

I almost want to laugh. There isn't a single thing in the world I think I could do fast right now. But nonetheless, Six goes racing around the SUV while I slowly drop to a knee and manage to crawl beneath it, flashing my hands on its undercarriage. Bernie Kosar gets to sniffing, starting at the bumper and moving his way forward. I spot it almost immediately, a small circular object no bigger than a quarter stuck to the plastic cover of the gas tank.

"Got it," I yell, plucking it off. I pull myself out and hand the device to Six while remaining on my back. She briefly studies it, then drops it in her pocket.

"Aren't you going to destroy it?"

"No," she answers. "Check again. We have to make sure there isn't a second, or a third."

I crawl back under with my hands blazing, scooting from the back of the SUV to the front. I don't see anything.

"You're sure?" she asks when I stand.

"Yes."

We get back in and speed away. It's two o'clock in the morning, and Sam heads west. With Six's instructions, he keeps the SUV between eighty-five and ninety, and I can't help but worry about police. After thirty miles, he jumps onto an interstate and drives south.

"We're almost there," she says. Two miles later she tells Sam to get off the interstate. "Stop! Right here, stop!" Sam slams the brakes beside an idling semi whose owner is pumping gas. Six goes invisible and steps out, leaving the door ajar.

"What's she doing?" Sam asks.

"I don't know."

After a few seconds the open door slams shut. Six reappears and tells Sam to get us back onto the highway, this time heading north. She's relaxed a bit, no longer holding a white-knuckled grip on the dashboard.

"Are you really going to make me ask what you just did?" I say.

She glances over. "That truck was on its way to Miami. I stuck the tracking device on the underside of its trailer. Hopefully they'll lose a few hours trailing him south while we drive north."

I shake my head. "Should be an interesting night for that trucker."

Once we're past the Ocala exits, Six tells Sam to get off and park behind a strip mall a few minutes from the interstate.

"We sleep here tonight," Six says. "Actually, we'll take turns sleeping."

Sam opens his door and turns his body sideways to dangle his feet out of the SUV. "Um, guys? I probably should have mentioned this earlier, but well, I got cut pretty bad back there and it's really starting to hurt and I think I'm about to pass out."

"What?" I scramble out of the vehicle and stand in front of him. He pulls up the dirty right leg of his jeans to reveal a wound above the knee that's slightly smaller than a credit card, though probably an inch deep. Dried and fresh blood cover his knee and shin.

"Good lord, Sam," I say. "When did that happen?"

"Right before I got ahold of that Mog's sword. I kind of pulled it out of my leg."

"All right, come on, get out of the car," I say. "Get on the ground."

Six shoves her head under Sam's armpit and helps him to the ground.

I open the back and retrieve the healing stone from the Chest. "Better hold on to something, man. This might . . . sting." Six offers her hand, and he takes it. The second I press the stone to his wound he writhes in agony as every muscle tightens. It seems like he's going to pass out. The skin around his wound turns white, then black, then to the bright red color of blood; and I immediately regret attempting to use the stone on a human. Did Henri ever say it won't work on them? I'm trying to remember as Sam lets out a long-winded groan that empties him of air. The outer edge of the wound seals inward and then disappears altogether. Sam relaxes his grip on Six's hand, and he slowly regains his breath. After a minute he's able to sit up.

"Man, do I ever want to be an alien," he finally says. "You guys get to do way too many cool things."

"You had me worried there for a second, buddy," I say. "Wasn't sure if it would work on you since some of the other stuff from the Chest doesn't."

"Me either," Six adds. She leans over and kisses him on his dirty cheek. Sam lies back down and sighs. Six laughs and rubs her hand over his head of stubble, and I'm surprised by how much jealousy bubbles inside me.

"Do you want to go to the hospital?" I ask.

"I want to stay right here," he says. "Forever."

"You know what? We were pretty lucky we were out on that walk," Six says after we settle back into the SUV.

"You're right," I say.

Sam places his right cheek on his headrest so he can look at both of us. "Why were you guys out walking in the first place?"

"I couldn't sleep. Neither could Six," I answer, which technically is the truth, but it doesn't take away the guilt. I know that Sarah is the girl for me, but I can't seem to stop these new feelings I have.

Six sighs. "You know what this means, right?"

"What?"

"They've probably opened my Chest."

"You don't know that for sure."

"No, I don't. But after I grabbed that rock from your Chest and it started pulsing and hurting my hand, I haven't been able to shake the feeling I got from it. And it just now came to me that it probably has something to do with my Chest."

"They've had your Chest for three years now," I say. "So you think it's possible for them to open the Chests without us, without us being dead?"

She shrugs. "I don't know. Maybe? But I have this feeling that they got into mine and that when I touched that stone it somehow led the scouts to our house."

"Why send so few?" Sam asks between yawns. "I mean, why not wait for reinforcements before attacking?"

"Maybe they got scared and panicked?" Six offers.

"Maybe one of them wanted to be the hero," I say.

Six rolls down her window and listens. When she's satisfied, she says, "Regardless. Next time there will be more of them. Pikens and krauls and whatever else they can throw at us."

"You're probably right," Sam whispers. He's drifting off. "I'll tell you one thing. This being on the run is really wearing me down."

"Try doing it for eleven years," I say.

"I think I'm a little homesick," he mumbles.

I lean forward and see that in his lap he's holding his father's old glasses, the ones with the thick lenses he used to wear in Paradise.

"It's not too late to go back, Sam. You know that, right?"

He frowns. "I'm not going back." It's with far less conviction this time around than when he had first said it in the North Carolina motel. "Not until I find my dad. Or until I at least learn what happened to him."

His dad? Six mouths to me, confused.

Later, I mouth back.

"Fair enough," I say. "We'll figure it out eventually." I turn back to Six. "So, where do we head tomorrow morning?"

"Now that it seems they opened my Chest, I guess we'll see where the wind carries us. It hasn't let me down yet," she says in a wistful sort of tone, then glances over at me. "Did you know that if it wasn't for the wind and my need for caffeine one night in Pennsylvania, the night before the attack in Paradise, I'd have never gotten there in time?"

"What are you talking about?" I ask.

"I was drifting through the Midwest, sensing you guys were in Ohio or in West Virginia or Pennsylvania after I found some news online of what I thought was probably the handiwork of Mogs in Athens near that college; but after a few weeks of coming up empty, I was certain I'd lost your trail. I figured you guys had taken off for California or Canada by that point. So there I was, standing in the parking lot of this strip mall, tired and lost, practically broke, when this huge gust of wind ripped past me and blew open the door to a coffee shop on my left. I thought I would refuel and get back out there and figure something out, but in the corner of the shop was an open computer for customers. I bought a large coffee and started searching the internet. Sure enough, I found an article about the house on fire that you jumped out of."

I'm embarrassed to know how easy it was to find me. No wonder Henri wanted to keep me home or at school all the time.

"If it wasn't for that gust of wind opening that door, I would have probably ended up in a diner instead, sipping coffee until daylight. I wrote down all the information I could find on you guys and then I ran down the street looking for an all-night copy place.

That's when I sent the fax and the letter with my number, to try to warn you guys or, at the very least, to tip you off so you could brace yourselves until I got there. And I arrived just in the nick of time."

CHAPTER
EIGHTEEN

THE WIND CARRIES US NORTH TO AN ALABAMA
motel where we stay two nights, again thanks to Sam
using one of my identities. From there we drive west
and spend a night beneath the stars in an open field in
Oklahoma, which we follow up with two more nights
in a Holiday Inn on the outskirts of Omaha, Nebraska.
And from there, for no apparent reason—at least for no
reason she'll admit to—Six drives one thousand miles
east to rent a log cabin nestled in the mountains of
the Maryland panhandle, a mere five-minute drive to the
West Virginia border, and three short hours from the
Mogadorian cave. We're exactly 197 miles from Paradise, Ohio, where our journey first began. Half a tank
of gas from Sarah.

Before my eyes even open, I can already feel it's
going to be a tough day, one of those days when the

reality of Henri's death will hit me like a sledgeham-
mer and no matter what I do, the pain won't leave. I've
been having these days more often. Days filled with
remorse. Filled with guilt. Filled with a genuine sadness to know I'll never talk to him again. The thought
cripples me. I wish I could change it. But as Henri once
said, "Some things can never be undone." And then
there's Sarah, and the terrible guilt that's crept in since
leaving Florida for allowing myself to get so close to Six
that I almost kissed her.

I take a deep breath, finally opening my eyes. The
pale morning light enters the room. *Henri's letter,* I
think. I have no choice but to read it now. It's too dangerous to delay it any longer. Not after almost losing it
in Florida.

I slip my hand beneath the pillow and remove the
diamond-bladed dagger and the letter. I've been keeping both of them close to me. I stare at the envelope for a
moment, trying to imagine under what circumstances
the letter was written. Then I sigh, knowing it doesn't
really matter and that I'm just wasting time, and with
the dagger I make a clean cut along the envelope's seal
and remove the pages. Henri's perfect handwriting fills
five yellow legal-sized sheets with thick black ink. I
take a deep breath, and then let my eyes fall upon the
top sheet.

January 19

J —

    I've written this letter many times over the years, never knowing whether it might be my last, but if you're reading this now, then surely the answer is yes. I'm sorry, John. I truly am. We Cêpans who came, our duty was to protect you nine at all costs, including our lives. But as I put down these words at our kitchen table, mere hours after you saved me in Athens, I know it's never been duty that has kept you and me together, but rather love that will always be a stronger bond than any obligation. The truth is that my death was always going to happen. The only variables were when and how, and if it hadn't been for you, then I would have certainly died today. Whatever the circumstances of my death, please don't blame yourself. I never expected to survive here, and when we left Lorien all those years ago, I knew I'd never be going back.

    In the time between me writing these words and you reading them, I wonder how much you've discovered. I'm confident you now know that I kept a lot from you. Probably more than I should have. For most of your life I wanted you to stay focused, to train hard. I wanted to give you as normal a life on Earth as I could. I'm sure you'll find that idea laughable, but to know the full truth would have added a world of stress during an already-stressful time.

Where to begin? Your father's name was Liren. He was brave and powerful, and he lived his life with integrity and purpose. As you witnessed during your visions of the war, he carried out these traits until the very end, even when he knew the war was unwinnable. And that's about all any of us can really hope for, to die with our dignity, to die with honor and valor. To die knowing we did everything we could. That was the epitome of who your father was. It's the epitome of who you are, too, even if you don't necessarily believe it.

I sit up, my back flat against the headboard, rereading my father's name over and over. The lump in my throat expands into a rock. I wish Sarah was here urging me to read on, her head on my shoulder. I focus my eyes on the next paragraph.

When you were just a small child, your father came around even when he wasn't supposed to. He adored you, and he could sit for hours watching you play in the grass with Hadley (I wonder now, have you discovered Bernie Kosar's true identity?). And while I'm sure you don't remember much of those youthful days, I can safely say you were a happy boy. For a brief while, you had the sort of childhood all children deserve, though not all receive.

While I spent considerable time with your father, I met your mother only once. Her name was Lara and, like your father, she was reserved and maybe even a little shy. I tell you this now because I want you to know who you are and who you come from. You come from a simple family of simple means, and the truth that I've always wanted to share with you is that we didn't leave Lorien because of where we happened to be that day. Our being at the airfield, it wasn't sheer happenstance. We were there because when the attack began, the Garde rallied together to get you there. Many sacrificed their lives in the process. There were supposed to be ten of you, though as you know only nine made it off.

Tears blur my vision. I slide my fingers over my mother's name. Lara. Lara and Liren. I wonder what my Loric name was, if it also started with an *L*. I wonder, if there wasn't a war, if I would have had a younger sister or brother. So much has been taken from me.

When the ten of you were born, Lorien rec-
ognized your strong hearts, your wills, your
compassion, and in turn she bestowed the ten of
you with the roles you're all meant to assume: the
roles of the original ten Elders. What this means
is that, in time, those of you left will grow to be
far stronger than anything Lorien has ever seen
before, far stronger even than the original ten
Elders from whom you've received your Inheri-
tances. The Mogadorians know this, which is why
they're hunting you so feverishly now. They've
grown desperate and have flooded this planet
with spies. I never told you the truth because I
feared it might drive you to arrogance and that
you might be led astray, and there's far too much
danger out there looking for you to risk that. I urge
you . . . become strong, grow into the role you are
meant to assume, and then find the others. Those
of you left, you can still win this war.

The last thing I have to tell you is that we didn't
move to Paradise by chance. Your Legacies were
delayed and I had begun to worry, and when my
worry grew to a full-out panic when the third scar
appeared—knowing you are next—I decided to
seek out the one man who might hold the key to
finding the others.

When we arrived on Earth there were nine

humans waiting for us who understood our situation and our need to scatter. They were allies of the Loric, and the last time we were here—fifteen years ago—they were all given a transmission device that would turn itself on only if it came into contact with one of our ships. They were there that night to provide us guidance in the transition from Lorien to Earth, to help us get started. None of us had ever been here before. When we stepped off the ship, we were each given two pairs of clothes, a packet of instructions to help us learn this planet's ways, and a slip of paper with an address on it. The addresses were a place to start, not to stay, and none of us knew where the others were headed. Ours led us to a small town in Northern California. It was a nice, quiet place fifteen minutes from the coast. I taught you to ride a bike there, and fly a kite, and more simple things like tying your shoes, which I had to first teach myself. We stayed six months, and then we went about our way, as I knew we must.

The man who met you and me, our guide, was from here, from Paradise; and I sought him because I was desperate to know where the others first went. But when we arrived here, the dark stars must have fallen, because the man was already gone.

This man who met us that first day, who gave us a cultural guide to follow and who set us up in our first homes, his name was Malcolm Goode. Sam's father.

What I'm telling you now, John, is that I believe Sam was right; I believe his father was abducted. For Sam's sake, I can only hope he's still alive. And if Sam's still with you, I ask that you tell him this information, and I hope he finds comfort in hearing it.

Become who you're meant to become, John. Grow strong and powerful and never forget for a minute the things you've learned along the way. Be noble, confident, and brave. Live with the same sort of dignity and valor that you inher-ited from your father, and trust in your heart and your will, as Lorien trusts in it still to this day. Never lose faith in yourself, and never lose hope; remember, even when this world throws its worst and then turns its back, there is still always hope.

And I'm certain, someday, you'll make it back home.

With love,
Your Friend and Cêpan,
-H

Blood pounds in my ears; and despite what Henri has written, I know in my heart that if we'd left Paradise when he'd wanted to, then he'd still be alive. We'd still be together. He came to the school to save me, because it was his duty to, and because he loved me. And now he's gone.

I take a deep breath, wipe my face with the back of my hand, and then walk from my room. Despite his bad leg, Sam insisted on taking the second floor, even when Six and I offered to take it instead. I go up the stairs now and knock on his door. I enter and flip his bedside lamp on, and I see his father's old glasses on the nightstand. Sam stirs.

"Sam? Hey, Sam. Sorry to wake you up, but there's some major shit you need to know."

That gets his attention and he pulls off the blanket. "Tell me then."

"First, you have to promise not to get mad. I want you to know that I had no idea of any of what I'm about to tell you until just now. And whatever Henri's reasons were for not telling you to your face, you have to forgive him."

He scoots up the mattress until his back rests on the headboard. "Damn, John. Tell me already."

"Promise me."

"Fine, I promise."

I hand him the letter. "I should have read it sooner,

Sam. I'm really sorry I didn't."

I leave the room and close his door to give him the privacy he deserves. I'm not sure how he'll react. There's no telling how a person will accept the answer to the question they've asked most of their life, the question that's haunted them.

I walk down the stairs and slip out the back door with Bernie Kosar, who runs into the forest. I sit on the top of a picnic table. I can see my breath in the cool February air. Darkness is pushed to the west, while the morning light bleeds in from the east. I stare up at the half-moon and wonder if Sarah is looking at it, or if any of the others might be seeing it. Me and the others, the five still alive, are meant to assume the roles of the Elders. I still don't entirely understand what that means. Then I close my eyes and lift my face towards the sky. I stay that way until the door slides open behind me. I turn, expecting to see Sam, but it's Six. She climbs up on the picnic table and sits next to me. I offer her a weak smile, but she doesn't return it.

"I heard you walk out here. Is everything okay? Did you and Sam have a fight or something?" she asks.

"What? No. Why?"

"All I know is he's crying on the couch downstairs and he won't talk to me."

I pause before telling her. "I finally read the letter Henri left behind. There's some stuff about Sam he and

I haven't told you. It's about his dad."

"What about his dad? Everything okay?"

I turn my body so our knees touch. "Listen. When I met Sam in school he was pretty obsessed with the disappearance of his dad, who just didn't come home from the grocery store one day. They found his truck and his glasses on the ground next to the truck. You know those glasses that you see him carrying around all the time?"

Six turns to look inside the back door. "Wait. Those are his dad's?"

"Yeah. And so the deal is that Sam is pretty convinced he was abducted by aliens, which I always thought was crazy; but I, I don't know, I let him go on believing it because who am I to crush the dude's hope of finding his dad again? I was waiting for Sam to tell you all this, but I just read Henri's letter, and you wouldn't believe what was in there."

"What?"

I tell her everything, about Sam's dad being a Loric ally who met Henri and me when the ship landed, why Henri moved us to Paradise.

Six slides off the top of the picnic table and lands awkwardly on the bench. "That is just so totally random that Sam is here. In there."

"I don't think it is. I mean, think about it. It just so happens that of *all* the people in Paradise I'm drawn to for a best friend, it happens to be Sam? I think we were destined to meet."

"Maybe you're right."

"Pretty cool that his dad helped us that night, right?"

"The coolest. Remember when he said he had these feelings growing inside him about being with us?"

I do. "But here's the thing. In Henri's letter he says that Sam's dad actually *was* abducted, or maybe even killed, by the Mogadorians."

We sit in silence watching the sun slowly come up over the horizon. Bernie Kosar jogs out of the forest and rolls onto his back to have his belly rubbed. "Hey there, Hadley." He flips onto his feet instantly when I say it, tilting his beagle head. "Yeah," I say, jumping down to scratch his chin with both hands. "I know." Sam walks out. His eyes are red. He sits next to Six on the bench.

"Hi, Hadley," Sam says to Bernie Kosar. BK barks in response and licks his hands.

"Hadley?" Six asks.

The dog barks again in approval.

"I always knew it," Sam says. "Always. From the day he disappeared."

"You were right all this time," I say.

"Do you mind if I read the letter?" Six asks. Sam hands it to her. I aim my right palm at the front page and turn on its light. She reads the letter in its radiance, then folds the pages and hands them back.

"I'm really sorry, Sam," she says.

I add, "Henri and I wouldn't have survived if it wasn't for your dad."

Six then turns to me. "You know, it's ridiculous that your parents were Liren and Lara. Or it's ridiculous I didn't realize that myself. Do you remember me from Lorien, John? Your parents and my parents—their names were Arun and Lyn—they were best friends. I know we weren't around our parents all that often, but I remember going to your house a few times. You were just a toddler at the time, I think."

It takes me a few seconds to remember what Henri once told me. It was the day Sarah had gotten back from Colorado, the day we confessed being in love with one another. After she left, Henri and I were eating dinner and he said, *Though I don't know her number, or have any idea where she is, one of the children who came to Earth with us was the daughter of your parents' best friends. They used to joke that it was fate that the two of you would end up together.*

I almost tell Six what Henri said, but remembering how that conversation came about because of my feelings for Sarah brings back the same guilt I've felt since Six and I went for our walk.

"Yeah, that is pretty crazy. I don't really remember it, though," I say.

"Regardless, this is some heavy stuff about the

Elders and how we're supposed to assume their roles. No wonder the Mogs are so relentless," she says.

"Definitely makes sense."

"We have to go back to Paradise," Sam interrupts.

"Yeah, right." Six laughs. "What we need to do is find the others somehow. We need to get back on that laptop. Train some more."

Sam stands. "No, I'm serious, guys. We have to go back. If my dad left something behind, that transmission device, I think I know how to find it. When I was seven, he told me that my future was mapped on the sundial. I would ask him what he was talking about, and he'd just say that if the dark stars ever fell, I was supposed to find the Ennead and read the map by my birth date on the sundial."

"What's an Ennead?" I ask.

"It's a group of nine deities in Egyptian mythology."

"Nine?" Six asks. "Nine deities?"

"And what sundial?" I ask.

"It's starting to make sense to me now," Sam says. He begins walking around the picnic table as he puts it together in his head, Bernie Kosar nipping at his heels. "I used to get *so* frustrated because he was always saying all this weird stuff that only he understood. A few months before he disappeared, my dad dug a well in our backyard and he said it would collect the rainwater from the gutters and whatever; but after the concrete was poured, he put this elaborate-looking sundial on the stone lid. Then he stood looking down at the well and he said to me. 'Your future's mapped on the sundial, Sam.'"

"And you never checked it out?" I ask.

"Sure I did. I twisted the sundial around, trying my date and time of birth and a few other things, but nothing ever happened. I thought it was just a stupid well with a sundial on it after a while. But now that I read Henri's letter, the part about the dark stars, I know that it has to be some kind of clue to all this. It's like he told me without telling me," Sam beams. "He was so smart."

"So are you," I say. "This could very well be suicide, us going back to Paradise, but I don't think we have much of a choice now."

CHAPTER
NINETEEN

I WAKE WITH CLENCHED TEETH, A SOUR TASTE IN my mouth. I tossed and turned all night, not only because the Chest is finally in my possession and I'm anxious to try to talk Adelina into opening it with me this morning, but also because I revealed too much to too many people. I put my Legacies on full display. How much would they all remember? Will I be exposed before breakfast? I sit up and see Ella in her bed. Everyone is still asleep in the room, except for Gabby, La Gorda, Delfina, and Bonita. Their beds are empty.

My feet are about to touch the ground when Sister Lucia appears in the doorway, her hands on her hips, her mouth twisted into a frown. We make eye contact and I lose my breath. But then she takes a couple steps backwards and allows the four girls from the nave to wobble into the room, dazed and bruised, their clothes ripped and dirty. Gabby stumbles to her bed and falls face-first onto it, the pillow enveloping her head. La Gorda rubs her double chin and lies back onto her bed with a grunt, and Bonita and Delfina slowly crawl under their covers. As soon as all four girls are motionless, Sister Lucia yells that it's time to get up. "And that means everyone!"

As I try to pass by Gabby on the way to the bathroom, she flinches.

La Gorda stands at the mirror inspecting the discoloration of her skin. When she sees my reflection over her shoulder, she immediately turns on the faucet and tries to focus on washing her hands. I can get used to this. I don't really want to intimidate people, but I like the idea I might be left alone.

Ella skips out of one of the bathroom stalls and waits her turn at the sinks to wash up. I worry that she's going to be scared of me because of what I did in the nave, but the moment she sees me Ella dramatically flexes her right hand over her head. I lean into her ear. "So you're okay?"

"Thanks to you," she says loudly.

I catch La Gorda's eyes in the mirror. "Hey," I whisper. "Last night is our little secret. Everything that happened last night is our secret, okay? Don't tell anyone."

She puts her finger to her closed lips and I feel better, but there is something about the way La Gorda looked at me that doesn't sit well.

I'm so preoccupied by what might be in the Chest that I forego my morning internet search for news on John and

Henri Smith. I don't have the patience to wait for morning Mass to see Adelina so I walk from room to room looking for her, but she's nowhere to be found. The first bell rings for morning Mass.

I shuffle in beside Ella in one of the last rows and wink at her. I locate Adelina in the front row. Halfway through Mass, Adelina looks over her shoulder and makes eye contact with me. When she does, I point up to the nave's nook where she hid the Chest so many years ago. Her eyebrows raise.

"I couldn't understand what you were saying," Adelina says after Mass. The two of us stand under a stained glass window of Saint Joseph on the left side of the nave, and we're bathed in a patchwork of muted yellows, browns, and reds. Her eyes match the seriousness of her posture.

"I found the Chest."

"Where?"

I nod my head up and to the right.

"I am the one who was supposed to decide when you're ready, and you are *not* ready. Not even close," she says angrily.

I pull my shoulders back and set my jaw. "I was never going to be ready in your eyes because you stopped believing, *Emmalina*."

The name catches her off guard. She opens her mouth and stops before letting loose whatever tirade is on her tongue.

"You have no idea what I'm going through in here with these other girls. While you're walking around holding onto your Bible and praying and counting the beads on your rosary, you don't care at all that I'm getting bullied, that I have just one friend, that all the Sisters hate me, and that there's a whole world out there that I'm supposed to be defending! Two worlds, actually! Lorien and Earth need me and they need you, and I'm holed up in here like an animal in the zoo and you don't even care."

"Of course I care."

I start to cry. "No you don't! No you don't! Maybe you cared back when you were Odetta and maybe a little when you were Emmalina; but ever since you've been Adelina and I've been Marina, you haven't cared about me or the other eight or what we're supposed to be doing here. I'm sorry, but I can't stand you talking to me about salvation when that's *all* I'm trying to achieve. I'm trying to protect us. I'm trying to do so much good, and you act as if I'm evil or something!"

Adelina takes a step forward, her arms open for a hug, but something causes her to retreat and take a step back. Her shoulders bounce as she starts to cry. My arms immediately wrap around her and we embrace.

"What's wrong? Why isn't Marina in the cafeteria?"

We turn to see Sister Dora with her arms crossed over her chest. A copper crucifix hangs over her wrists.

"Go," Adelina whispers. "We'll talk about this later."

I wipe my face and rush past Sister Dora. As I leave the nave I can hear snippets of a heated argument brewing between Sister Dora and Adelina, their voices echoing off the vaulted ceiling, and I run my hands through my hair in hope.

Before sneaking back into the sleeping quarters last night, I floated the Chest down the narrow dark hallway to the left of the nave, past the ancient statues cut into the rock wall. It now sits hidden atop the narrow tower of the north belfry, secure behind the padlocked oak door. It's safe there for the moment; but if I can't convince Adelina to open it with me soon, I'll have to find another location.

Ella is nowhere to be found in the cafeteria, and I worry that my Legacy has somehow backfired and she's at the hospital.

"She's in Sister Lucia's office," a girl says when I ask the girls at the table nearest the door. "There was a married couple with her. I think they're going to adopt her or something." She pours a spoonful of soggy eggs onto her plate. "So lucky."

My knees buckle, and I catch myself from falling to the ground by gripping the edge of the table. I have no right to be so upset at the thought of Ella leaving the orphanage, but she's my one friend. Of course I knew she would be on the Sisters' short list of adoptable girls; Ella is seven and sweet and cute and wonderful to be around.

I truly hope she finds a home, especially after losing her parents; but I'm not ready to let her go, regardless of how selfish it is.

It was determined when Adelina and I arrived that I'd never be adopted, but I sit there now wondering if it might have been better if I was eligible. Maybe someone would have fallen in love with me.

I realize that even if Ella is adopted today, it'll take some time for all the paperwork to be reviewed and accepted, which means she'll be here a week, maybe two, maybe three. But it still breaks my heart, and makes me even more determined to leave this place as soon as I get the Chest opened.

I slump out of the cafeteria and find my coat, then sneak through the double doors and march down the hill, not caring that I'm skipping school. I keep an eye out for the man with the Pittacus book, staying on the sidewalk behind the vendors on Calle Principal, bouncing from shadow to shadow.

As I walk past El Pescador, the village restaurant, I look down the cobblestone alley and see the lid of a trash can teeter and then crash to the ground. The trash can itself begins to quake and wobble, and I hear something scraping at its insides. A pair of black-and-white paws curl over the lip of the can. It's a cat, and when he struggles over the edge and lands on the alley floor, I see a long gash running along his right side. An eye is swollen shut.

It looks as though he is about to fall over from exhaustion or starvation, and he just lies in a pile of trash as if he's given up.

"You poor thing," I say. I know I'm going to heal him before I take my first step down the alley. He purrs when I kneel down next to him, and when I place my hand on his fur there isn't resistance. The iciness flows quickly from me to the cat, quicker than it did to Ella or my own cheek, and I don't know if the Legacy is getting stronger or if it works faster on animals. His legs straighten and paws spread wide, and his breathing picks up until it melts into a loud purr. I gently turn the cat over to inspect his right side and see that it's completely healed and covered with a lush coat of black fur. The eye that was swollen shut is now open and looking up at me. I name him Legacy and say, "If you want a ride out of town, Legacy, then we should talk. Because I think I'm leaving soon, and I could use the company."

I'm startled by a figure appearing at the end of the alley, but it's just Héctor pushing his mother in the wheelchair.

"Ah, Marina of the sea!" he yells.

"Hi, Héctor Ricardo." I walk towards them. His mother looks slumped and distant, and I worry she's gotten worse.

"Who is your friend? Hello, little man." Hector bends down to scratch Legacy's chin.

"Just some company I've picked up along the way."

We walk quietly, chatting about the weather and Legacy, until arriving at Héctor and his mother's front door. "Héctor? Have you seen the man with the mustache and book at the café recently?"

"No, I have not," he says. "What is it about this man that bothers you so much?"

I pause. "He just looks like somebody I know."

"Is that everything?"

"Yes." He can tell I'm lying but also knows enough not to pry. I know he'll be on the lookout for the man I believe is a Mogadorian; I just hope he doesn't get hurt.

"It was good to see you, Marina. Remember that today is a school day." He winks. I nod sheepishly, and he unlocks his front door, backing inside, pulling his sick mother along with him.

The coast is clear over my shoulder and I continue with my walk for a while, thinking about the Chest, when I will be able to talk again with Adelina. I also think about John Smith on the run, Ella and her possible adoption, my fight last night in the nave. At the end of Calle Principal, I stare at the school building, hating the front door and the windows, angry at all the time I've spent inside when I should have been on the move, changing my name with each new country. I wonder what I would name myself in America.

Legacy meows around my feet as I make my way back through the village. I am still walking in the shadows, studying the street blocks ahead of me. I peek inside the window of the café, hoping and not hoping to see the Mogadorian with the thick mustache. He's not there, but Héctor already is, and he's laughing at something the woman at the next table just said. I'm going to miss Héctor just as much as I'll miss Ella. I have two friends, not one.

Ducking under the window as I pass, I can't help but look down at Legacy's lush black-and-white fur coat. Less than an hour ago the cat was lying in an alley, bleeding on a pile of trash, and now he's a ball of energy. My ability to heal and breathe new life into plants and animals and humans is an enormous responsibility. Fixing Ella made me feel more special than I ever had before, and it wasn't because I felt like a hero, but because I helped someone who needed it. I slink a few doors down the street and Héctor's laugh travels through the café window and wraps itself around my shoulders, and I know what I need to do.

The front door is locked, but when I go around to the back of Héctor's house, the first window I try opens with ease. Legacy licks his paws as I climb up and through the window. Jitters attack; I have never broken into someone's house before.

The house is small and dark inside, and the air is heavy. Every foreseeable surface is covered with Catholic figurines. I find Héctor's mother's room in no time. She lies on a twin bed in the far corner, her blankets slowly rising with each breath. Her legs are twisted at unnatural angles, and she looks frail. Pill bottles line a small nightstand, along with rosary beads, a crucifix, a miniature statue of the Virgin Mary with her hands held in prayer, and ten or so saints I don't know the names of. I drop to my knees beside Carlotta's sleeping body. Her eyes flutter open and scan the air. I freeze and hold my breath. I've never talked to her before, though when she finds me crouching beside her, a glint of recognition registers. She opens her mouth to speak.

"Shhh," I say to her. "I'm a friend of Héctor's, Señora Ricardo. I don't know if you can understand me, but I'm here to help you."

She accepts what I have told her with fluttering eyelids. I reach up and caress the side of her cheek with the back of my left hand, and then I rest it on her forehead. Her gray hair is dry and brittle. She closes her eyes.

My heart's pounding, and I can see a noticeable shake in my hand when I lift it and place it on her stomach; and it's then that I can feel how weak and sick she really is. The cold tingle crawls up my spine and spreads down my arms and into the tip of each finger. I grow dizzy. My breathing quickens, and my heart beats even faster. I begin to sweat despite the prickly chill turning my skin cold. Carlotta's eyes open, and a low groan escapes her open mouth.

I close my eyes. "Shhh, it's okay, it's okay," I say to

comfort the both of us. And then, with the icy chill radiating from me to her, I begin to pull the sickness away. It retreats stubbornly, clinging tightly to her insides, reluctant to loosen its grip; but finally even the stubborn bits let go.

Slight tremors cause Carlotta to convulse and shake, and I do my best to hold her down. I open my eyes just in time to see the ashen color of Carlotta's face change to a pink glow.

Vertigo sweeps through me. I lift my hands from her body and fall backwards to the floor. My heart thuds so violently that it scares me, like it's about to break free from my body. But in time it slows, and when I finally pull myself to my feet, I see Carlotta's sitting up with a bewildered look, as though trying to remember where she is and how she'd gotten here.

I rush into the kitchen and drink three glasses of water. When I walk back, Carlotta is still gathering her bearings. I make another quick decision—I go to the nightstand and rifle through the ten or so pill bottles, finding the label I'm looking for: WARNING: MAY CAUSE DROWSINESS. I open it, take four pills, and shove them in my pocket.

"What's going on?" Carlotta asks. She is frantic. "Where am I? Who are you?"

I don't answer her, and instead walk from the room. But before I leave, I turn and look at Carlotta once more. She's watching me with her healed, untwisted legs dangling over the bed as though she's about to stand.

I rush out of the house and find Legacy sleeping underneath the back window. Keeping to the alleys and side streets, I make my way back to the orphanage with the cat in my arms, wondering how Héctor will react when he finds his mother cured. The problem, however, is that in a village this small, secrets don't last very long. My only hope is that nobody saw me come or go, and that Carlotta won't remember what really happened.

Outside the double doors, I unzip my coat halfway and carefully place Legacy inside. I know just where I can keep him safe: up in the north belfry with the Chest. *The Chest,* I think. *I have to get it open.*

CHAPTER TWENTY

BEING IN LOVE IS A VERY STRANGE THING. Your thoughts constantly drift towards this other person, no matter what you're doing. You could be reaching for a glass in the cupboard or brushing your teeth or listening to someone tell a story, and your mind will just start drifting towards their face, their hair, the way they smell, wondering what they'll wear, and what they'll say the next time they see you. And on top of the constant dream state you're in, your stomach feels like it's connected to a bungee cord, and it bounces and bounces around for hours until it finally lodges itself next to your heart.

That's how I've felt since the first day I met Sarah Hart. I can be training with Sam or trying to find my shoes in the back of our SUV, and the thought of Sarah's face and her lips and ivory skin take over me. I can be giving directions from the backseat and *still* be one hundred percent focused on the way it feels when the top of Sarah's head rests just under my chin. And I can be surrounded by twenty Mogs, my palms just starting to light up, and I'll be analyzing every line of conversation from Thanksgiving dinner at Sarah's.

But what's even more insane is that as we drive the speed limit towards Paradise at nine o'clock at night, as we drive right towards Sarah and her blond hair and blue eyes, I'm also thinking about Six. I'm thinking about the way she smells, the way she looks in her training outfits, how we almost kissed back in Florida. My stomach also hurts because of Six. Not only because of her, but because of the fact my best friend also has a crush on her. I need to buy some antacids the next time we stop.

While Sam drives we debate Henri's letter and talk about how cool Sam's dad is for not only helping the people of Lorien but also for giving Sam a riddle to find the transmitter device in case anything were to happen to him. And still I'm going back and forth between Sarah and Six in my head.

We're two hours from Paradise when Six asks, "But what if it's nothing, though? I mean, what if there's nothing down in that well but some weird birthday present or *anything* else but the transmitter. We're risking a lot, like *a lot* a lot, by showing up in Paradise like this."

"Trust me," Sam says. He drums his thumbs on the steering wheel and turns up the stereo. "I've never been so certain of anything in my entire life. And I get straight As, thank you very much."

I think the Mogadorians are there waiting, in far greater numbers than what we faced in Florida, watching everything that might lead them to us. And if I'm going to be honest with myself, the only reason I'm willing to take this risk is because of the possibility of seeing Sarah.

I lean forward in the backseat and pat Sam's right shoulder. "Sam, no matter what happens with that well and sundial, Six and I owe you big-time for what your dad did for us. But I really, really, really, really hope that it leads to a transmitter."

"Don't worry," Sam says.

Highway lights come and go. Bernie Kosar's floppy ears fall from the edge of the seat as he sleeps. I'm nervous about seeing Sarah. Nervous about being so close to Six.

"Hey, Sam?" I ask. "You wanna play a game?"

"Yeah, sure."

"What do you think Six's Earth name is?"

Six whips her head over her shoulder, her raven hair slapping her right cheek, and she frowns at me in mock anger.

"She has one?" Sam laughs.

"Just guess," I say.

"Yeah, Sam," Six says. "Guess."

"Um, Stryker?"

I laugh so hard Bernie Kosar jumps up to look out the nearest window.

"Stryker?" Six yells.

"Not Stryker, then? Okay, okay. I don't know, something like Persia or Eagle or . . ."

"Eagle?" Six yells. "Why would I be Eagle?"

"You're such a badass, you know." Sam laughs. "I just figured you would be like a Starfire or like Thunder Clap or something really badassy."

"Exactly!" I shout. "That's totally what I thought, too!"

"So what is it then?" he asks.

Six crosses her arms and looks out the passenger-side window. "I'm not telling you until you make a real guess with a real girl's name. Eagle, Sam? Give me some credit."

"What? I'd name myself Eagle if I had the chance," Sam says. "Eagle Goode. That sounds pretty awesome, right?"

"It sounds like a brand of cheese," Six says. We all laugh at that.

"Okay. Uh, Rachel?" Sam says. "Britney?"

"Ew, yuck," she says.

"Fine. Rebecca? Claire? Oh, I know. Beverly."

"You are insane." Six laughs. She punches Sam's thigh, and he howls and rubs at it dramatically. He hits her back, a couple of knuckles on her left bicep, and she feigns severe pain.

"Her name is Maren Elizabeth," I say. "Maren Elizabeth."

"Aw, you gave it away," he says. "I was going with Maren Elizabeth next."

"Yeah, right," she says.

"No, I was, I was! Maren Elizabeth's pretty cool. Do you want us to start calling you that? Four goes by John, right Four?"

I scratch Bernie Kosar's head. I don't think I could get used to calling him Hadley, but maybe I could get used to calling Six Maren Elizabeth. "I think you should take on a human name," I say. "If not Maren Elizabeth, then something else. I mean, at least for when we're in front of strangers."

Everyone grows silent, and I reach behind me into the Chest for the velvet bag holding Lorien's solar system. I set the six planets and the sun in my palm and watch them hover and glow to life. As the planets begin to orbit their sun, I find that I am able to dim the brightness of their glow with my mind. I intentionally lose myself in them, successfully forgetting just for a few moments that I might be seeing Sarah soon.

Six turns to look at the faint solar system that floats in front of my chest, and then she finally says, "I don't know; I still like the name Six. Maren Elizabeth was when I was a different person, and right now Six just feels right. It can be short for something if someone asks."

Sam looks over. "For what? Sixty?"

I set out seven mugs and a kettle on the stove. While waiting for the water to boil, I crush three of the pills I stole from Héctor's mother into a fine powder with the rounded back side of a metal spoon. Ella stands beside me watching as she always does when it's my turn to make the Sisters' nightly tea.

"What are you doin'?" she asks.

"Something I'm probably going to regret," I say. "But something I have to do."

Ella flattens a piece of crumpled paper on the table and places the tip of her pencil on it. Immediately she's drawing a perfect picture of the seven teacups I've lined up. From what I can get out of her, she met with a couple in Sister Lucia's office who said they had "a lot of love to give." I'm not sure how long the meeting lasted, but Ella says they're coming back tomorrow. I know what it means and I pour the boiling water from the kettle as slowly as I can, trying to prolong my time with her.

"Ella? How often do you think about your parents?" I ask.

Her brown eyes grow wide. "Today?"

"Sure. Today, or any other day?"

"I don't know . . ." She trails off. After a pause, she adds, "A million times?"

I bend down to hug her, and I don't know if it's because of how sorry I feel for her or how sorry I feel for myself. My parents are dead, too. The victims of a war I'm supposed to continue someday.

I scoop the crushed pills into Adelina's teacup, regretting that I've resorted to drugging her. There's no other choice. She can stand by and wait for death if that's what she chooses, but I refuse to give up or to go down without a fight, without doing everything within my power to survive.

With the tray teetering in my hands, I leave Ella at the table and make my rounds. One by one I hand the tea out around the orphanage, and when I'm ushered into the Sisters' quarters to deliver Adelina her tea, I carefully shove her cup towards the front edge. She takes it with a polite nod. "Sister Camila is feeling ill this evening and I have been asked to sleep in the children's quarters tonight for her."

"Okay," I say. As I think about the possibilities of

Adelina and me being in the same room tonight, I watch her take a long sip from her teacup. I can't tell if I just made a huge mistake or helped my cause immensely.

"I will see you soon then," she says. Then she winks at me. I'm taken aback, almost dropping the two remaining cups from my tray to the floor.

"O-okay," I stutter.

When curfew comes a half hour later, nobody falls asleep right away, and instead many girls whisper to one another in the dark. I lift my head every few minutes to look at Adelina lying on her bed across the room. Her wink has left me confused.

Ten more minutes pass. I can tell most everyone is still awake, including Adelina. She's usually quick to fall asleep when she's on duty, so the fact that she's still up tells me that she's also waiting for everyone in the room to fall asleep. Now I think her wink definitely meant she wanted to resume our conversation. The room falls silent, and I wait before I lift my head. Adelina hasn't moved in the last half hour, so I move the left legs of her bed off the ground and tip her slightly. Suddenly she raises her left arm above her like a white flag of surrender, and she points to the doorway.

I toss the covers aside, stand, then tiptoe from the room. When I reach the hall I slink a few paces into the shadows, holding my breath, hoping this isn't some sort of trap Adelina and Sister Dora have set up. After thirty seconds, Adelina enters the hallway. Her walk is labored and she sways from side to side.

"Come with me," I whisper, taking her hand. I haven't held her hand in years, and it brings back the memory of us huddling together on the boat to Finland, when I was sick and she was strong. We were once so close you couldn't slide a piece of paper between us. Now the mere touch of her hand feels alien.

"I'm so tired," Adelina confesses as we climb to the second floor; we're halfway to the north wing and the belfry protected by the padlock. "I don't know what's wrong with me."

I do. "Do you want me to carry you?"

"You can't carry me."

"Not with my arms," I say.

She's too tired to argue. I focus on her feet and legs, and a few seconds later I've lifted Adelina off the floor and begin to float her down the dusty corridors. We pass the ancient statues cut into the rock wall and enter the narrower hallway in silence. I worry that she's fallen asleep, but then she says, "I can't believe you're using telekinesis to fly an old lady like me down the hall. Where are we going?"

"I had to hide it," I whisper. "We're almost there, I promise."

I unlock the padlock and it falls from the oak door's handle, and soon I'm following a floating Adelina up the stone stairway that circles around the north tower leading to the belfry. I can hear Legacy faintly meowing from the top.

I open the door to the belfry and set Adelina gently down next to the Chest. She props her left arm up on the Chest lid and leans her head against it; I can see she has just about lost her battle with the pills, and I'm angry with myself now for tricking her. Legacy climbs into her lap and licks her right hand. "How is there a cat in here?" she mumbles.

"Don't ask. Listen, Adelina, you're almost completely asleep, and I need you to open the Chest with me before you are, okay?"

"I don't think I have . . ."

"Have what?" I ask.

"Have it in me right now, Marina." Her eyes are closed.

"Yes, you do."

"Put your hand on the Chest's lock. Put my hand on the other side."

I press my palm against the side of the lock and it feels warm. I use telekinesis to pull her right hand away from Legacy's tongue and onto the other side of the lock. She interlocks her fingers with mine. A second passes. The lock snaps open.

"Uh, guys? Something is, uh, something's totally happening back here." The seven orbs that hover in front of my chest in the backseat of the SUV are speeding up, and I can no longer control them. It gets so bright that I have to cover my eyes.

"Hey, hey! Dude, cut it out!" Sam barks. "I'm trying to drive up here."

"I don't know what's going on!"

"Pull over!" Six yells.

Sam rips the vehicle onto the shoulder of the road and slams on the brakes, stone and gravel crunching and pinging us. The six planets and one sun dim in brightness, and the planets start to whip around the sun at such a rate that it's hard to focus on any single one. With each orbit the planets are absorbed into the sun until it's the size of a basketball. The new globe rotates as though on an axis, and then it produces a flash of light so bright that I'm momentarily blinded. It slowly dims, and sections of its surface raise and recede until what's left behind is a perfect replica of Earth itself, all seven continents, all seven seas.

"Is that . . . ?" Sam asks. "That looks like Earth."

The planet spins near my head, and on its third or fourth rotation I see a small pinprick of pulsing light.

"Do you guys see that little light?" I ask. "Look at Europe."

"Oh, yeah," Sam says. He waits for another rotation

and then squints. "I would say that's in what? Spain or Portugal? Can someone reach the laptop? Hurry."

With my eyes still on the globe and the tiny pulsing light, I crash my hand around behind me until I find the laptop. I hand it to Six, who hands it Sam. He looks up at the globe hovering in the backseat, types and looks up. "Well, it's definitely in Spain, and it looks to be close to . . . Well, the closest city seems to be a place called León. But that's, that's slightly off. We're looking at the Picos de Europa Mountains for sure. Anyone ever heard of them?"

"Definitely not," I say.

"Me neither," Six says.

"Is that maybe our ship?" I ask.

"No way, not in Spain. Well, at least I highly doubt it," she says. "I mean, if it is our ship then why would it just start glowing now, showing us where it is? That wouldn't make any sense. Besides, you've looked at these things how many times?"

"A dozen," I say. "Maybe more."

Sam hugs his headrest and raises his eyebrows. "Right. So it's as if something just activated it."

Six and I look at each other.

"It could definitely be one of the others," Sam says.

"Could be," Six says. "Or it could be a trap." She looks at Sam. "Has there been any suspicious news from Spain?"

He shakes his head. "Not as of five hours ago. But I'll check again right now." He starts typing on the keyboard.

"Before you do that, let's get off the main road before someone notices there's a glowing planet of Earth floating in the car," I say. "We're pretty damn close to Paradise, remember?"

Adelina snores and I feel guilty, but for the first time in my life I see the Inheritance I should have received years ago. Rocks and gems of different colors, different sizes and shapes. A pair of dark gloves and a pair of dark glasses, both made of materials I've never seen before. There's a small tree branch with the bark pared away, and under that there is an odd circular device with a glass lens and floating needle not unlike a compass. But it's a glowing red crystal that has me most intrigued. Once I look at it I can't look away, and I slowly reach down and take it in my hand; it's warm and tingly in my palm. For a brief second the red light brightens, and then it fades and begins to slowly pulse at the same rate I breathe.

The crystal grows hotter, brighter, and it begins to emit a low hum. I panic, nervous that one of my Legacies has activated a Loric grenade. "Adelina!" I yell. "Wake up! Wake up, please!"

She furrows her brow and her snoring intensifies.

With my free hand I shake her shoulder. "Adelina!"

I shake her harder, and as I do I drop the crystal. It bounces hard on the belfry's stone floor and rolls towards the doorway. As it falls from the first stair to the second, the red light stops pulsing. As it falls from the second stair to the third, it stops glowing altogether. And as it falls to the fourth stair, I chase after it.

Sam zips us down a dark dirt road. The globe continues to whir in my face. The tiny pulsing light continues to try to tell us something. We come to a stop, and Sam kills the engine and lights.

"So, I'm thinking it's one of you guys," Sam says, turning around. "It's another number. And that number is in Spain."

"We have no way of knowing that," Six says.

Sam nods at the globe. "Okay, look. You guys were meant to stay apart from one another when you first arrived, right? That's how it worked. You all go off in hiding until your Legacies develop and you train and everything. And then what? Then you get together and you fight together. So this light right here, maybe that's a signal to get together, or more likely, it's a distress signal from one of the remaining numbers. Or, guys, maybe Number Five or Number Nine just opened up their Chest for the first time, and because we have this thing running at the same time, we can communicate."

"Maybe they see we're in Ohio, then?" I ask.

"Shit. Maybe. Possibly. But seriously, think about it. If the Elders were going to give you all this stuff in your Chests, then they'd give you something to communicate with each other. Right? Maybe we just unlocked the key somehow, and we've got the location of someone who needs our help," he says.

"Or maybe one of the others is getting tortured and they're being forced to contact us and it's a trap," Six says.

Just as I'm about to agree, the edges of Earth grow fuzzy and then the entire globe vibrates with a female voice that says, "Adelina! *¡Despierta! ¡Despierta, por favor!* Adelina!"

I'm about to yell back, but the globe suddenly shrinks, re-forms into the seven orbs and returns to normal.

"Whoa, whoa, whoa! What just happened?" I ask.

"I'd say the signal has been cut," Sam says.

"Who was that girl? And who's Adelina?" Six asks.

I catch the stone after it bounces off the ninth stair, but no matter what I do it doesn't glow like it did before. I shake it in my palm. I blow on it. I set it in Adelina's open hand. It doesn't change from its new faint blue color, and I'm worried I broke it. I carefully set it back inside the Chest and pick up the short tree branch.

With a deep breath, I stick the branch out one of the two windows and I concentrate on the opposite end. There's a bit of a magnetic force happening; but before I can really test it or figure it out, I hear the oak door at the bottom of the tower creak open.

CHAPTER
TWENTY-ONE

WHILE WE DRIVE, I TRY A FEW MORE TIMES TO regain the signal with the globes, but every time I get the solar system up and running they just orbit like normal. It's almost midnight and I'm about to rifle through the other stones and objects in my Chest, but it's then I see the scattered lights of a town on the horizon. A sign passes on my right just like it did a few months ago when Henri was behind the wheel:

WELCOME TO PARADISE, OHIO
POPULATION 5,243

"Welcome home," Sam whispers.

I press my forehead against the window and recognize a dilapidated barn, an old sign for apples, a green pickup still for sale. A warm feeling comes over my entire body. Of all the places I've ever lived, Paradise has been my favorite. It's where I made my first best friend. It's where I developed my first Legacy. It's where I fell in love. But Paradise was also where I met my first Mogadorians. Where I had my first real battle and felt real pain. It's the place where Henri died.

Bernie Kosar jumps onto the seat next to me, and his tail wags at an amazing rate. He shoves his nose through the small crack in his window, and he sniffs furiously at the familiar air.

As we take the first side road on the left and make several more turns, backtracking here and there, making sure we're not being followed, finding the best and least conspicuous place to leave the SUV, we go over the plan once more.

"After we get the transmitter we go right back to the car and we leave Paradise immediately," Six says. "Right?"

"Right," I say.

"We don't make contact with *anyone* else; we just go. We leave."

I know she's referring to Sarah, and I bite my lip. Finally after all these weeks on the run, I'm back in Paradise and I'm told I can't see Sarah.

"Got it, John? We leave? Right away?"

"Lay off already. I know what you're getting at."

"Sorry."

Sam parks the SUV on a dark street under a maple

tree two miles from his house. My shoes drop to the asphalt, my lungs take their first real breath of Paradise air and I instantly want to go back to how it was, back to Halloween, back to coming home to Henri, back to sitting on my couch next to Sarah.

We don't take any chances of losing my Chest in an unguarded car, so Six opens the back door and lugs it onto her shoulder. Once comfortable, she makes herself invisible.

"Wait," I say. "I want something out of there first. Six?"

Six reappears and I open the Chest and retrieve the dagger, slipping it into the back pocket of my jeans. "Okay. Now I'm ready. Bernie Kosar, buddy, are you ready?"

Bernie Kosar transforms into a small brown owl, and he flaps his way onto a low branch of the maple tree.

"Let's do this already." Six picks up my Chest and disappears again.

Then we run. With Sam trailing at a good pace, I jump a fence and pick up speed on the edge of the nearest field. After a half mile, I'm veering into the forest, loving the way the branches break off my chest and arms, how the tall patches of grass whip my jeans. I look over my shoulder often, and Sam is never farther than forty yards behind me, jumping over logs, sliding under branches. There is a noise beside me, but before I can reach for my dagger Six whispers that it's just her. I see a swatch of grass part down the middle and I follow.

Luckily, Sam lives on the outskirts of Paradise with large yards separating each neighbor. I stop just inside the lip of the forest when his house comes into view. It's a small, modest house with white aluminum siding and black shingles, a thin chimney on its right side, a tall wooden fence enclosing the backyard. Six materializes and sets down my Chest.

"That it?" she asks.

"That's it."

Thirty seconds later, Bernie Kosar lands on my shoulder. Four minutes go by until Sam lumbers through a line of brush and stands next to us, out of breath, his palms planted firmly on his thighs. He looks up at his house in the distance.

"How are you feeling?" I ask.

"Like a fugitive. Like a bad son."

"Think about how proud your dad would be if we pull this off," I say.

Six turns herself invisible to run reconnaissance, checking the shadows of the nearby houses, the backseats of every car on the street. She returns and says everything looks okay, but there are some motion sensor lights on the house on the right. Bernie Kosar flies away, perching himself on the highest point of the roof.

Six grabs Sam's hand and they turn invisible. I tuck the Chest under my arm and quietly follow them to the back fence. They reappear, and Six goes over first, then Sam. I toss the Chest over and climb quickly after. We duck behind an overgrown shrub, and I survey the backyard and its trees, high grass, a big tree stump, a rusty swing set, and an antique wheelbarrow on its side. There's a back door on the left side of the house and two dark windows on the right.

"There it is," Sam whispers, pointing.

What I first thought was a tree stump peeking out of the middle of the yard is actually, upon closer inspection, a wide stone cylinder. Squinting, I see a triangular object sticking up off its top.

"We'll be right back," Six whispers to Sam.

My hand in Six's, I turn invisible and say, "Okay, Eagle Goode. Guard that Chest as if my life depends on it. Because it does."

Six and I carefully walk through the high grass towards the well, and then kneel in front of it. Numbers border the circumference of the sundial—one through twelve on the left side and another one through twelve on the right, zero at the top—and the numbers are surrounded by a series of lines. I'm about to grip the middle triangle and twist randomly when I hear Six gasp.

"What?" I whisper, raising my eyes to the dark back windows.

"In the middle. Look. The symbols."

I study the sundial again, and my breath is caught in my throat. They're faint and easy to overlook, but in the middle of the circle are nine shallow Loric symbols. I recognize the numbers one through three because they match the scars on my ankle, but the others are new to me.

"What's Sam's birthday again?" I ask.

"January fourth, nineteen ninety-five."

The triangle clicks like a lock as I turn it right to the Loric number one. I turn it left, swallowing hard as I aim it at what must be number four. My number. Then I rotate the triangle to one, nine, back around to nine again, and five. Nothing happens for a few seconds, and then the sundial begins to hiss and smoke. Six and I step back and watch as the stone lid of the well flips back and opens with a loud echoing crack. When the smoke clears, I see a ladder inside.

Sam is jumping up and down near the fence. One hand over his mouth, the other raised in a fist.

One of the dark windows of the house turns yellow. Bernie Kosar lets out two long *hoo*s from the roof. Before I can think, Six yanks me forward, and soon I'm visible and descending the ladder inside the well. Six follows, pulling the lid almost closed above her. I illuminate my palms and see we're twenty feet from a cement floor.

"What about Sam?" I whisper.

"He'll be fine. Bernie Kosar's up there."

We reach the floor and find ourselves in a short hall-way that curves to the left. The air is musty. I shine my palms back and forth as we walk through the curve; and when the hallway straightens again, we see there's a room ahead with a cluttered desk and hundreds of papers pinned to the wall. I'm about to run inside, but that's when my lights catch a long white object in the doorway.

"Is that . . ." Six trails off.

I'm stuck in my tracks. It's an enormous bone. Six pushes me forward and I pull the dagger from my back pocket.

"Ladies first?" I offer.

"Not this time."

With a running start, I jump over the bone and immediately light up the room with my hands. A yell escapes my mouth as I take in the skeleton sitting against the wall. Six jumps inside, and when she sees it, she stumbles backwards into the desk.

The skeleton is over eight feet tall, with giant feet and hands. Thick blond hair falls from the top of its skull and reaches past its wide shoulder blades. Around its neck hangs a blue pendant similar to mine.

"That's not Sam's dad," Six says.

"Definitely not."

"Then who is it?"

I step forward and examine the pendant. The blue Loralite stone is slightly larger than mine, but everything else is the same. I stare at it and feel an overwhelming connection to whoever this was. "I'm not sure, but I think he was a friend." I reach over his head and retrieve the pendant, handing it to Six.

We move to the desk. I don't know where to start. A heavy layer of dust covers stacks of papers and writing utensils. The writing on the papers pinned to the wall above the desk is in every language but English. I recognize a few Loric numbers, but nothing else. A white electronic tablet sits on a dilapidated wooden chair, and I pick it up and press my fingers over its black screen. Nothing happens.

Six opens the top drawer to find more papers, and as she grabs the second drawer's handle, an explosion aboveground knocks us off our feet. A long crack travels along the room's ceiling and then the concrete buckles. Chunks fall all around us.

"Run!" I yell.

With the pendant around her neck, Six tears a dozen papers from the wall and I stuff the white tablet in the back of my waistband. We scramble up the ladder and peek out the sliver of space between the well and the sundial. Dozens of Mogs. Smoldering fires. Bernie Kosar has transformed himself into a tiger with the curling horns of a ram. A Mog's arm is in his teeth. Sam is no longer at the fence, and neither is my Chest.

I'm about to burst out of the well when Six launches herself past me in a tornado of clouds. The sundial lid whips backwards, and she rips through a huddle of five Mogs, sending them across the yard. I pull myself out of the well and close it as she picks up a gleaming Mog sword, turning invisible.

I use my telekinesis to toss three armed Mogs standing near the well against the house. They explode into thick ash, and when I turn I see a shirtless man frozen in the back door with a shotgun in his hands. Behind him stands Sam's frightened mom in a nightgown.

Six materializes next to two Mogs running at me with glowing cannons, and she swings the sword through both their necks. Then she uses her telekinesis to throw the wheelbarrow at another, turning him into a pile of ash. I toss two Mogs against another, and Six impales all three in one quick motion. Bernie Kosar leaps into the middle of the yard and digs his teeth into a few Mogs struggling to their feet.

"Where's Sam?" I yell.

"Here!"

I twist to see Sam lying on his stomach under a charred shrub. Blood runs down his scalp.

"Sam!" his mom yells from the doorway.

He struggles to his knees. "Mom!"

His mom yells again, but a Mog reaches down and pulls Sam up by his shirt. I concentrate and uproot the rusty swing set, but before one of its metal poles can spear the Mog in the chest, he tosses Sam over the fence.

With an intensity I've never seen in her before, Six slices through the remaining Mogs. She's covered in ash when she jumps over the fence after Sam. I leap onto Bernie Kosar and we follow.

Sam is on his back in the neighbor's yard. Motion sensor lights flood over him. I jump off Bernie Kosar and pick him up.

"Sam? Are you okay? Where's my Chest?"

He opens his eyes halfway. "They got it. I'm sorry, John."

"There!" Six points to several Mogs running through a field towards the forest.

I set Sam on Bernie Kosar's back, but he pushes himself off. "I'm okay. I swear."

From the other side of the fence, Sam's mom yells, "Sam!"

"I'll be back, Mom! I love you!" And then he's the first to run towards the Mogs. Six and I catch up easily, but she veers right to plunge her sword into an approaching Mog. Four more are thirty yards ahead of her; and with the large pendant bouncing around her neck, she charges, with Bernie Kosar at her heels.

Sam and I enter the muddy field, and two Mogs cut off our path. Over my shoulder I see two more separating and marching in our direction at strategic angles. The others have entered the forest at two different sections, and I can't see who has the Chest. I pull the dagger out of my back pocket. The handle wraps around my hand.

I run ahead, and the two Mogs in front of me run, too, their swords bouncing and cutting into the empty field behind them. When we're less than five yards apart I leap with my dagger above my head. As I start to fall, a huge tree zips underneath me, ramming both Mogs and killing them. Six. As I hit the ground again I turn to see her running towards Sam and the two Mogs who circle him.

The one on Sam's left tackles him around the waist. Six tears the Mog off and throws him far into the field, where he immediately gets back on his feet and charges.

I sneak up behind the other Mog and hammer my dagger into the back of his neck, pulling it out at an angle that slices down through his shoulder blade. He falls to a pile of ash that blows onto my shoes.

Bernie Kosar pounces on the other Mog and quickly he has a tongue coated in thick ash.

"We have to get back to the car and get out of here," Six says. "There must be more on their way—they were waiting for us."

"We have to get my Chest first," I say.

"Then we're going to have to split up," Six says. With her soot-covered sword, she points at the two sections of forest the Mogs disappeared into. "Bernie Kosar, you're with me." Bernie Kosar shrinks into a hawk, and he and Six head left.

Sam and I enter the forest in the other direction. Soon we hear twigs cracking, and we run in that direction. I speed ahead and hurdle a series of dead trees to see four Mogs trying to escape through a small clearing. In the moonlight, I still can't see if any of them hold my Chest.

I slide down the hill on my side, crushing saplings, creating a small landslide of loose rock. I hear Sam crashing after me.

They're halfway through the small clearing. It's dense, with grass six feet tall, and I run through it at full speed. Sam yells for me to tell him what direction I'm headed in, but instead I keep running and aim my lit palm straight up into the sky as a beacon. "Okay! Got it!" he yells.

Finally, right before the clearing becomes forest again, I can almost reach one. I dive for his legs and slice through the bottom of his muddy khakis and sever his Achilles tendon, causing him to roar onto his back. I climb up his flailing body and stab him in the chest, killing him.

Sam trips over my legs and falls on his face. "You get it?"

"No. Come on!"

Using one hand as a flashlight and the other as a machete, I race through the forest with ease, not caring how close Sam stays behind me. In less than a minute, I see another Mog struggling over a fallen log. From twenty-five yards away, I lift the log high off the ground, tip it, and force the Mog to teeter and fall head-first. I crash through weeds to find him motionless on his stomach. I can already tell he doesn't have my Chest. I kill him with two stabs of my dagger.

"John?" Sam yells in the darkness. "Dude?"

I again shine my palm in the air, and I'm scanning the trees when Sam arrives.

"Tell me you got it?"

"Not yet," I say.

"No Chest," Sam mutters.

"I just hope Six had better luck." I reach behind me and pull the white tablet out to show Sam. "But I do have this."

He grabs it out of my hand. "From the well?"

"That's not all we found. Wait until I tell you what else—" I suddenly recognize where we are. I stop walking. I even stop breathing.

Sam grabs my shoulder and says, "Whoa, dude.

What's going on? You feeling something? Like maybe somebody just opened your Chest?"

As far as I can tell, my Chest hasn't been opened. The feeling brewing inside me is something entirely different. "We're near Sarah's house."

CHAPTER
TWENTY-TWO

AFTER THE DOOR AT THE BOTTOM OF THE TOWER creaks open, I hear footsteps. I hear echoed breathing. Whoever it is, it'll be impossible to hide a drugged Adelina, a cat, and a Chest stuffed with alien weapons and artifacts. I slowly set the branch back into the Chest and close the lid. Legacy creeps to the edge of the belfry floor and then sits and stares down into the darkness. We're all silent, but then Adelina rolls out a long, droning snore.

The footsteps in the circular stairway speed up. I give Adelina a few shakes to wake her up. She falls onto her side.

What do I do? I mouth to Legacy. The cat jumps on top of the Chest and then jumps back off again only to purr around my feet. It isn't an answer, but it does give me an idea. I lean down and set Legacy on top of the Chest and then scramble up into one of the two windows where the cool air penetrates my pajamas and instantly causes my teeth to chatter. The footsteps are getting closer.

With my mind, I raise the Chest high in the air, and Legacy's claws scrape at the lid for a safe footing. I have to duck as I float the Chest up and over me and out the window. Immediately after I set the Chest quietly on the frosty lawn ten stories below, Legacy jumps off and runs into the darkness. I then float Adelina up and over me, her nightgown brushing the top of my head, and carefully I set her down next to the Chest.

The footsteps are loud now. I swing my legs over the edge of the window. Using whatever concentration I can still muster, I am able to levitate myself a few centimeters above the cold stone. I push out into the swirling wind. Before I lower myself away from the tower, I see the mustached Mogadorian from the café round the last turn of the stairway and stomp into the belfry.

My concentration buckles and then snaps into a million little pieces. I go into a wild free-fall until the last moment, when I press my hands in front of my chest and set my mind on floating like a feather. My right knee lands a hair from Adelina's shivering body.

I panic. I either have to try to get the Chest and Adelina down into the village for hiding—but it is the middle of the night and we are in our nightclothes and I can only see a few lonely windows lit in town—or I have to quickly find a place to hide us within the orphanage. It will take the Mogadorian less time to descend the tower than it did for him to race up it, but he still has a long hallway to travel and another flight of stairs to run down to make it to the first floor. I stick my head through the double doors, and once I see the coast is clear, I drape Adelina over the Chest and float them into the nave. My strength is waning immensely, but I am somehow able to summon just enough power to get the Chest, Adelina and me tucked away up into the farthest recess of the drafty, cold and damp nook where the Chest had originally been hidden.

I am beginning to think I led the Mogadorian right to me by opening the Chest. Perhaps the red pulse of the crystal I dropped is some kind of transmitter. Adelina will know what it is, what to do. To combat the fear that an evil alien race is coming directly for me, to somehow apologize to Adelina for drugging her, and to gather a little warmth, I rest my head on Adelina's chest and wrap my arms around her waist.

Hours later, I hear Adelina grunt and shuffle her legs underneath mine.

"Adelina?" I whisper. "Are you awake?"

"Who is that? Marina?"

I whisper, "Adelina, you have to be really, really quiet."

"Why?" she whispers. "And where are we?"

"We're in the nave where you hid the Chest. But please listen to me. They're here. The Mogadorians came for me last night after I opened the Chest, and I had to hide us."

"How did you open up the Chest by yourself? It doesn't work that way."

"You told me how to do it. You were sleep-talking," I lie. I could tell her I drugged her, but I'm not ready for that argument.

Her confusion is evident in her voice. "I don't remember. . . . I, I remember getting out of bed and then . . . I guess that's about it. You opened up the Chest? What was inside?"

"A lot of things, Adelina. So much. There are all these stones and all these jewels, and one of them lit up in my hand and started flashing, and I think that's why the Mogadorian showed up."

"What Mogadorian? What happened?" Adelina tries to sit up, but I stop her before she hits her head on the low ceiling.

I whisper, "I saw a man in the café a few days ago who had a book about Pittacus, and he kept staring at me. He had this hat on and this big mustache, and I could just tell he was from Mogadore. And then last night after I opened the Chest in the north belfry, he showed up."

"How did we escape?"

"I used my telekinesis to float us out the window and into the yard, and then I used it to get us up here."

"We have to get out of here," she whispers. "We have

to leave Santa Teresa immediately."

My excitement is immediate. I hug her in the dark, and to my surprise she hugs me back. Adelina crawls to the lip of the nook and I follow her with the Chest hovering behind me. When the nave appears empty, Adelina asks me to lower her to the floor. Then I carefully drop the Chest over the lip and set it silently next to Adelina's bare feet. I'm about to levitate down when Sister Dora appears at the back of the nave and marches towards Adelina.

"Where have you been?" she barks. "You left your post all night. How could you do such a thing? And what is this luggage doing in here?"

"I had to get some fresh air, Sister Dora," Adelina says softly. "I'm sorry I left my post."

I can see Sister Dora's eyes narrow. "With Marina?"

"What?"

"I had four girls wake me up in the middle of the night saying that Marina snuck out last night and that you left with her."

Adelina starts to speak, but Ella suddenly appears behind Sister Dora and tugs on her dress.

"Sister Dora? I just saw Marina," she lies.

"Where?"

"In the bedroom, sleeping."

Sister Dora bends down and snatches Ella by the arm, and the terrified look on Ella's face causes something to shift inside me. "You're a little liar! I just came from the sleeping quarters, and *no* one is in there. You're making up excuses for her."

"Sister Dora, that's enough," Adelina says.

But Sister Dora begins dragging Ella away so forcefully that her feet hardly touch the ground. "We're going up to the office, and you're going to learn that you don't lie here."

Tears stream down Ella's cheeks. From the nook's opening, I stare at Sister Dora's hand and pry her fingers away from Ella's bicep. Sister Dora yells in pain, and then peers down at Ella with surprise and confusion. She grabs Ella again.

Adelina jogs over to them, and before I can send Sister Dora all the way down the main aisle on her back, Adelina grabs her wrist.

Sister Dora rips her arm away. My heart jumps into my throat with Adelina's newfound alliance to me and my friend.

"Don't you ever touch me again," Sister Dora challenges her. "You don't even belong here, Adelina. And neither does that juvenile demon you brought with you."

Adelina smiles calmly. "You're right, Sister Dora. Perhaps Marina and I don't belong here, and perhaps we will leave this very morning. But would you please be so kind as to let go of Ella first?" Her voice, while cordial and patient, contains a hint of venom.

"How dare you!" Sister Dora scoffs. "Why, you're no more than an orphan yourself. We took you in when no one else wanted you!"

"We're all the same in the Lord's eyes. Surely you acknowledge as much?"

Sister Dora moves to take another step, but Adelina again grabs her arm. The two women stare into each other's eyes.

"I will be talking about this with Sister Lucia. You will be thrown out of here so fast you won't have a chance to pray for forgiveness."

"I already said I'd be leaving this morning. And I will *always* have the chance to pray for forgiveness." Adelina reaches her hand out to Ella, and she takes it. Sister Dora hesitates before reluctantly letting go of Ella's arm. "I'll not only pray that Marina forgives me for being such a terrible guardian, but I'll also pray that God forgives you for forgetting your purpose here."

They continue to stare into each other's eyes for a few more seconds before Sister Dora pivots and huffs out of the nave. Once she's out of sight and Ella has her back to me, I float to the ground.

"Hi, Ella," I say.

"Marina!" She lets go of Adelina's hand, runs and hugs me. "Where were you?"

"Adelina and I had to talk alone," I say, pulling away from her. I look up at Adelina. "We had to talk about our future."

Adelina squints, then looks down at her dirty night-gown and becomes embarrassed. "Marina, go pack your things and put that Chest somewhere safe. We're leaving very soon."

When Adelina walks away, Ella grabs my hand and squeezes it. "The bad men were here last night, Marina."

"I know, I saw him. That's why we're leaving." As soon as I say it I know I will ask Adelina if we can take Ella with us.

"I saw all three of them," Ella whispers.

I gasp. "There's three of them?"

"They were at the window last night, looking at your bed."

A shiver runs up my spine. I float the Chest back up into the nook and run to the sleeping quarters, dodging huddles of girls in the hallway whispering to each other about something that happened in the village.

"They were right there," she says, pointing at the window.

"Three of them, you're sure?"

She nods her head. "Yes, and they saw me at the window watching them. Then they ran away."

"What did they look like?" I ask.

"They were tall and had really long hair. And their jackets went almost to their shoes," she says.

"With mustaches, right? They had mustaches?"

"I don't think so. I don't remember mustaches," she says.

I'm confused, but I know I don't have much time before Adelina shows up with a bag of the belongings she's collected over the past eleven years. I'm about to race into the shower when Analee, another girl, stops me in my tracks.

"School is canceled today. That girl Miranda Marquez was found strangled inside the school this morning."

I sit down on my bed, shocked. Miranda Marquez is a dark-haired girl who lives in the village and sits beside me in Spanish history class. Our teacher, Maestra Muñoz, often confuses us for each other because Miranda is skinny and tall like me, and her hair is the same length as mine. It takes me a second to realize that whoever killed Miranda might have mistaken her for me. Someone might have tried to kill me last night.

"This is really . . . this is bad," I whisper.

Analee says, "Plus, I heard one of the Sisters say that some villagers saw people flying through the air last night and now there are all these news vans out there doing a report on it."

This is all happening so fast. The Mogadorians have found me. They found my cave. I was being reckless with my Legacies and witnesses saw me and Adelina leave the belfry window. A girl from my school might be dead because of me, and Adelina and I are leaving the orphanage in the middle of winter without a place to stay.

I take the fastest hot shower of my life and wait for Adelina.

CHAPTER
TWENTY-THREE

"WE'RE NOT GOING TO SARAH'S," SAM SAYS, following me along the edge of the forest. "We got this tablet thing, possibly the transmitter we were after, and we're going back to help Six."

I step towards him. "Six can handle herself. I'm right here and Sarah's right here. I love her, Sam, and I'm going to see her. I don't care what you say."

Sam backs down, and I keep walking towards Sarah's house. Sam says, "Do you really love her though, John? Or are you in love with Six? Which one?"

I twist around and shine my palm in his face. "You think I don't love Sarah?"

"Hey, come on!"

"Sorry," I mutter, lowering my palm.

He rubs his eyes. "It's a valid question, man. I see you and Six flirting all the time, *all the time*, and you do it right in front of me. You know I like her, and you don't even care. *And* to top it all off you already have like the hottest girlfriend in Ohio."

"I do care," I whisper.

"You care about what?"

"I care that you like Six, Sam. But you're right—I like her too. I wish I didn't, but I do. It's stupid and cruel to you, but I can't stop thinking about her. She's cool and she's beautiful and she's Loric, which is like, extracool. But I *love* Sarah. And that's why I have to see her."

Sam grabs my elbow. "You can't, man. We have to go back and help Six. Think about it. If they were waiting for us at my place, then even more of them are waiting for us at Sarah's."

I gently pull my elbow away from his grip. "You got to see your mom, right? You saw her in the backyard?"

"Yeah," he sighs. His eyes find his shoes.

"You got to see your mom, so I get to see Sarah."

"That doesn't make as much sense as you think it does. We got the transmitter, remember? This is why we're in Paradise. It's the only reason." Sam hands me the tablet, and I stare at its blank screen. I touch every inch of it. I try telekinesis. I hold it to my forehead. The tablet remains off.

"Let me try," Sam says. As he fumbles with the tablet, I tell him about the ladder, the huge skeleton with the pendant, and the desk and wall covered in papers.

"Six grabbed a handful of the papers, but it's not like we can read them," I say.

"So my dad had a secret underground lair?" Sam smiles for the first time in hours, handing the tablet back. "He was so cool. I'd really like to look at the papers Six took."

"Absolutely," I say. "Right after I see Sarah."

Sam opens his arms in astonishment. "What can I do to change your mind? Just tell me."

"Nothing. There's nothing you can do to stop me."

The last time I was at Sarah's house it was Thanksgiving Day. I remember walking up the driveway and seeing Sarah wave from the front window.

"Hey, handsome," she said when she opened the door, and I turned around to look over my shoulder to pretend she meant it for someone else.

Her house looks completely different at two in the morning. With every window dark, with the garage doors closed, the house looks cold and empty. Uninviting. Sam and I are on our bellies in the shadow of a house on the corner, and I don't know how I'm going to talk to her.

I pull the prepaid cell phone I've had turned off for days out of my jeans. "I could text her until she wakes up."

"That's actually a pretty good idea. Just do this

already so we can get out of here. I swear, Six is going to kill us, or worse, maybe she's about to be killed by a swarm of Mogs and we're here lying in the grass about to go through a scene from *Romeo and Juliet*."

I power up the phone and type: **I promised I'd come back. U up?**

We count to thirty after I send it, and then I type: **I love you. I'm here.**

"Maybe she thinks you're pranking her," Sam whispers after we wait another thirty seconds. "Say something only you would know."

I try: **Bernie Kosar misses you.**

Her window lights up. Then my phone buzzes with a text: **Is it really you? You're in Paradise?**

I pull up a handful of grass, I'm so excited.

"Chill out," Sam whispers.

"I can't help it."

I respond: **I'm outside. Meet me at the playground in 5?**

My phone buzzes immediately: **I'll be there. :)**

Sam and I are hiding behind a Dumpster at the end of the street when Sarah takes her first steps onto the concrete playground. From the moment I see her, I'm breathless, flooded with emotions. She's twenty yards away, wearing dark jeans and a black fleece jacket. A white winter hat is pulled over her head, but I can still see her long blond hair, and it brushes over her shoulders in the slight wind. Her flawless complexion glows in the lone playground bulb, and I feel instantly self-conscious about being covered in dirt and Mog ash. I take a step away from the Dumpster, but Sam grabs my wrist and holds me back.

"John, I know this is going to be really hard," he whispers. "But we have to be back in those woods in ten minutes. I'm serious. Six is counting on us."

"I'll do my best," I say, not even thinking of the repercussions at this point. Sarah is right there, and I'm so close I can practically smell her shampoo.

I watch Sarah turn her head back and forth looking for me. Finally she sits down on a swing and twists herself, the ropes above her becoming taut. Sarah starts to spin slowly, and I shuffle around the perimeter of the playground, pausing behind trees, watching her. She looks so beautiful. So perfect.

I wait until she's facing the other direction before stepping out of the shadows, and when she twists around again, there I am.

"John?" The toes of Sarah's sneakers scrape on the concrete to stop her from twisting back around.

"Hey, beautiful," I say. I can feel my smile reaching the corners of my eyes.

Sarah covers her mouth and nose with her hands.

I walk towards her and she tries to get off of the swing, but its ropes are too taut for her to escape.

I jump forward and catch the swing's ropes in my

hands. I twist her towards me and raise my arms, lifting her and the seat so her face lines up with mine. I lean in and kiss her, and the instant our lips meet, it's as if I'd never left Paradise.

"Sarah," I say into her ear. "I've missed you so, so, so much."

"I can't believe you're here. This can't be real."

I kiss her again, and I don't stop while I twist us both around and around until the ropes above her separate. Sarah pushes off from the seat and lands in my arms. I kiss her cheeks and her neck, and she runs her hands over my head, gripping my short hair between her fingers.

I set her down and she says, "Somebody got a haircut."

"Yeah, it's my whole tough-guy-on-the-run look. What do you think? You into it?"

"I am," she says, pressing her palms to my chest. "But you could be bald for all I care."

I take a step back to cement this image of Sarah. I note the brightness of the stars behind her, the tilt of her winter hat. Her nose and cheeks are red from the cold; and as she bites her lower lip and stares at me, a small cloud of breath floats from her mouth. "I've thought about you every single day, Sarah Hart."

"I promise I've thought about you twice as much."

I lower my head until our foreheads touch. We stay

this way wearing ridiculous grins until I ask, "How are you? What are things like for you around here right now?"

"Better now."

"It's so hard being away from you," I say, kissing her cold fingers. "I'm constantly thinking about what it feels like to touch you and hear your voice. I've come close to calling you every single night."

Sarah cups my chin and runs her thumbs over my lips. "I've sat in my dad's car so many times just wondering where you are. All I needed to know was which direction and I would've started to drive."

"I'm right here. Right in front of you," I whisper.

She drops her hands. "I want to come with you, John. I don't care. I can't go on like this."

"It's way too dangerous. We *just* finished battling fifty Mogs over at Sam's place. That's what life is like with me right now. I can't put you in the middle of all this."

Her shoulders shake, and tears dot the corners of her eyes. "I can't stay here, John. Not with you out there and me not knowing if you're dead or alive."

"Look at me, Sarah," I say. She raises her head. "There's no way I'm going to die. Knowing that you're here waiting for me, it's like a force field. We're going to be together. Soon."

Her lip quivers. "It's so hard. Everything is awful right now, John."

"Everything's awful? What do you mean?"

"People are jerks. Everyone's saying hateful things about you, and they say a lot of things about me, too."

"Like what?"

"That you're a terrorist and a murderer and you hate the United States. Guys at school call you names like Bomb Smith. My parents say you're dangerous and I'm never supposed to talk to you again no matter what; and as an added bonus, there's a reward on your head, so people are always talking about shooting you."

She puts her head down. "I can't believe you have to put up with all that, Sarah," I say. "At least you know the truth."

"I've lost almost every friend I had. Plus I'm at a new school where everyone just thinks I'm this weirdo."

I'm devastated. Sarah was the most popular, most beautiful, most liked girl at Paradise High School. Now she's an outcast.

"Things won't always be this way," I whisper.

She can't hold back the tears any longer. "I love you so much, John. But I can't imagine how we're going to get out of this mess. Maybe you should turn yourself in."

"I'm not turning myself in, Sarah. I just can't. We'll get out of it. Of course we will. My one and only love, Sarah. I promise, if you wait for me, things will get better."

But the tears don't stop. "How long do I wait, though? And what happens when things do get better? Will you go back to Lorien?"

"I don't know," I finally say. "Paradise is the only place I want to be right now, and you're the only person I want to be with in the future. But if we're able to somehow defeat the Mogadorians, then yes, I have to go back to Lorien. But I don't know when that will be."

Sarah's phone buzzes in her pocket, and she pulls it halfway out to check the screen.

"Who's texting you so late?" I ask.

"Just Emily. Maybe you should just turn yourself in and tell them you're not a terrorist. I don't want to lose you over and over, John."

"Listen to me, Sarah. I can't turn myself in. I can't sit in a police station and try to explain how an entire school was destroyed and how five people were killed. How am I supposed to explain Henri? Those documents they found in our house? I can't get arrested. I mean, Six would absolutely kill me right now if she knew I was here talking to you."

Sarah sniffs and wipes her tears away with the backs of her hands. "Why would Six kill you if she knew you were here?"

"Because she needs me right now and it's dangerous for me to be here."

"She needs you? *She* does? I need you, John. I need

you here to tell me everything is going to be okay, that all this is worth it."

Sarah walks slowly over to a bench marked with initials. I sit down next to her and lean my shoulder onto hers. We're out of the light and I can't see her face very well.

I don't know where it comes from, but Sarah leans away from me and says, "Six is very pretty."

"She is," I agree. I shouldn't have, but it just fell out of my mouth. "Not as pretty as you, though. You're the prettiest girl I know. You're the prettiest girl I've ever seen."

"But you don't have to stay away from Six like you have to with me."

"When we go on walks we have to be invisible, Sarah! It's not like we can just hold hands and walk down the street. We have to hide from the entire world. I'm hiding just as much when I'm with her as when I am with you."

Sarah shoots off of the bench and turns around. "You go on walks with her? *Do you* hold her hand when you two walk down the street?"

I stand up and approach her with my arms out, the sleeves of my coat still caked with dirt. "We have to. It's the only way I can be invisible."

"Have you kissed her?"

"What?"

"Answer me." There's something new in her voice. It's a mixture of jealousy and loneliness, and enough anger to give each word a kick.

I shake my head. "Sarah, I love you. I don't really know what else to say. I mean, nothing's happened." A tsunami of discomfort crashes into me, and I rifle through my vocabulary to piece together the right words.

She's furious. "It was a simple question, John. Have you kissed her?"

"I haven't kissed Six, Sarah. We haven't kissed. I love *you*," I say, and then I cringe at the acidity of the words, the sentence sounding far worse than I thought it would.

"I see. Why was that question so hard for you to answer, John? My life just keeps getting better and better. Does she like you?"

"It doesn't matter, Sarah. I love you, so Six doesn't matter. No other girls matter!"

"I feel like such an idiot," she says, crossing her arms.

"Stop, please. Sarah, you're misinterpreting everything."

"Am I, John?" she asks, turning her head and staring fiercely at me with tears in her eyes. "I've gone through so much for you."

I reach out and try taking Sarah's hand, but she

snatches it away the instant our fingers touch.

"Don't," she says, a hard edge in her voice. Her phone buzzes again in her jacket pocket, but she doesn't make a move to check it.

"I want to be with you, Sarah," I say. "Nothing I say right now seems to come out right. All I can really say is that I've spent weeks missing you terribly, and there hasn't been a single day that I didn't think about calling you or writing a letter." I feel wobbly. I can tell I'm losing her. "I love you. Don't doubt that for a second."

"I love you, too," she cries.

I close my eyes and breathe in the cool air. A bad feeling rushes over me; a prickly feeling that starts in my throat and claws its way into my shoes. When I open my eyes, Sarah has taken several steps away from me.

There's a noise to my left, and I whip my head to see Sam. His eyes are downcast, and he bobs his head in a way that tells Sarah and me that he'd rather not be approaching but he has to.

"Sam?" Sarah asks.

"Hey, Sarah," he whispers.

Sarah wraps her arms around him.

"It's really good to see you," he says into her hair. "But, Sarah, I'm sorry. I'm really, really sorry and I know you guys haven't seen each other in a long time, but John and I need to go. We're in a lot of danger. You have no idea."

"I sort of do." She pulls off of him, and just as I prepare to start reassuring her how much I love her, just as I'm about to start saying good-bye, chaos erupts.

Everything happens so fast I'm unable to take it all in completely, the scenes randomly skipping like a movie reel gone mad. Sam is tackled from behind by a man in a gas mask. The blue jacket he wears has the letters *FBI* on the back. Someone wraps their arms around Sarah and whisks her away from me. A metallic shell skids across the grass and lands at my feet, and the white smoke billowing from both ends burns my eyes and throat. I can't see. I hear Sam gag. I stumble away from the canister and fall to my knees next to a plastic slide. When I lift my head I see over a dozen officers surrounding me, all with guns drawn. The masked officer who tackled Sam has his knee on Sam's back. A voice through a megaphone blasts: "Don't move! Put your hands on the top of your head and get on your stomach! You are under arrest!" As I place my hands on the top of my head, cars that have been parked on the street the entire time we were there suddenly come to life; their headlights turn on, red lights flash from dashboards. Cop cars screech around the corner, and an armored vehicle with SWAT written on its side jumps the curb and slams on its brakes in the middle of the basketball court. Men yell and pile out of it at an alarming rate, and that's when someone kicks me in my stomach.

Handcuffs are clicked around my wrists. Above me I hear the whir of a helicopter.

My mind grabs hold of the only explanation it can come up with.

Sarah. The text messages. That wasn't Emily. The police were talking to her. What little of my heart that didn't break when Sarah backed away from me now shatters.

I shake my head with my face against the concrete. I feel someone remove my dagger. Hands take the tablet from my waistband. I watch as Sam is pulled off the ground by his arms, and our eyes meet for a brief second. I can't tell what he's thinking.

Cuffs are slapped around my ankles, and a chain connects to the cuffs around my wrists. I'm jerked up from the ground. The cuffs are too tight and dig into my wrists. A black hood is pulled over my head and secured around my throat. I can't see a thing. Two officers grab my elbows while another shoves me forward.

"You have the right to remain silent," one of them begins as I'm led away, and I'm thrown into the back of a vehicle.

CHAPTER
TWENTY-FOUR

AFTER FIVE MINUTES, I GET UP OFF MY BED AND look in the wardrobe to see if there are any clothes I want to take with us. I'm holding a black sweater when I decide I can't leave without saying good-bye to Héctor.

I rip another girl's jacket from the wall, one with a hood, and write a quick note to Adelina: *Had to say good-bye to someone in town first.*

The double doors open into the chilly air, and once I see the police cars and news vans lining Calle Principal, I feel better. The Mogadorians wouldn't try anything with so many witnesses. I walk through the gate with the hood over my head. The door to Héctor's house is cracked open, and I knock softly on the door frame. "Héctor?"

A woman answers. "Hello?"

The door swings open and it's Héctor's mother, Carlotta. Her black-and-gray hair is pinned carefully around her head, and her face is pink and smiling. She's wearing a beautiful red dress and a blue apron. The house smells like cake.

"Is Héctor home, Señora Ricardo?" I ask.

"My angel," she says. "My angel has returned."

She remembers what I did for her, how I cured her disease. I feel embarrassed by the way she's looking at me, but she bends down for a hug and I can't resist. "My angel has returned," she says again.

"I'm so happy you're feeling better, Señora Ricardo."

The tears that fall from her eyes are almost too much, and soon my own eyes swell with water. "You're welcome," I whisper. There's a meow behind Carlotta, and I lean over to see Legacy trotting towards me from the kitchen with milk dripping from his chin. He purrs against my shins and I bend down to pet his coat.

"When did you get a cat?" I ask.

"This morning he comes to my door, and I think he is so sweet. I've named him Feo."

"It's good to see you, Feo."

"He's a good cat," she says, her hands now on her hips. "Very hungry boy."

"I'm so glad you two found each other. Carlotta, I'm very sorry but I have to leave. I need to speak with Héctor. Is he home?"

"He's at the café," she says. The disappointment of Héctor drinking so early in the morning must be evident on my face, because Carlotta adds, "Only coffee now. He's drinking coffee."

I hug her good-bye and she kisses both of my cheeks.

The café is packed. I reach for the door, but just before I pull it open, something stops me dead in my tracks: Héctor's sitting at a small table, but I notice him only in my periphery. My eyes are glued to who's sitting in the chair opposite him—the Mogadorian from last night. He's now clean shaven, and his black hair has been lightened to a chestnut color, but there's no mistaking him. He's just as tall and muscular as before, just as broad shouldered, just as dark and brooding, with the same heavy brows. I don't need the killer's description to know he matches it perfectly, with or without the dyed hair or missing mustache.

I let go of the door and step backwards. *Oh Héctor*, I think. *How could you?*

My legs shake; my heart pounds. As I'm standing there watching them, the Mogadorian turns and sees me at the window. My flesh turns cold. The world seems to stop; I'm stuck, rooted in place, incapable of moving a muscle. The Mogadorian watches me, causing Héctor to turn my way as well, and it's only upon seeing his face that I'm shocked into action.

I stumble backwards then, turn and run, but before I've made it far, I hear the café door open. I don't turn around.

If the Mogadorian is following me, I don't want to know.

"Marina!" Héctor yells. "Marina!"

Four officers ride with me. I touch my fingertips to the heavy chains. I'm certain I could break them if I wanted to, or I could simply unlock the cuffs with telekinesis; but the thought of Sarah empties me of the energy required for such an undertaking. *She couldn't have turned me in. Please don't let it have been her.*

The first drive takes twenty minutes, and I have no idea where we are. I'm pulled out and shoved into a second vehicle which I assume is more secure, meant for longer transport. The second drive takes forever— two hours, maybe three—and by the time we finally stop and I'm again jerked out, the sickness over what Sarah may have done has grown to the point that it's nearly unbearable.

I'm guided into a building. After each turn I have to wait for a door to be unlocked. I count four of them, and the air changes with each new corridor, becoming staler the farther I'm led. Finally I'm pushed into a cell.

"Sit," one of them orders.

I sit on a bed. The hood is removed but the shackles remain. Four officers exit and slam the door shut. The two larger ones take seats outside my cell, while the other two leave.

The cell is small, ten feet by ten feet, and contains

the bed I'm sitting on, covered in yellow stains, and a metal toilet and sink. Nothing else. Three of its four walls are solid concrete, and there's a small window at the very top of the back wall.

Despite the filthy mattress, I lie down, close my eyes, and wait for my mind to slow down.

"John!" Sam's voice yells out.

My eyes snap open. I rush to the front of the cell, grabbing hold of the bars. "Right here," I yell back.

"Shut up!" the larger of the two guards yells, pointing his nightstick at me. Down the corridor, somebody yells at Sam, too. He doesn't say anything else, but at least I know he's close.

I reach my hand through the bars of my cell and press my palm against the flat metal surface of the lock. I close my eyes, focus my telekinesis to feel its inner workings, and yet I feel nothing other than a vibration that hurts my head the harder I concentrate.

The cell—it's electronically controlled. I can't open it with telekinesis.

I run as fast as I can back to the orphanage, the hood ballooning with air behind me, and as I gain speed the clouds and blue sky above me melt into a bright white.

I burst through the double doors and run to the sleeping quarters. Adelina's sitting on my bed, the note folded on her lap. A small suitcase sits at her feet. When she sees me, she jumps up and hugs me.

"You have to look at this," she says, handing me the paper. I unfold it to see that it's not my note after all but a photocopied picture.

It takes me a second to realize what the picture is of, and when I recognize it my heart sinks. Someone has burned an enormous and intricate symbol into the side of a nearby mountain. With its careful lines and sharp angles, it's an exact replica of the scars around my ankle.

The sheet falls from my hand and slowly floats to the ground.

"That was found yesterday, and the police are handing these copies out looking for information," Adelina says. "We have to go now."

"Yes, absolutely. I need to talk to you about Ella first," I say.

Adelina tilts her head. "What about Ella?"

"I want her to come with—"

Before I can finish my sentence, I'm rocked off my feet by a thundering crash. Adelina falls as well and slams her shoulder into the ground. There's been an explosion, somewhere within the orphanage. Several girls run into the room screaming; others run past the doorway looking for refuge elsewhere. I hear Sister Dora yell for everyone to go to the south wing.

Adelina and I get to our feet and head for the hallway, but then another explosion hits, and suddenly I can feel cold wind. I can't hear what Adelina is saying above the screams, but I follow her gaze to the roof, where there's now a jagged hole the size of a bus. As I'm staring, a tall man in a trench coat with long red hair walks to the edge of the hole. He points at me.

CHAPTER TWENTY-FIVE

THE INTERROGATION ROOM IS WARM AND PITCH-black. I rest my head on the table in front of me and try not to fall asleep; but after being up all night, I can't help myself. Instantly, I feel a vision forming and hear the whispers. I feel myself floating up through the darkness, then, as if shot through a cannon, I blaze through a shadowy tunnel. Black turns to blue. Blue turns to green. The whispers follow me, growing weaker the farther down the tunnel I go. Suddenly, I'm jolted to a stop and everything falls silent. A gust of wind appears with a bright light, and when I look down, I realize I'm standing on the snowy peak of a mountain.

The view is spectacular, with mountains stretching for miles. There's a deep green valley below me and a crystal blue lake. I'm drawn to the lake and begin descending when I see tiny bursts of light surrounding it. As if I'm wearing binoculars, my vision is suddenly

magnified and I see hundreds of heavily armed Mogadorians shooting at four running figures.

My anger is immediate and colors blur as I run down
the mountain. A few hundred yards from the lake, the
sky growls above me with a black wall of clouds. Bolts
of lightning crash into the valley and thunder roars.
I'm knocked off my feet as lightning strikes all around
me, and that's when I see the glowing eye form and
stare down from the clouds.

"Six!" I yell, but the thunder drowns me out. I know
it's her, but what is she doing here?

The clouds part, and someone drops into the valley.
My vision magnifies again, and I see that I was right:
Six stands furious between the advancing army of
Mogs and two young girls and two older men. Her arms
are above her head, and a steady sheet of rain falls.

"Six!" I yell again, and a pair of hands grabs my
shoulders from behind.

My eyes snap open and I whip my head off the table.
The lights in the interrogation room are on, and there's
a tall man with a round face standing above me. He's
wearing a dark suit with a badge clipped to his belt. In
his hands is the white tablet.

"Chill out, kid. I'm Detective Will Murphy, FBI. How
we doing today?"

"Never better," I reply, dazed by the vision. Who was
Six protecting?

"Good," he says. The detective sits, a pen and legal pad in front of him. He carefully displays the tablet on the left side of the table.

"So," he begins, slowly drawing it out. "Six what? What do you have six of?"

"What?"

"You were yelling the number six in your sleep. You want to tell me what that's all about?"

"It's my golf handicap," I say. My mind tries to conjure up the faces of the two girls behind Six in the valley, but they're fuzzy.

Detective Murphy chuckles. "Yeah, right. How about you and me have a little chat? Let's start with the birth certificate you gave to Paradise High. It's counterfeit, John Smith. In fact, we can't find a single thing about you prior to you showing up in Paradise several months ago," he says, squinting as though expecting some reply. "Your social security number belongs to a dead man in Florida."

"Was there a question there?"

His grin turns into a smirk. "Why don't you start by telling me your real name."

"John Smith."

"Right," he says. "Where's your father, John?"

"Dead."

"How convenient."

"Actually, it's probably the most inconvenient thing

that's ever happened to me up until now."

The detective writes something on the notepad. "Where are you originally from?"

"The planet Lorien, three hundred million miles away."

"Must have been a long trip, John Smith."

"Took almost a year. Next time I'm bringing a book."

He drops his pencil on the table, interlocks his fingers behind his head, and leans back. Then he pushes forward again and holds up the tablet. "You want to tell me what this thing is?"

"I was hoping you could tell me. We found it in the woods."

He holds it by its edge and whistles. "You found this in the woods? Where at in the woods?"

"Near a tree."

"Are you going to be a wiseass with every question?"

"That depends, detective. Are you working for them?"

He sets the tablet back on the desktop. "Am I working for who?"

"The Morlocks," I say, the first thing I remember from English class.

Detective Murphy smiles.

"You can smile, but they'll probably be here soon," I say.

"The Morlocks?"

"Yes, sir."

"Like from *The Time Machine*?"

"That's the one. That's like our Bible."

"And let me guess; you and your friend, Samuel Goode, you're members of the Eloi?"

"The Loric, actually. But for our purposes today, the Eloi will be fine."

The detective reaches into his pocket and slams my dagger on the table. I stare at its four-inch diamond blade as if I've never seen it before. I could easily kill this man just by moving my eyes from the blade to his neck, but I need to free Sam first. "What's this for, John? Why would you need a knife like this?"

"I don't know what knives like that are for, sir. Whittling?"

He picks up his notepad and pencil. "Why don't you tell me what happened in Tennessee."

"Never been," I say. "I hear it's a nice place, though. Maybe I'll visit when I'm out of here, take a tour, see the sites. Any suggestions?"

He nods, tosses the notepad onto the table, and then launches the pencil at me. I deflect it without lifting a finger, sending it bouncing against the wall; but the detective doesn't notice, and leaves through the steel door with the tablet and my dagger.

Soon I'm shoved back into my old cell. I have to get out of here.

"Sam?" I yell.

The guard who's been sitting outside my cell jumps off his chair and swings the nightstick at my fingers. I let go of the bars just before they're crushed.

"Shut up!" he orders, pointing his nightstick at me.

"You think I'm afraid of you?" I ask. Getting him inside my cell sounds like a pretty good option.

"I could give a damn, peewee. But if you keep it up, you're gonna regret it real fast."

"You couldn't hit me if you tried; I'm too quick and you're too fat."

The guard chuckles. "Why don't you just sit back on your bed and shut your mouth, huh?"

"You know I can kill you any time I want to, right? Without even lifting a finger."

"Oh yeah?" he replies. The guard steps forward. His breath smells rancid, like stale coffee. "What's stopping you then?"

"Apathy and a broken heart," I say. "Both of those will go away eventually, though, and that's when I'll just get up and leave."

"I can hardly wait, Houdini," he says.

I'm extremely close to taunting him inside, and as soon as he unlocks the door, Sam and I are as good as free.

"You know who you look like?" I ask.

"Tell me," he says.

I turn around and bend over.

"That's it, punk!" The guard reaches for a control panel on the wall, and as he's stomping towards the door of my cell, an earsplitting blast rattles the entire jail. The guard stumbles into the bars and smacks his forehead, falling to his knees. I drop and instinctively roll beneath the bed. Pandemonium erupts—yells and gunshots, clanking metal, and loud bangs. An alarm goes off, and a blue light flashes in the corridor.

I roll onto my back and twist my hands to get a firm grip on the chain binding my wrists. While using my legs as leverage, I straighten myself and snap the chain binding my hands and feet in two. I use telekinesis to unlock my cuffs and drop them to the floor. I do the same with the pair around my ankles.

"John!" Sam yells from down the hall.

I crawl to the front of the cell. "Right here!"

"What's going on?"

"I was going to ask you the same thing!" I yell back.

Other prisoners shout through their cell bars, too. The guard who fell in front of my cell grunts and struggles to his feet. Blood flows from a gash on his head.

The ground shakes again. It's more violent and lasts longer than the first time, and a fog of dust barrels down the corridor from the right. I'm temporarily blinded, but reach my hand through the bars and yell to the guard, "Let me out of here!"

"Hey! How'd you get your cuffs off?"

I see he's disoriented, wavering a few steps to his right, a few to his left, ignoring the other guards who run by him with guns drawn. He's covered in dust.

A thousand gunshots come from the right end of the corridor. A roar of a beast answers them.

"John!" Sam screams in a pitch I've never heard from him before.

I make eye contact with the guard and yell, "We're all going to die in here if you don't let me out!"

The guard looks towards the roars and terror spreads across his face. He slowly reaches for his gun, but before he can touch the grip it floats away from him. I know that trick—I saw that in Florida on a midnight walk—and I watch as the guard spins in confusion and runs.

Six becomes visible in front of my door, the large pendant still around her neck, and from the second I see her face I know she's pissed at me. I also see that she's in a very big hurry to get me out of here.

"What's down there, Six? Is Sam okay? I can't see anything," I say.

She looks down the corridor and concentrates on something, and a set of keys comes floating down the corridor, right into her hands. She inserts them into a metal panel on the wall. My door unlocks. I run out of my cell and I'm finally able to see down the corridor.

It's extremely long, with at least forty cells between me and the exit. But the exit is gone, as is the wall it should be on, and I'm staring at the giant horned head of a piken. Two guards are in its mouth, and drool mixed with blood falls from its razor-sharp teeth.

"Sam!" I yell, but he doesn't answer. I turn to Six. "Sam's down there!"

She disappears before my eyes, and five seconds later I watch another cell slide open. Sam rushes towards me. I yell, "Okay, Six! Let's trash this thing!"

Inches from my nose, Six's face appears. "We're not fighting the piken. Not here."

"Are you kidding me?" I ask.

"There's more important stuff we have to do, John," she barks. "We have to get to Spain immediately."

"Now?"

"Now!" Six grabs my hand and pulls me after her until I'm running at a full clip. Sam is right behind me, and we're able to get through two sets of doors with Six's keys. As the second one is flung open, we're faced with seven Mogs running with cylindrical cannonlike tubes and swords. Instinctively, I reach for my dagger, but it's not there. Six throws me the guard's gun then holds me and Sam back. She lowers her head in concentration. The lead Mog is spun around, and his sword slices across the two behind him, turning them to ash. Six then kicks the Mog in the back and he falls on his own sword. She's invisible before he dies.

Sam and I duck the first tube's blast, and the second one singes the collar of my shirt. I shoot, emptying my pistol as I slide into the piles of ash. I kill one Mog and then pick up his dropped tube. Hundreds of lights spark to life the second my finger finds the trigger, and a green beam cuts through another Mog. I aim for the last two, but Six has already appeared behind them, lifting both to the ceiling with telekinesis. She slams them against the ground in front of me, then back to the ceiling and then again on the ground. My jeans are covered in their ash.

Six unlocks another door and we enter a large room with dozens of cubicles on fire. Holes smolder in the ceiling. Mogs are shooting at police, and police are firing back. Six wrestles a sword away from the nearest Mog and cuts off his arm, and then she jumps over a burning cubicle wall. I blast the stumbling one-armed Mog in the back with my tube, and he falls into a black heap of ash.

I see an unconscious Detective Murphy on the ground. Six darts through the maze of cubicles, swinging her sword so fast it blurs. Mogs turn to ash all around her. Police retreat through a door on the far left as Six slices through a circle of Mogs closing in on her. I shoot and shoot, destroying those on the perimeter.

When the room is clear, we run down an empty

hallway under a shower of sparks.

"There!" Sam points to a giant hole leading out into a parking lot. We don't hesitate, each one of us jumping through sparks and smoke; and before I sprint into the cold morning, I see my dagger and the tablet sitting on the desk in the office. I reach over and scoop them both up, and seconds later I'm following Six and Sam into a deep ditch that provides us plenty of cover.

"We're not going to talk about that right now," Six says, her arms pumping fast. She dropped the sword a mile back. I tossed the Mog tube under a bush.

"But do you have it, though?"

"John, not right now."

"But do you—"

Six comes to an abrupt halt.

"John! You want to know where your Chest is?"

"In the trunk of the car?" I ask, my eyebrows raised in apology.

"Nope," she says. "Try again."

"Hidden in a Dumpster?"

Six lifts her arms above her head and a gust of wind sends me flying until I hit a massive oak tree. She marches towards me, fists at her sides. "How is she?"

"Who?" I ask.

"Your girlfriend, you asshole! Was it worth it? Was it worth leaving me surrounded by Mogs fighting to get *your* Chest back to see precious little Sarah? Was it worth getting arrested for? Did you get enough kisses to make up for getting your face slapped all over the news again?"

"No," I mumble. "I think Sarah turned us in."

"I think so, too," Sam says.

"And you!" Six spins around to raise her finger at Sam. "You went along with it! I thought you were smarter than that, Sam. You're supposed to be some kind of genius, and you think it's a good idea to go to the one place in the whole world that the police would definitely be watching?"

"I've never called myself a genius," Sam says, picking up the tablet I dropped, brushing dirt from it. Six keeps walking. "And, Six, I had no choice. Seriously. I tried as hard as I could to get John to go back and look for you and help."

"He did," I mutter, standing. "Don't blame Sam."

"Well, John, while you two lovebirds were hugging and kissing, I was getting my ass kicked doing you a favor. I would have died if Bernie Kosar didn't grow into this giant elephant-bear animal and help. They have your Chest. And I'm sure by this point it's sitting right next to mine in the cave in West Virginia."

"Then that's where I'm going," I say.

"No, we're going to Spain. Today."

"No, we're not!" I shout, brushing off my sleeves.

"Not until I have my Chest back."

"Well, I'm going to Spain," she says.

"Why now?" Sam asks.

Our SUV comes into view. "I was just online. It's serious over there. Somebody burned a huge symbol into the mountainside over Santa Teresa and it looks exactly like the brands around our ankles. Someone needs our help and I'm going."

We hop in the car and Six drives slowly down the road, and Sam and I hide in the footwells of the backseat. Bernie Kosar barks from the passenger seat, happy to be riding shotgun for a change.

Sam and I pass the laptop back and forth, both of us reading the article about Santa Teresa twice, three times. The burning symbol on the mountain is no doubt Loric. "What if it's a trap?" I ask. "My Chest is more important right now." It might be selfish, but before I leave the continent, I want my Inheritance. The possibility that the Mogs might open my Chest is just as urgent to me as whatever is going on in Spain.

"I need to know how to get to the cave," I say.

"John! Get real. You're really not going to come with me to Spain?" Six asks. "After reading all that, you're going to let me and Sam go alone?"

"Guys, get this. Also out of Santa Teresa, there's a woman reported to have been cured, out of the blue, of an incurable degenerative disease. Santa Teresa is, like, an epicenter of activity right now. I bet every member of the Garde are on their way," Sam says.

"If that's the case," I say, "then I'm definitely not going. I'm getting my Chest back."

"That's insane," Six says.

I scramble over the passenger seat and open the glove compartment. My fingers find the stone I'm looking for, and I drop it in Six's lap before hiding in the footwell again.

She lifts the pale yellow stone above the wheel, turning it over in the sunlight, and laughs. "You had the Xitharis out?"

"I figured it might come in handy," I say.

"These don't last long, remember," she says.

"How long?"

"An hour, maybe a little more."

The news is discouraging, but it could still give me the advantage I need. "Can you charge it, please?"

When Six holds the Xitharis to her temple, I know she's agreed to let me go after the Chests while she heads to Spain.

CHAPTER
TWENTY-SIX

I DO IT WITHOUT EVEN THINKING. THE SECOND the man points at me from the edge of the hole in the roof, I send two metal bed frames rocketing towards him. The second one is a direct hit. He falls forward and into the sleeping quarters; and when he hits the stone floor, to my amazement, he turns into a pile of dirt or ash.

"Run!" Adelina screams.

We crash into the hallway, pushing against the flow of the other girls and Sisters heading to the south wing for safety. I take hold of Adelina's hand and guide us to the nave and down the center aisle.

"Where are we going?" Adelina yells.

"We're not leaving without the Chest!"

Another explosion rocks the foundation of the orphanage and my hip crashes into a pew.

"I'll be right back," I whisper, releasing her hand, floating towards the nook.

Six tells us we're close to Washington, DC, and that makes sense. I am considered an armed and dangerous terrorist; no wonder I was taken to the nation's capital for questioning.

"There's a flight leaving Dulles International in less than an hour," she says, turning the wheel. "I'm getting on that plane. Sam, are you with me or are you with John?"

Sam places his forehead on the backseat and closes his eyes.

"Sam?" Six asks.

"I'm thinking, I'm thinking," he says. After a minute, he raises his head and looks right at me. "I'm going with John."

I mouth *Thank you.*

"It'll be easier for me to get there alone, anyway," Six says, but she sounds hurt.

"You'll be fighting with more experienced Garde members," I reassure her. "Plus, it's probably going to take two of us to get both of our Chests out of there."

Bernie Kosar barks from the front seat.

"Yeah, buddy," I say. "You're a part of this team, too."

The Chest is gone. My entire body sweats with panic. I almost vomit. Did the Mogadorians know it was up here the whole time? Why didn't they trap me in here when they had the chance? I float back onto the nave floor.

"It's gone, Adelina," I whisper.

"The Chest?"

"It's gone." I hug her and bury my face in her shoulder. She pulls something up over her head. It's a pale blue, almost transparent amulet attached to a beige cord. She carefully slips it over my hair until the amulet touches my neck. It's both cold and warm at the same time against my skin, and then it glows brightly. My breath is taken away.

"What is it?" I ask, covering the glow with my hands.

"Loralite, the most powerful gem on Lorien, found only at its core," she whispers. "I've hidden it this whole time. It's yours, and there's no use in hiding it any longer. *They* know who you are, with or without the amulet. I'll never forgive myself for not training you properly. Never. I'm sorry, Marina."

"It's okay," I say, feeling tears well up behind my eyes. All these years, this was all I had wanted from her. Understanding. Companionship. The acknowledgment of shared secrets.

We get closer to the airport, and the fear of splitting up weighs heavily on us. Sam tries to distract himself by studying the papers Six took from his dad's office. "I wish I could spread these out in some library's reference section."

"After West Virginia," I say. "I promise."

Six gives me and Sam careful instructions on how to find the map that'll take us to the cave. The rest of the trip passes in silence. We pull into a McDonald's parking lot a mile from Dulles.

"There are three things you guys have to know."

I sigh. "Why do I have the feeling that none of these things are going to be good?"

She ignores me and writes something on the back of a receipt. "First, here's the address that I'll be at in exactly two weeks at five p.m. Meet me there. If I'm not there, or, if for some reason you aren't, then return in another week and I'll do the same. If one of us doesn't make it after the second week, then I think we can assume the other isn't coming." She hands it to Sam, who reads it and shoves it into his jeans pocket.

"Two weeks, five p.m.," I say. "Got it. The second thing?"

"Bernie Kosar can't go into the cave with you."

"Why not?"

"Because it'll kill him. I don't understand it completely, but the Mogadorians control their beasts by filtering some sort of gas throughout the cave that only affects animals. If one leaves its designated place, it drops dead. When I finally got out, there was a heap of dead animals right at the cave's entrance. Animals that had gotten too close."

"Gross," Sam says.

"And the last thing?"

"Their cave is equipped with every detection device you can think of. Cameras, motion detectors, body temperature gauges, infrared. Everything. The Xitharis will allow you to get past everything; but once it's out of juice, look out, because they're going to find you."

"Where do we go?" I ask Adelina. Now that the Chest is gone, I feel directionless. Even with the amulet around my neck.

"We go to the belfry, and you use your telekinesis to get us into the yard. Then we run."

I take her hand and start running when a ball of fire suddenly roars from the back of the nave. The fire takes hold of the back pews and rages towards the high ceiling. The nave is now brighter than it is during Sunday Mass. A man in a trench coat with long blond hair walks confidently out of the northern hallway, our path to freedom, and every muscle in my body seems to come unwound at the same time; every inch of skin breaks out with goose bumps.

He stands watching us, the flames attacking several more rows of pews, and then a sneer slowly breaks across his face. From the corner of my eye, I can see Adelina reach into her dress and remove something, but I can't tell what it is. She stands beside me, her eyes aimed at the back of the nave. And then, ever so gently, she reaches up and pushes me behind her.

"I can't make up for lost time, or for the wrongs that I've done," she says. "But I'm certainly going to try. Don't let them catch you."

Just then the Mogadorian comes charging towards us, right down the center aisle. He's far larger than he looked from a distance, and he lifts a long sword that glows a fluorescent green color.

"Get as far from here as you can," Adelina says without turning. "Be brave, Marina."

Six places the Xitharis into the console's cupholder and then slides out of the SUV. "I'm running late," she says as she closes her door.

Sam and I both exit the vehicle after carefully studying the parking lot, the other cars, the people milling about.

I round the front of the hood and watch as Six hugs Sam.

"Kick some ass over there," he says.

They separate and she says, "Sam, thank you for helping us even when you don't have to. Thank you for being so amazing."

"*You're* amazing," he whispers. "Thanks for letting me tag along."

To my surprise and Sam's, Six steps forward and kisses him on the cheek. They smile at each other, and once Sam sees me over Six's shoulder, he blushes, opens the driver's door, and climbs inside.

I don't want her to go. As much as it pains me to admit it, I know I might never see her again. She looks at me with a certain tenderness that I'm not sure I've ever seen from her before.

"I like you, John. For the past few weeks, I've tried convincing myself that I don't, especially because of Sarah and how much of an idiot you can be . . . but I do. I do like you."

The words knock me over. I hesitate, then say "I like you, too."

"Do you still love Sarah?" she asks.

I nod. She deserves the truth. "I do, but it's all really confusing. She may have turned me in, and she may never want to see me again because I told her I thought you were pretty. But Henri once said that the Loric fall in love once in their life. And so that means I will always love Sarah."

Six shakes her head. "Don't take offense at what I'm about to say, okay? But Katarina never told me that. In fact, she told me stories about *multiple* loves she had on Lorien over the years. I'm sure Henri was a great man, and there's no doubt that he loved you with everything he had; but it sounds like he was a romantic and wanted you to follow in his footsteps. If he had one true love, then he wanted you to have one, too."

I'm silent, taking in her theory and pushing Henri's to the side.

She can tell I'm struggling with her words. "What I'm saying is, when the Loric fall in love, a lot of times it is for life. Obviously, it was for Henri. But not always."

And with that last sentence, Six steps towards me and I step towards her. The kiss that eluded us at the end of our walk in Florida now connects us with a passion I thought I'd reserved for Sarah and Sarah alone. I never want this kiss to end, but Sam turns on the engine and we separate.

"Sam likes you, too, you know," I say.

"And I like Sam."

I cock my head. "But you just said you like me."

She pushes me on my shoulder. "You like me *and* Sarah. I like you *and* Sam. Deal with it."

She turns invisible, but I can sense she's still in front of me.

"Please be careful over there, Six. I wish we could all stay together."

Her voice comes out of the air. "Me, too, John; but whoever is in Spain needs help. Can't you feel it?"

I can tell she's already gone by the time I say, "Yes."

___

I try to move, but I'm rooted in place. A glint of light in Adelina's hand catches my gaze, and I realize that what she removed from her dress was a kitchen knife. She runs towards the Mogadorian, and I start running down a pew the other way. With precision I've never seen before from her, she drops to the ground as the Mogadorian leaps and swings his sword for her throat. He misses her entirely, and as she comes back up she catches him flush with the knife's blade across his right thigh. Dark blood spurts out, but it does little to slow the Mogadorian; he turns and brings the sword back down. Adelina rolls forward, and it's with nothing short of awe that I watch her pass the knife across the Mogadorian's other leg as the momentum pushes her to her feet. How can I leave Adelina to fight alone?

I stop running, clench my hands into fists, but before I can do anything the man's left hand is wrapped around Adelina's throat, lifting her off the ground. His right hand drives the sword through her heart.

"No!" I yell, jumping on top of the pew's bench, rushing down the wood towards them.

Adelina's eyes shut, and with her very last breath, she thrusts her arm up and the knife's blade cuts an arc in the air in front of her. It falls from her hand and clatters to the floor. For a second I think she's missed, but I'm wrong. The cut was made so cleanly that a full two seconds pass before the dark blood spills out. He drops Adelina and falls to his knees, both hands clutched to the front of his throat to stop the bleeding, but the blood simply cascades through his fingers. I walk towards him and take a deep breath. I raise my hand and lift Adelina's knife from off the floor. I let it hover for a brief moment, and just as his eyes widen at the sight of it, I plunge it into his chest. He disintegrates before my eyes, his body turning to ash and spreading across the floor.

I drop to my knees and take Adelina's lifeless body into my arms, cupping the back of her head and pulling her to me. Our cheeks touch and I begin to cry. She's gone, and regardless of my recently discovered Legacy, I know there isn't anything I can do to bring her back. I need help.

CHAPTER
TWENTY-SEVEN

A GROWL COMES FROM MY LEFT, AND I LIFT MY head to see another man in a trench coat with long brown hair. I rush to my feet as the Mogadorian lifts his hand. A flash of light comes from it and hits me hard in the left shoulder, sending me flying backwards. The pain is instant and blinding. It runs down my arm, white-hot as though electricity has hit the bone and travels through it. My left hand feels dead, and with my right I reach up and touch the new gash on my shoulder. I lift my head and look up hopelessly at the Mogadorian.

The charm, I think. Adelina told me when we traveled that I couldn't be killed unless it was in the order set by the Elders. This wound could be bad enough to kill me. I look down at my ankle to see if there are six scars instead of the three I've been living with for the last several months, but nothing has changed. Then how can I be killed? How can I be hurt this badly . . .

unless *the charm has been broken.*

My eyes meet the Mogadorian's, and he bursts into a heap of ash. For a crazy moment I think the intensity of my own thoughts is what killed him, but then I see that standing just behind him is the Mogadorian from the café. The one with the book, the one I've been running from. I don't understand. Does their selfishness run so deep that they'll kill one another to be the one who kills me?

"Marina," he says.

"I, I can kill you," I say in a shaky voice full of sorrow. The blood continues flowing from my shoulder and runs down my arm. I look over at Adelina's body and start to cry.

"I'm not who you think I am," he says, jogging over to me and reaching out his hand. "Time is extremely short," he says. "I'm one of you, and I'm here to help."

I take his hand. What other choice do I have? He pulls me up, and from the nave before any others arrive. He leads me down the northern hallway and to the second floor, heading towards the belfry tower. My shoulder screams in pain with each step.

"Who are you?" I ask. A hundred different questions race through my head. If he's one of us, then why did it take him so long to tell me? Why torture me into believing he was one of them? Can I even trust him?

"Shhh," he whispers. "Keep quiet."

The musty hallway is silent, and as it narrows, I hear dozens of heavy footsteps on the floor below us. Finally, we reach the oak door. It opens just a crack, and a girl's head sticks out. I gasp. Auburn hair, curious brown eyes, small features. She's older by years, but there's no mistaking that it's her.

"Ella?" I ask.

She looks eleven years old, maybe twelve. Her face, which brightens at the sight of mine, is more slender now. Ella pulls the door open so we can enter.

"Hi, Marina," she says in a voice I don't recognize.

The man pulls me in, shutting the door. He wedges a thick wooden board between the door and the bottom stair, and the three of us rush up the circular stone steps. When we get to the belfry, I take another look at Ella. All I can do is stare at her, wide-eyed and confused, no longer feeling the blood rolling down my arm, dripping from my fingertips.

"Marina, my name is Crayton," the man says. "I'm sorry about your Cêpan. I wish I had gotten there sooner."

"Adelina's dead?" the older version of Ella asks.

"I don't understand," I say, still staring at Ella.

"We'll explain it all to you, I promise. There isn't much time. You're losing a lot of blood," Crayton says. "You can heal people, correct? Can you heal yourself?"

With all the confusion and running, I hadn't considered healing myself, but when I place the palm of my right hand over the gaping wound, I try it. The iciness tickles as the gash closes itself and the dead numbness is pushed from my hand and arm. After thirty seconds, I'm as good as new.

"Please be more careful with this," Crayton says. "It's far more vital than you know."

I look to where he's pointing. "My Chest!"

There's an explosion nearby. The tower sways, and dust and rocks drop from the ceiling and walls. More rocks fall as another blast takes me off my feet. I use my telekinesis to stop their descent, and I fling them out the window.

"They're searching for us, and it's not going to take long until they realize where we are," he says. He looks at Ella, and then at me. "She's one of you. A member of the Garde from Lorien."

"But she's not old enough," I say, shaking my head, unable to replace the younger version I've come to know with this older one. "I don't get it."

"Do you know what an Aeternus is?"

I shake my head.

"Show her, Ella."

While standing in front of me, Ella begins to change. Her arms shorten and her shoulders narrow; she loses twenty centimeters of height, and her weight drops significantly. The shrinking of her face shocks me the most, and quickly she looks like the tiny girl I've come to love.

"She's an Aeternus," Crayton says. "She's able to move

back and forth between different ages."

"I—I didn't know that was possible," I stutter.

"Ella's eleven years old," he says. "She came with me on a second ship from Lorien that left after yours. She was just a baby, only hours old. Loridas, the last remaining Elder, sacrificed himself so that Ella could assume his role and grow into his powers."

As I'm looking at Crayton, Ella slips her hand into mine as she's done so many times before; but it feels different now. I glance over and see that she's returned to the older, taller version of herself. Recognizing my discomfort, Ella shrinks back down, the four years quickly melting away until she's seven again.

"She's the tenth child," he says. "The tenth Elder. We created a rumor about her backstory, her parents dying in a car accident, and we sent her here to live with you to watch over you and be the eyes I needed."

"I'm sorry I couldn't tell you the truth, Marina," she says in her soft voice. "But I'm the best secret-keeper in the whole world, just like you said."

"I know you are," I say.

"I was just waiting for Adelina to give you your Chest," she says, smiling.

"Do you know who the tenth Elder was?" Crayton asks. "Changing his age is how Loridas was able to live as long as he did, even after the other Elders had passed away. Each time he grew old, he made himself young again, and assumed the vitality that comes with it."

"Are you Ella's Cêpan?"

"Only in the surrogate sense of the word. Since she was just born, she hadn't been assigned a Cêpan yet."

"I thought you were a Mogadorian," I say.

"I know, but only because you misinterpreted the clues. This morning when I was talking to Héctor, I was trying to show you I was a friend."

"But why didn't you just come and get me when you arrived? Why send Ella in?"

"I tried approaching Adelina first, but she cast me out the second she knew who I was, and we needed you to have your Chest. I couldn't pull you away without it," he says. "So I sent Ella in, and she started looking for it even before you asked her to. The Mogadorians have known your general location for a good while now, and I've done my best to keep them off your trail. Killing some, well, killing most, but also planting stories in villages hundreds of miles away, about kids doing amazing things, like about a boy who lifted a car above his head and a girl who could walk across a lake. It was working until they discovered you were in Santa Teresa; but even then, they still didn't know which one you were. Then Ella found the Chest and you opened it, and that's when I came here, to talk to you in private. When you opened the Chest, it led the Mogadorians right here."

"Because I opened the Chest?"

"Yes. Go ahead, open it up now."

I let go of Ella's hand and grab hold of the lock. I'm sick thinking that I'm able to open it on my own, now that Adelina is dead. I remove the lock and toss the lid open. The small crystal is still glowing a faint blue.

"Don't touch that," he says. "The fact that it's glowing means a Macrocosm is in orbit somewhere. If you touch it now, it will tell them exactly where you are. I don't know whose Macrocosm is operational, but I'm pretty sure the Mogadorians have stolen somebody's," he finishes. I haven't the slightest idea of what he's talking about.

"Macrocosm?" I ask.

He shakes his head, frustrated. "There isn't time to explain it all," he says. "Relock it." He opens his mouth to say more, but is interrupted by banging on the door at the bottom of the stairs. We can hear muffled bursts of foreign voices.

"We have to go," Crayton says, rushing to the back of the room and grabbing a large black suitcase. He flings it open, revealing ten different guns, a handful of grenades, several daggers. He shrugs his coat to the floor and reveals a leather vest, and he rushes to strap every piece of weaponry to it before slipping his coat back on.

The Mogadorians ram the door below with a heavy object, and we hear footsteps enter the stairwell. Crayton removes one of the guns and snaps a clip into it.

"The burning symbol on the mountain," I say. "Was it you?"

He nods. "I waited too long, I'm afraid, and when you opened the Chest it became impossible to slip away under their gaze. So I created the biggest beacon I could, and now we have to hope the others have seen it, and that they're on the way. Otherwise . . ." He trails off. "Well, otherwise we're out of options. We have to get to the lake now. It's our only chance."

I have no idea what lake he's talking about, or why he wants to go there, but my whole body is trembling. I just want to get away.

The footsteps are closer. Ella grabs hold of my hand, back to her eleven-year-old self. Crayton pulls the slide on the gun, and I hear a bullet clicking into place. He aims it at the belfry's entryway.

"You have a very good friend in town," he says.

"Héctor?" I ask, suddenly understanding why the two of them were talking in the café this morning. Crayton wasn't spreading lies, but rather telling the truth.

"Yes, and let's hope he keeps his word."

"Héctor will," I say, certain that's true regardless of what Crayton has asked him to do. "It's in his name," I add.

"Grab the Chest," Crayton says.

I reach down and take the Chest in my left arm just as

we hear the footsteps reach the last curves of the stairwell.

"Both of you, stay close to me," Crayton says, his eyes moving from Ella to me. "She was born able to change ages, but she's young and hasn't developed any Legacies yet. Keep her close. And don't let go of that Chest."

"Don't worry, Marina. I'm fast," she says, smiling.

"You two ready?"

"Ready," Ella says, tightening her hand around mine.

"They're all going to be wearing body armor that would stop almost every bullet here on Earth," Crayton says, "but I've soaked mine in Loricyde, and there isn't a shield here that could stop them. I'm going to mow every damn one of them down." His eyes narrow. "Keep your fingers crossed that Héctor's outside the gates waiting for us."

"He'll be there," I say.

Then Crayton pulls the trigger, and he doesn't let go until every bullet's been fired.

CHAPTER
TWENTY-EIGHT

WE KEEP THE WINDOWS DOWN, SAYING LITTLE, unnerved by the task ahead. Sam keeps a firm grip on the wheel as the highway winds through Virginia.

"You think Six will make it?" Sam asks.

"I'm sure she'll make it, but who knows what she'll find."

"That was a hell of a kiss you two had."

I open my mouth and then shut it. A minute later I say, "She likes you, too, you know."

"Yeah, as a friend."

"Actually, Sam, she *like-likes* you."

Sam blushes. "Sure. I could tell by the way she shoved her tongue in your mouth."

"She kissed you, too, dude. I *saw* it." I slap him in the chest with the back of my hand, and I can see he's replaying the kiss in his mind. "After I kissed her I asked if she knew you liked her and—"

We're jerked over the double yellow line on the road. "You did *what*?"

"Dude, relax. Don't kill us." Sam glides us back onto our side of the road. "She said she liked you, too."

A devilish grin spreads across Sam's face. "Interesting. It's kind of hard to believe this," Sam finally says.

"God, Sam. Why would I lie about it?"

"No, I can't believe that this whole thing is real. That you're real or that Six is real, or that a hostile race of aliens has scattered themselves across the planet and nobody seems to know it. I mean, they've hollowed out a mountain in the middle of the state. How has it not been found? What did they do with all the dirt and rocks they removed? Even as scarcely populated as parts of West Virginia are, surely somebody had to stumble across it at some point. Hikers or hunters. Pilots of small planes. What about satellite imaging? And who knows how many other base camps or outposts or whatever you want to call them they have on Earth. I just don't understand how they move about so freely."

"I agree," I say. "I don't know how either, but something tells me we probably don't know the half of it. You remember the very first conspiracy theory you told me?"

"No," Sam says.

"We were talking about an entire Montana town

being abducted, and you said the government allowed abductions in exchange for technology. Remember now?"

"Vaguely. Sure."

"Well, that makes sense now. Maybe technology has nothing to do with it, and maybe the government isn't allowing abductions; but I really think some agreement has to be in place. Because you're right, there's no way they're traveling unnoticed. There are way, way, way too many of them."

Sam doesn't respond. I look over and see that he's smiling.

"Sam?" I ask.

"I was just thinking of where I might be at this exact moment if you guys hadn't come along. Probably alone in my basement, collecting more conspiracy theories and wondering if my dad's still alive. That's how it was for years. But what's awesome is that I really do believe he's alive now. He's somewhere, John. I know it. And I know it because of you guys."

"I hope so," I say. "It's pretty cool that Henri came to Ohio to try to find him, and you and I became friends almost immediately. It's like fate."

Sam smiles. "Or a cosmic aligning."

"Nerd," I say.

After a pause, Sam asks, "Hey, John? You're positive that skeleton in the well wasn't my dad, right?"

"Absolutely, dude. He was Loric and huge. Bigger than any human."

"What's your best guess, then? Who was it?"

"I really don't know. I just hope he wasn't too important."

Four hours pass, and finally we see a sign pointing the way to Ansted, six miles ahead. We fall silent. Sam makes the turn and navigates a precarious two-lane road that twists up the mountain until we pass the town's border. We drive through it and turn left at the only stoplight in town.

"Hawks Nest, right?"

"Yep, a mile or two down the road," Sam says, and it's there we'll find the map that Six drew three years ago.

The map is exactly where Six said it would be, hidden at Hawks Nest State Park, overlooking the New River. Exactly forty-seven steps down the Gysp Trail, Sam, Bernie Kosar, and I reach a tree with *E6* deeply carved into its side. From there, we leave the trail, taking thirty steps past the tree to the right. That's followed by a hard left turn, and then, a tenth of a mile away, we see a tree that towers over the others. In the small gap at the base of its twisted trunk, safely tucked away in a black plastic box, is the map that leads to the cave.

We make our way back to the SUV and drive another fifteen miles, ultimately pulling down a muddy, deserted road. It's the closest any road can get us, five miles due north of the cave. Sam takes the address Six wrote out of his pocket and puts it in the glove compartment. "On second thought." He removes it and puts it back into his pocket. "As safe as anywhere," he says.

I drop the Xitharis and some duct tape into Six's backpack that she left behind, and Sam slips the bag over his shoulders. I flip my dagger over in my hand and then stuff it into my back pocket.

We step out and I lock the doors, Bernie Kosar running circles around my legs. There's only a few hours left of daylight, which doesn't leave us much time. Even with the benefit of my hands, I can't imagine finding the cave without the sun to help us along.

Sam holds the map in his hands. At its right side Six has drawn a heavy X. A winding path five miles long connects the X with where we are now, marked on the map's left side. Along the way we'll skirt a riverbed while passing various landmarks noted for their physical descriptions, all of which are carefully marked to keep us on track. Turtle Rock. Fisherman's Pole. Circle Plateau. King's Throne. Lover's Kiss. Lookout Point.

Sam and I lift our heads at the same time, and we both see the rock a quarter mile away with an uncanny resemblance to a turtle's shell. Bernie Kosar barks.

"I guess we know which direction to head first," Sam says.

And off we go, following the path set by the map. There's no trail, nothing that might allude to these mountains having been trampled by beings of another world, or even by beings of this one. Once we reach Turtle Rock, Sam spots a fallen tree that hangs over the cliff side at a forty-five degree angle, and thus looks like a fishing pole patiently waiting for a bite. And we hike on, following the trail as the sun lowers in the western sky.

Each step taken is another chance to turn around and walk away. But neither of us does. "You're a hell of a friend, Sam Goode," I tell him.

"You're not so bad yourself," he replies. And then, "I can't stop my hands from shaking."

After passing King's Throne, which is a tall slender rock that looks like a high-back chair, I immediately spot two tall trees leaning against one another at slight angles, their branches appearing like arms wrapped around each other in an embrace. And I smile, for a brief moment forgetting how terribly scared I am.

"Only one more to go," Sam says, pulling me back into the clutches of reality.

We reach Lookout Point five minutes later. All told, the hike has taken an hour and ten minutes, and the shadows are long and stretched as the last light of dusk drains away. Without warning, a deep growl bellows beside me. I look down. Bernie Kosar's teeth are flashed, his fur bristling along his spine, his eyes pointed in the direction of the cave. He begins backing away from it.

"It's okay, Bernie Kosar," I say, patting his back.

Sam and I drop to the ground and lay on our stomachs, both staring across the small valley at the cave's almost indiscernible entrance. It's far larger than I'd imagined, probably twenty feet wide and tall, but also much better hidden. There's something covering it, a net or a tarp maybe, making it blend in with its surroundings; you'd have to know it's there to be able to see it.

"Perfect location," Sam whispers.

"Totally."

My nervousness quickly turns to full-blown terror. As mysterious as the cave is, one thing I know for sure is that there'll be no shortage of things—weapons, beasts or traps—that could kill us. I could die within the next twenty minutes. And Sam could, too.

"Whose idea was this, anyway?" I ask.

Sam snorts. "Yours."

"Well, I have some stupid ideas sometimes."

"True, but we have to get your Chest somehow."

"There's so much in there that I don't even know how to use yet . . . but maybe they do," I say. Then something catches my eye.

"Look at the ground in front of the entrance," I say, pointing to a smattering of dark objects by the cave's entrance.

"At the rocks?"

"Those aren't rocks. Those are dead animals," I say.

Sam shakes his head. "Great," he says.

I shouldn't be surprised since Six told us about it, but the sight of them fills me with even more dread, which I didn't think possible. My mind races.

"All right," I say, sitting up. "There's no time like the present."

I kiss the top of Bernie Kosar's head, then run my hand down the length of his back, hoping this won't be the last time I ever see him. He tells me not to go, and I communicate back that I have to, no other choice. "You're the best, BK. I love you, buddy."

Then I stand. I take the bottom of my shirt in my right hand so I can remove the Xitharis from the bag without touching it.

Sam messes with the buttons on his digital watch, putting it in stopwatch mode. We won't be able to read its face once we're invisible, but when the hour is up, the watch will beep—though I imagine by then we'll have figured it out.

"Ready?" I ask.

Together we take our first step, then a second, and

then we're hiking down the trail that may very well lead to our imminent doom. I turn around only once, when I've nearly reached the cave, and see Bernie Kosar staring at us.

CHAPTER
TWENTY-NINE

WE GET AS CLOSE TO THE CAVE AS WE CAN WITH-out being seen, and we duck behind a tree. I place the Xitharis stone on the sticky side of a section of duct tape. Sam watches with his fingers pinched around his stopwatch.

"Ready?" I ask.

He nods. I press the Xitharis and the tape to the very bottom of my sternum. I vanish instantly and Sam hits the watch's button, eliciting a soft digital beep. I snatch Sam's hand, and together we lurch around the tree and speed to the cave. It's all about the task at hand now, and with that in mind I'm no longer as nervous.

The cave is covered with a large camouflage tarp. We navigate through the graveyard of dead animals, being careful not to step on any, which is hard to do without the luxury of seeing your feet. There are no

Mogs outside, and I hurry forward and flick the tarp aside a little too forcefully. Sam and I stumble in and four guards jump up from their seats and raise cylindrical cannons like the one that was held to my forehead that night in Florida. We stand as still as statues for a brief moment, and then quietly sneak past, hoping they'll attribute the tarp's sudden disturbance to the outside wind.

There's a cool breeze coming from a ventilation system and the air is oddly fresh, which I hadn't expected considering it's laced with poisonous gas. The gray walls are polished smooth like flint; electrical conduit connects dim lights evenly spaced twenty feet apart.

We pass several more scouts and slither by undetected. The anxiety of the ticking clock racks us both with stress. We jog, we sprint, we tiptoe, we walk. And when the tunnel narrows and declines steadily, we sidestep down it. The cool air grows hot and stifling, and a crimson glow at the end of the tunnel comes into view. We shuffle towards it until finally reaching the cave's beating heart.

The cavernous hall is far larger than I'd imagined based on Six's description. A long, continuous ledge runs along the circular walls and spirals all the way, from top to bottom, giving the overall appearance of a beehive; and the place is every bit as busy as one, too—there are literally hundreds of Mogs in sight, crossing the precarious stone arched bridges, entering and exiting tunnels. The deep floor and the vast ceiling are separated by a half mile, and Sam and I are situated very close to the middle. Two massive pillars sprout up from the floor and reach all the way to the ceiling, keeping the whole thing from caving in. The number of passageways around us is endless.

"My God," Sam whispers in awe, taking it all in. "It'd take months to explore this entire thing."

My eyes are drawn to the lake of glowing green liquid down below. Even from so far away, the heat off of it makes it hard to breathe. But despite the near roasting temperatures, twenty to thirty Mogs work around it, retrieving carts full of the bubbling stuff and quickly taking it away. Past the green lake, my eyes focus on something else.

"I think we can pretty much guess what we'll find down that tunnel with the giant bars," I whisper. It's three times the height and width of the passageway that carried us here, and a checkered pattern of heavy iron bars covers it, keeping caged whatever beasts are inside. We can hear them howl from below, deep and almost sorrowful. One thing is immediately clear: their numbers are far from few.

"It'll literally take months," Sam says again in a disbelieving whisper.

"Well, we have less than an hour," I whisper back. "So we better hurry."

"I think we can put a big X through all those dark narrow tunnels that look obstructed."

"I agree. We should start with the one directly across from us," I say, looking at what appears to be the central room's main artery, wider and better lit than the others, the one with the greatest number of Mogs coming and going. The bridge over to it is just a long arch of solid rock that, at most, is two feet wide. "Think you can make it across that archway?"

"We're about to find out," Sam replies.

"Lead or follow?" I ask.

"Let me lead."

Sam takes his first few steps uncertainly. Since we have to keep our hands locked, for the first forty feet or so we shuffle along sideways. It takes forever, and if we're to get to the other side and back again, there's no way we can do it at this pace.

"Just don't look down," I say to Sam.

"Don't be cliché," he responds, squaring his body. We move ahead slowly, and I wish I could see my feet for just this obstacle. I'm so focused on not falling that I don't feel Sam stop ahead of me, which causes me to stumble into him, nearly knocking us both off the bridge.

"What are you doing?" I ask, my heart thudding in

my chest. I look up and see why he's stopped. Racing towards us is a Mogadorian soldier. He comes charging across in a jog, and he's already so close there's hardly time to react.

"There's nowhere to go," Sam says. The soldier continues forward, cradling a wrapped bundle in his arms, and when he's close enough I feel Sam crouch. A second later, the Mog's feet are swept out from under him, completely catching the soldier off guard. He falls over the side of the bridge and catches himself with one hand as the bundle he was carrying drops away. The Mog cries out in pain as my invisible foot crushes his fingers, and he lets go and drops through the air, splattering far below with a sickly thud.

Sam races us forward before any further calamities arise. Every single Mog in the area has stopped in midstride, staring at one another with confused expressions. I wonder if they believe what just happened was an accident, or if they're now on alert.

Sam squeezes my hand in relief when we've made it across, and he lurches ahead, having gained a world of confidence from killing the soldier.

The next corridor is wide and busy, and it doesn't take long for Sam and me to realize we're heading in the wrong direction; the rooms we pass are exclusively private, and the entire wing seems to be where the Mogs live: caves with beds, a large open cafeteria with hundreds of tables, a shooting range. We rush down a nearby corridor, but the result is the same. And then we try a third.

We follow the winding tunnel deeper into the mountain. Several tributaries lead away from the main drag, and Sam and I randomly turn down them based on nothing more than gut feeling. Aside from the main hall we entered, the rest of the mountain is nothing more than an interconnected network of damp stone corridors, off of which various rooms house research centers with examination tables, computers and shiny, sharp instruments. We pass several scientific laboratories that we both wish we had the time to investigate further as we rush by. We've probably run a mile, maybe two, and with each new corridor that turns up nothing, stress floods my veins.

"We can't have more than fifteen minutes left, John."

"I'm aware of that," I whisper, desperate and irritated and quickly losing hope.

When we take the next turn and rush up a steady incline, we pass the thing I'd feared most: a room full of prison cells. Sam stops in midstride and keeps a firm grip on my hand, causing me to stop as well. Twenty to thirty Mogadorians guard more than forty cells, all lined up in a row, with heavy steel doors. In front of each door, there's a bubbling blue force field pulsing with electricity.

"Look at all those cells," Sam says. I know he's thinking of his dad.

"Wait a second," I say, the solution flashing into my head from out of nowhere. It's so obvious.

"What?" Sam asks.

"I know where the Chest is," I say.

"Seriously?"

"So stupid of me," I whisper. "Sam, if you could pick just one place in this entire hellhole where you'd absolutely refuse to go, where would that place be?"

"In the pit with the howling beasts," he answers without a second's hesitation.

"Exactly," I say. "Come on, let's go."

I lead him back up the corridor that'll empty out at the cave's center; but before we've left the cells behind, a door clangs open and Sam jerks his hand to stop me.

"Look," he says.

The nearest cell door stands wide-open. Two guards enter. They speak angrily for ten seconds in their native tongue, and when they exit they're clutching the arms of a pale, emaciated man in his late twenties. He's weak to the point of having trouble walking, and Sam's grip tightens as the guards shove him forward. One of them unlocks a second door, and all three disappear through it.

"Who do you think they have locked up in there?" he asks as I pull him forward.

"We gotta go, Sam," I say. "We don't have the time."

"They're torturing humans, John," he says when we finally reach the central hive. "Human beings."

"I know," I say, scanning the mammoth room for the quickest route down. There are Mogs everywhere, but I've become so used to passing by them that they no longer bother me. And besides, something tells me I'm about to find far scarier things than scouts and soldiers.

"People with families who probably have no idea where they've disappeared to," Sam whispers.

"I know, I know," I say. "Come on, we'll talk about it when we're out of here. Maybe Six will have some sort of plan."

We sprint around the spiral ledge and start down a tall ladder, but find it's nearly impossible to do so while holding the person's hand above you. I look down. There's still a far way to go.

"We have to jump," I say to Sam. "Otherwise it'll take ten minutes to get all the way down there."

"Jump?" he asks incredulously. "It'll kill us."

"Don't worry," I assure him. "I'll catch you."

"How the hell are you going to catch me if I'm holding your hand the whole time?"

But there isn't time to argue or debate. I take a deep breath, and leap from the ledge a hundred feet above the cave's bottom. Sam howls, but the continuous clatter of manufacturing drowns out the noise. My feet hit the unyielding stone, and the force knocks me backwards; but I keep a firm grip on Sam, who lands on top of me.

"Never again are we doing that," he says, standing.

The ground floor is so hot it's nearly impossible to breathe, but we sprint around the green lake towards the massive gate keeping the beasts locked away. When we reach it, a cool wind gusts through the bars, and I realize that the regular blasts of fresh air prevent any of the gas from entering this tunnel.

"John, I really don't think there's any time left," Sam pleads.

"I know," I say, letting a group of ten or so Mogs exit ahead of us.

We enter a dark tunnel. The walls look mucus covered, and barred chambers line each side of the shaft. Down the middle of the ceiling ten huge industrial fans blow, all pointed towards the entry we just came through, keeping the air cool and moist. Some of the locked chambers are small, though others are large, and bursting out of them all are feral and ferocious sounds. In the cage on our left are twenty to thirty krauls jumping over one another while letting loose shrill yips. Imprisoned on our right is a pack of demonic-looking dogs the size of wolves, with yellow eyes and no hair. Beside them stands a creature that looks like a troll, complete with a wart-covered nose. In a larger cell across the way a massive piken not unlike the one who busted through the prison wall that morning paces back and forth, sniffing the air.

"We might as well not even bother with these smaller rooms," I say. "If my Chest is here, it'll be in the biggest room at the end of this tunnel. I don't even want to take a guess at what kind of beast needs a door that large to fit through."

"We're down to seconds, John."

"We better hurry then," I say, pulling Sam forward while quickly taking in the different horrors corralled here: gargoylelike winged creatures, monsters with six arms and red skin, several more pikens standing twenty feet tall, a wide reptilian mutant with trident-shaped horns, a monster with skin so transparent that its internal organs are on display.

"Whoa," I say, stopping at a group of rounded tanks and vessels, most of which are silver, though two are copper colored and lined with heat gauges. Some kind of boiler room, I guess.

"So that's what's keeping this place going," Sam says.

"This has to be it," I reply. The tallest silo goes to the ceiling, and every tank is connected with heavy pipes, spouts, and aluminum ducts. Beside the silo, a control panel is affixed to the wall with a heap of electrical wires pouring out.

"Come on," Sam says, impatiently jerking my hand.

Together we run the rest of the way to the tunnel's

end. There's a massive door, forty to fifty feet tall and wide, made entirely of steel. To its right is a small wooden door. It's unlocked, and instantly I see why.

"Holy God," Sam whispers, taking in the beast's enormity.

I'm momentarily stunned myself, and all I can do is stare at it: a hulking mass slumped in the room's far corner. Its eyes are closed and it breathes rhythmically. The beast must be fifty feet tall when standing, and from what I can tell its dark body is shaped like a man's, but with much longer arms.

"I want nothing to do with this place," Sam says.

"You sure?" I ask, nudging him so his gaze leaves the monster. "Look."

There, in the center of the room, at eye level atop a thick stone pedestal, is my Chest. And right beside it sits a second one, almost identical in appearance. Both of them there for the taking. Except for the iron bars around them, which are housed beneath a humming and crackling electrical force field surrounded by a moat of the steaming green liquid. And the slumbering giant.

"That's not Six's Chest," I say.

"What are you talking about? Who else's would it be?" Sam asks, confused.

"They found us, Sam. In Florida, they found us by opening Six's Chest."

"Right, I know."

"But look at the padlock on it. Why would they put the lock back on a Chest that they probably had a hell of a time getting into in the first place? I think that one's never been opened."

"Maybe you're right."

"It could be any of ours," I whisper, shaking my head while staring up at them both. "Number Five's or Nine's or anyone's who isn't dead yet."

"So they stole the Chest and didn't kill the Garde?"

"Like they did with me. Or maybe the Mogs caught one of them and they're being held here like Six was," I say.

Sam doesn't get a chance to answer, because just then the alarm on his wristwatch begins to beep. Three seconds later it's followed by the whine of a hundred sirens echoing off the walls of the cave.

"Aw hell," I say, turning my head. "I can see you, Sam."

He nods, a panicked look on his face. He lets go of my hand. "I can see you, too."

When I look over Sam's shoulder, the beast's eyes have come open—blank and white—narrowing in our direction.

CHAPTER THIRTY

THE GUNFIRE MAKES MY EARS RING LONG AFTER it's stopped. Smoke rises from the end of the barrel, but Crayton wastes no time and drops the gun's clip and snaps another in place. Heaping mounds of ash have given the air a thick haze. We stand waiting, Ella and I behind Crayton. He keeps the gun raised, his finger hovering on the trigger. A Mogadorian climbs into the entryway with a cannon of his own, but Crayton fires first, cutting him in half and hurling him backwards. The Mogadorian explodes before he hits the wall. A second jumps into view, wielding the same flashing weapon that tore my shoulder downstairs, but Crayton disposes of it before any light comes forth.

"Well, they know where we are now. Come on," he yells, rushing forward and down the stairs before I can offer to float us out the window. Ella and I follow, still holding hands. Crayton stops after the second curve of the stairwell, pressing his fingers to his eyes. "There's too much ash in my eyes. I can't see anything," he says. "Marina, take the lead. If there's anything up ahead, yell and get the hell out of the way."

I keep the Chest tucked beneath my left arm and Ella stays in the middle, holding my hand and Crayton's. I lead them down and out the broken oak door just as the tower above us explodes.

I scream, ducking down and pulling Ella with me. Crayton instinctively begins firing. The gun unloads a rapid stream of ammunition—eight to ten bullets per second—and I can see an entire group of Mogadorians drop. Crayton stops firing.

"Marina?" he asks, nodding his head forward without seeing me.

I turn and study the hallway, thick with ash. "I think it's clear," I say; and the second the words leave my mouth, a Mogadorian leaps out of an open doorway and fires, sending a flashing white meteor raging towards us too bright to look at. We drop just in time, and the white death misses us by a hair. Crayton quickly lifts the gun and returns a barrage of bullets, killing the Mogadorian instantly.

I lead us forward. I have no idea how many of them Crayton just killed, but the ash stands thick on the floor, covering our feet and ankles. We pause at the top of the steps. Light from the windows comes through the fading ash, and Crayton has cleared his eyes. He takes the lead position, clutching the gun tightly to his chest while staying hidden behind the corner. Once we turn, all that separates us from the door leading outside are these steps, a short hallway, the back of the nave, and the main vestibule. Crayton takes a deep breath, nods his head, and then turns, dropping the barrel of the gun, ready to fire. But there's nothing to fire at.

"Come on," he grunts.

We follow him and he escorts us across the nave's rear, which is black with fire damage. For a brief moment I glimpse Adelina's body, looking small from as far away as we are. My heart aches seeing her. *Be brave, Marina,* her words echo.

An explosion erupts against the outside wall on our right side. The stones blow inward, and I instinctively lift my hand and prevent any of them from hitting Ella and me. But Crayton gets hit hard, and he smashes against the wall to our left, landing with a grunt. The gun rattles away from him, and a Mogadorian enters the cathedral through the newly created hole. He's holding a cannon; and in one fluid motion, I heave the Mogadorian backwards with my mind, bring Crayton's gun into my hand, and pull the trigger. The gun's kick is a lot harder than I expected, and I almost drop it; but I recover quickly and keep firing until the Mogadorian is reduced to ash.

"Here," I say, pushing the gun into Ella's hands; and

in the comfortable way she takes it, I can tell she's no stranger to firearms.

I rush to Crayton. His arm is broken, and blood seeps from gashes on his head and face. But his eyes are open and he seems alert. I slap my hands on his wrist and close my eyes, the iciness crawling over my body and extending to Crayton. I watch the bones in his arm move under the skin, and the gashes on his face seal and disappear. His chest expands and contracts so fast I think his lungs are going to explode, but then he's calm again. He sits up and moves his arm fluidly.

"Nice job," he says.

He takes the gun from Ella, and we climb through the hole in the wall and out into Santa Teresa's front grounds. I don't see a single person as Ella and I run ahead and pass through the iron gates while Crayton sweeps his gun back and forth, looking for any reason to fire it. My eyes are drawn over Crayton's left shoulder to a quick burst of red from the cathedral's roof. With a loud blast, the discharged rocket surges towards Crayton. I stare at the rocket's tip and raise my hands, concentrating harder than I ever have, and at the very last instant I'm able to slightly alter the rocket's path. It misses him and angles off towards a mountain, where it hits it with a plume of fire. Crayton rushes us through the gates with eyes alert and the gun aimed. He pulls up and spins around.

He shakes his head, and from behind us we hear the

church doors thrust open.

"He isn't here," Crayton says, and just before he turns around to begin firing, the sound of squealing tires pierces the air. The plastic covering that had kept the truck concealed falls off and its back side fishtails as Héctor, wide-eyed behind the wheel, floors it. He comes racing our way and slams on the brakes when he reaches us. The truck screeches to a halt, and Héctor reaches across the seat and throws open the passenger-side door. I toss my Chest beside Héctor, and Ella and I jump in. Crayton stays out just long enough to empty his gun at the Mogadorians emerging from the church door. Several drop, but there are far too many to get them all. Crayton jumps in and slams the door, and the tires bite into the cobblestones in an attempt to find traction. There's the sound of another rocket nearing, but the tires catch and we go racing down Calle Principal.

"I love you, Héctor," I say. I can't help it; the sight of him behind the wheel fills me with such warmth that it brims over the edge.

"I love you, too, Marina. I always told you, stick with Héctor Ricardo; he'll take care of you."

"I never doubted it once," I say, which is a lie; I had doubted it this morning.

We reach the bottom of the hill and fly past the signs announcing the town limits.

I twist around to peer out the back window as Santa

Teresa quickly fades behind us. I know it's the last time I'll ever see it and though I've waited years to leave, it now holds the sacredness of being Adelina's last resting place. Soon the town is gone, left behind.

"Thank you, Señorita Marina," Héctor says.

"For what?"

"I know it was you who cured my dear mother. She told me it was you, that you were her angel; and I'll never be able to repay you for it."

"You already have, Héctor. I was very happy to help."

He shakes his head. "I haven't yet, but I'm sure going to try."

While Crayton refills both clips and takes inventory of his ammo, Héctor navigates the windy and unpredictable road. We bounce and skid along the sharp turns and sudden hills. But despite the speed, it doesn't take long for a convoy of vehicles to be seen in the distance behind us.

"Don't worry about them," Crayton says. "Just get us to the lake."

Even though the truck is barreling down the road, the convoy closes the gap. After ten minutes, a flash of light sails just over the truck and explodes into the countryside ahead of us. Héctor instinctively jerks his head down.

"My God!" he says.

Crayton turns around and breaks the back window with the butt of his gun, then fires. The lead vehicle is upended, which makes us all cheer in celebration.

"That should keep them far enough back," Crayton says, quickly reloading the gun's clip.

And it does for a few minutes, but as the road grows more precarious and twists down the mountain at sharp declines, the vehicles catch right back up to us. Héctor mutters under his breath as he whips around each bend, the gas pedal buried, the truck's back tires swinging frighteningly over the edge of the towering cliff.

"Careful, Héctor," Crayton says. "Don't kill us before we get there. At least give us a chance."

"Héctor is in control," Héctor replies, bringing no comfort whatsoever to Crayton, who keeps a white-knuckled grip on the headrest in front of him.

The only refuge is the road's perpetual turns, which keep the Mogadorians from getting a straight shot, though they try anyway.

As we race around a particularly sharp bend, Héctor can't turn us quickly enough and we go off the edge of the road. At a seventy-five-degree angle, the truck races down the dense mountainside, smashing through saplings, bouncing off boulders, barely avoiding thick trees. Ella and I scream. Crayton yells as he flies forward and slams into the windshield. Héctor doesn't say a word; he clenches his teeth and maneuvers us around and over obstacles until we miraculously land on another road. The truck's hood is severely dented and smoking, but the engine is still running.

"This is a, uh, shortcut," Héctor says. He tries the gas pedal, and we quickly rumble down the new road.

"I think we lost them," says Crayton, looking up the cliff.

I pat Héctor's shoulder and laugh. Crayton sticks the barrel of his gun out the back window and waits.

Eventually the lake comes into view. I wonder why Crayton believes the lake will save us.

"What's the big deal about the lake?" I ask.

"You didn't think I'd come to find you with just Ella, did you?"

For a moment I think to tell him that up until a few hours ago I thought he had come to kill me. But soon the Mogadorians appear behind us again, and Crayton turns around while Héctor's eyes dart up to the rearview mirror.

"This is going to be close," Crayton says.

"We'll get out of it, Papa," Ella says, looking at Crayton; and hearing her call him that fills my heart with affection. He smiles warmly at her, then nods. Ella squeezes my hand. "You'll love Olivia," she says to me.

"Who's Olivia?" I ask, but she doesn't get a chance to answer before the road turns at a ninety-degree angle and declines sharply towards the lake ahead. Ella tenses in my arms as the road ends, and Héctor barely lets up on the gas as the truck rams straight through a chain-link gate that surrounds the lake. We hit a slight bump, and the truck's tires leave the ground entirely before landing with a thud and bouncing on the shore. Héctor speeds straight for the water, and just before we reach it, he slams on the brakes and brings us skidding to a stop. Crayton shoulders open the passenger-side door and dashes towards the lake, rushing straight into the water until it reaches his knees. With the gun still in his left hand, he hurls an object as far as he can with his right and begins muttering something in a language I don't understand.

"Come on!" he screams, thrusting his hands up in the air as though offering encouragement. "Come on, Olivia!"

Héctor, Ella, and I rush out and run up near him. I have the Chest under my arm and in an instant I see that the water has begun to crest and bubble in the lake's middle.

"Marina, do you know what a Chimæra is?"

But I don't get to answer, because just then a lone Mogadorian vehicle, a tanklike Humvee with a gun mounted on top, erupts onto the scene and speeds down the hill. As it comes right at us, in the water, Crayton unloads a barrage of bullets into the windshield. The vehicle instantly goes out of control, crashing straight into the back of Héctor's truck. It creates a deafening bang, followed by the crush of grinding metal and breaking glass. As the dozens of other vehicles in the convoy rumble down the last hill and begin firing, the world erupts in fire and smoke as explosions rock the beach, causing all four of us to hit the ground. Sand and water rain down, and we scramble back to our feet. Crayton snags me by the collar.

"Get out of here!" he yells.

I take Ella's hand and we run as fast as we can around the left side of the lake. Crayton begins firing; but it's not one gun that I hear but two, and I can only hope it's Héctor's finger pulling the second trigger.

We race towards a cluster of trees sloping down from the mountainside, jutting out all the way to the water's bank. Our footsteps slap on the wet stones, and Ella's accelerated pace matches my own. Gunfire continues to rattle through the air; and just as it lets up, a loud animal roar booms over our head, causing me to stop short. I turn to look at the creature able to create such a paralyzing call, knowing it's not of this world. A long, muscular neck protrudes ten or fifteen stories out of the water, the flesh a gleaming gray. At the end of it, a giant lizard head separates its pebbled lips to show an enormous set of teeth.

"Olivia!" Ella cheers.

Olivia rears her head and lets loose another earsplitting roar, and in the middle of it, a series of high-pitched yipping sounds roll down from the mountain. I look up and see a pack of small beasts descending towards the lake.

I gasp. "What are those?" I ask Ella.

"Krauls. Lots of them."

Olivia's neck is fully emerged and thirty stories high

now, and as the rest of her body surfaces, her neck widens and her torso thickens. The Mogadorians immediately fire at her, and Olivia slams her head down on several at a time, creating large piles of ash. I can see the dark figures of Crayton and Héctor, both with guns blazing. The Mogadorians fall back as a hundred krauls enter the lake and swim towards Olivia. The creatures leap out of the water and attack. Many claw their way up Olivia's back and rip at the base of her neck. The lake water is soon streaked with blood.

"No!" Ella screams.

She tries running back, but I grab hold of her arm.

"We can't go back," I say.

"Olivia!"

"That's suicide, Ella. There're too many."

Olivia roars in pain. She whips her head at her sides and back, trying to crush or bite the black krauls that have blanketed her. Crayton aims his gun at the beasts, but he lowers his weapon when he realizes he would most likely shoot Olivia in the process. He and Héctor instead fire on the army of Mogadorians lining up and preparing for a new attack.

Olivia wavers left and right, howls at the mountains, and backs herself up into the middle of the lake and slowly sinks in a wave of red. The krauls detach and swim towards the Mogadorians.

"No!" I hear Crayton yell above the chaos. I watch him

try to enter the lake but Héctor pulls him back onto the shore.

"Duck!" Ella screams, pulling me down by the arm. A whoosh of air passes over us. A giant black hoof smashes the ground next to me, and I look up to see a horned monster. Its head is as large as Héctor's truck, and when the giant roars, my hair flaps in my face.

"Come on!" I yell. We race towards the trees.

"Split up," Ella says. I nod and dart left, towards an ancient beech tree with gnarled limbs. I set the Chest down and instinctively lift my hands and then pull them apart. To my surprise the beech trunk opens, creating a hollow space that looks just big enough for two people and a Chest to fit.

I look over my shoulder to see the creature chasing Ella through a dense line of trees. I toss the Chest in the open trunk, and with telekinesis I pick up two trees and send them like missiles at the creature's back. They splinter against its dark skin with a loud crash, knocking it to its knees. I run and grab Ella's shaking hand, pulling her in the other direction. The beech tree with my Chest comes into view.

"The tree, Ella! Get inside!" I yell. She sits atop the Chest and tries to make herself as compact as she can, shrinking down to a younger age.

"That's a piken, Marina! Get in!" she pleads; and before she can say another word, I close the trunk up around her, leaving just enough room so she can see.

"I'm sorry," I say through the small crevice, hoping the giant didn't see where I've stashed the Chest and hidden my friend.

I turn and run trying to lead the piken away, but it soon catches up and knocks me from behind. The force of the hit is shocking, and I fall down a steep slope until my arm finds a boulder to hook around. I look over my shoulder to see that I'm less than a meter from a rocky cliff.

The piken appears at the top of the slope. There it shuffles sideways until it's positioned directly above me. It roars so loudly my mind blanks. I hear Ella scream my name in the distance, but I can't breathe, let alone yell back.

It marches down the slope. I raise one of my hands and uproot a small spindly tree near me and launch it at the giant's chest. It impales its chest, and it's enough for the piken to lose its footing; and it falls sideways, shrieking and barreling right at me. I close my eyes and prepare for the impact; but instead of smashing me under its weight and knocking me over the cliff, its body hits the boulder I'm holding on to and then bounces *over* me. I whip my head over my shoulder to see the piken fall down the rocky cliff.

I'm finally able to concentrate enough to float myself up the slope. I hurry back towards the beech tree—to

Ella and my Chest—and I hear the cannon's blast a split second before I'm shot. The pain is double anything I've felt before, and all I can see is red and flashes of white. I roll around uncontrollably, writhing in agony.

"Marina!" I hear Ella scream.

I roll onto my back and stare at the sky. Blood drips out of my mouth and nose. I can taste it. I can smell it. A few birds circle overhead. As I wait to die, I watch as the sky is taken over by a colossal group of dark, heavy clouds. The clouds crash and roll on top of each other, pulsing as if they're breathing. I think I'm hallucinating, seeing visions before I die, when a massive drop of water hits me on the right cheek. I blink as another hits me above my eyes, and then a bolt of lightning splits the sky in two.

A huge Mogadorian in gold-and-black armor stands over me smiling. He presses a cannon against my temple and spits on the ground; but before he pulls the trigger, he looks up at the looming storm. I quickly place my hands on the gaping wound in my abdomen, feeling the icy familiarity surge under my skin. Then the oncoming rain washes over me as the clouds become a solid wall of darkness.

CHAPTER THIRTY-ONE

BY THE LOOK ON SAM'S FACE I CAN TELL HE'S just about lost all faith in getting out of here alive. My own shoulders sag as I stare into the massive white eyes of the beast that's rising to its feet in front of us. It takes its time, stretching its muscular neck, veins as thick as Roman columns protruding on both sides. The dark skin on its face is dry and cracked like the stone jutting above its head. With its long arms, it has the look of an alien gorilla.

By the time the giant has pushed itself into a full standing position, fifty feet tall, the handle of my dagger has melted itself around my right hand.

"Flank it!" I yell. Sam runs left and I dart right.

Its first move is towards Sam, who immediately turns and runs along the circular edge of the moat. The beast lumbers after him, and that's when I sprint towards it and slide my dagger right and left, cutting small chunks from its calves. It rears its head and smashes its nose against the ceiling, and then swings a hand down at me, one of its fingers connecting with my back leg. I'm sent spinning into the wall, where I land on my left shoulder, dislocating it.

"John!" Sam yells.

The giant swings for me again, but I'm able to jump out of the path of its fist; the giant may be powerful, but it's slow. Still, the cave we're in is not large enough to run very far so, slow or not, it still has the advantage.

I don't see Sam anywhere as I stagger from boulder to boulder. The giant has a hard time following me; and once I figure I have enough time, I slowly raise my left arm above my head and rotate my hand so my palm is on the back of my head. The pain shoots from my neck to my heels; and before I give in to it, I keep reaching and feel my dislocated shoulder pop back into place. A sense of relief comes over me, but it's short-lived as I look up to see the giant's palm right above my head.

I raise my dagger and its blade punctures the beast's palm, but it's not enough to stop it from wrapping its fingers around me. It picks me up, and the strength of its squeeze causes the dagger to fall to the ground. I hear its diamond blade clang; and as I'm turned upside down, I search for it so I can use my telekinesis to retrieve it.

"Sam! Where are you?"

I'm disoriented as the beast turns me right side up again, and it holds me a few feet above its nose. Then I see Sam emerge from a fissure in the wall. He runs and picks up my blade, and a second later the giant squeals in shock and pain. It squeezes me hard, and I push back against its fingers as much as I can. As it stumbles backwards, I'm able to free my shoulders, arms, and hands. I turn on the lights of my palms and shine my Lumen directly into its eyes. It's instantly blinded and backs into a wall, and that's when I'm able to pull the rest of my body free and jump.

Sam tosses me my dagger and I charge at the beast, plunging the blade into the skin between every toe. The giant howls. It bends over, and when it does I shine my Lumen again into its eyes. It loses its balance, and I make a boulder behind it dislodge and slam into its lower back. The beast pitches forward, its long arms straight out to break its fall. Its massive hands land in the moat of steaming green liquid—and the sound of its searing flesh comes a second later. I watch as the beast crashes into the base of the electrical force field and the thick stone pedestals holding the Chests. The crash disrupts the force field and sends the pedestals flying across the room, breaking against the stone. The beast lies unmoving.

"Tell me you planned that," Sam says, following me towards the Chests.

"I wish I could," I say.

I open my Chest to find everything inside, including the coffee can of Henri's ashes and the volatile crystal that's wrapped in the towel. "Looks good," I say. Sam picks up the other Chest.

"What happens when we go through that door?" Sam says, nodding to the small wooden door we came in through.

We killed the beast and we have the Chests, but we can't turn ourselves invisible and just stroll by a hundred Mogs. I open my Chest and handle different crystals and objects, but again I have no idea what most of them do, and the ones I do know how to use can't exactly get me through a mountain of aliens. Looking around the room, I'm losing hope. But it's after studying the giant's melting skin and disintegrating bones that I get an idea.

With my dagger back in my jeans pocket, I slowly approach the moat of bubbling green liquid. I take a deep breath and carefully dip a finger in it. Just as I'd hoped, it's scalding hot but merely tickles my skin like fire. It's like green lava.

"Sam?"

"Yeah?"

"When I say open the door, I want you to open it and get out of the way immediately."

"What are you going to do?" he asks.

Visions of Henri running the Loric crystal over me as I lie on the coffee table, my hands in open flames, run through my mind, and I dunk my hand into the moat and pick up a dripping scoop of the green lava. I close my eyes and concentrate, and when I open them the liquid is hovering over my hand in a perfect flaming ball.

"This, I guess," I say.

"Wicked."

Sam runs over to the wooden door, and I nod to show him I'm ready.

He rips the door open and dives to his right. A cluster of heavily armed Mogs are running our way; but when they catch sight of the fiery green ball coming their way, they try to turn around. As the ball is about to splash on the chest of the first Mog, I use my mind to spread it out like a fiery blanket. Several Mogs are hit, and after a moment of burning torture, they turn to ash.

I wing ball after ball of green lava at more Mogs, knocking them down. Sam collects a pile of their guns, and once there's a lull in the advancement, I grab two more balls of green liquid and run out the door. Sam follows me with a long black gun under each arm.

The number of Mogs running down the dark tunnel is staggering; and with the flashing lights and piercing sirens, it's a sensory overload. Sam pulls both triggers and mows down row after row of Mogs, but they keep coming. When he's out of bullets, Sam grabs two more guns.

"I could use some help here!" Sam yells, mowing down another line of Mogs.

"I'm thinking, I'm thinking!" The mucus-covered walls of the tunnel don't appear to lend themselves to spreading a decent fire, and I don't have enough of the green lava in my hands to do enough damage. To my left are the silver gas tanks and silos with their heavy pipes, spouts and aluminum ducts. Next to the tallest of the silos I eye the control panel with electrical wires pouring out. I can hear the screams and roars of the beasts in the barred chambers farther down the hall, and wonder how hungry they are.

I toss a flaming ball at the control panel and it disintegrates in a storm of sparks. The bars of the chambers lining the walls begin to rise, and that's when I toss the other green ball at the base of the gas tanks and silos.

I grab hold of Sam and sprint with him back into the giant's chamber. As the explosion erupts, I whip Sam against the stone section between the wooden door and the rising steel gate, and allow the advancing wave of flames to sweep over me. My ears are flooded with the crackle and hum of fire.

Dozens of krauls burst from their open chamber and attack a series of unsuspecting Mogs from behind; several pikens stomp into the tunnel with roars and swinging arms; the reptilian mutant with horns charges towards the back of the tunnel, plowing over Mogs and krauls under the legs of the pikens; the gargoylelike winged creatures buzz at the ceiling, swooping down to take a bite out of anything they can; and the monster with transparent skin sinks its rows of teeth into the calf of a piken. That all happens in a matter of seconds, then they're overtaken by a sea of fire.

After a few minutes, once the fire escapes up the spiral cavern at the end of the tunnel to continue to wreak havoc throughout the mountain, the long corridor in front of me is littered with ash piles and black monster bones. I extinguish the fire surrounding me and brush my hands off onto my thighs.

Sam is singed, but otherwise okay.

"Brilliant, dude," he says.

"Let's just try to get the hell out of here, and *then* we can celebrate."

I stick my Chest under my arm and Sam picks up the other. We race through the fire's destruction; the stench of death is choking. The charred ladder at the end of the tunnel appears stable, and with only one free hand apiece, we climb with difficulty. Our feet hit the burned and blackened spiral ledge, and we sprint around and around until we reach the cave's center.

The inferno I unleashed did much more damage than I thought it would, and we see piles upon piles of ash; but we also see hundreds of Mogs crawling out of different corridors and tunnels on their hands and knees, burned or still on fire, barking in pain, unable to pick up their guns, unable to do anything as we jump over them. There are other soldiers racing above us on ledges, some with weapons in their arms, others with the wounded.

I'm confused which way the exit is; and as I lead us through a series of tunnels with my pendant swinging around my neck, Sam and I each pick up a discarded gun. We run with them chest high, firing at anything that gets in our way. Even though we don't know where we're going, we don't stop moving until we come to the cells with human prisoners. That's when I know for certain we've gone the wrong way. I pull Sam in the other direction, but he plants his feet and stops me. I can see the concern and hope on his face. The cells have their steel doors stuck a foot above the floor and the bubbling blue force fields have disappeared.

"They're open, John!" he yells, tossing his Chest at my feet. I drop my gun and pick up the other Chest, and Sam finally says what I knew he was thinking: "What if my dad's here?"

I look into Sam's eyes, and I know we have to check. He runs along the left side of the corridor, yelling into each cell for his dad. I'm investigating the cells on the right when a boy my age with long black hair sticks his head under a door. When he sees me, he puts a hand cautiously into the corridor.

"The force field is really gone?" he shouts.

"I think so!" I yell.

Sam hoists his gun over his shoulder and ducks his head under the boy's cell door. "Do you know a man named Malcolm Goode? Forty years old, brown hair? Is he here? Have you seen him?"

"Shut up and stand back, kid," I hear the boy say. There's a grittiness to his voice, something that makes me uneasy, and I immediately pull Sam to the side. The boy grips the bottom of the door and rips it from the wall, tossing it into the corridor like a Frisbee. The ceiling cracks and boulders fall, and I use telekinesis to shield Sam and me from being crushed. Before I can say a word, the boy emerges clapping the dust off his hands. He's taller than I am, shirtless and muscular.

Sam steps forward, and to my surprise he aims his gun at the boy's head. "Just tell me! Do you know my dad? Malcolm Goode? Please!"

The boy looks past Sam and his weapon, focusing on the Chests under my arms. That's when I notice the three scars on his leg. They're just like mine. He's one of us.

I drop the other Chest to the ground in shock. "What number are you? I'm Four."

He squints at me and then offers his hand. "I'm Nine.

Good job staying alive, Number Four."

He reaches for the Chest I've dropped. Sam lowers his gun, retreating down the corridor, stopping every few seconds to look inside a cell. Nine places his hand on the Chest's lock and it instantly shakes and snaps open. A yellow glow lights up his face when he opens the lid.

"Hell, yeah." He laughs, placing a hand inside. Nine pulls out a tiny red rock and shows it to me. "You have one of these?"

"I don't know. Maybe." I'm embarrassed by how little I understand the items in my own Chest.

Nine places the rock between his knuckles and aims his fist at the nearest wall. A white cone of light appears, and instantly we can see through the wall and into an empty jail cell.

Sam runs in our direction. "Wait! You have X-ray vision?"

"What number is the nerd?" Nine asks me, digging around in his Chest again.

"That's Sam. He's not Loric, but he's our ally. He's looking for his dad."

He tosses Sam the red rock. "This will make shit go faster, Sammy. Just aim and squeeze."

"He's human, dude," I say. "He can't use this stuff."

Nine places his thumb on Sam's forehead. Sam's hair blows upward and I can smell electricity in the air.

Sam stumbles backwards. "Whoa."

Nine ducks his hands back into his Chest. "You've got about ten minutes. Get to it."

I'm amazed that Nine has the ability to transfer powers to humans. Sam runs down the corridor, inspecting cells with a flick of the wrist. When he gets to the large metal door at the end, he aims the rock at it, exposing more than a dozen armed Mogs on the other side, and one is twisting together exposed wires in an open keypad.

"Sam!" I yell picking up my gun. "Get back!"

Whoosh. The door rises and the Mogs rush forward. Sam sprints away, firing over his shoulder.

"You have any other Legacies yet?" I ask Nine over the sound of my gun.

He winks, and then he's gone, running along the cracked ceiling at super speed. The Mogs don't notice Nine until he's dropped behind them, and by then it's too late. He's a tornado, ripping through them with a ferocity I didn't know Loric possessed; even Six would be impressed. Sam and I stop firing, letting Nine dismember each Mog with his bare hands.

When he's finished, Nine runs back along the left wall of the corridor before circling to the ceiling and then to the right wall, a cloud of ash trailing him.

"Antigravity," Sam says. "Now *that's* a cool Legacy."

Nine skids to a stop in front of his Chest and kicks it

shut. "I can also hear pretty well. For miles."

"Okay, let's go," I say, scooping up my Chest. Nine easily places his on his huge shoulder and grabs a gun from the floor.

"What about those other cells?" he asks Sam, pointing down the corridor. A hundred or more cell doors line the walls past where the Mogs had entered.

"We have to go," I say, knowing we're already pushing our luck. It's only a matter of seconds before we'll be surrounded. But there's no persuading Sam.

He runs under the large door, still holding the red rock. Another dozen Mogs suddenly emerge from a hidden tunnel entrance between us. Sam braces himself against the wall and fires. I see a few of the Mogs burst into ash, but then my view is blocked by a swarm of drooling krauls.

Focusing my thoughts on a boulder, I whip it at the krauls, smashing all but a few. Nine catches a kraul by its back legs, and slams the beast against the wall. He crushes another two, and when he's done he turns to me, laughing. I'm about to ask him what's so funny when he launches a boulder right at me. I barely jump out of the way, and a moment later my back is covered with black ash.

"They're everywhere!" He laughs.

"We have to get to Sam!" I try to run past Nine when an enormous piken hand snatches us both.

"Sam!" I yell. "Sam!"

Sam doesn't hear us over the sound of his gun. The piken pulls us in the other direction, and, in what feels like slow motion, I lose sight of my best friend. Before I can yell again, the piken throws us down the opposite tunnel. I hit the wall and land on one Chest and the other lands on top of me. The wind is knocked out of me; and when I look up, I see Nine spitting blood out. He's grinning.

"Are you crazy?" I ask. "You're enjoying this?"

"I've been locked up for over a year. This is the best day of my life!"

Two pikens duck into the tunnel, blocking our direct path back to Sam. Nine wipes the blood from his chin and opens his Chest. He pulls out a short silver pipe, and it expands violently at both ends until it's over six feet long and glowing red. He runs toward the pikens with the pipe over his head. I stand to join him but feel a jolt of pain in my ribs. I dig inside my Chest for my healing stone, but by the time I find it Nine has killed both pikens. Running back along the ceiling, he twirls the pipe at his side, and when he's twenty feet away he yells for me to move. The glowing red pipe sails over my head like a javelin, impaling a piken in the stomach.

"Don't mention it," Nine says before I can utter a word.

More pikens squeeze into the far end of the tunnel, and when I turn around to run, a flock of transparent birds with razor-sharp teeth is flying towards us. Nine grabs a strand of green stones from his Chest and flings it towards the flock. It hovers in the air and, like a black hole, sucks the birds into it.

He closes his eyes and the stones zip towards the pikens, spinning and unleashing the flock of birds into their faces. Nine points at me and yells, "Boulder them!"

I follow his lead, rocketing boulder after boulder at the mayhem. The pikens and the birds collapse under our barrage.

Several more pikens push their way into the tunnel, roaring. I grab Nine's arm to keep him from charging.

"They're just going to keep coming," I say. "We have to find Sam and get out of here. Number Six is meeting us."

He nods and we run. At the next opening we veer left, unsure if we're making progress or getting even more lost. More and more enemies appear behind us with every new turn. Nine trashes every tunnel we pass through, bringing down ceilings and collapsing walls with telekinesis and perfectly thrown boulders.

We come to a long, low-arching bridge of solid rock, similar to the one Sam and I shuffled along earlier, and below is a steaming pool of green lava. Charging across the other side of the narrow bridge is a thick line of Mogs, and behind us several pikens are racing down the tunnel, straight towards us.

"Where do we go?" I shout as we step onto the bridge.

Nine says, "We go under."

Nine grabs my hand as we reach the peak of the bridge, and my world literally flips upside down until we're running along the underside of the arch. Without warning Nine lets go of me, but my shoes still firmly grip the belly of the bridge somehow. I reach over my head and scoop up a pile of the green lava, and by the time we're standing on the other side of the room, I have a perfect green ball of fire in my hand. I wing it at the Mogs on the bridge and visualize it spreading over them. I can hear the sizzling of their flesh when we duck into another cave.

I'm out of breath when we reach a steep decline. I'm judging the grade of the drop when I'm hit with a blast from behind. I topple forward and fall at an amazing speed, and when the ground finally levels out, my recently dislocated shoulder hits it first.

I roll onto my stomach in unimaginable pain. The blast hit me square in the back, and my muscles are stuck in an uncontrollable spasm. I can hardly breathe, let alone search my Chest for my healing stone. The only thing I can do is stare at the slivers of moonlight that appear and disappear at the end of the tunnel. The tarp. It's flapping in the forest wind. I'm back to where I started.

I hear the sound of rocks crumbling behind me. I'm in more pain than I thought imaginable, and all I can think about is leaving the mountain. "Straight ahead. It's the exit. We can regroup out there," I manage.

If we can make it outside, then I can heal myself, hide our Chests in the forest. And maybe BK can come back in with us now that we've destroyed the gas tanks. The four Mogs who guarded the entrance are gone, and Nine jumps out through the tarp and into the forest. I follow. The stench from the dead animal carcasses hits us fast, and we both gag as Nine jogs into a line of trees. I collapse against a trunk. I need five minutes, I think. Then we're going back in for Sam. Guns and hands blazing.

Nine digs around his Chest and I close my eyes. Tears roll down my face. I'm startled by something rough touching my left hand. I open my eyes to see it's Bernie Kosar in his beagle form, licking my fingers.

"I don't deserve that," I tell him. "I'm a coward. I'm cursed."

He notices my injuries and tears, and then sniffs Nine's face before expanding into a horse.

"Whoa!" Nine jumps back. "What the hell are you?"

"Chimæra," I whisper. "He's a good guy. He's Loric."

Nine quickly pets BK's muzzle and then presses a healing stone to my back. As it works through my system, I notice a menacing storm brewing over the mountain.

The sky suddenly rages with lightning and booming thunder, and I'm so grateful Six has returned that I stand, ignoring the remaining pain in my back. The clouds shift and stretch in a way I've never seen before, though, and the sky feels suddenly evil. This isn't Six. She's not back to help.

I watch the funnel cloud that I've only seen in my worst visions form.

Bernie Kosar rears backward as a perfectly spherical spaceship, milky white like a pearl, sweeps down through the tornado's eye. The ship lands right in front of the mountain's entrance, sending tremors through the ground. In the same way as I had seen in my visions, a door appears from out of nowhere on the ship's side, simply melting away. The Mogadorian leader from my visions, he's here.

Nine gasps. "Setrákus Ra. He's here. This is it."

I'm silent, frozen in fear. "So that's his name," I finally whisper.

"That *was* his name. For every day they tried to torture me and my Cêpan, I'm going to stab him with this." The red pipe glows in Nine's hand. Its ends expand with rotating blades. "I'm going to kill him.

And you're going to help me."

Setrákus Ra walks towards the cave's entrance but stops before going in, one massive silhouette, stark and spectral. Through the raging wind and torrential rain, he turns, lifting his gaze in our general direction. Even from as far away as I am, the faint glow of the three pendants is unmistakable around his thick neck.

Nine and I charge out of the trees with Bernie Kosar galloping behind, but it's too late. Setrákus Ra has disappeared into the cave and the same bubbling blue force field that covered the prison cell doors appears over the entrance.

"No!" Nine yells. He slides to a stop and stabs the ground with his pipe.

With my dagger in my hand, I keep going. I hear Nine scream for me to stop, but all I can think about is killing Setrákus Ra, saving Sam and his dad and ending this war, right here, right now. When I hit the blue force field, everything goes black.

CHAPTER
THIRTY-TWO

THUNDER ROLLS, FOLLOWED BY BRILLIANT STREAKS of lightning, and in their glare I see the clouds expand and drop. Rain falls in heavy sheets, and the armored Mogadorian looks down at me. He presses the cannon against my blue pendant and says something I can't understand. My wound in my stomach has almost healed, and I hear Ella yell my name over the thunder.

If I'm going to die, then I need to release Ella first. One of us needs to live to tell the others. I cautiously lift my hands and envision the trunk separating, when a bolt of lightning cracks in the distance. Less than a second later, the bolt strikes the Mogadorian standing over me, and he turns to ash and is swept away in the wind.

I climb to my feet and see that I've opened the beech tree's trunk halfway. I continue to separate the tree as I run towards it. "Ella? Are you okay?"

She spills out of the trunk and falls into my arms. "I

couldn't see you," she says, squeezing me. "I thought I lost you."

"Not yet," I say, grabbing my Chest. "Come on."

We turn to run, and see Crayton and Héctor coming towards us. Héctor's been hurt, and his arm is over Crayton's shoulders for support. The wind and rain are raging. Behind them, the first wave of Mogadorians and krauls are charging up the shore after them. When I see this, I break away a large limb from a dead tree and hurl it hard at the closest pack of krauls. It knocks down several, but they're back up again in no time. A Mogadorian soldier throws a grenade that I intercept midair with my mind and send right back into his stomach. It explodes, throwing several Mogadorians and krauls to the ground in soggy bits of ash. I send tree after tree, rock after rock, knocking many to the ground, killing more.

"Help me!" Crayton yells.

I rush to take Héctor from him. He has a bite wound in his stomach and a bullet hole in his arm, and both are bleeding badly.

"Come on, everyone!" Crayton yells, pulling bullets from his coat pocket and quickly sliding them into his gun's empty clip. "We have to get to the dam!"

I open my mouth to respond, but an enormous lightning bolt snaps over us. It spreads across the sky like the veins of the gods, leaving the distinct taste of metal in the air. A deafening clap of thunder reverberates off the mountains. The wind and rain cease, and the clouds rotate around and around in a massive maelstrom, until a dark, glowing eye forms, staring at us from high over the mountaintops. The Mogadorians are just as mesmerized as we are. The wind kicks up again, and the dark clouds and the thunder and lightning come with it, slow at first, but quickly gaining speed, heading our way. A perfect storm, beautiful at its cataclysmic heart, unlike anything I've ever seen before. All any of us can do is watch the thick clouds rolling towards us with a deep growl.

"What's happening?" I scream over the gale force winds.

"I don't know!" Crayton replies. "We're going to need to find some cover!"

But he doesn't move, and neither does anyone else. Héctor seems to have forgotten all about the pain of his wounds as he watches, too.

"Go!" Crayton finally yells, and then he spins around and fires on the Mogadorians to cover us as we run over a slight hill and then down into a valley. I see the dam on my right, which connects two lower mountains. It's too far away to realistically believe we'll reach it. Héctor's face has turned white and he's fading fast, and I start looking for a place to rest so I can heal him. Crayton's gun falls silent. I look behind me fearing the worst, but he's merely out of ammo. He chucks the gun over his shoulder and catches up to us.

"We're not going to make it to the dam!" He yells. "Run to the lake!"

The rain starts up again as the four of us change direction. Bullets zip into our grassy footprints and ricochet off boulders. The clouds shift over us with a roar. A second later it's as if we've gone under a bridge: the rain just stops. I look over my shoulder and see that just a few paces back, the rain still falls heavy and hard. The wind picks up significantly, and suddenly the Mogadorians behind us are stuck in the worst rainstorm I've ever seen. They completely disappear in a blur.

Our shoes slip over the sand on the shore, and Ella and Crayton dive into the water headfirst.

"I can't do it, Marina," Héctor says, stopping before his feet reach the water.

I drop my Chest and grab his arm and say, "I can fix you, Héctor. You can make it."

"It wouldn't make any difference. I don't know how to swim."

"I'm Marina of the sea, Héctor. Remember?" I allow the iciness to spread from my fingertips to the bullet hole in his arm. I watch it turn from black and gray and red to a tan patch of wrinkled skin. I quickly concentrate on the bite wound on his stomach beneath his shirt, and Héctor suddenly stands up straight with energy. I look into his eyes. "As the Queen of the sea, I will swim with you."

"But you have that," Héctor says, pointing at the Chest.

"You'll have to hold it then," I say, dropping it into his arms.

We jog into the water until our feet no longer touch the lake floor, and then I wrap my right arm around Héctor's chest and paddle with my left. Héctor hugs the Chest to his stomach, and he floats on his back, his head just above water. Ella and Crayton tread water in the middle of the lake, and I pull Héctor towards them.

The clouds overhead dissipate, shrinking into a hundred wispy lines of gray in the sky. The advancing Mogadorians are no longer a blur in a rainstorm, and the moment they can see they charge at the lake with dozens of krauls yipping in front of them.

A tiny black speck falls from above as the last cloud disappears, and the closer the speck gets, the more it appears to be a human.

Wearing a large blue pendant around her neck, she lands on the shore, rippling the sand. It's a strikingly beautiful girl with raven-colored hair; and the second I see her I know she's the one I've been dreaming of, the one I painted on the cave's wall.

"She's one of us!" I shout.

The girl looks around, we make eye contact, and then she vanishes a moment later. I'm shocked, crushed, believing I must have imagined her.

"Where'd she go?" Ella asks.

The moment I realize Ella saw her, too, that I hadn't imagined her, I watch as the two nearest krauls are somehow yanked backwards in the air. They're hovering, yipping and snarling at something behind them, and then they slam into each other until they fall limp. One kraul goes sailing into the legs of two soldiers, and the other is swung in the air, connecting with other krauls and soldiers.

"Invisibility. She has the Legacy of invisibility." Crayton breathes.

She's invisible? I'm amazed and jealous at the same time, but most of all I'm grateful. Every kraul that touches the water is yanked backwards by an unseen hand and slammed into the hard sand or a Mogadorian soldier. A dropped cannon rises from the grass and starts firing in all directions. Kraul after kraul is destroyed. Dozens of Mogadorians burst into clouds of ash.

Cannon blasts come from the other side of the lake, and I spin to see twenty or more Mogadorians wading in up to their waists. Rays of light hit the water all around us, creating enough steam that I can barely see Héctor in front of me.

"Ella?" I shout.

"Over here!" she yells from my left.

"Take Héctor."

She wraps her arm around Héctor's chest. "Why?"

"Because I'm not going to stay out here while that girl

fights all by herself. This is my war, too."

Before anyone can stop me, I sink below the surface and the water instantly tickles my lungs. I swim deeper until the green-blue color of the lake becomes gray. I see the hulking body of Olivia below me; she's lying lifeless on the lake floor, clouds of blood billowing from the hundreds of bite wounds on her back.

I head towards the opposite shore and after a minute I can see the legs of the Mogadorians. I swim next to the one farthest on the left. I plant my feet in the muddy bottom and launch myself out of the water. The Mogadorian doesn't have enough time to react as I toss him towards the middle of the lake with my mind. I float his cannon into my hands, shoot him, and never let go of the trigger. The Mogadorians along the lake burst into ash, and when I've killed them all, I aim towards the hundreds near the vehicles.

There's movement in the water behind me and I'm too slow; a kraul jumps and sinks its teeth into my side. The pain is immediate and horrible, as if someone was holding a hot branding iron to my ribs. The beast whips me headfirst into the water and then against the sand of the shore. I catch my breath and scream as it arcs me back over and into the water again. I'm sure this is how I will die, but suddenly the kraul's mouth widens and releases me. I fall onto my stomach on the shore and watch as the kraul's mouth continues to widen until I hear bones snapping. The raven-haired girl materializes before my eyes, her hands on the beast's quivering lips. She looks back at me before yanking the jaws completely vertical, killing the kraul.

"Are you okay?" the girl asks me.

I lift up my shirt and place a hand on my wound. "I will be in a second."

She ducks a blast from a cannon. "Good. What number are you?"

"Seven."

"I'm Six," she says before vanishing.

The iciness spreads from my fingers over my body, but I know I won't be able to heal myself completely before the oncoming wave of Mogadorian soldiers reaches me. I roll into the lake and stay underwater. My wound is almost healed when I rise above the surface.

Number Six is on top of one of the armored Humvees with a glowing sword. She's fighting several soldiers at once: hacking off body parts, blocking cannon fire with her blade, using telekinesis to aim a floating cannon high above her so it blasts through dozens of Mogadorians on the formation's edge. She then hurls her sword into a crowd, impaling three soldiers at once. Number Six grabs the large gun mounted on top of the vehicle and mows down dozens of Mogadorians in seconds.

There are only twenty or thirty soldiers left. Maybe four krauls. Number Six holds one hand over her head while the gun in the other shoots and destroys the Humvees along the shore. Dark clouds form over the mountains and bolts of lightning crack and split the ground near her. The Mogadorians show fear for the first time, and I watch a few drop their weapons and run towards the woods.

"Out of the water!" I yell, fearful of the lightning. Ella drags Héctor to the edge of the lake and Crayton follows.

I reach the shore near Number Six and pick up two cannons. I struggle to keep my footing as I press both triggers, turning more soldiers to ash, destroying two of the krauls. An injured soldier hiding behind a wrecked Humvee tosses a grenade at Number Six's back, but I'm able to shoot it in the air. The explosion rotates Number Six and the mounted gun, and a moment later the injured soldier is nothing but ash.

I can't keep my eyes off of Number Six. Her strength is mesmerizing. The blue pendant bounces around as the gun in her one hand cuts down more and more soldiers. She rotates to her left and blows a kraul into bits, and then she rotates to her right and takes out several more Mogadorians with a bolt of lightning.

The valley is bright and smoky. It's damp and charred. I look around me and can't believe that victory will be ours in just a matter of seconds. Crayton races over and I toss him one of my guns, and instantly he's killing soldiers retreating into the woods. Héctor runs with my Chest, and soon he and Ella stand behind me. I nod towards

Number Six and smile at my friends, thinking that the worst is over; but that's when Ella raises her eyes over my head and her face turns white.

"Pikens!" Ella yells.

Four of the horned monsters run down the mountainside at full speed. Directly below them, Number Six is preoccupied with the few remaining soldiers and the kraul. I uproot as many silver firs as I can and send them like rockets. Four hit the lead one and it falls backwards into the path of the other three, and it's crushed and killed in the stampede.

"Number Six!" I shout. She hears me, and I point to the pikens rumbling down into the valley. She spins with the gun and blows the knees off the monster on the left. It tumbles down faster than the other two can run, and Number Six jumps from the Humvee a moment before the dead piken flattens it with an echoing crunch.

Crayton and I shoot our cannons at the other two, but they're too fast, splitting up when they reach the valley floor. The clouds roar when Number Six stands, and an enormous bolt of lightning crashes into one of the pikens, cutting off its arm. It bellows and falls to its knees, but quickly regains its balance and charges ahead with blood spurting from its side. The other piken dodges Crayton's fire and rushes in from the other direction. We all run towards Number Six, but Héctor is too slow with my Chest in his arms. The piken closes in, and before I can help, the one-armed monster reaches down and snatches Héctor and my Chest in its fist.

"No!" I scream. "Héctor!"

I'm in such shock that when the piken throws a lifeless Héctor and my Chest into the lake, I don't use my telekinesis to stop either from sinking.

Number Six has killed the other piken. She turns towards us now and holds both hands up to the sky. A lightning bolt severs the monster's head from its body.

For the first time all day, there is silence. I lean into Number Six, look at Ella and Crayton and the fire and destruction behind them, and I know that these quiet moments are about to become rare in my life.

"Your Chest, Marina," Crayton says. "You have to go get it."

I turn to Number Six and hug her. "Thank you. Thank you, Number Six."

"I'm sure we'll get a chance to do it again sometime." She wraps her arms around my shoulders. "And just call me Six."

"I'm Marina. This is Crayton and Ella. She's Number Ten."

Ella steps forward and shrinks to her seven-year-old body. She extends her small hand towards Six, who has her mouth open, speechless.

Crayton starts to explain Ella and the second ship to Six as I walk into the lake. I feel its coolness for the first time. I swim to the middle and dive, descending until the water is devoid of any light and my feet touch the muddy floor. I circle the bottom until I see my Chest. I rock it back and forth to dislodge it from the mud's suction. Swimming with one arm, I start to ascend. When the water turns blue, I see Héctor's body and wrap my other arm around his waist.

Ella and Crayton stand with Six on the shore. I drop the Chest and slap my wet hands on Héctor's shin, arm, neck, all around his crushed back, hoping and praying the icy feeling will arrive in my fingers.

"He's dead," Crayton says, pulling on my shoulders.

I don't give up. Hating myself for not trying the same thing on Adelina, I touch Héctor's face. I run my hand through his gray hair. I even levitate him a few centimeters off the sand and try it all over again, but it's true. He's gone.

CHAPTER
THIRTY-THREE

I'M HOVERING OVER GRASS. I'M FLOATING OVER a river. I feel wretched and stiff, and every time I dare to open my eyes, I'm either bouncing over a log or gliding up a rocky hill. There's a constant noise, and it takes me several minutes to realize it's the sound of Bernie Kosar's hooves. I'm draped over his back and we're moving quickly through the mountains.

"You awake?" Nine asks. I raise my head to see him sitting behind me, both of our Chests under his arms.

"I don't know what I am," I say, closing my eyes. "What . . . what happened?"

"You ran right into the blue stuff. That's the last thing on Earth, or Lorien, or anywhere, you want to do." He sounds pissed, like I just tore him away from his own birthday party.

"What about Setrákus Ra?" I ask.

"Somewhere in the mountain, the coward. I couldn't

find another way in. And I looked."

I push myself up BK's hide in a panic. "Where's Sam?"

"Not a chance, Four. Your buddy is either long gone, or he's hanging upside down staring at the wrong end of a knife."

I vomit. Bernie Kosar quickly lowers himself so I can slide off his back, and then I vomit some more. Nine tries to explain the sickness will go away soon, that he's gone through it several times when he tried to escape his cell, that the healing stone seems to be powerless against the force field's effects, but I'm too dizzy with visions of Sam being tortured to listen. My sickness is from my betrayal, not from some Mogadorian force field. I don't think I'll ever be able to forgive myself. It's my fault he went in there, and it's my fault he was left behind. I turned my back on my best friend.

"We have to go back," I say. "Sam would go back for me."

"Not a chance. Not yet. You're too much of a mess and like you said before, we need numbers."

I pull myself to my feet but fall onto my hands and knees almost immediately. "You don't even know where we are."

"We're a couple of miles from your car," Nine says. He must see the confusion on my face, because he smiles and pats Bernie Kosar's back. "Turns out I can talk to animals. Who knew? Bernie Kosar here is leading the way. Let's jet."

I'm too weak to protest and I climb back up. Bernie Kosar gallops as fast as he can, his belly brushing the tops of shrubs and felled trees as he hurdles us over obstacles. My body aches and I clutch his side as we zigzag up and down the mountains and hills, splashing through two fast-moving rivers. The stars slowly reveal themselves, high in the sky, and I know that one of them, far, far away, is the slight glimmer of Lorien's own sun, shining its bright light upon a hibernating planet.

"So, what's our next move?" Nine asks as we trot among the shadows.

I'm silent, wondering what Henri would say our next move would be. I wonder what kind of look would be on his face. Would he beam with pride over me retrieving the Chests, rescuing a member of the Garde and killing so many Mogs in the process, or would he be disappointed in me for not taking on the leader when I had the chance, and for leaving Sam behind?

Visions of Sam locked behind one of those steel doors come to me every few seconds, and I watch my tears glide down BK's neck. I hate to think it, but I'd rather he die than be tortured for information about me.

I try to blame Sarah for turning us in to the police, but I can only blame myself for contacting her when everyone told me not to. I keep quiet and dig my heels into Bernie Kosar's hide and he picks up the pace.

Six is somewhere in Spain, hopefully with another member of the Garde. Part of me wants to get on a plane, to go directly to her, but with my escape from a federal facility and my face still on the FBI's Most Wanted List, I don't see how it's possible.

We make it to the SUV, and I painfully dismount. I unlock the back door and Nine quietly loads both Chests into the trunk. Crawling across the backseat, disgusted with myself, I ask Nine if he'll drive.

"I was hoping you'd ask," Nine replies. I hand him the keys and feel the engine come to life.

Something is under my body, and I shift to my side to find Sam's dad's glasses. I hold them above my head, and I let the moon reflect in the lenses. I suck in a deep breath and whisper, "We'll see each other again soon, Sam. I promise." And then, when I think things can't get much worse, it hits me almost harder than the blue force field. "Oh shit! Six's address for when we meet. It was in Sam's pocket. I'm so stupid! How are we going to find each other now?"

Over his shoulder, Nine says, "Don't worry, Four. Things are happening for a reason. If we're supposed to meet up with Six or Five or whoever, we will. And if Sam is supposed to still be a part of all this, he will be."

Bernie Kosar jumps into the backseat in his beagle

form and licks my cheek. I pat his head and let out a long-drawn sigh, in utter disbelief that after everything that's gone wrong in the last forty-eight hours, I've also managed to lose the address Six had written down. I look out the window to see the wind is blowing to the north, and I wonder if it might be telling me something, or, at the very least, pointing me in the right direction as Six believes it's done for her.

"Head north," I say. "I think north would be good."

"You got it, boss." Nine steps on the gas and I look over at Bernie Kosar, who has curled up and fallen asleep.

We bury Héctor's body at the bottom of the dam, where the white concrete meets the grass.

"He once told me that the key to change is letting go of fear," I say, looking into the eyes of Ella, Crayton and Six. "I don't know if I've let go of fear just yet, but the change is happening. It's definitely happening. And I can only hope that you all can help me through it."

"We're a team," Ella says. "Of course we will."

After we say our good-byes, we climb the dam's ladder. We stand on top of the dam, peering down into the valley and the lake. On the other side of the dam is a series of locks holding back a much larger lake, and I can't help but think it's a metaphor for the way I'm feeling right now. In front of me lies my past, small and distant and dotted with carnage, threatened to be flooded at any time. Behind me and my fellow Garde members, the future is massive and held back by unnatural forces.

I turn to Six and ask, "Do you know a John Smith in Ohio? Is he one of us?"

Her smile is wide. "I do know John. He's Number Four."

I reach for Ella's hand on my right and Six's on my left, and we stand there letting the mountain breeze whip our hair around our faces. Ella looks over at Six and asks, "Can we go to America?"

"The charm is broken. I don't see why we can't all be together now." Six shrugs, turning back to the lake below.

Crayton joins us. "I hate to say this, but it's the calm before the storm, ladies. We're winning far too many battles for them to ease up now. You're getting too strong for them, and they'll be throwing everything they have at you. No more small armies with a few hundred soldiers and a couple of clumsy beasts. Their ruler will be here soon. Setrákus Ra."

"Who?" I ask.

"Setrákus Ra." Crayton shakes his head. "And I don't think we're ready for him."

"Then it's settled," I say. "We're going to Ohio to be with John Smith."

"West Virginia, actually. In exactly two weeks," Six says.

"I'm not sure that's wise just yet." Crayton begins walking away. "We need to gather the others first."

Six walks after him. "That sounds good and all, but I have no idea where they are."

"I do," Crayton says, not turning around. "I also know where our Chimæras are. If Setrákus Ra thinks this is going to be easy, he's got another thing coming."

We follow him, taking the first of many steps down the opposite side of the dam.

DESPERATE FOR MORE?

The Mogadorians found and killed Numbers One, Two, and Three. Then they found Number Six. They followed her, they hunted her down—and they caught her. *I Am Number Four: The Lost Files: Six's Legacy* is the riveting story of Six's harrowing capture by the Mogadorians. Available exclusively as an ebook.

HARPER
An Imprint of HarperCollinsPublishers

www.iamnumberfourfans.com

SEVEN THINGS *NOT* TO DO

1. Run. Although we believe half of the extraterrestrial races who visit Earth are peaceful, running away from them—or towards them—could cause them to become aggressive. Stay where you are and let them make the first move. Don't blow your chance at making peaceful contact!

2. Stand still when they are aggressive. Rule #1 ends at the first sign of aggression. Use your instincts and if the extraterrestrials charge you or raise a weapon, run to a safe location.

3. Invite them inside. They could see this as a trap, or they could accidentally destroy your home. Remember that extraterrestrials possess powers we can't even imagine and might damage everything you own purely by accident. Also, if you bring them inside, that removes the possibility of other witnesses seeing them. The more people who witness your interaction, the more credible you and your story are.

4. Attempt to shake hands. They can see this as an attack. There is a story of a man in Pensacola, Florida, who found an alien in his backyard. As soon as he offered to shake its hand, his right arm went numb and he was never able to use that arm again. It was permanently paralyzed, and the doctors haven't found a cure. Mimic what the aliens do instead.

DO NOT SEARCH FOR THIS MOUNTAIN.

We believe we are all in grave danger. The more we learn, the more we will share in our next issue of They Walk Among Us. . . .

It looks like a normal mountain in West Virginia. Just feet below its jagged peak, however, we have been told, there sits an alien headquarters so large and so technologically advanced that we believe it's only a matter of time before the aliens inside advance on—and destroy—the entire human race.

Our exclusive source has been on the inside. We have seen his drawings and maps, and we are certain that he is to be completely trusted. "I've seen too much to think they are peaceful," he said. He described seeing aliens with guns and savage alien beasts. He was shot at and dodged all but one of their lasers while escaping. His scars could have ONLY come from alien weaponry.

Checking dozens of thermal satellite images from three different governments—the USA, Mexico, and Russia—we found a mountain deep in the Monongahela National Forest in West Virginia that showed never-before-recorded levels of heat and gas. When we showed these images (since removed from the internet) to our source, he confirmed it was the same mountain he was in.

was camping nearby," he said. "I set up my tent, when I went out looking for firewood I saw this t blue light in the distance." He walked towards saw it came from a cave in the base of a in. "I was about to touch the light, but then eared before I could reach it, like it knew I I discovered a hidden way INTO the cave, when I saw all the aliens." They shot at sers, he said, were yellow and loud—and out of the cave he ran for several miles.

WHEN ENCOUNTERING AN EXTRATERRESTRIAL

5. Use flash photography. Unfortunately most alien encounters happen at night, and that makes them harder to document. We advise you to try to take video because others can learn so much more from film than from photographs. But if you must take pictures instead of video, NEVER use flash photography. The flash can startle the alien. If you don't have a video camera, try to lead the alien towards an outside light instead, or occupy it until the sun rises before taking a photo.

6. Board their ship. There are many conflicting stories about what happens inside an alien spacecraft. Some people have just been given a tour of the ship, others have been able to travel to galaxies far away on the spacecraft, but some people have become part of horrible experiments that involve torture and permanent damage to their bodies and brains. You can't risk it. Also, if you board their ship, you may never come back.

7. Forget to document the encounter. The worst possible thing you can do when encountering an extraterrestrial is to not document EVERYTHING that happened. Yes, write down what they looked like and what they sounded like, also what they smelled like and how the group reacted to their movements. Always try to video footage or photographs. Try to use cell phone as a recording device by your voicemail and letting it record with alien says and what you say back. When counter is over, immediately seclude and write down everything that happ that before even talking to someone cause your memories could be influen

00:00 / 12:12

TORNADOES DETERMINED TO BE ALIEN ABDUCTION DEVICES

Two highly accredited exobiologists have determined that tornadoes have been used as powerful alien abduction devices for hundreds of years. Dr. Bruce Gregory and Dr. Everett Chatterton, both of the International Veritas Institute, say that extraterrestrial civilizations have been creating tornadoes as tools and diversions to bring humans aboard their spaceships in the daylight.

"Sometimes aliens can't wait until nightfall, when most alien abductions happen." Dr. Chatterton said over the phone. "They create these tornadoes to mask and control their abductions right out in the open." The aliens create the perfect atmosphere with the tornadoes. The sky is darkened and the chaotic winds and heavy rain drive many people into their basements, eliminating most witnesses; and when the aliens find a single human or animal alone, they can maneuver the tornado right over them, then fly them up through the doors on the bottom of their ship. The aliens also send victims back to Earth in tornadoes, sometimes dropping them miles away from where they found picked up.

Dr. Gregory went on to explain that many abductees over the years never been recovered. "These are the people they've chosen to take back to their planets for various reasons. We'll never know what the

"It's been the perfect charade," Dr. Gregory then said. "It's only we've been able to document and film them taking a decoy for that we set out in a field in rural Illinois." The exobiologists said the mannequin's abduction—they outfitted the mannequin w

THEY WALK AMONG US

-- *An Urgent Letter to the Readers of They Walk Among Us* --

What you are holding in your hands is not just the next issue of *They Walk Among Us*. In front of you is something much bigger.

It is with great sadness that I inform you that the long-time editors of *They Walk Among Us*—who dedicated their lives to exposing the truth about extraterrestrial civilizations—are missing. Their offices have been torn apart. Documents and computers are gone.

We can only assume that one of their stories was too close to the truth. They knew too much and they were silenced. I am picking up where they left off and I promise that the truth will come out. Stay tuned.

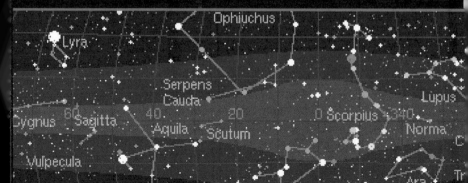

I know that continuing *They Walk Among Us* puts my life in immediate danger, but in respect to the former editors, and to you, we will continue on.

THE MOGADORIAN RACE HUNTS DOWN SPECIFIC EARTHLINGS

WE HAVE NEW DETAILS ON THE MOGADORIANS, A VICIOUS RACE OF ALIENS.

As previously reported, we know that THE Mogadorians have been on Earth for over ten years, looking to expose Earth's weaknesses so they can inhabit the planet. But we now know that is only part of their plan. We are told that they are, first and foremost, ferociously hunting down a small group of specific Earthlings.

Those hunted are NOT world leaders. There have been no attempts on any heads of state OF powerful nations. The scientific community appears to be safe as well, and at this time we have found no direct connection from this Mogadorian mission to the disappearance of the former They Walk Among Us editors. According to our sources, the Mogadorians are busy combing the planet looking for NINE specific teenagers.

We don't know who these nine are or what they look like, and we don't know where they live. We can only assume destroying these nine is vital to the Mogadorians' success. These nine teenagers may be future warriors, intellectuals, astronauts, leaders, linchpins, etc., who are predestined to take down the Mogadorian race and save Earth and maybe even the galaxy. We are rooting for these nine, wherever they are, to RISE and become intergalactic legends.